OUTSTANDING PRAISE FOR
FREDERICK FORSYTH AND HIS NOVELS

"With quick, sure images, Forsyth creates indelible impressions of characters."
—*The New York Times*

"When it comes to espionage, international intrigue, and suspense, Frederick Forsyth is a master."
—*The Washington Post*

AVENGER

"*Avenger* is proof Forsyth can still tell a suspenseful tale better than anyone."
—*Forth Worth Star-Telegram*

"It's a pleasure to watch Forsyth build his complicated plot. The author is indeed a watchmaker [with] the wheels and levers all working perfectly together."
—*Houston Chronicle*

"*Avenger* is another gem from a master craftsman."
—*Rocky Mountain News*

"[A] creative rebirth for the venerable author of 1971's *The Day of the Jackal.*"
—*Time Out New York*

D0035440

MORE...

"A gripping, powerful thriller from the master, surpassing the mark he set with *The Day of the Jackal*."

—*Pages*

"A suspense-filled, adrenaline-driven ride that leaves the reader exhausted yet never happier."

—*Rendezvous*

"Just for fun, I thought I would read fifty pages of Clancy's latest and Forsyth's new book, *Avenger*, and decide which one demanded my immediate attention. Forsyth won hands down."

—*Ocala Star-Banner*

"*The Day of the Jackal, The Dogs of War, The Odessa File*—these Forsyth blockbusters helped define the international conspiracy thriller . . . Forsyth's extraordinary care with detail, his solid voice, and his exquisite pacing make this a totally engrossing thriller."

—*Booklist* (starred review)

"The great Forsyth of *The Day of the Jackal* returns . . . [and] the pages burn by."

—*Kirkus Reviews*

THE VETERAN

"Each of the stories in this volume is Forsyth in top form. The writing exceeds expectations, the stories are never less than compelling, and the suspense in each of them is nonstop."

—Otto Penzler, a Penzler Pick for September 2001

"A smooth and satisfying read for anyone who likes his or her thrills in small packages."

—*Providence Journal*

"Lucid, vivid, and delightfully readable, Forsyth is a master word-spinner and a master of meticulous detail."

—*The Los Angeles Times*

"The five stories in this book . . . deserve to be classics themselves. Combining sharp detail, fully realized characters, and clever last-minute twists, these small gems are polished to perfection . . . Forsyth has always been a masterful plotter, with a special affection for using elements that appear to come from out of left field but somehow work just perfectly. Fans of his novels will be utterly thrilled by this collection. Readers unfamiliar with his writings couldn't find a better introduction. Revenge, mystery, murder, deception—all the main themes of Forsyth's best novels are represented here in stories that showcase the author's ability to capture character and generate suspense in remarkably few words."

—*Booklist* (starred review)

"A good read. What is surprising is the thematic and geographical range of these pieces, all narrated in a solid realist style with sharply observed detail and engrossing, sometimes surprising, plots. Always suspenseful, the stories take us into disparate worlds."

—*Library Journal*

Also by Frederick Forsyth

AVENGER

FREDERICK FORSYTH

St. Martin's Paperbacks

NOTE: If you purchased this book without a cover you should be aware that this book is stolen property. It was reported as "unsold and destroyed" to the publisher, and neither the author nor the publisher has received any payment for this "stripped book."

AVENGER

Copyright © 2003 by Frederick Forsyth.

All rights reserved. No part of this book may be used or reproduced in any manner whatsoever without written permission except in the case of brief quotations embodied in critical articles or reviews. For information address St. Martin's Press, 175 Fifth Avenue, New York, NY 10010.

Library of Congress Catalog Card Number: 2003053163

ISBN: 0-312-99722-1
EAN: 80312-99722-9

Printed in the United States of America

St. Martin's Press hardcover edition / September 2003
St. Martin's Paperbacks edition / August 2004

St. Martin's Paperbacks are published by St. Martin's Press, 175 Fifth Avenue, New York, NY 10010.

10 9 8 7 6 5 4 3 2 1

For the Tunnel Rats,
You guys did something I could never force myself
to do

PROLOGUE
THE MURDER

It was the seventh time they had pushed the American boy down into the liquid excrement of the cesspit that he failed to fight back and died down there, every orifice filled with unspeakable filth.

When they were done, the men put down their poles, sat on the grass, laughed, and smoked. Then they finished off the other aid worker and the six orphans, took the relief agency off-road, and drove back across the mountain.

It was May 15, 1995.

PART ONE

PART ONE

1

THE HARDHAT

He leaned into the gradient and once again fought the enemy of his own pain. It was a torture and a therapy. That was why he did it.

Those who know often say that of all the disciplines the triathlon is the most brutal and unforgiving. The decathlete has more skills to master, and putting the shot needs more brute strength; but for fearsome stamina and the capacity to meet the pain and beat it, there are few trials like the triathlon.

The runner had risen as always on training days well before dawn. He drove his pickup to a distant New Jersey lake, dropping off his racing bicycle on the way, chaining it to a tree for safety. At two minutes after five, he set the chronometer on his wrist, pulled the sleeve of the neoprene wetsuit down to cover it, and entered the icy water.

It was the Olympic triathlon that he practiced, with distances measured in metric lengths. A fifteen-hundred-meter swim—as near as dammit one mile—out of the water, strip fast to undershirt and shorts, mount the racing bike, then forty kilometers crouched over the handlebars, all of it at the sprint. He had long ago measured the mile along the lake from end to end and knew exactly which tree on the far bank marked the spot he had left the bike. He had marked out his forty kilometers along the country roads, always at that empty hour, and knew which tree was the point to abandon the bike and start the run. Ten kilometers was the run, and there was a farm gatepost that marked the two-clicks-to-go point. That morning he had just passed it. The last two kilometers were uphill, the final heartbreaker, the no-mercy stretch.

The reason it hurt so much is that the muscles needed are all different. The powerful shoulders, chest, and arms of a swimmer are not normally needed by a speed cyclist or marathon man. They are just extra poundage that has to be carried.

The speed-blurred driving of the legs and hips of a cyclist are different from the tendons and sinews that give the runner the rhythm and cadence to eat up the miles underfoot. The repetitiveness of the rhythms of one exercise does not match those of the other. The triathlete needs them all, then tries to match the performances of three specialist athletes one after the other.

At age twenty-five it is a cruel event. At the age of fifty-one, it ought to be indictable under the Geneva Convention. The runner had passed his fifty-first the previous January. He dared a glance at his wrist and scowled. Not good; he was several minutes down on his best. He drove harder against his enemy.

The Olympians were looking at just under two hours; the New Jersey runner had clipped two hours twenty. He was almost at that time now, and he still had almost two kilometers to go.

The first houses of his hometown came into view around

a curve in Highway 30. The old, prerevolution village of Pennington straddles Route 31, just off Interstate 95, running down from New York, through the state, and on to Philadelphia, Baltimore, then Washington.

There is not much to Pennington, one of a million neat, clean, tidy, neighborly small towns that make up the overlooked and underestimated heart of the United States. A single major crossroads at the center where West Delaware Avenue crosses Main Street, several well-attended churches of three denominations, a First National Bank, a handful of shops, and off-the-street residences scattered down the tree-clothed byroads.

The runner headed for the crossroads, half a kilometer to go. He was too early for a coffee at the Cup of Joe or breakfast at Vito's Pizza, but even had they been open he would not have stopped.

South of the junction he passed the Civil War vintage, white clapboard house with the shingle of Calvin Dexter, attorney-at-law, next to the door. It was his office, his shingle, and his law practice, save for the occasions when he took time off and went away to attend to his other practice. Clients and neighbors accepted that he took fishing vacations now and then, knowing nothing of the small apartment under another name in New York City.

He drove his aching legs that last five hundred yards to reach the turning into Chesapeake Drive at the south end of town. That was where he lived, and the corner marked the end of his self-imposed Calvary. He slowed, stopped, and hung his head, leaning against a tree, sucking in oxygen to heaving lungs. Two hours, thirty-six minutes. Far from his best. That there was probably no one within a hundred miles who, aged fifty-one, could come near it was not the point. The point, as he would never dare to explain to the neighbors who grinned and cheered him on, was to use the pain to combat the other pain, the always pain, the pain that never went away, the pain of lost child, lost love, lost everything.

The runner turned into his street and walked the last two

hundred yards. Ahead of him he saw the paperboy hurl a heavy bundle onto his porch. The kid waved as he cycled past, and Cal Dexter waved back.

Later he would take his motor scooter and go retrieve his truck. With the scooter in the rear, he would drive home, picking up the racing bike along the road. First he needed a shower, some high-energy bars, and the contents of several oranges.

On the stoop he picked up the bundle of mail and newspapers, broke them open, and looked.

Calvin Dexter, the wiry, sandy-haired, friendly, smiling attorney of Pennington, New Jersey, had been born with close to nothing in terms of a worldly advantage.

He'd been created in a Newark slum, rife with roaches and rats, and came into the world in January 1950, the son of a construction worker and a waitress at the local diner. His parents, according to the morality of the age, had had no choice but to marry when a meeting in a neighborhood dance hall and a few drinks too many had led to things getting out of hand and his own conception.

His father was not a bad man, by his lights. After Pearl Harbor he had volunteered for the armed forces, but as a skilled construction worker he had been deemed more useful at home, where the war effort involved the creation of thousands of new factories, dockyards, and government offices.

He was a hard man, quick with his fists, the only law on many blue-collar jobs. But he tried to live by the straight and narrow, bringing his pay straight home unopened, trying to raise his toddler son to love Old Glory, the Constitution, and Joe DiMaggio.

But when the Korean War ended, the job opportunities gradually slipped away. Only the industrial blight remained, and the unions were in the grip of the Mob.

Calvin was five when his mother left. He was too young to understand why. He knew nothing of the loveless union his parents had had, accepting with the philosophical endurance of the very young that people always shouted and quarreled. He knew nothing of the traveling salesman who had promised her bright lights and better frocks. He was simply told she had "gone away."

He had accepted that his father was now home each evening, looking after him instead of having a few beers after work, staring glumly at a foggy television screen. It was not until his teens that he learned his mother, abandoned in her turn by the traveling salesman, had tried to return but been rebuffed by his angry and bitter father.

When Calvin was seven, his father hit upon an idea to solve the problem of a home and the need to search for work far and wide. They moved out of the walk-up tenement in Newark and acquired a second-hand trailer. This became his home for ten years.

Father and son moved from job to job, living in the trailer, the scruffy boy attending whichever local school would take him. It was the age of Elvis Presley, Del Shannon, Roy Orbison, the Beatles, over from a country Cal had barely heard of. It was the age of Kennedy, the Cold War, and Vietnam.

The jobs came and the jobs were completed. They moved through the northern cities of East Orange, Union, and Elizabeth; then on to work outside New Brunswick and Trenton. For a time they lived in the Pine Barrens while Dexter Senior was foreman on a small project. Then they headed south to Atlantic City. Between the ages of eight and sixteen, Cal attended nine schools in as many years. His formal education could fill an entire postage stamp.

But he became wise in other ways; streetwise, fightwise. Like his departed mother, he did not grow tall, topping out at five feet, eight inches. Nor was he heavy and muscular like his father, but his lean frame packed fearsome stamina and his fists a killer punch. Once he challenged the booth fighter in a fairground sideshow, knocked him flat, and took the twenty-dollar prize.

A man who smelt of cheap aftershave approached his father and suggested the boy attend his gym with a view to becoming a boxer, but they moved on to a new city and a new job.

There was no question of money for vacations, so when school was out, the kid just went to the construction site with his father. There he made coffee, ran errands, did odd jobs. One of the "errands" involved a man who told him there was a vacation job taking envelopes to various addresses across Atlantic City and saying nothing to anyone. So for the summer vacation of 1965, he became a bookie's runner.

Even from the bottom of the social pile, a smart kid can still look. Cal Dexter could sneak unpaying into the local movie house and marvel at the glamour of Hollywood, the huge rolling vistas of the Wild West, the shimmering glitz of the screen musicals, the crazy antics of the Martin and Lewis comedies.

He could see in the television ads perfect houses with stainless-steel kitchens and smiling families in which the parents seemed to love each other. He could look at the gleaming limousines and sports cars on the billboards above the highway.

He had nothing against the hard hats of the construction sites. The men were gruff and crude, but they were kind to him, or most of them were anyway. On-site he, too, wore a hard hat, and the general presumption was that once out of school he would follow his father in the building trades. But he had other ideas. Whatever life he had, he vowed, it would be far from the crash of the trip-hammer and the choking dust of cement mixers.

Then he realized that he had nothing to offer in exchange for that better, more moneyed, more comfortable life. He thought of the movies but assumed all actors were towering men, unaware that most were well under five feet nine. This thought only came to him because some barmaid said she thought he looked a bit like James Dean, but the building workers roared with laughter so he dropped the idea.

Sports and athletics could get a kid out of the street and on the road to fame and fortune, but he had been through all his schools so fast he had never had a chance to make any of the school teams.

Anything involving a formal education, let alone qualifications, was out of the question. That left other kinds of working-class employment—waiter, bellhop, grease monkey, delivery-van driver—the list was endless, but for all the prospects most of them offered, he might as well stay with construction. The sheer brutalism and danger of the work made it better paid than most.

Or there was crime. No one raised on the waterfronts or construction sites of New Jersey could possibly be unaware that organized crime, running with the gangs, could lead to a life of big apartments, fast cars, and easy women. The word was, it hardly ever led to jail. He was not Italian-American, which would preclude full membership in the Mob aristocracy, but there were others who had made good.

He quit school at seventeen and started the next day at his father's work site, a housing project outside Camden. A month later the driver/operator of the bulldozer fell ill. There was no substitute. It was a skilled job.

Cal looked at the interior of the cab. It made sense. "I could work this," he said.

The foreman was dubious. It would be against all the rules. Any inspector chancing along and his job would be history. On the other hand, the whole team was standing around needing mountains of earth shifted.

"There's an awful lot of levers in there."

"Trust me," said the kid.

It took about twenty minutes to work out which lever did what function. He began to shift dirt. It meant a bonus, but it was still not a career.

In January 1968, he turned eighteen, and the Vietcong launched the Tet Offensive. He was watching television in a bar in Camden. After the newscast came several commercials and then a brief recruitment film made by the army. It mentioned that, if you shaped up, the army would give you an education. The next day he walked into the

U.S. Army office in Camden and said, "I want to join the army."

Back then every American youth would, failing some pretty unusual circumstances or voluntary exile, become liable for compulsory draft just after his eighteenth birthday. The desire of just about every teenager and twice that number of parents was to get out of it. The master sergeant behind the desk looked bemused.

"I'm volunteering," Cal said. That caught his attention.

The master sergeant drew a form toward him, keeping eye contact like a ferret that does not want the rabbit to get away. "Well, that's fine, kid. That's a very smart thing to do. Take a word of advice from an old sweat?"

"Sure."

"Make it three years instead of the required two. Good chance of better postings, better career choices." He leaned forward as one imparting a state secret. "With three years, you could even avoid going to Vietnam."

"But I want to go to Vietnam," said the kid in the soiled denims. The master sergeant thought this one over. "Right," he said very slowly. He might have said, "There's no accounting for taste." Instead he said, "Hold up your right hand . . ."

Thirty-three years later, the former hard hat pushed four oranges through the juicer, rubbed the towel over his wet head again, and took the pile of papers with the juice through to the sitting room.

There was the local paper, another from Washington, and one from New York, and, in a wrapper, a technical magazine. It was this he went to first.

Vintage Airplane is not a big-circulation organ, and in Pennington it could only be obtained by mail order. It catered to those with a passion for classic and World War II airplanes. The runner flicked to the small want-ads section. He stopped, the juice halfway to his mouth, put down the glass, and read the item again. It said: "AVENGER.

Wanted. Serious offer. No price ceiling. Please call."

There was no Pacific War Grumman Avenger torpedo dive-bomber out there to be bought. They were in museums. Someone had uncovered the contact code. There was a number. It had to be a cell phone. The date was May 13, 2001.

2
THE VICTIM

Ricky Colenso was not born to die at the age of twenty in a Bosnian cesspit. It should have never ended that way. He was born to get a college degree and live out his life in the States, with a wife and children and a decent chance at life, liberty, and the pursuit of happiness. It went wrong because he was too kindhearted.

Back in 1970, a young and brilliant mathematician called Adrian Colenso secured tenure as an associate professor of math at Georgetown University. He was twenty-five, remarkably young for the post.

Three years later, he gave a summer seminar in Toronto, Canada. Among those attending, even though she understood little of what he was saying, was a stunningly pretty student called Annie Edmond. She was smitten and arranged a blind date through close friends.

Professor Colenso had never heard of her father, which both puzzled and delighted her. She had already been urgently pursued by half a dozen fortune hunters. In the car back to the hotel, she discovered that apart from an amazing grasp of quantum calculus, he also kissed rather well.

A week later he flew back to Washington, D.C. Miss Edmond was not a young lady to be denied. She left her job, obtained a sinecure at the Canadian Consulate, rented an apartment just off Wisconsin Avenue, and arrived with ten suitcases. Two months later they married. The wedding was a blue-chip affair in Windsor, Ontario, and the couple honeymooned in Caneel Bay, in the U.S. Virgin Islands.

As a present, the bride's father bought the couple a large country house on Foxhall Road, off Nebraska Avenue, in one of the most rustic and therefore sought-after areas of the District. It was set in its own wooded two-acre plot, with pool and tennis court. The bride's allowance would cover its upkeep, and the groom's salary would just about do the rest. They settled down into loving domesticity.

Baby Richard Eric Steven was born in April 1975 and was soon nicknamed Ricky.

He grew up like millions of other American youngsters in a secure and loving parental home, doing all the things that boys do: spending time at summer camps, discovering and exploring the thrills of girls and sports cars, worrying over academic grades and looming examinations.

He was neither brilliant like his father nor dumb. He'd inherited his father's quirky grin and his mother's good looks. Everyone who knew him rated him a nice kid. If someone asked him for help, he would do all he could. But he should never have gone to Bosnia.

He graduated from high school in 1994 and was accepted at Harvard for the following autumn. That winter, watching on television the sadism of ethnic cleansing and the aftermath of the refugees' misery and relief programs in a faraway place called Bosnia, he determined that he wanted to help in some way.

His mother pleaded that he should stay in the States;

there was plenty to do right at home if he wanted to exercise his social conscience. But the images he had seen of gutted villages, wailing orphans, and the blank-eyed despair of the refugees had affected him deeply, and Bosnia it had to be.

A few calls from his father established that the world agency for him was the United Nations High Commissioner for Refugees (UNHCR), with a big office in New York. Ricky begged that he be allowed to join for the summer at least and went to New York to inquire about procedures for enlistment.

By early spring of 1995, as the old federation of Yugoslavia tore itself apart, three years of civil war had gutted the province of Bosnia. The UNHCR was there in strength, with a staff of about four hundred "internationals" and several thousand locally recruited staffers. The outfit was headed up by a former British soldier, the full-bearded and restlessly energetic Larry Hollingworth, whom Ricky had seen on television. He wanted to join and help in some way.

The New York office was kind but less than enthusiastic. Amateur offers came in by the sackload, and the personal visits were several dozen a day. This was the United Nations; there were procedures; six months of bureaucracy, enough filled-out forms to break the springs of a pickup, and as Ricky would have to be in Cambridge by autumn, probably refusal at the end.

The dejected young man was heading down again in the elevator at the start of the lunch hour when a middle-aged secretary gave him a kindly smile. "If you really want to help in there, you'll have to get over to the regional office in Zagreb," she said. "They take people on locally. It's much more relaxed right on the spot."

Croatia had also once been part of the disintegrating Yugoslavia, but it had secured its separation, was now a new state, and many organizations were based in the safety of its capital, Zagreb. One of them was the UNHCR.

Ricky had a long call with his parents, got their grudging permission, and flew New York–Vienna–Zagreb. But the

reply was still the same; forms to fill out; only long-term
commitments were really sought. Summertime amateurs
were a lot of responsibility and made precious little contribution.

"You really should try one of the nongovernmental organizations," suggested the regional controller, trying to be
helpful. "They meet right next door at the café."

The UNHCR might be the world body, but that was far
from the end of it. Disaster relief is an entire industry and,
for many, a profession. Outside of the United Nations and
individual government efforts come the nongovernmental
organizations (NGOs). There were over three hundred
NGOs involved in Bosnia.

The names of no more than a dozen would ring a bell
with the general public: Save the Children (British), Feed
the Children (American), Age Concern, War on Want, Mé-
decins Sans Frontières—they were all there. Some were
faith-based, some secular, and many of the smaller ones
had simply come into being for the Bosnian civil war, im-
pelled by TV images beamed endlessly into the West. At
the extreme bottom end were single trucks driven across
Europe by a couple of sturdy youths who had had a collection round in their local bar. The jumping-off point for
the drive on the last leg into the heart of Bosnia was either
Zagreb or the Adriatic port of Split.

Ricky found the café, ordered a coffee and a slivovitz
against the bitter March wind outside, and looked around
for a possible contact. Two hours later a burly, bearded
man, built like a trucker, walked in. He wore a plaid mack-
inaw and ordered coffee and cognac in a voice Ricky placed
as coming from North or South Carolina. He went up and
introduced himself. He had struck lucky.

John Slack was a dispatcher and distributor of relief aid
for a small American charity called Loaves-n-Fishes, a recently formed offshoot of Salvation Road, which itself was
the corporate manifestation in the sinful world of the Reverend Billy Jones, television evangelist and saver of souls
(for the appropriate donation) of the fine city of Charleston,

South Carolina. He listened to Ricky as one who had heard it all before.

"You drive a truck, kid?"

"Yes." It was not quite true, but he reckoned a big off-road was like a small truck.

"You read a map?"

"Of course."

"And you want a fat salary?"

"No. I have an allowance from my grandpa."

John Slack's eyes twinkled. "You don't want anything? Just to help?"

"That's right."

"OK, you're on. Mine's a small operation. I go and buy relief food, clothes, blankets, mainly in Austria. I truck it down to Zagreb, refuel, and then head into Bosnia. We're based at Travnik. Thousands of refugees down there."

"That suits me fine," said Ricky. "I'll pay all my own costs."

Slack threw back what remained of his coffee and cognac. "Let's go, kid," he said.

The truck was a ten-ton German Hanomag, and Ricky got the hang of it before the border. It took them ten hours to Travnik, spelling each other at the wheel. Around midnight they arrived at the Loaves-n-Fishes compound just outside the town. Slack threw him several blankets.

"Spend the night in the cab," he said. "We'll find you a billet in the morning."

The Loaves-n-Fishes operation was indeed small. It involved a second truck about to leave for the north to collect more supplies with a monosyllabic Swede at the wheel; one small, shared compound wired with chain-link fencing to keep out pilferers, a tiny office made out of a workman's portable cabin, a shed called a warehouse for unloaded but not yet distributed food, and three locally recruited Bosnian staffers. Plus two new black Toyota Landcruisers for small-cargo aid distribution. Slack introduced him all around, and by afternoon Ricky had found lodging with a Bosnian widow in the town. To get to and from the compound, he

bought a ramshackle bicycle from the stash he kept in a
money belt around his waist. John Slack noticed the belt.

"Mind telling me how much you keep in that pouch?"
he asked.

"I brought a thousand dollars," said Ricky trustingly,
"just in case of emergencies."

"Shit. Just don't wave it around, or you'll create one.
These guys can take the summer off on that."

Ricky promised to be discreet. Postal services, he soon
discovered, were nonexistent. Inasmuch as no Bosnian state
existed, no Bosnian post office had come into being and
the old Yugoslav services had collapsed. John Slack told
him any driver running up to Croatia or on to Austria would
mail letters and cards for everyone. Ricky wrote a quick
card from the bundle he had bought at the Vienna airport
and thrown into his haversack. This the Swede took north.
Mrs. Colenso received it a week later.

Travnik had once been a thriving market town, inhabited
by Serbs, Croats, and Bosnian Muslims. Their presence
could be discerned by the churches. There was a Catholic
one for the departed Croats, an Orthodox one for the also-
departed Serbs, and a dozen mosques for the majority, Muslims, the ones still called Bosnians.

With the coming of the civil war, the triethnic community, which had lived in harmony for years, was shattered.
As pogrom after pogrom was reported across the land, all
interethnic trust evaporated.

The Serbs quit and retreated north of the Vlasic mountain range that dominates Travnik, across the Lasva River
valley and into Banja Luka on the other side.

The Croats were also forced out, and most went ten
miles down the road to Vitez. Thus three single-ethnic
strongholds were formed. Into each poured the refugees of
that particular ethnic group.

In the world media, the Serbs were portrayed as the perpetrators of all the pogroms, though they had also seen Serb
communities butchered when isolated and in the minority.
The reason was that in the old Yugoslavia the Serbs had

had dominant control of the army; when the country fell apart, they simply grabbed 90 percent of the heavy weaponry, giving them an insuperable edge.

The Croats, also no slouches when it came to slaughtering non-Croat minorities in their midst, had been granted irresponsibly premature recognition by the German chancellor Helmut Kohl; they could then buy weapons on the world market.

The Bosnians were largely unarmed and kept that way on the advice of European politicians. As a result, they suffered most of the brutalities. In late spring 1995, it would be the Americans who, sick and tired of standing by and doing nothing, would use their military power to give the Serbs a bloody nose and force all parties to the conference table at Dayton, Ohio. The Dayton Agreement would be implemented that coming November. Ricky Colenso would not see it.

By the time Ricky reached Travnik, it had stopped a lot of shells from Serb positions across the mountains. Most of the buildings were shrouded in planks leaning against the walls. If hit by an "incomer," they would be splintered to matchwood but save the house itself. Most windows were missing and had been replaced by plastic sheeting. The brightly painted main mosque had somehow been spared a direct hit. The two largest buildings in town, the gymnasium (high school) and the once famous music school, were stuffed with refugees.

With virtually no access to the surrounding countryside and thus access to growing crops, the refugees, about three times the original population, were dependent on the aid agencies to survive. That was where Loaves-n-Fishes came in, along with a dozen other smaller NGOs in the town.

But the two Landcruisers could be piled with up to five hundred pounds of relief aid and still make it to various outlying villages and hamlets, where the need was even greater than in Travnik center. Ricky happily agreed to haul the sacks of food and drive the off-roads into the mountains to the south.

Four months after he had sat in Georgetown and seen
on the television screen the images of human misery that
had brought him here, he was happy. He was doing what
he came to do. He was touched by the gratitude of the
weary peasants and their brown, saucer-eyed children when
he hauled sacks of wheat, maize, powdered milk, and soup
concentrates into the center of an isolated village that had
not eaten for a week.

He believed he was paying back in some way for all the
benefits and comforts that a benign God, in whom he firmly
believed, had bestowed upon him at his birth simply by
creating him an American.

He spoke not a word of Serbo-Croat, the common language of all Yugoslavia, nor the Bosnian patois. He had no
idea of the local geography, where the mountain roads led,
where was safe and where it could be dangerous.

John Slack paired him with one of the local Bosnian
staffers, a young man with reasonable, school-learned English, called Fadil Sulejman, who acted as his guide, interpreter, and navigator.

Each week through April and the first two weeks of May
Ricky dispatched either a letter or card to his parents; and
with greater or lesser delays, depending on who was heading north for resupplies, they arrived in Georgetown bearing Croatian or Austrian stamps.

It was in the second week of May that Ricky found
himself alone and in charge of the entire depot. Lars, the
Swede, had had a major engine breakdown on a lonely
mountain road in Croatia, north of the border but short of
Zagreb. John Slack had taken one of the Landcruisers to
help him out and get the truck back into service.

Fadil Sulejman asked Ricky for a favor.

Like thousands in Travnik, Fadil had been forced to flee
his home when the tide of war swept toward it. He explained that his family home had been a small farm in an
upland valley on the slopes of the Vlasic range. He was
desperate to know if there was anything left of it. Had it
been torched or spared? Was it still standing? When the

war began, his father had buried family treasures under a barn. Were they still there? In a word, could he visit his parental home for the first time in three years?

Ricky happily gave him time off, but that was not the real point. With the tracks up the mountain slick with spring rain, only an off-road would make it. That meant borrowing the Landcruiser.

Ricky was in a quandary. He wanted to help, and he would pay for the gas. But was the mountain safe? Serbian patrols had once ranged over it, using their artillery to pound Travnik below.

That was a year ago, Fadil insisted. The southern slopes, where his parents' farmhouse was situated, were quite safe now. Ricky hesitated and then, moved by Fadil's pleading, wondering what it must be like to lose your home, he agreed. With one proviso: He would come, too.

In fact, in the spring sunshine, it was a very pleasant drive. They left the town behind and went up the main road toward Donji Vakuf for ten miles before turning off to the right.

The road climbed, degenerated into a track, and went on climbing. Beech, ash, and oak in their spring leaf enveloped them. It was, thought Ricky, almost like the Shenandoah where he had once gone camping with a school party. They began to skid on the corners, and he admitted they would never have made it without the four-wheel drive.

The oak gave way to conifers, and at five thousand feet they emerged into an upland valley, invisible from the road far below, a sort of secret hideaway. In the heart of the valley, they found the farmhouse. Its stone smokestack had survived, but the rest had been torched and gutted. Several sagging barns, unfired, still stood beyond the old cattle pens. Ricky glanced at Fadil's face and said, "I am so sorry."

They dismounted by the blackened firestack, and Ricky waited as Fadil walked through the wet ashes, kicking here and there at what was left of the place he was raised in. Ricky followed him as he walked past the cattle pens and the cesspit, still brimming with its nauseous contents, swollen by the rains, to the barns where his father might have buried the family treasures to save them from marauders. That was when they heard the rustle and the whimper.

The two men found them under a wet and smelly tarpaulin. There were six of them, small, cringing, terrified, aged about ten down to four. Four little boys and two girls, the oldest apparently the surrogate mother and leader of the group. Seeing the two men staring at them, they were frozen with fear. Fadil began to talk softly. After a while the girl replied.

"They come from Gorica, a small hamlet about four miles from here along the mountain. I used to know it."

"What happened?"

Fadil talked some more in the local lingo. The girl answered, then burst into tears.

"Men came, Serbs, paramilitaries."

"When?"

"Last night."

"What happened?"

Fadil sighed. "It was a very small hamlet. Four families, twenty adults, maybe twelve children. Gone now, all dead. When the firing started, their parents shouted that they should run away. They escaped in the darkness."

"Orphans? All of them?"

"All of them."

"We must get them into the truck, down to the valley," said the American.

They led the children, each clinging to the hand of the next eldest up the chain, out of the barn into the bright spring sunshine.

At the edge of the trees they saw the men. There were ten of them and two Russian GAZ off-roads in army camouflage. The men were also in cammo—and heavily armed.

Three weeks later, scouring the mailbox but facing yet another day with no card, Mrs. Annie Colenso rang a number in Windsor, Ontario. It answered on the second ring. She recognized the voice of her father's private secretary.

"Hi, Jean. It's Annie. Is my dad there?"

"He surely is, Mrs. Colenso. I'll put you right through."

3
THE MAGNATE

There were ten young pilots in A Flight crew hut and another eight next door in B Flight. Outside on the bright green grass of the airfield, two or three Hurricanes crouched with that distinctive hunch-backed look caused by the bulge behind the cockpit. They were not new, and fabric patches revealed where they had taken combat scars high above France over the previous two weeks.

Inside the huts the mood could not have been in greater contrast to the warm summer sunshine of June 25, 1940, at Coltishall Field, Norfolk, England. The mood of the men of 242 Squadron, Royal Air Force, known simply as the Canadian squadron, was about as low as it had ever been, and with good cause.

Two Four Two had been in combat almost since the first

shot was fired on the western front. They had fought the losing battle for France from the eastern border back to the Channel coast. As Hitler's great blitzkrieg machine rolled on, flicking the French army to one side, the pilots trying to stem the flood would find their bases evacuated and moved farther back even while they were airborne. They had to scavenge for food, lodgings, spare parts, and fuel. Anyone who has ever been part of a retreating army will know that the overriding adjective is that of chaos.

Back across the Channel in England, they had fought the second battle, above the sands of Dunkirk, as beneath them the British army sought to save what it could from the rout, grabbing anything that would float to paddle back to England, whose white cliffs were enticingly visible across the flat, calm sea.

By the time the last Tommy was evacuated from that awful beach and the last defenders of the perimeter passed into German captivity for five years, the Canadians were exhausted. They had taken a terrible beating: nine killed, three wounded, three shot down and taken prisoner.

Three weeks later they were still grounded at Coltishall, without spares or tools, all abandoned in France. Their CO, Squadron Leader "Papa" Gobiel, was ill, had been for weeks, and would not return to command. Still, the Brits had promised them a new commander, who was expected any time.

A small open-topped sports car emerged from between the hangars and parked near the two timber crew huts. A man climbed out, with some difficulty. No one went out to greet him. He stumped awkwardly toward A Flight. A few minutes later he was out of there and heading for B hut. The Canadian pilots watched him through the windows, puzzled by the rolling walk with feet apart. The door opened and he appeared in the aperture. His shoulders revealed his rank of squadron leader. No one stood up.

"Who's in charge here?" he demanded angrily.

A chunky Canuck hauled himself upright a few feet from where Steve Edmond sprawled in a chair and surveyed the newcomer through a blue haze. "I guess I am," said Stan Turner. It was early days. Stan Turner already had two confirmed kills to his credit but would go on to score a total of fourteen and a hatful of medals.

The British officer with the angry blue eyes turned on his heel and lurched away toward a parked Hurricane. The Canadians drifted out of their huts to observe.

"I do not believe what I am watching," muttered Johnny Latta to Steve Edmond. "The bastards have sent us a CO with no bloody legs."

It was true. The newcomer was stumping around on two prosthetics. He hauled himself into the cockpit of the Hurricane, punched the Rolls-Royce Merlin engine into life, turned into the wind, and took off. For half an hour he threw the fighter into every known aerobatic maneuver in the textbook and a few that were not yet there.

He was good in part because he had been an aerobatic ace before losing both legs in a crash long before the war and partly just because he had no legs. When a fighter pilot makes a tight turn or pulls out of a power dive, both ploys being vital in air combat, he puts heavy g-forces on his own body. The effect is to drive blood from the upper body downward, until blackout occurs. Because this pilot had no legs, the blood had to stay in the upper body, nearer the brain, and his squadron would learn that he could pull tighter turns than they could. Eventually he landed the Hurricane, climbed out, and stumped toward the silent Canucks.

"My name is Douglas Bader," he told them, "and we are going to become the best bloody squadron in the whole bloody air force."

He was as good as his word. With the Battle of France lost and the battle of the Dunkirk beaches a damn close-run thing, the big one was coming; Hitler had been promised by his Luftwaffe chief, Goering, mastery of the skies to enable the invasion of Britain to succeed. The Battle of Britain was the struggle for those skies. By the time it was over, the Canadians of 242, always led into combat by their legless CO, had established the best kill-to-loss ratio of all.

By late autumn, the German Luftwaffe had had enough and withdrew back into France. Hitler snapped his anger at Goering and turned his attention east to Russia.

In three battles, France, Dunkirk, and Britain, spread over only six months of the summer of '40, the Canadians had racked up eighty-eight confirmed kills, sixty-seven in the Battle of Britain alone. But they had lost seventeen pilots, and all but three were Canucks.

Fifty-five years later Steve Edmond rose from his office desk and crossed once again, as he had done so many times down the years, to the photo on the wall. It did not contain all the men he had flown with; some had been dead before others arrived. But it showed the seventeen Canadians at Duxford one hot and cloudless day in late August at the height of the battle.

Almost all gone. Most of them KIA during the war. The faces of boys from nineteen to twenty-two stared out, vital, cheerful, expectant, on the threshold of life, yet mostly never destined to see it.

He peered closer. Benzie, flying on his wingtip, shot down and killed over the Thames estuary, September 7th, two weeks after the photo. Solanders, the boy from Newfoundland, dead the next day.

Johnny Latta and Willie McKnight, standing side by side, would die wingtip to wingtip somewhere over the Bay of Biscay in January 1941.

"You were the best of us all, Willie," murmured the old man. McKnight was the first ace and double ace, the "natural"; nine confirmed kills in his first seventeen days of combat, twenty-one air victories when he died ten months after his first mission, aged just twenty-one.

Steve Edmond had survived to become extremely rich, certainly the biggest mining magnate in Ontario. But all through the years he had kept the photo on the wall, when he lived in a shack with a pick for company, when he made his first million dollars, when (especially when) *Forbes* magazine pronounced him a billionaire.

He kept it to remind him of the terrible fragility of that thing we call life. Often, looking back, he wondered how he had survived. Shot down the first time, he had been in the hospital when 242 Squadron left in December 1941 for the Far East. When he was fit again, he was posted to Training Command.

Chafing at the bit, bombarding higher authority with requests to fly combat again, he had finally been granted his wish in time for the Normandy landings, flying the new Typhoon ground-attack fighter-bomber, very fast and very powerful, a fearsome tank killer.

The second time he was shot down was near Remagen as the Americans stormed across the Rhine. He was among a dozen British Typhoons giving them cover in the advance. A direct hit to the engine gave him a few seconds to gain height, lose the canopy, and throw himself out of the doomed airplane before it blew up.

The jump was low and the landing hard, breaking both his legs. He lay in a daze of pain in the snow, dimly aware of round steel helmets running toward him, more keenly aware that the Germans had a particular loathing of Typhoon pilots, and the people he had been blowing apart were an SS panzer division, not known for their tolerance.

A muffled figure stopped and stared down at him. A voice said, "Well, lookee here." He let out his pent-up breath in relief. Few of Adolf's finest spoke with a Mississippi drawl.

The Americans got him back across the Rhine dazed with morphine, and he was flown home to England. When the legs were properly set, he was judged to be blocking up a bed needed for fresh incomers from the front, so he was sent to a convalescent home on the South Coast, there to hobble around until repatriation to Canada.

He enjoyed Dilbury Manor, a rambling Tudor pile steeped in history, with lawns like the green baize of a pool table and some pretty nurses. He was twenty-five that spring and carried the rank of wing commander.

Rooms were allocated at one per two officers, but it was

a week before his roommate arrived. He was about the same age, American, and wore no uniform. His left arm and shoulder had been smashed up in a gunfight in northern Italy. That meant covert ops, behind enemy lines, special forces.

"Hi," said the newcomer, "Peter Lucas. You play chess?"

Steve Edmond had come out of the harsh mining camps of Ontario, joining the Royal Canadian Air Force in 1938 to escape the unemployment of the mining industry when the world had no use for its nickel. Later that nickel would be part of every aircraft engine that kept him aloft. Lucas had come from the New England top social drawer, endowed with every advantage from the day of his birth.

The two young men were sitting on the lawn with a chess table between them when the radio through the dining hall window, speaking in the impossibly posh accent of the BBC newsreaders in those days, announced that Adm. Karl Doenitz had just signed the instruments of unconditional surrender; it was May 8, 1945.

The war in Europe was over. The American and Canadian sat and remembered all the friends who would never go home, and each would later recall it was the last time he cried in public.

A week later they parted and returned to their respective countries. But they formed a friendship in that convalescent home by the English coast that would last for life.

It was a different Canada when Steve Edmond came home, and he was a different man, a decorated war hero returning to a booming economy. His father had been a miner and his grandfather before that. The Canadians had been mining copper and nickel around Sudbury since 1885, and the Edmonds had been part of the action for most of that time.

Steve Edmond found he was owed a fat wedge of pay by the air force and used it to put himself through college, the first of his family to do so. Not unnaturally he took mineral engineering as his discipline and threw a course in

metallurgy into the pot as well. He was near the top of his
class in both in 1948 and was snapped up by Inco, the
International Nickel Company and principal employer in
the Sudbury Basin.

Formed in 1902, Inco had helped make Canada the pri-
mary supplier of nickel to the world, and the company's
core was the huge deposit outside Sudbury, Ontario. Edmond joined as a trainee mine manager. Steve would have
remained a mine manager living in a comfortable but run-
of-the-mill framehouse in a Sudbury suburb but for the rest-
less mind that was always telling him, "there must be a
better way."

College had taught him that the basic ore of nickel,
which is pentlandite, is also a host to other elements: plat-
inum, palladium, iridium, ruthenium, rhodium, tellurium,
selenium, cobalt, and silver and gold also occur in pentlandite. Edmond began to study the rare earth metals, their
uses, and the possible market for them. No one else both-
ered. This was because the percentages were so small their
extraction was uneconomical, so they ended up in the slag
heaps. Very few knew what rare earth metals were.

Almost all great fortunes are based upon one genius idea
and the guts to go with it. Hard work and luck also help.
Steve Edmond's idea was to go back to the laboratory when
the other young mine managers were helping with the bar-
ley harvest by drinking it. What he came up with was a
process now known as "pressure acid leaching." Basically,
it involved dissolving the tiny deposits of rare metals out
of the slag, then reconstituting them back to metal.

Had he taken this to Inco, he would have been given a
pat on the back, maybe even a slap-up dinner. Instead, he
resigned his post and booked a third-class train seat to Toronto and the Bureau of Patents. He was thirty and on his
way.

He borrowed, of course, but not too much, because what
he had his eye on did not cost much. When every exca-
vation of pentlandite ore became exhausted, or at least ex-
ploited until it became uneconomical to go on, the mining

companies left behind huge slag heaps called "tailing dams." The tailings were the rubbish; no one wanted them. Steve Edmond did. He bought them for pennies.

He founded Edmond Metals, Ems—known on the Toronto Exchange simply as Emmys—and the price went up. He never sold out, despite the blandishments, never took the gambles proposed to him by banks and financial advisers. That way he avoided the hypes, the bubbles, and the crashes. By forty, he was a multimillionaire; and by sixty-five, in 1985, he had the elusive mantle of billionaire.

He did not flaunt it, never forgot where he came from, gave much to charity, avoided politics while remaining affable to them all, and was known as a good family man.

Over the years there were indeed a few fools who, taking the mild-mannered exterior for the whole man, sought to cheat, lie, or steal. They discovered, often too late from their point of view, that there was as much steel in Steve Edmond as in any airplane engine he had ever sat behind.

He married once, in 1949, just before his big discovery. He and Fay were a love match, and it stayed that way until motor neuron disease took her away in 1994. There was one child, their daughter, Annie, born in 1950.

In his old age, Steve Edmond doted on her as always, approved mightily of Prof. Adrian Colenso, the Georgetown University academic she had married at twenty-two, and loved to bits his only grandson, Ricky, then aged twenty.

Most of the time Steve Edmond was a contented man with every right to be so, but there were days when he felt tetchy, ill at ease. Then he would cross the floor of his penthouse office suite high above the city of Windsor, Ontario, and stare again at the young faces in the photo, faces from far away and long ago.

The internal phone rang. He walked back to his desk. "Yes, Jean."

"It's Mrs. Colenso on the line."

"Fine. Put her through." He leaned back in the padded

swivel chair as the connection was made. "Hi, darling. How are you?"

The smile dropped from his face as he listened. He came forward in the chair until he was leaning on the desk.

"What do you mean missing? . . . Have you tried phoning? . . .Bosnia? No lines . . . Annie, you know kids nowadays don't write . . . maybe it's stuck in the mail over there . . . yes, I accept he promised faithfully . . . alright, leave it to me. Who was he working for?"

He took a pen and pad and wrote what she dictated. When he put the phone down, he thought for a moment, then called his chief executive officer. "Among all those young Turks you employ, do you have anyone who understands researching on the Internet?" he asked. The executive was stunned.

"Of course. Scores."

"I want the name and private number of the head of an American charity called Loaves-n-Fishes. No, just that. And I need it fast."

He had it in ten minutes. An hour later he came off a long call from a gleaming building in Charleston, South Carolina, headquarters of one of those television evangelists, the sort he despised, raking in huge donations from the gullible against guarantees of salvation.

Loaves-n-Fishes was the pompadoured savior's charity arm, which appealed for funds for the pitiful refugees of Bosnia, then gripped by a vicious civil war. How much of the donated dollars went to the wretched and how much to the reverend's fleet of limousines was anyone's guess. But if Ricky Colenso had been working as a volunteer for Loaves-n-Fishes in Bosnia, the voice from Charleston informed him, he would have been at their distribution center at a place called Travnik.

"Jean, do you remember a couple of years back a man in Toronto lost a couple of old masters in a burglary at his country home? It was in the papers. Then they reappeared. Someone at the club said he used a very discreet agency to track them down and get them back. I need his name. Call me back."

This was definitely not on the Internet, but there were other nets. Jean Searle, his private secretary of many years, used the secretaries' net and one of her friends was secretary to the chief of police.

"Rubinstein? Fine. Get me Mr. Rubinstein in Toronto or wherever."

That took half an hour. The art collector was found visiting the Rijksmuseum Amsterdam to stare, once again, at Rembrandt's *The Night Watch*. He was taken from his dinner table, given the six-hour time difference, but he was helpful.

"Jean," said Steve Edmond when he had finished, "call the airport. Get the Grumman ready. Now. I want to go to London. No, the English one. By sunrise."

4
THE SOLDIER

Cal Dexter had hardly finished taking the oath of allegiance when he was on his way to boot camp for basic training. He did not have far to go; Fort Dix was right there in New Jersey.

In the spring of 1968, tens of thousands of young Americans were pouring into the army, 15 percent of them unwilling draftees. The drill sergeants could not have cared less. Their job was to turn this mass of shorn-to-the-skull young male humanity into something resembling soldiers before passing them on, just three months later, to their next posting.

Where they came from, who their fathers were, what their level of education, was of glorious irrelevance. Boot camp was the greatest leveler of them all, barring death. That would come later—for some.

Dexter was a natural rebel, but he was also more street-wise than most. The chow was basic, but it was better than he had had on many construction sites, so he wolfed it down.

Unlike the rich boys, he had no problem with dormitory sleeping, open-doored ablutions, or the requirement to keep all his gear very, very neatly in one small locker. Most useful of all, he had never had anyone clear up after him, so he expected nothing of the sort in camp. Some others, accustomed to being waited upon, spent a lot of time jogging around the parade square or doing push-ups under the eyes of a displeased sergeant.

That said, Dexter could see no point in most of the rules and rituals, but he was smart enough not to say so. And he absolutely could not see why sergeants were always right and he was always wrong.

The benefit of signing on voluntarily for three years became plain very quickly. The corporals and sergeants, who were the nearest thing to God in basic training camp, learned of his status without delay and eased up on him. He was, after all, close to being "one of them." Mama-spoiled rich boys had it worst.

Two weeks in, he had his first assessment panel. That involved appearing before one of those almost invisible creatures, an officer. In this case, a major. "Any special skills?" asked the major for what was probably the ten thousandth time.

"I can drive bulldozers, sir," said Dexter.

The major studied his forms and looked up.

"When was this?"

"Last year, sir. Between leaving school and signing on."

"Your papers say you are just eighteen. That must have been when you were seventeen."

"Yes, sir."

"That's illegal."

"Lordy, sir, I'm sorry about that. I had no idea."

Beside him he could feel the ramrod-stiff corporal trying to keep a straight face. But the major's problem was solved.

"I guess it's engineering for you, soldier. Any objections?"

"No, sir."

Very few said good-bye at Fort Dix with tears in their eyes. Boot camp is not a vacation. But they did come out, most of them, with a straight back, square shoulders, a buzz-cut head, the uniform of a private soldier, a knapsack, and a travel pass to their next posting. In Dexter's case it was Fort Leonard Wood, Missouri, for Advanced Individual Training.

That was basic engineering; not just driving a bulldozer, but driving anything with wheels or tracks, engine repair, vehicle maintenance, and had there been time, fifty other courses besides. Another three months later, he achieved his Military Occupational Specialty certificate and was posted to Fort Knox, Kentucky.

Most of the world only knows Fort Knox as the U.S. Federal Reserve's gold depository, fantasy Mecca of every daydreaming bank robber and subject of numerous books and films. But it is also a huge army base and home of the Fort Knox Armor School. On any base that size there is always some building going on or tank pits to be dug or a ditch to be filled in. Cal Dexter spent six months as one of the post engineers at Fort Knox before being summoned to the Command Office.

He had just celebrated his nineteenth birthday; he carried the rank of private first class. The commanding officer looked grim, as one about to impart bereavement. Cal thought something might have happened to his father.

"It's Vietnam," said the major.

"Great," said the PFC. The major, who would happily spend the rest of his career in his anonymous marital home on the base in Kentucky, blinked several times.

"Well, that's all right then," he said.

Two weeks later Cal Dexter packed his knapsack, said good-bye to the buddies he had made on the post, and boarded the bus sent to pick up a dozen transferees. A week later he walked down the ramp of a C5 Galaxy and into the sweltering, sticky heat of Saigon Airport, military side.

Coming out of the airport, he was riding up front with the bus driver. "What do you do?" asked the corporal, as he swung the troop bus between the hangars.

"Drive bulldozers," said Dexter.

"Well, I guess you'll be an REMF like the rest of us around here."

"REMF?" queried Dexter. He had never heard the word before.

"Rear-echelon motherf****r," supplied the corporal.

Dexter was getting his first taste of the Vietnam status ladder. Nine-tenths of the GIs who went to Vietnam never saw a Vietcong, never fired a shot in anger, and rarely even heard one fired. The fifty thousand names of the dead on the memorial wall by the Reflecting Pool in Washington, D.C., with few exceptions, come from the other 10 percent. Even with a second army of Vietnamese cooks, launderers, and bottle washers, it still took nine GIs in the rear to keep one out in the jungle trying to win the war.

"Where's your posting?" asked the corporal.

"First Engineer Battalion, Big Red One."

The driver gave a squeak like a disturbed fruit bat. "Sorreee," he said. "Spoke too soon. That's Lai Khe, edge of the Iron Triangle. Rather you than me, buddy."

"It's bad?"

"Dante's vision of hell, pal."

Dexter had never heard of Dante and assumed he was in a different unit. He shrugged.

There was indeed a road from Saigon to Lai Khe; it was Highway 13 via Phu Cuong, up the eastern edge of the Triangle to Ben Cat, and then on another fifteen miles. But it was unwise to take it unless there was an armored escort, and even then never at night. This was all heavily forested country and was teeming with Vietcong ambushes. When Cal Dexter arrived inside the huge defended perimeter that housed the First Infantry Division, the Big Red One, it was by helicopter. Throwing his knapsack once again over his shoulder, he asked directions for the headquarters of the First Engineer Battalion.

On the way he passed the vehicle park and saw something that took his breath away. Accosting a passing GI, he asked, "What the hell is that?"

"Hogjaw," said the soldier laconically. "For ground clearing."

Along with the Twenty-fifth "Tropic Lightning" Infantry Division out of Hawaii, the Big Red One tried to cope with what purported to be the most dangerous area of the whole peninsula, the Iron Triangle. So thick was the vegetation, so impenetrable for the invader, and such a protective labyrinth for the guerrilla, that the only way to try to level the playing field was to clear the jungle.

To do this, two awesome machines had been developed. One was the tankdozer, an M-48 medium tank with a bulldozer blade fitted up front. With the blade down, the tank did the pushing while the armored turret protected the crew inside. But much bigger was the Rome Plow or "hogjaw."

This was a terrible brute if you happened to be a shrub or a tree or a rock. A sixty-ton tracked vehicle, the D7E was fitted with a specially forged, curving blade, whose protruding, hardened-steel lower edge could splinter a tree with a three-foot trunk.

The solitary driver/operator sat in his cabin way up top, protected by a "headache bar" above him to stop falling debris from crushing him, and with an armored cab to fend off sniper bullets or guerrilla attack.

The "Rome" in the name had nothing to do with the capital of Italy, but came from Rome, Georgia, where the brute was made. And the point of the Rome Plow was to make any piece of territory that had received its undivided attention unusable as a sanctuary for Vietcong ever again.

Dexter walked to the battalion office, threw up a salute, and introduced himself. "Morning, sir. PFC Calvin Dexter reporting for duty, sir. I'm your new hogjaw operator. Sir."

The lieutenant behind the desk sighed wearily. He was nearing the end of his one-year tour. He had flatly refused

to extend. He loathed the country, the invisible but lethal
Vietcong, the heat, the damp, the mosquitoes, and the fact
that once again he had a prickly heat rash enveloping his
private parts and rear end. The last thing he needed with
the temperature nudging ninety was a joker.

But Cal Dexter was a tenacious young man. He badgered
and pestered. Two weeks after arriving on post, he had his
Rome Plow. The first time he took it out, a more experienced driver tried to offer him some advice. He listened,
climbed high into the cab, and drove it on a combined
operation with infantry support all day. He handled the towering machine his way, differently and better.

He was watched with increasing frequency by a lieutenant, also an engineer, but who seemed to have no duties to
detain him, a quiet young man who said little but observed
much.

"He's tough," said the officer to himself a week later.
"He's cocky, he's a loner, and he's talented. Let's see if he
chickens out easily."

There was no reason for the big machine gunner to hassle
the much smaller plow driver, but he just did. The third
time he messed with the PFC from New Jersey, it came to
blows, but not out in the open. Against the rules. But there
was a patch of open ground behind the mess hall. It was
agreed they would sort out their differences, bare-knuckled,
after dark.

They met by the light of headlamps, with a hundred
fellow soldiers in a circle, taking bets mostly against the
smaller man. The general presumption was that they would
witness a repeat of the slugging match between George
Kennedy and Paul Newman in *Cool Hand Luke*. They were
wrong.

No one mentioned Queensberry Rules so the smaller
man walked straight up to the gunner, slipped beneath the
first head-removing swing, and kicked him hard under the
kneecap. Circling his one-legged opponent, the dozer driver

landed two kidney punches and a knee in the groin. When the big man's head came down to his level, he drove the middle knuckle of his right hand into the gunner's left temple, and for the gunner, the lights went out.

"You don't fight fair," said the stakeholder, when Dexter held out his hand for his winnings.

"No, and I don't lose either," he said. Out beyond the ring of lights the officer nodded at the two MPs with him, and they moved in to make their arrest. Later the limping gunner got his promised twenty dollars.

Since Dexter declined to name his opponent, thirty days in the cooler was the penalty. He slept perfectly well on the unpadded slab in the cell and was still asleep when someone started running a metal spoon up and down the bars. It was dawn.

"On your feet, soldier," said a voice. Dexter came awake, slid off the slab, and stood to attention. The man had a lieutenant's single silver bar on his collar. "Thirty days in here is really boring," said the officer.

"I'll survive, sir," said the ex-PFC, now busted back to private.

"Or you could walk now."

"I think there has to be a catch to that, sir."

"Oh, there is. You leave behind the big, jerk-off toys and come and join my outfit. Then we find out if you're as tough as you think you are."

"And your outfit, sir?"

"They call me Rat Six. Shall we go?"

The officer signed the prisoner out, and they adjourned for breakfast to the smallest and most exclusive mess hall in the whole First Division. No one was allowed in without permission, and there were at that time only fourteen members. Dexter made fifteen, but the number would go down to thirteen in a week when two more were killed.

There was a weird emblem on the door of the "hootch" as they called their tiny club. It showed an upright rodent with snarling face, phallic tongue, a pistol in one hand, and a bottle of liquor in the other. Dexter had joined the Tunnel Rats.

For six years, in a constantly shifting sequence of men, the Tunnel Rats did the dirtiest, deadliest, and by far the scariest job in the Vietnam War; yet so secret were their doings and so few their number that most people today, even Americans, have hardly or never heard of them.

There were probably not more than 350 over the period, a small unit among the engineers of the Big Red One, an equal unit drawn from the Tropic Lightning Twenty-fifth Division. A hundred never came home at all. About a further hundred were dragged, screaming, nerves gone, from their combat zone and consigned to trauma therapy, never to fight again. The rest went back to the States and, being by nature taciturn, laconic loners, seldom mentioned what they had done.

Even the United States, not normally shy about its war heroes, cast no medals and raised no plaques. They came from nowhere, did what they did because it had to be done, and went back to oblivion. And their story all started because of a sergeant's tired ass.

The United States was not the first invader of Vietnam, nor the last. Before the Americans were the French, who colonized the three provinces of Tonkin (north), Annam (center), and Cochin China (south) into their empire, along with Laos and Cambodia.

But the invading Japanese ousted the French in 1942, and after Japan's defeat in 1945, the Vietnamese believed that at last they would be united and free of foreign domination. The French had other ideas and came back. The leading independence fighter (there were others at first) was the Communist Ho Chi Minh. He formed the Vietminh resistance army and the Vietnamese went back to the jungle to fight on, and on and on, for as long as it took.

A stronghold of resistance was the heavily forested farming zone northwest of Saigon, running up to the Cambodian border. The French accorded it their special attention (as would the Americans later) with punitive expedition after expedition. To seek sanctuary the local farmers did not flee; they dug.

They had no technology, just their antlike capacity for hard work, their patience, their local knowledge, and their cunning. They also had mattocks, shovels, and palm-weave baskets. How many million tons of dirt they shifted will never be calculated. But dig and shift, they did. By the time the French left after their 1954 defeat, the whole of the Triangle was a warren of shafts and tunnels. And no one knew about them.

The Americans came, propping up a regime the Vietnamese regarded as puppets of yet another colonial power. They went back to the jungle and back to guerrilla warfare. And they resumed digging. By 1964, they had two hundred miles of tunnels, chambers, passages, and hideouts—and all underground.

The complexity of the tunnel system, when the Americans finally began to comprehend what was down there, took one's breath away. The shafts were so disguised as to be invisible at a few inches' range at the level of the jungle floor. Down below were up to five levels of galleries, the lowest at fifty feet, linked by narrow, twisting passages that only a Vietnamese, or a small, wiry Caucasoid, could crawl through.

The levels were linked by trap doors, some going up, others heading down. These, too, were camouflaged to look like blank end-of-tunnel walls. There were stores, assembly caverns, dormitories, repair shops, eating halls, and even hospitals. By 1966, a full combat brigade could hide down there, but until the Tet Offensive that number was never needed.

Penetration by an aggressor was discouraged. If a vertical shaft was discovered, there could well be a cunning booby trap at the bottom. Firing down the tunnels served no purpose; they changed direction every few yards so a bullet would go straight into the end wall.

Dynamiting did not work; there were scores of alternate galleries within the pitch-black maze down there, but only

a local would know them. Gas did not work; they were
fitted with water seals, like the U-bend in a lavatory pipe.

The network ran under the jungle from the suburbs of
Saigon almost to the Cambodian border. There were various other networks elsewhere but nothing like the tunnels
of Cu Chi, named after the nearest town.

After a monsoon, the laterite clay was pliable, easy to
dig, scrape back, and drag away in baskets. Dry, it set like
concrete.

After the passing of Kennedy, Americans arrived in really significant numbers and no longer as instructors but for
combat, starting in the spring of 1964. They had the numbers, the weapons, the machines, the firepower—and they
hit nothing. They hit nothing because they found nothing,
just an occasional VC corpse if they got lucky. But they
took casualties, and the body count began to mount.

At first it was convenient to presume the VC were peasants by day, lost among the black pajama–clad millions,
switching to guerrillas at night. But why so many casualties
by day and no one to fire back at? In January 1966, the
Big Red One decided to raze the Iron Triangle once and
for all. It was Operation Crimp.

They started at one end, fanned out, and moved forward.
They had enough ammunition to wipe out Indochina. They
reached the other end and had found no one. From behind
the moving line, sniper fire started and the GIs took five
fatalities. Whoever was firing had only old, bolt-action Soviet carbines, but a bullet through the heart is still a bullet
through the heart.

The GIs turned back and went over the same ground.
Nothing. No enemy. They took more fatalities, always in
the back. They discovered a few foxholes, a brace of air-
raid shelters, empty, offering no cover. More sniper fire but
no running figures in black to fire back at.

On day four, Sgt. Stewart Green, massively fed up as
were his comrades around him, had sat down for a rest. In
two seconds he was up, clutching his butt. Fire ants, scor-
pions, snakes, Vietnam had them all. He was convinced he

had been stung or bitten. But it was a nail head. The nail
was part of a frame, and the frame was the hidden door to
a shaft that went straight down into blackness. The U.S.
Army had discovered where the snipers were going. They
had been marching over their heads for two years.

There was no way of fighting the Vietcong living and
hiding down there in the darkness by remote control. The
society that in three years would send two men to walk on
the moon had no technology for the tunnels of Cu Chi.
There was only one way to take the fight to the invisible
enemy.

Someone had to strip down to thin cotton pants and with
pistol, knife, and torch, go down into that pitch-black, stinking, airless, unknown, unmapped, booby-trapped, deadly,
hideously claustrophobic labyrinth of narrow passages with
no known exit and kill the waiting Vietcong in their own
lair.

A few men were found, a special type of man. Big, burly
men were of no use. The 95 percent who feel claustrophobic were no use. Loud mouths, exhibitionists, look-at-me's
were no use. The ones who did it were quiet, soft-spoken,
self-effacing, self-contained personalities, often loners in
their own units. They had to be very cool, even cold, possessed of icy nerves, and almost immune to panic, the real
enemy below ground.

Army bureaucracy, never afraid to use ten words where
two will do, called them "Tunnel Exploration Personnel."
They called themselves the Tunnel Rats.

By the time Cal Dexter reached Vietnam, they had been
in existence for three years, the only unit whose Purple
Heart ratio was 100 percent.

The commanding officer of the moment was known as
Rat Six. Everyone else had a different number. Once
joined, they kept to themselves and everyone regarded them
with a kind of awe, as men will be awkward in the company
of one sentenced to die.

Rat Six had been right in his gut guess. The tough little
kid from the construction sites of New Jersey with his

deadly fists and feet, Paul Newman eyes, and steel nerves, was a natural.

He took him down into the tunnels of Cu Chi and within an hour realized that the recruit was the better fighter. They became partners underground where there were no ranks and no "sirs," and for nearly two tours they fought and killed down in the darkness until Henry Kissinger met Le Duc Tho and agreed America would quit Vietnam. After that there was no point.

To the rest of the Big Red One, the pair became a legend, spoken of in whispers. The officer was "the Badger" and the newly promoted sergeant was "the Mole."

5
THE TUNNEL RAT

In the army, a mere six years in age difference between two young men can seem like a generation. The older man appears almost a father figure. Thus it was with the Badger and the Mole. At twenty-five, the officer was six years older. More, he came from a different social background with a far better education.

His parents were professional people. After high school he had spent a year touring Europe, seeing ancient Greece and Rome, historical Italy, Germany, France, and Britain.

He had spent four years in college getting his degree in civil and mechanical engineering before facing the draft. He, too, had opted for the three-year commission and gone straight to OCS at Fort Belvoir, Virginia.

Fort Belvoir was then churning out junior officers at a hundred a month. Nine months after entering, the Badger had emerged as a second lieutenant, rising to first when he shipped to Vietnam to join the First Engineer Battalion of the Big Red One. He, too, had been headhunted for the Tunnel Rats, and in view of his rank, quickly became Rat Six when his predecessor left for home. He had nine months of his required one-year Vietnam tour to complete, two months less than Dexter did.

But within a month it was clear that once the two men went into the tunnels, their roles were reversed. The Badger deferred to the Mole, accepting that the young man had a sense for danger, the silent menace around the next corner, the smell of a booby trap, that no college degree could match and which might keep them both alive.

Before either man had reached Vietnam, the U.S. High Command had realized that trying to blow the tunnel system to smithereens was a waste of time. The dried laterite was too hard, the complex too extensive. The continuous switching of the tunnel direction meant explosive forces could only reach so far and not far enough.

Attempts had been made to drown the tunnels with flooding, but the water just soaked through the tunnel floors. Due to the water traps, gas failed as well. The decision was made that the only way to bring the enemy to battle was to go down there and try to find the headquarters network of the entire Vietcong War Zone C.

This, it was believed, was down there somewhere, between the southern tip of the Iron Triangle at the junction of the Saigon and Thi Tinh Rivers and the Boi Loi Woods at the Cambodian end. To find that headquarters, to wipe out the senior cadres, to grab the huge harvest of intelligence that must be down there—that was the aim and, if it could be achieved, a prize beyond rubies.

In fact, the headquarters was under the Ho Bo Woods, upcountry by the bank of the Saigon River, and was never found. But every time the tankdozers or the Rome Plows uncovered another tunnel entrance, the Rats went down into hell to keep looking.

The entrances were always vertical, and that created the

first danger. To go down feet first was to expose the lower half of the body to any VC waiting in the side tunnel. He would be happy to drive a needle-pointed bamboo spear deep into the groin or entrails of the dangling GI before scooting backward into the darkness. By the time the dying American had been hauled back up, with the haft of the spear scraping the walls and the venom-poisoned tip ripping at his bowels, his chances of survival were minimal.

To go down head first meant risking the spear, bayonet, or point-blank bullet through the base of the throat.

The safest way seemed to be to descend slowly until the last five feet, then drop fast and fire at the slightest movement inside the tunnel. But the base of the shaft might be twigs and leaves, hiding a pit with punji sticks. These were embedded bamboo spears, also venom-tipped, that would drive straight through the sole of a combat boot, through the foot, and out the instep. Being fishhook carved and barbed, they could hardly be withdrawn. Few survived them either.

Once inside the tunnel and crawling forward, the danger might be the VC waiting around the next corner but more likely the booby traps. These were various, of great cunning, and had to be disarmed before progress could be made.

Some horrors needed no Vietcong at all. The nectar bat and black-bearded tomb bat were both cave dwellers and roosted through the daylight in the tunnels until disturbed. So did the giant crab spider, so dense on the walls that the wall itself appeared to be shimmering with movement. Even more numerous were the fire ants.

None of these were lethal; that honor went to the bamboo viper, whose bite meant death in thirty minutes. The trap was usually a yard of bamboo embedded in the roof, jutting downward at an angle and emerging by no more than an inch.

The snake was inside the tube, head downward, trapped and enraged, its escape blocked by a plug of kapok at the lower end. Threaded through this was a length of fishing line, heading through a hole in a peg in the wall on one side, thence to a peg across the tunnel. If the crawling GI touched the line, it would jerk the plug out of the bamboo above him and the viper would tumble onto the back of his neck.

And there were the rats, real rats. In the tunnels they had discovered their private heaven and bred furiously. Just as the GIs would never leave a wounded man or even a corpse in the tunnels, the Vietcong hated to leave one of their casualties up above for the Americans to find and add to the cherished "body count." Dead VC were brought below and entombed in the walls in a fetal position before being plastered over with wet clay.

But a skim of clay will not stop a rat. They had their endless food source and grew to the size of cats. Yet the Vietcong lived down there for weeks or even months on end, challenging the Americans to come into their domain, find them, and fight them.

Those who did it and survived became accustomed to the stench as well as to the hideous life-forms. It was always hot, sticky, cramped, and pitch dark. And it stank. The VC had to perform their bodily functions in earthenware jars; when full, these were buried in the floors and capped with a plug of clay. But the rats scratched them open.

Coming from the most heavily armed country on earth, the GIs who became Tunnel Rats had to cast all technology aside and return to primal man. One commando knife, one handgun, one flashlight, a spare magazine, and two spare batteries were all that would fit down there. Occasionally a hand grenade would be used, but these were dangerous, sometimes lethal for the thrower. In tiny spaces, the boom could shatter eardrums, but worse, the explosion would suck out all the oxygen for hundreds of feet. A man could die before more could filter in from outside.

For a Tunnel Rat to use his pistol or flashlight was to give his position away, to announce his coming, never knowing who crouched in the darkness up ahead, silent and waiting. In this sense, the VC always had the edge. They only had to stay silent and wait for the man crawling toward them.

Most nerve-racking of all, and the source of most deaths, was the task of penetrating the trap doors that led from level to level, usually downward.

Often a tunnel would come to a dead end. Or was it a dead end? If so, why dig it in the first place? In the dark, with fingertips feeling nothing ahead but laterite wall, no side tunnel to left or right, the Tunnel Rat had to use his flashlight. This would usually reveal, skillfully camouflaged and easily missable, a trap door in the wall, floor, or ceiling. Either the mission was aborted, or the door had to be opened.

But who waited on the other side? If the GI's head went through first and there was a Vietcong waiting, the American's life would end with a throat cut from side to side or the lethal bite of a garroting noose of thin wire. If he dropped downward feet first, it could be the spear through the belly. Then he would die in agony, his screaming torso in one level, ruined lower body in the next one down.

Dexter had the armorers prepare him small, tangerine-sized grenades with a reduced explosive charge from the standard issue but with more ball bearings. Twice in his first six months he lifted a trap door, tossed in a grenade with a three-second fuse, and pulled the door back down. When he opened the trap door a second time and went through with his flashlight on, the next chamber was a charnel house of torn bodies.

The complexes were protected from gas attack by water traps. The crawling Tunnel Rat would find a pool of rank water in front of him. That meant the tunnel continued on the other side of the water.

The only way through was to roll onto one's back, slide in upside down, and pull your body along with your fingertips scrabbling at the roof. The hope was that the water ended before the breath in your lungs did. Otherwise, the Tunnel Rat could die fifty feet under, drowned, upside down, in blackness. The way to survive was to rely on a partner.

Before entering the water, the point man would tie a lanyard to his feet and pass it back to his partner. If he did not give a reassuring tug on it within ninety seconds of entering the water, confirming that he had found air on the other side of the trap, his buddy had to pull him back without delay because he would be dying down there.

Through all this misery, discomfort, and fear, there occurred a moment now and again when the Tunnel Rats hit the mother lode. This would be a cavern, sometimes recently vacated in a hurry, which had clearly been an important subheadquarters. Then boxes of papers, evidence, clues, maps, and other mementoes would be ferried back to the waiting Intelligence experts from G2.

Twice the Badger and the Mole came across such Aladdin's caves. Senior brass, unsure how to cope with such strange young men, handed out medals and warm words. But the Public Affairs people, normally avid to tell the world how well the war was going, were warned off. No one mentioned a word. One facility trip was arranged, but the "guest" from PA got fifteen yards down a "safe" tunnel and had hysterics. After that, silence reigned.

But there were long periods of no combat for the Rats as for all the other GIs in Vietnam. Some slept the hours away, or wrote letters, longing for the end of their tour and the journey home. Some drank the time away or played cards or craps. Many smoked, and not always Marlboros. Some became addicts. Others read.

Cal Dexter was one of those. Talking with his officer partner he realized how blighted his formal education was and started again from square one. He found he was fascinated by history. The base librarian was delighted and impressed, and prepared a long list of must-read books, which he then obtained from Saigon.

Dexter worked his way through Attic Greece and Ancient Rome, learned of Alexander, who had wept that, at thirty-one, he had defeated the known world and there were no more worlds to conquer.

He learned of Rome's decline and fall, of the Dark Ages, medieval Europe, the Renaissance, and the Enlightenment, the Age of Elegance and the Age of Reason. He was particularly fascinated by the early years of the birth of the American colonies, the Revolution, and why his own country had had a vicious civil war just ninety years before he was born.

He did one other thing in those long periods when monsoons or orders kept him confined to base. With the help of the elderly Vietnamese who swept and cleaned the "hootch" for them all, he learned workaday Vietnamese until he could speak enough to make himself understood and understand more than that.

Nine months into his first tour, two things happened. He took his first combat wound, and the Badger ended his twelve-month stint.

The bullet came from a VC who had been hiding in one of the tunnels as Dexter came down the entrance shaft. To confuse such a waiting enemy, Dexter had developed a technique. He threw a grenade down the shaft, then went in fast, hand over fist. If the grenade did not blow away the false floor of the shaft, then there was no punji-stick trap down there. If it did, he had time to stop before he hit the spikes.

The same grenade ought to shred any VC waiting out of sight. On this occasion, the VC was there but standing well down the passage with a Kalashnikov AK-47. He survived the blast but was injured and fired one shot at the fast-falling Tunnel Rat. Dexter hit the deck with his pistol out and fired back three times. The VC went down, crawled away, but was found later, dead. Dexter was nicked in the upper left arm, a flesh wound that healed well but kept him above ground for a month. The Badger's problem was more serious.

Soldiers will admit it, policemen will confirm it; there is no substitute for a partner you can utterly rely on. Since

they had formed their partnership in the early days, the
Badger and the Mole did not really want to go into the
tunnels with anyone else. In nine months, Dexter had seen
four Rats killed down there. In one case, the surviving Tunnel Rat had come back to the surface screaming and crying.
He would never go down a tunnel again, even after weeks
with the psychiatrists.

But the body of the one who never made it was still
down there. The Badger and the Mole went in with ropes
to find the man and drag him out to be sent home for a
Christian burial. His throat had been cut. No open casket
for him.

Of the original thirteen, four more had quit at the end
of their time. Eight down. Six recruits had joined. They
were back to eleven in the whole unit.

"I don't want to go down there with anyone else," Dexter told his partner when the Badger came to visit him in
the base clinic.

"Nor me if it were the other way around," said the
Badger. They settled it by agreeing that if the Badger extended for a second one-year tour, the Mole would do the
same in three months. So it was done. Both accepted a
second tour and went back to the tunnels. The division's
commanding general, embarrassed by his own gratitude,
handed out two more medals.

There were certain rules down in those tunnels that were
never broken. One was: Never go down alone. Because of
his remarkable hazard antennae, the Mole was usually up
at point with the Badger several yards behind. Another rule
was: Never fire off all six shots at once. It tells the VC you
are now out of ammo and a sitting duck. Two months into
his second tour, in May 1970, Cal Dexter nearly broke them
both and was lucky to survive.

The pair had entered a newly discovered shaft up in the
Ho Bo Woods. The Mole was up front and had crawled
three hundred yards along a tunnel that changed direction
four times. He had fingertip felt two booby traps and disconnected them. He failed to notice that the Badger had

confronted his own personal pet hatred, two tomb bats that had fallen into his hair and had stopped, unable to speak or go on.

The Mole was crawling alone when he saw, or thought he saw, the dimmest of glows coming from around the next corner. It was so dim he thought his retina might be playing tricks. He slithered silently to the corner and stopped, pistol in his right hand. The glow also stayed motionless, just around the corner. He waited like that for ten minutes, unaware that his partner was lying, frozen with fear, out of sight behind him. Then the Mole decided to break the standoff. He lunged around the corner.

Ten feet away was a Vietcong on his hands and knees. Between them was the source of light, a shallow lamp of coconut oil with a tiny wick floating in it. The VC had evidently been pushing it along the floor to accomplish his mission, checking out the booby traps. For half a second the two enemies just stared at each other, then both reacted.

With the back of his fingers, the Vietnamese flicked the dish of hot nut oil straight at the American's face. The light was snuffed out at once. Dexter raised his left hand to protect his eyes and felt the searing oil splash across the back of his knuckles. With his right hand he fired three times as he heard a frantic scuffling sound retreating down the tunnel. He was sorely tempted to use the other three rounds, but he did not know how many more there were down there.

Had the Badger but known it, they were crawling toward the headquarters complex of the Vietcong's entire Zone Command. Guarding it were fifty diehards.

Back in the States while all this was going on was a covert little unit called the Limited War Laboratory. Throughout the Vietnam War, they dreamed up splendid ideas to help the Tunnel Rats, though none of the scientists had ever been down a tunnel. They shipped their ideas over to Vietnam, where the Rats, who did go down in the tunnels, tried them out, found them gloriously impractical, and shipped them back again.

In the summer of 1970, the Limited War Laboratory came up with a new kind of gun for close-quarter work in a confined space. And at last they had a winner. It was a .44 Magnum handgun modified down to a three-inch barrel so as not to get in the way, but with special ammunition.

The very heavy slug of this .44 was divided into four segments. They were held together as one by the cartridge, but on emerging from the barrel separated to make four slugs instead of one. The Tunnel Rats found it very good for close-quarter work and likely to be deadly in the tunnels because if fired twice it would fill the tunnel ahead with eight projectiles instead of two. They had a far greater chance of hitting the Vietcong.

Only seventy-five of these guns were ever made. The Tunnel Rats used them for six months, then they were withdrawn. Someone had discovered that they probably contravened the Geneva Convention. So the seventy-four traceable Smith & Wesson revolvers were sent back to the States and never seen again.

The Tunnel Rats had a short and simple prayer. "If I have to take a bullet, so be it. If I have to take a knife, tough luck. But please, Lord, don't ever bury me alive down there."

It was in the summer of 1970 that the Badger was buried alive. Either the GIs should not have been down there, or the B-52 bombers out of Guam should not have been bombing from thirty-thousand feet. But someone had ordered the bombers, and that someone forgot to tell the Tunnel Rats. It happens. Not a lot, but no one who has ever been in the armed forces will fail to recognize a FUBAR—f*cked up beyond all repair.

It was the new thinking, to destroy the tunnel complexes by caving them in with massive explosions dropped by B-52s. This had partly been caused by the change in psychology.

Back in the States the tide of opinion was now comprehensively against the Vietnam War. The parents were now joining their children in the antiwar demonstrations.

In the war zone, the Tet Offensive of thirty months earlier had not been forgotten. The morale was simply drib-
bling away into the jungle. It was still unspoken among the
High Command, but the mood was spreading that this war
could not be won. It would be three more years before the
last GI would board the last plane out of there; but by the
summer of 1970, the decision was made to destroy the tunnels in the "free strike zones" with bombs. The Iron Triangle was a free strike zone.

Because the entire Twenty-fifth Infantry Division was
based there, the bombers had instructions that no bomb
should fall closer than two miles from the nearest U.S. unit.
But that day the High Command forgot about the Badger
and the Mole, who were in a different division.

They were in a complex outside Ben Suc, in the second
level down, when they felt rather than heard the first
"crump" of bombs above them. Then another, and the earth
began to rock around them. Forgetting the VC, they
crawled frantically toward the shaft going up to level one.

The Mole made it and was ten yards toward the final
shaft up to daylight when the roof came down. It was behind him. He yelled, "Badger!" There was no reply. He
knew there was a small alcove twenty yards ahead because
they had passed it coming down. Drenched in sweat he
dragged himself into it and used the extra width to turn
around and head back.

He met the dirt pile with his fingertips. Then he felt a
hand, then a second, but nothing beyond that except fallen
earth. He began to dig, hurling the slag behind him but
blocking his exit as he did so.

It took him five minutes to liberate his partner's head,
five more to free the torso. The bombs had ceased, but up
top the falling debris had blocked the air flues. They began
to run out of oxygen.

"Get out of here, Cal," hissed the Badger in the darkness. "Come back with help later. I'll be OK."

Dexter continued scrabbling at the dirt with his fingertips. He had lost two nails entirely. It would take over an

hour to get help. His partner would not survive half that time with the air flues blocked. He put on his flashlight and shoved the lamp in his partner's hand.

"Hold that. Direct the beam back over your shoulder."

By the yellow light he could see the mass covering the Badger's legs. It took another half hour, then the crawl back to daylight, squeezing past the rubble he had cast behind him as he dug. His lungs were heaving, his head spinning; his partner semiconscious. Then he crawled around the last corner and felt the air.

In January 1971, the Badger reached the end of his second tour. Extension for a third year was forbidden, but he had had enough anyway. The night before he flew back to the States, the Mole secured permission to accompany his partner into Saigon to say farewell. They went into the capital with an armored convoy. Dexter was confident he could hitch a lift back in a helicopter the next day.

The two young men had a slap-up meal then toured the bars. They avoided the hordes of prostitutes but concentrated on some serious drinking. At two in the morning they found themselves, feeling no pain, somewhere in Cholon, the Chinese quarter of Saigon across the river. There was a tattoo parlor still open and available for business, especially in dollars. The Chinaman was wisely contemplating a future outside Vietnam.

Before they left him and took the ferry back across the river, the young Americans had each gotten a tattoo. On the left forearm, it showed a rat, not the aggressive rat on the door of the "hootch" at Lai Khe, but a smart-ass rat, facing away from the viewer but looking back over his shoulder with a broad wink, trousers down, a mooning rat. They were still laughing until they sobered up. Then it was too late.

The Badger flew back to the States the next morning. The Mole followed ten weeks later, in mid-March. On April 7, 1971, the Tunnel Rats formally ceased to exist.

That was the day Cal Dexter, despite the urging of several senior officers, mustered out of the army and returned to civilian life.

6

THE TRACKER

There are very few military outfits more secretive than the British Special Air Service, but if there is one that makes the tight-lipped SAS look like *The Jerry Springer Show*, it is the Det.

The Fourteenth Independent Intelligence Company, also called the Fourteenth Intelligence or the Detachment or the Det, is an army unit drawing its recruits from right across the board, with (and unlike the all-male SAS) quite a proportion of women soldiers.

Although it can, if need be, fight with lethal efficiency, the main tasks of the Det are to locate, track to lair, survey, and eavesdrop on the bad guys. They are never seen, and their planted listening devices are so advanced they are rarely found.

A successful Det operation would involve tailing a ter-

rorist to the main hive, entering secretly at night, planting
a "bug," and listening to the bad people for days or weeks
on end. In this manner the terrorists would be likely to
discuss their next operation.

Tipped off, the slightly noisier SAS could then mount a
sweet little ambush and, as soon as the first terrorist fired
a weapon, wipe them out. Legally. Self-defense.

Most of the Det operations up to 1995 had been in
Northern Ireland, where their covertly obtained information
had led to some of the IRA's worst defeats. It was the Det
who hit on the idea of slipping into a mortician's parlor
where a terrorist, of either Republican or Unionist persua-
sion, was lying in a casket and inserting a bug into the
coffin.

This was because the terrorist godfathers, knowing they
were under investigation, would rarely meet to discuss
planning. But at a funeral they would congregate, lean over
the coffin, and, covering their mouths from lip readers behind the telescopes on the hillside above the cemetery, hold
a planning conference. The bugs in the coffin would pick
up the lot. It worked for years.

In years to come, it would be the Det who carried out
the "Close Target Reconnaissance" on Bosnia's mass killers, allowing the SAS snatch squads to haul them off to
trial in The Hague.

The company whose name Steve Edmond had learned
from Mr. Rubinstein, the Toronto art collector who had
mysteriously recovered his paintings, was called Hazard
Management, a very discreet agency based in the Victoria
district of London.

Hazard Management specialized in three things and extensively used former Special Forces personnel among its
staff. The biggest income earner was Asset Protection. As
its name implies, their job was the protection of extremely
expensive property on behalf of very rich people who did
not want to be parted from it. This was only carried out for
limited-term special occasions, not on a permanent basis.

Next came Personnel Protection, PP as opposed to AP.

This was also only for a limited time span, although there was a small school in Wiltshire where a rich man's own personal bodyguards could be trained, for a substantial fee.

The smallest of the divisions in Hazard Management was known as L&R, Location & Recovery. This was what Mr. Rubinstein had needed: someone to trace his missing masterpieces and negotiate their return.

Two days after taking the call from his frantic daughter, Steve Edmond had his meeting with the chief executive of Hazard Management and explained what he wanted.

"Find my grandson. This is not a commission with a budget ceiling," he said.

The former director of Special Forces, now retired, beamed. Even soldiers have children to educate. The man he called in from his country home the next day was Phil Gracey, former captain in the Parachute Regiment and ten years a veteran of the Det. Inside the company, he was simply known as "the Tracker."

Gracey had his own meeting with the Canadian, and his interrogation was extremely detailed. If the boy was still alive, he wanted to know everything about his personal habits, tastes, preferences, even vices. He took possession of two good photographs of Ricky Colenso and the grand-father's personal cell-phone number. Then he nodded and left.

The Tracker spent two days almost continuously on the phone. He had no intention of moving until he knew exactly where he was going, how, why, and whom he sought. He spent hours reading written material about the Bosnian civil war, the aid program, and the non-Bosnian military presence on the ground. He struck lucky on the last.

The United Nations had created a military "peace-keeping" force—the usual lunacy of sending a force to keep the peace where there was no peace to keep, then forbidding them to create the peace, ordering them instead to watch the slaughter without interfering. The military were called UNPROFOR, and the British government had sup-

plied a large contingent. It was based at Vitez, just ten miles
down the road from Travnik.

The regiment assigned there in June 1995 was recent;
its predecessor had been relieved only two months earlier,
and the Tracker traced the colonel commanding the earlier
regiment to a course at Guards Depot, Pirbright. He was a
mine of information. On the third day after his talk with
the Canadian grandfather, the Tracker flew to the Balkans,
not straight into Bosnia (impossible) but to the Adriatic
resort of Split on the coast of Croatia. His cover story said
he was a freelance journalist, which is a useful cover being
completely unprovable either way. But he also included a
letter from a major London Sunday newspaper asking for
a series of articles on the effectiveness of relief aid—just
in case.

After twenty-four hours in Split, enjoying an unexpected
boom as the main jumping-off point for central Bosnia, he
had acquired a secondhand but tough off-road and a pistol.
Just in case. It was a long, rough drive through the mountains from the coast to Travnik, but he was confident his
information was accurate; he would run into no combat
zone, and he did not.

It was a strange combat, the Bosnia civil war. There
were rarely any lines, as such, and never a pitched battle,
just a patchwork quilt of monoethnic communities living in
fear; hundreds of fire-gutted, ethnically "cleansed" villages
and hamlets; and, roaming among them, bands of soldiery,
mostly belonging to one of the surrounding "national" ar-
mies but also including groups of mercenaries, freebooters,
and psychotic paramilitaries posing as patriots. These were
the worst.

At Travnik, the Tracker met his first reverse. John Slack
had left. A friendly soul with Age Concern said he believed
the American had joined Feed the Children, a much bigger
NGO, and was based in Zagreb. The Tracker spent the
night in his sleeping bag in the rear of the 4×4 and left
the next day for another grueling drive north to Zagreb, the
Croatian capital. There he found John Slack at the Feed the

Children warehouse. He was not much help.

"I have no idea what happened, where he went or why," he protested. "Look, man, the Loaves-n-Fishes operation closed down last month, and he was part of that. He vanished with one of my two brand-new Landcruisers, that is, 50 percent of my transportation.

"Plus, he took one of my three local Bosnian helpers. Charleston was not pleased. With peace moves finally in the offing, they did not want to start over. I told them there was still a lot to do, but they closed me down. I was lucky to find a billet here."

"What about the Bosnian?"

"Fadil? No chance he was behind it all. He was a good guy. Spent a lot of time grieving for his lost family. If he hated anyone, it was the Serbs, not the Americans."

"Any sign of the money belt?"

"Now that was stupid. I warned him. It was too much either to leave behind or carry around, but I don't think Fadil would kill him for that."

"Where were you, John?"

"That's the point. If I had been there, it would never have happened. I'd have vetoed the idea, whatever it was. But I was on a mountain road in southern Croatia trying to get a truck with a solid engine block towed to the nearest town. Dumb Swede. Can you imagine driving a truck with an empty oil sump and not noticing?"

"What did you discover?"

"When I got back? Well, he had arrived at the compound, let himself in, taken a Landcruiser, and driven off. One of the other Bosnians, Ibrahim, saw them both, but they didn't speak. That was four days before I returned. I kept trying his mobile, but there was no answer. I went apeshit. I figured they'd gone partying. At first I was more angry than worried."

"Any idea which direction?"

"Ibrahim said they drove north. That is, straight into central Travnik. From the town center the roads lead all over. No one in town remembers a thing."

"You got any ideas, John?"

"Yep. I reckon he took a call. Or more likely Fadil took a call and told Ricky. He was very compassion driven. If he had taken a call about some medical emergency in one of the villages high in the backcountry, he'd have driven off to try and help. Too impulsive to leave a message.

"You seen that country, pal? You ever driven through it? Mountains and valleys and rivers. I figure they went over a precipice and crashed into a valley. Come winter, when the leaves fall, I think someone will spot the wreckage down below among the rocks."

The Tracker went back to Travnik, set up a small office-cum-living quarters, and recruited a happy-to-be employed Ibrahim as his guide and interpreter.

He carried a satphone with several spare batteries and a scrambler device to keep communications covert. It was just for keeping in touch with his head office in London. They had facilities he did not.

He believed there were four possibilities, ranging from dumb via possible to likely. The dumbest of the four was that Ricky Colenso had decided to steal the Landcruiser, drive south to Belgrade in Serbia, sell it, abandon all his previous life, and live like a bum. He rejected it. It simply was not Ricky Colenso, and why would he steal a Land-cruiser if his grandpa could buy the factory?

Next up was that Sulejman had persuaded Ricky to take him for a drive then murdered the young American for his money belt and the vehicle. Possible. But as a Bosnian Muslim without a passport, Fadil would not get far in Croatia or Serbia—both hostile territory for him—and a new Landcruiser on the market would be spotted.

Three, they ran into person or persons unknown and were murdered for the same trophies. Among the out-of-control freelance killers wandering the landscape were a few groups of Mujehadin, Muslim fanatics from the Middle East come to "help" their persecuted fellow Muslims in Bosnia. It was known they had already killed two European mercenaries, even though they were supposed to be on the same side, plus one relief worker and one Muslim garage owner who declined to donate gas.

But way out on top of the range of probabilities was John Slack's theory. The Tracker had taken Ibrahim and, day by day, followed every road out of Travnik for miles into the backcountry. While the Bosnian drove slowly behind him, the Tracker scoured the road edges over every possible steep slope into the valleys below.

He was doing what he did best. Slowly, patiently, missing nothing, he looked for tire marks, crumbled edges, skid lines, crushed vegetation, wheel-flattened grass. Three times, with a rope tied to the Lada off-road, he went down into ravines where a clump of vegetation might hide a crushed Landcruiser. Nothing.

With binoculars he sat on road edges and scanned the valleys below for a glint of metal or glass. Nothing. By the end of an exhausting ten days he had become convinced that Slack was wrong. If a vehicle of that size had swerved off the road and over the edge, it would have left a trace, however small, even forty days later; and he would have seen that trace. There was no crashed vehicle lying in those valleys around Travnik.

He offered a big-enough reward for information to make the mouth water. Word about the prize spread in the refugee community, and hopefuls came forward. But the best he got was that the car had been seen driving through town. Destination unknown. Heading unknown.

After two weeks he closed his operation down and moved to Vitez, headquarters of the newly resident British army contingent.

He found a billet at the school that had been converted into a sort of hostel for the mainly British press. It was on a street known as TV Alley, just outside the army compound but safe enough if things turned nasty.

Knowing what most army men think of the press, he did not bother with his "freelance journalist" cover story, but sought a meeting with the commanding colonel on the basis of what he was, ex–Special Services.

The colonel had a brother in the elite Parachute Regiment of the British army. Common background, common interests. Not a problem. Anything he could do to help?

Yes, he had heard about the missing American boy. Bad show. His patrols had kept a lookout, but nothing. He listened to the Tracker's offer of a substantial donation to the Army Benevolent Fund. A reconnaissance exercise was mounted, a light aircraft from the artillery people. The Tracker went with the pilot. They flew over the mountains and ravines for more than an hour. Not a sign.

"I think you're going to have to look at foul play," said the colonel over dinner.

"Mujehadin?"

"Possibly. Weird swine, you know. They will kill you as soon as look at you if you're not a Muslim, or even if you are but not fundamentalist enough. May 15th? We'd only been here for two weeks. Still getting the hang of the terrain. But I've checked the Incident Log. There were none in the area. You could try the ECMM sitreps. Pretty useless stuff, but I've got a stack in the office. Should cover May 15th."

The European Community Monitoring Mission (ECMM) was the attempt of the European Union based in Brussels to horn in on an act they could influence in no way at all. Bosnia was a UN affair until finally, in exasperation, taken over and resolved by the Americans. But Brussels wanted a role, so a team of observers was created to give them one. This was the ECMM. The Tracker went through the stack of reports the next day.

The EU monitors were mainly armed forces officers loaned by the EU defense ministries with nothing better to do. They were scattered throughout Bosnia, where they each had an office, a flat, a car, and a living allowance. Some of the situation reports, or sitreps, read more like a social diary. The Tracker concentrated on anything filed May 15th or the three days following. There was one from Banja Luka dated May 16th that caught his eye.

Banja Luka was a fiercely Serbian stronghold well to the

north of Travnik and across the Vlasic mountain chain. The ECMM officer there was a Danish major, Lasse Bjerregaard. He had written that the previous evening, i.e., May 15th, he had been taking a drink in the bar of the Bosna Hotel when he witnessed a blazing row between two Serbs in camouflage. One had clearly been in a rage at the other and was screaming abuse at him in Serbian. He slapped the face of the junior man several times, but the offending party did not answer back, indicating the clear superiority of the slapper.

When it was over, the major tried to seek an explanation from the barman, who spoke halting English, which the Dane spoke fluently; but the barman shrugged and walked away in a very rude manner, which was unlike him. The next morning the uniformed men were gone, and the major never saw them again.

The Tracker thought it was the longest shot of his life, but he called the ECMM office in Banja Luka. Another change of posting; a Greek came on the line. Yes, the Dane had returned home the previous week. The Tracker called London suggesting they ask the Danish Defense Ministry. London came back in three hours. Fortunately, the name was not so common. Jensen would have been a problem. Major Bjerregaard was on furlough, and his number was in Odense.

The Tracker caught him that evening when he returned from a day on the water with his family in the summer heatwave. Major Bjerregaard was as helpful as he could be. He remembered the evening of May 15th quite clearly. There was, after all, precious little for a Dane to do in Banja Luka; it had been a very lonely and boring posting.

Every evening he had gone to the bar around 7:30 for a predinner beer. About half an hour later a small group of Serbs in camouflage had entered. He did not think they were Yugoslav army because they did not have unit flashes on their shoulders.

They seemed very full of themselves and ordered drinks all around, slivovitz with beer chasers, a lethal combination.

Several rounds of drinks later, the major was about to adjourn to the dining room because the noise was becoming
deafening when another Serb arrived. He seemed to be the
commander because the rest subsided.

He spoke to them in Serbian, and he must have ordered
them to come with him. The men began to swig their beers
and put their packs of cigarettes and lighters back in their
uniform pockets. Then one of them offered to pay.

The commander went berserk. He started screaming at
the subordinate. The rest went deathly quiet. So did the
other customers and the barman. The tirade went on, accompanied by two slaps to the face. Still no one protested.
Finally the leader stormed out. Crestfallen and subdued, the
others followed. No one else offered to pay for the drinks.

"Did the commander rage at anyone else?" asked the
Tracker.

"No, just at the one who had tried to pay," said the voice
from Denmark.

"Why him alone, Major? There is no mention in your
report as to any possible reason."

"Ah. Didn't I put that in? Sorry. I think it was because
the man tried to pay with a hundred-dollar bill."

7

THE VOLUNTEER

The Tracker packed his gear and drove north from Travnik. He was passing from Bosnian (Muslim) territory into Serb-held country. But a British Union Jack fluttered from a pennant above the Lada and with luck that ought to deter long-range potshots. If stopped, he intended to rely on his passport, proof that he was just writing about relief aid, and generous presents of Virginia-made cigarettes bought from the Vitez barracks shop. If all that failed, his pistol was fully loaded, close to hand, and he knew how to use it.

He was stopped twice, once by a Bosnian militia patrol as he left Bosnia-controlled country and once by a Yugoslav army patrol south of Banja Luka. Each time his explanation, documents, and presents worked. He rolled into Banja Luka five hours later.

The Bosna Hotel was certainly never going to put the
Ritz out of business, but it was about all the town had. He
checked in. There was plenty of room. Apart from a French
TV crew, he judged he was the only foreigner staying there.
At 7:00 that evening he entered the bar. There were three
other drinkers—all Serbs, and all seated at tables—and one
barman. He straddled the stool at the bar.

"Hallo. You must be Dusko."

He was open, friendly, charming. The barman shook the
proffered hand. "You been here before?"

"No, first time. Nice bar. Friendly bar."

"How you know my name?"

"Friend of mine was posted here recently. Danish fellow.
Lasse Bjaerregaard. He asked me to say hi if I was passing
through."

The barman relaxed considerably. There was no threat
here.

"You Danish?"

"No, British."

"Army?"

"Heavens no. Journalist. Doing a series of articles about
aid agencies. You'll take a drink with me?"

Dusko helped himself to his own best brandy. "I would
like to be a journalist one day. Travel. See the world."

"Why not? Get some experience on the local paper, then
go to the big city. That's what I did."

The barman shrugged in resignation. "Here? Banja
Luka? No paper."

"So try Sarajevo. Even Belgrade. You're a Serb. You
can get out of here. The war won't last forever."

"To get out of here costs money. No job, no money. No
money, no travel, no job."

"Ah yes, money, always a problem. Or maybe not."

The Englishman produced a wad of U.S. dollars, all hundreds, and counted them onto the counter.

"I am old-fashioned," he said. "I believe people should
help each other. It makes life easier, more pleasant. Will
you help me, Dusko?"

The barman was staring at the thousand dollars a few inches from his fingertips. He could not take his eyes off the money. He dropped his voice to a whisper. "What you want? What do you do here? You not reporter."

"Well, I am in a way. I ask questions. But I am a rich asker of questions. Do you want to be rich like me, Dusko?"

"What you want?" repeated the barman. He flicked a glance toward the other drinkers, who were staring at the pair of them.

"You've seen a hundred-dollar bill before. Last May. The fifteenth, wasn't it? A young soldier tried to settle the bar bill with it. Started one hell of a row. My friend Lasse was here. He told me. Explain to me exactly what happened and why."

"Not here. Not now," hissed the frightened Serb. One of the men from the tables was up and walking toward the bar. A wiping cloth flicked expertly down over the money. "Bar close at ten. You come back."

At half-past ten, with the bar closed and locked, the two men sat in a booth in half-darkness and talked.

"They were not the Yugoslav army, not soldiers," said the barman. "Paramilitary people. Bad people. They stay three days. Best rooms, best food, much drink. They leave but not pay."

"One of them tried to pay you."

"True. Only one. He was good kid. Different from others. I don't know what he was doing with them. He had education. The rest were gangsters . . . gutter people."

"You didn't object to them not paying for three days' stay?"

"Object? Object? What I say? These animals have guns. They kill, even fellow Serbs. They all killers."

"So when the nice kid tried to pay you, who was the one who slapped him around?"

He could feel the Serb go rigid in the gloom.

"No idea. He was boss man, group leader. But no name. They just call him 'Chief.' "

"All these paramilitaries have names, Dusko. Arkan and his Tigers. Frankie's Boys. They like to be famous. They boast of their names."

"Not this one. I swear."

The Tracker knew it was a lie. Whoever he was, the freelance killer inspired a sweat-clammy measure of fear among his fellow Serbs.

"But the nice kid . . . he had a name?"

"I never heard it."

"We are talking about a lot of money here, Dusko. You never see him again, you never see me again, you have enough to start up in Sarajevo after the war. The kid's name."

"He paid the day he left. Like he was ashamed of the people he was with. He came back and paid by check."

"It bounced? Came back? You have it?"

"No, it was honored. Yugoslav dinars. From Belgrade. Settlement in full."

"So, no check?"

"It will be in the Belgrade bank. Somewhere, but probably destroyed by now. But I wrote down his ID card number in case it bounced."

"Where? Where did you write it?"

"On the back of an order pad. In ballpoint."

The Tracker traced it. The pad, for taking long and complicated drink orders that could not be memorized, only had two sheets left. Another day and it would have been thrown away. In ballpoint, on the cardboard back, was a seven-figure number and two capital letters. Eight weeks old, still legible.

The Tracker donated a thousand of Mr. Edmond's dollars and left. The shortest way out of there was north into Croatia and a plane from Zagreb airport.

The old six-province Yugoslavia Federation had been disintegrating in blood, chaos, and cruelty for five years. In the north, Slovenia was the first to go, luckily without bloodshed. In the south, Macedonia had escaped into separate independence. But at the center, the Serbian dictator,

Slobodan Milosevic, was trying to use every brutality in the book to cling to Croatia, Bosnia, Kosovo, Montenegro, and his own native Serbia. He had still lost Croatia, but his appetite for power and war remained undiminished.

The Belgrade into which the Tracker had arrived in 1995 was still untouched. Its desolation would be provoked in the Kosovo war yet to come.

His London office had advised there was one private detective agency in Belgrade, headed up by a former senior police officer whom they had used before. He had endowed his agency with the not too original name of Chandler, and it was easy to find.

"I need," the Tracker told the investigator, Dragan Stojic, "to trace a young guy for whom I have no name but only the number of his state ID card."

Stojic grunted. "What did he do?"

"Nothing, so far as I know. He saw something. Maybe. Maybe not."

"That's it. A name?"

"Then I would like to talk to him. I have no car and no mastery of Serbo-Croat. He may speak English. Maybe not."

Stojic grunted again. It appeared to be his speciality. He had apparently read every Philip Marlowe novel and seen every movie. He was trying to be Robert Mitchum in *The Big Sleep*, but at five feet, four inches and bald, he was not quite there.

"My terms . . ." he began.

The Tracker eased another ten one-hundred-dollar bills across the desk. "I need your undivided attention," he murmured.

Stojic was entranced. The line could have come straight from *Farewell, My Lovely*.

"You got it," he said.

To give credit where credit was due, the dumpy ex-inspector did not waste time. Belching black smoke, his Yugo sedan, with the Tracker in the passenger seat, took them across town to the district of Konjarnik where the corner of Ljermontova Street was occupied by the police headquarters of Belgrade. It was, and remains, a big, ugly block in brown and yellow, like a huge, angular hornet on its side.

"You'd better stay here," said Stojic. He was gone half an hour and must have shared some conviviality with an old colleague, for there was the plummy odor of slivovitz on his breath. But he had a slip of paper.

"That card belongs to Milan Rajak, aged twenty-four. Listed as a law student. Father a lawyer, successful, upper-middle-class family. Are you sure you've got the right man?"

"Unless he has a doppelganger, he and his ID card bearing his photograph were in Banja Luka two months ago."

"What the hell would he be doing there?"

"He was in uniform. In a bar."

Stojic thought back to the file he had been shown but not allowed to copy.

"He did his National Military Service. All young Yugoslavs, aged eighteen through twenty-one, have to do that."

"Combat soldier?"

"No. Signal Corps. Radio operator."

"Never saw combat. Might have wished he had. Might have joined a group going into Bosnia to fight for the Serbian cause. A deluded volunteer? Possible?"

Stojic shrugged.

"Possible. But these paramilitaries are scumbags. Gangsters all. What would this law student be doing with them?"

"Summer vacation?" asked the Tracker.

"But which group? Shall we ask him?"

Stojic consulted his piece of paper. "Address in Senjak, not half an hour away."

"Then let's go."

They found the address without trouble, a solid, middle-class villa on Istarska Street. Years serving Marshal Tito and now Slobodan Milosevic had done Mr. Rajak Sr. no harm at all. A pale and nervous-looking woman in her forties, but looking older, answered the door.

There was an interchange in Serbo-Croat.

"Milan's mother," said Stojic. "Yes, he's in. What do you want? she asks."

"To talk to him. An interview. For the British press."

Clearly bewildered, Mrs. Rajak let them in and called to her son. Then she showed them into the sitting room. There were sounds of feet on the stairs and a young man appeared in the hall. He had a whispered conversation with his mother and came in. His air was perplexed, worried, almost fearful. The Tracker gave him his friendliest smile and shook hands. The door was still an inch open. Mrs. Rajak was on the phone speaking rapidly. Stojic shot the Englishman a warning glance, as if to say, "Whatever you want, keep it short. The artillery is on its way."

The Englishman held out the notepad from the bar in the north. The two remaining sheets on it were headed Hotel Bosna. He flicked the cardboard over and showed Milan Rajak the seven numbers and two initials.

"It was very decent of you to settle the bill, Milan. The barman was grateful. Unfortunately the check bounced."

"No. Not possible. It was cl . . ." He stopped and went white as a sheet.

"No one is blaming you for anything, Milan. So just tell me; what were you doing in Banja Luka?"

"Visiting."

"Friends?"

"Yes."

"In camouflage? Milan, it's a war zone. What happened that day two months ago?"

"I don't know what you mean." Then he broke into Serbo-Croat, and the Tracker lost him. He raised an eyebrow at Stojic.

"Dad's coming," muttered the detective.

"You were with a group of ten others. All in uniform. All armed. Who were they?"

Milan Rajak was beaded with sweat and looked as if he

was going to burst into tears. The Tracker judged this to be a young man with serious nerve problems.

"You are English? But you are not press. What are you doing here? Why you persecute me? I know nothing."

There was a screech of car tires outside the house, running feet up the steps from the pavement. Mrs. Rajak held the door open, and her husband charged in. He appeared at the door of the sitting room, rattled and angry. A generation older than his son, he did not speak English. Instead, he shouted in Serbo-Croat.

"He asks what you are doing in his house, why you harass his son," said Stojic.

"I am not harassing," said the Tracker calmly, "I am simply asking. What was this young man doing eight weeks ago in Banja Luka, and who were the men with him?"

Stojic translated. Rajak Senior began shouting.

"He says," explained Stojic, "that his son knows nothing and was not there. He has been here all summer, and if you do not leave his house he will call the police. Personally, I think we should leave. This is a powerful man."

"OK," said the Tracker. "One last question."

(At his request, the former director of Special Forces, who now ran Hazard Management, had had a very discreet lunch with a contact in the Secret Intelligence Service. The head of the Balkans Desk had been as helpful as he was allowed.)

"Were those men Zoran's Wolves? Was the man who slapped you around Zoran Zilic himself?"

Stojic had translated more than half before he could stop himself. Milan understood it all in English. The effect was in two parts. For several seconds there was a stunned, glacial silence. The second part was like an exploding grenade.

Mrs. Rajak emitted a single scream and ran from the room. Her son slumped in a chair, put his head in his hands, and started to shake. The father went from white to puce, pointed at the door, and started shouting a single word, which Gracey presumed meant "Out." Stojic headed for the door. The Tracker followed.

As he passed the shaking young man, he stooped and slipped a card into his top jacket pocket. "If you ever change your mind," he murmured, "call me. Or write. I'll come."

There was a strained silence in the car back to the airport. Dragan Stojic clearly felt he had earned every dime of his thousand dollars. As they drew up at International Departures, he spoke across the car roof at the departing Englishman.

"If you ever come back to Belgrade, my friend, I advise you not to mention that name. Not even in jest. Especially not in jest. Today's events never took place."

Within forty-eight hours the Tracker had completed and filed his report to Stephen Edmond, along with his list of expenses. The final paragraphs read:

> I fear I have to admit that the events that led to your grandson's death, the manner of that death or the resting place of the body will probably never be discovered. And I would be raising false hopes if I said I thought there was a chance that your grandson was still alive. For the present and the foreseeable future, the only judgment has to be: missing, presumed killed.
>
> I do not believe that he and the Bosnian accompanying him crashed off some road in the area and into a ravine. Every possible such road has been personally searched. Nor do I believe the Bosnian murdered him for the truck or the money belt or both.
>
> I believe they inadvertently drove into harm's way and were murdered by person or persons unknown. There is a likelihood that these persons were a band of Serbian paramilitary criminals believed to have been in the general area. But without evidence, identification, a confession, or court testimony, there is no possibility of charges being brought.

*It is with the deepest regret that I have to
impart this news to you, but I believe it to be
almost certainly the truth.*
I have the honor to remain, sir,
Your obedient servant,

Philip Gracey.

It was July 22, 1995.

8
THE LAWYER

The main reason Calvin Dexter decided to leave the army was one he did not explain because he did not want to be mocked. He had decided he wanted to go to college, get a degree, and become a lawyer. As for funds, he had saved several thousand dollars in Vietnam and he could seek further help under the terms of the GI Bill.

There are few "ifs" and "buts" about the GI Bill; if an American soldier leaving the army for reasons other than dishonorable discharge wishes to apply, then his government will pay to put him through college. The allowance paid, rising over the past thirty years, can be spent by the student any way he wants, so long as the college confirms he is in full-time attendance.

Dexter reckoned that a rural college would probably be

cheaper, but he wanted a university with its *own* law school as well, and if he was ever going to practice law, then there would be more opportunities in New York than in New Jersey. After scouring fifty brochures, he applied to Fordham University, New York City.

He sent in his papers in the late fall, along with the vital discharge document, the DD214 with which every GI left the army. He was just in time.

In the spring of 1971, though the sentiment against the Vietnam War was already high, and nowhere higher than in academia, the GIs were not seen as being to blame, rather as victims.

After the chaotic and undignified pullout of 1973, sometimes referred to as a scuttle, the mood changed. Though Richard Nixon and Henry Kissinger sought to put the best spin on things that they could, and though a disengagement from the unwinnable disaster that Vietnam had become was almost universally welcomed, it was still seen as a defeat.

If there is one thing the average American does not want to be associated with too often, it is defeat. The GIs coming home post-1971 thought they would be welcomed, as they had done their best, they had suffered, they had lost good friends; instead, they met a blank wall of indifference, even hostility. The Left was more concerned with My Lai.

Dexter's papers were considered, along with all the other applicants that summer, and he was accepted for a four-year degree course in political science. In the category of "life experience," his three years in the Big Red One were considered a positive, which would not have happened twenty-four months later.

The young veteran found a cheap, one-room walk-up in the Bronx, not far from the Rose Hill campus. He calculated that if he walked or used public transport, ate frugally, and used the long summer vacation to go back to the construction industry, he could make enough to survive until graduation. Among the construction sites on which he worked over the next three years was the new wonder of the world, the slowly rising World Trade Center.

The year 1974 was marked by two events that were to change his life. He met and fell in love with Angela Marozzi, a beautiful, vital, life-loving Italian-American girl working in a flower shop on Bathgate Avenue. They married that summer and, with their joint income, moved to a larger apartment.

That autumn, still one year from graduation, he applied for admission to the Fordham University School of Law, a faculty within the university, but separate in its location and administration, across the river in Manhattan. It was far harder to get into, having few places and being much sought after.

Law school would mean three more years of study after graduation in 1975 to the law degree, then the bar exam, and finally the right to practice as an attorney-at-law in the state of New York.

There was no personal interview involved, just a mass of papers to be submitted to the Admissions Committee for their perusal and judgment. These included school records right back to grade school, which were awful, more recent grades from college, a self-written assessment, and references from present advisers, which were excellent. Hidden in this mass of paperwork was his old DD214.

He made the short list, and the Admissions Committee met to make the final selection. There were six of them, headed by Prof. Howard Kell, at seventy-seven well past retirement age, bright as a button, a professor emeritus, and the patriarch of them all.

It came to one of two for the last available place. The papers marked Dexter as one of those. There was a heated debate. Professor Kell rose from his chair at the head of the table and wandered to the window. He stared out at the blue summer sky.

"Tough one, eh, Howard? Who do you favor?"

The old man tapped a paper in his hand and showed it to the senior tutor. The tutor read the list of medals and gave a low whistle.

"He was awarded those before his twenty-first birthday."

"What the hell did he do?"

"He earned the right to be given a chance in this law school, that's what he did," said the professor.

The two men returned to the table and voted. It would have been three against three, but the chairman's vote counted double in such a contingency. He explained why. They all looked at the DD214.

"He could be violent," objected the politically correct dean of studies.

"Oh, I hope so," said Professor Kell. "I'd hate to think we were giving these away for nothing nowadays."

Cal Dexter received the good news two days later. He and Angela lay on their bed; he stroked her growing belly and talked of the day he would be a wealthy lawyer and they would have a fine house out in Westchester or Fairfield County.

Their daughter, Amanda Jane, was born in the early spring of 1975, but there were complications. The surgeons did their best, but the outcome was unanimous. The couple could adopt, of course, but there would be no more natural pregnancies. Angela's family priest told her it was the will of God, and she must accept His will.

Cal Dexter graduated in the top five of his class that summer and in the autumn began the three-year course in law. It was tough, but the Marozzi family rallied around; Mama baby-sat Amanda Jane so that Angela could wait tables. Cal wanted to remain a day student rather than revert to night school, which would extend the law course by an extra year.

He labored through the summer vacations in the first two years but in the third managed to find work as a legal assistant with the highly respectable Manhattan law firm of Honeyman Fleischer.

That summer of 1978 his father died. They had not been close after Cal's return from Vietnam, for the parent had never understood why his son could not return to the construction sites and be content with a hard hat for the rest of his life.

But he and Angela had visited, borrowing Mr. Marozzi's car, and shown Dexter Senior his only grandchild. When the end came, it was sudden. A massive heart attack felled the building laborer on a work site. His son attended the humble funeral alone. He had hoped his dad could attend his graduation ceremony and be proud of his educated son, but it was not to be.

He graduated that summer and, pending his bar exam, secured a lowly but full-time position with Honeyman Fleischer, his first professional employment since the army seven years earlier.

Honeyman Fleischer prided itself on its impeccable liberal credentials, and to prove its lively social conscience, fielded many pro bono assignments for the poor and vulnerable.

That said, the senior partners saw no need to exaggerate and kept their pro bono work to a few of their lowest paid newcomers. That autumn of 1978, Cal Dexter was as lowly in the legal pecking order at Honeyman Fleischer as one could get.

Dexter did not complain. He needed the money, he cherished the job, and covering the down-and-outs gave him a wide spectrum of experience, rather than the narrow confines of one single specialty. He could defend on charges of petty crime, negligence claims, and a variety of other disputes that eventually went to a court of appeal.

It was that winter that a secretary popped her head around the door of his cubbyhole office and waved a file at him.

"What's that?" he asked.

"Immigration appeal," she said. "Roger says he can't handle it."

Dexter's supervising associate chose the pro bono cream, if ever any cream appeared, for himself. Immigration matters were definitely the skimmed milk.

Dexter sighed and buried himself in the details of the new file. The hearing was the next day.

9

THE REFUGEE

There was a charity in New York in those years called Refugee Watch. "Concerned citizens" was how it would have described its members; do-gooders was the less admiring description.

Its self-appointed task was to keep a weather eye open for examples of the flotsam and jetsam of the human race who, washed up on the shores of America wished to take literally the words written on the base of the Statue of Liberty and stay.

Most often, these were forlorn, bereft people, refugees from a hundred climes, usually with a most fragmentary grasp of the English language, and who had spent their last savings in the struggle to survive.

Their immediate antagonist was the Immigration and Naturalization Service, the formidable INS, whose collective philosophy appeared to be that 99.9 percent of the applicants were frauds who should be sent back whence they came, or at any rate somewhere else.

The file tossed onto Cal Dexter's desk that early winter of 1978 concerned a couple fleeing from Cambodia, Mr. and Mrs. Hom Moung.

In a lengthy statement by Mr. Moung, who seemed to speak for them both, translated from the French—which was the French-educated Cambodian's language of choice— his story emerged.

Since 1975, a fact already well-known in the United States and later to become better known through the film *The Killing Fields*, Cambodia had been in the grip of a mad and genocidal tyrant called Pol Pot and his fanatical army, the Khmer Rouge.

Pot had some harebrained dream of returning his country to a sort of agrarian Stone Age. Fulfillment of his vision involved a pathological hatred of the people of the cities and anyone with any education. These were destined for extermination.

Mr. Moung claimed he had been headmaster of a leading lycée or high school in the capital, Phnom Penh, and his wife a staff nurse at a private clinic. Both fitted firmly into the Khmer Rouge category for execution.

When things became impossible, they went underground, moving from safe house to safe house among friends and fellow professionals, until the latter had all been arrested and taken away.

Mr. Moung claimed he would never have been able to reach the Vietnamese or Thai borders because in the countryside, infested with Khmer Rouge and informers, he would not have been able to pass for a peasant. Nevertheless, he had been able to bribe a truck driver to smuggle them out of Phnom Penh and across to the port of Kompong Son. With his last remaining savings, he persuaded the captain of a South Korean freighter to take them out of the hell that his homeland had become.

He did not care or know where the *Inchon Star* was

headed. It turned out to be New York harbor, with a cargo of teak. On arrival, he had not sought to evade the authorities but had reported immediately and asked permission to stay.

Dexter spent the night before the hearing hunched over the kitchen table while his wife and daughter slept a few feet away behind a wall. The hearing was his first appeal of any kind, and he wanted to give the refugee his best shot. After the statement, he turned to the response of the INS. It had been pretty harsh.

The local INS Almighty in any U.S. city is the district director, and his office is the first hurdle. The director's colleague in charge of the file had rejected the request for asylum on the strange grounds that the Moungs should have applied to the local U.S. Embassy or Consulate and waited in line, according to American tradition.

Dexter felt this was not too much of a problem; all U.S. staff had fled the Cambodian capital years earlier when the Khmer Rouge stormed in.

The refusal at the first level had put the Moungs into deportation procedure. That was when Refugee Watch heard of their case and took up the cudgels.

According to procedure, a couple refused entry by the district director's office at the exclusion hearing could appeal to the next level up, an administrative hearing in front of an asylum hearing officer.

Dexter noted that at the exclusion hearing, the INS's second ground for refusal had been that the Moungs did not qualify under the five necessary grounds for proving persecution: race, nationality, religion, political beliefs, and/or social class. He felt he could now show that as a fervent anti-Communist—and he certainly intended to advise Mr. Moung to become one immediately—and as head teacher, he qualified on the last two grounds at least.

His task at the hearing in the morning would be to plead with the hearing officer for a relief known as Withholding of Deportation, under Section 243(h) of the Immigration and Nationality Act.

In tiny print at the bottom of one of the papers was a note from someone at Refugee Watch that the asylum hearing officer would be a certain Norman Ross. What he learned was interesting.

Dexter showed up at the INS building at 26 Federal Plaza to meet his clients over an hour before the hearing. He was not a big man himself, but the Moungs were smaller, and Mrs. Moung was like a tiny doll. She gazed at the world through lenses that seemed to have been cut from the bottoms of Coca-Cola bottles. His papers told him they were forty-eight and forty-five, respectively.

Mr. Moung seemed calm and resigned. Because Cal Dexter spoke no French, Refugee Watch had provided a female interpreter.

Dexter spent the preparation hour going over the original statement, but there was nothing to add or subtract.

The case would be heard not in a real court but in a large office with chairs imported for the occasion. Five minutes before the hearing, they were shown in.

As he surmised, the representative of the district director represented the arguments used at the exclusion hearing to refuse the asylum application. There was nothing to add or subtract. Behind his desk, Mr. Ross followed the arguments already before him in the file, then raised an eyebrow at the novice sent down by Honeyman Fleischer.

Behind Dexter, Mr. Moung muttered to his wife, "We must hope this young man can succeed, or we will be sent back to die." But he spoke in his own native language.

Dexter dealt with the DD's first point; there had been no U.S. diplomatic or consular representation in Phnom Penh since the start of the killing fields. The nearest would have been in Bangkok, Thailand, an impossible target that the Moungs could never have reached. He noted a hint of a smile at the corner of Ross's mouth as the man from the INS went pink.

His main task was to show that faced with the lethal fanaticism of the Khmer Rouge, any proven anti-Communist like his client would have been destined to tor-

ture and death. Even the fact of being a head teacher with
a college degree would have guaranteed execution.

What he had learned during the night was that Norman
Ross had not always been Ross. His father had arrived
around the turn of the century as Samuel Rosen, from a
shtetl in modern Poland, fleeing the pogroms of the tsar
then being carried out by the Cossacks.

"It is very easy, sir, to reject those who come with nothing, seeking not much but the chance of life. It is very easy
to say 'No' and walk away. It costs nothing to decree that
these two Orientals have no place here and should go back
to arrest, torture, and the execution wall.

"But I ask you, supposing our fathers had done that, and
their fathers before them, how many, back in the homeland-
turned-bloodbath, would have said, 'I went to the land of
the free, I asked for a chance of life, but they shut their
doors and sent me back to die.' How many, Mr. Ross? A
million? Nearer ten. I ask you, not on a point of law, not
as a triumph for clever lawyer semantics, but as a victory
for what Shakespeare called 'the quality of mercy,' to decree that in this huge country of ours there is room for one
couple who have lost everything but life and ask only for
a chance."

Norman Ross eyed him speculatively for several
minutes. Then he laid his pencil down on his desk like a
gavel and pronounced, "Deportation withheld. Next case."

The lady from Refugee Watch excitedly told the Moungs
in French what had happened. She and her organization
could handle procedures from that point on. There would
be administration, but no more need for advocacy. The
Moungs could now remain in the United States under the
protection of the government, and eventually a work permit, asylum, and, in due course, naturalization, would come
through.

Dexter smiled at her and said she could go. Then he
turned to Mr. Moung and said, "Now let us go to the caf-
eteria and you can tell me who you really are and what you

are doing here." He spoke in Mr. Moung's native language, Vietnamese.

At a corner table in the basement café, Dexter examined the Cambodian passports and ID documents. "These have already been examined by some of the best experts in the West and pronounced genuine. How did you get them?"

The refugee glanced at his tiny wife. "She made them. She is of the Nghi."

There is a clan in Vietnam called Nghi, which for centuries supplied most of the scholars of the Hue region. Their particular skill, passed down through generations, was for exceptional calligraphy. They created court documents for their emperors.

With the coming of the modern age, and especially when the war against the French began in 1945, their absolute dedication to patience, detail, and stunning draftsmanship meant the Nghi could transmute to become some of the finest forgers in the world.

The tiny woman with the bottle glasses had ruined her eyesight because, for the duration of the Vietnam War, she had crouched in an underground workshop creating passes and identifications so perfect that Vietcong agents had passed effortlessly through every South Vietnamese city at will and had never been caught.

Cal Dexter handed the passports back. "Like I said upstairs, who are you really, and why are you here?"

The wife quietly began to cry, and her husband slid his hand over hers. "My name," he said, "is Nguyen Van Tran. I am here because, after three years in a concentration camp in Vietnam, I escaped. That part at least is true."

"So why pretend to be Cambodian? America has accepted many South Vietnamese who fought with us in that war."

"Because I was a major in the Vietcong."

Dexter nodded slowly. "That could be a problem," he admitted. "Tell me everything."

"I was born in 1930, in the deep south, up against the Cambodian border. That is why I have a smattering of

Khmer. My family was never Communist, but my father was a dedicated Nationalist. He wanted to see our country free of the colonial domination of the French. He raised me the same way."

"I don't have a problem with that. Why turn Communist?"

"That is my problem. That is why I have been in a camp. I didn't. I pretended to."

"Go on."

"As a boy before World War II, I was raised under the French lycée system, even as I longed to become old enough to join the struggle for independence. In 1942, the Japanese came, expelling the French even though Vichy France was technically on their side. So we fought the Japanese.

"Leading in that struggle were the Communists under Ho Chi Minh. They were more efficient, more skilled, more ruthless than the Nationalists. Many changed sides, but my father did not. When the Japanese departed in defeat in 1945, Ho Chi Minh was a national hero. I was fifteen, already part of the struggle. Then the French came back.

"Then came nine more years of war. Ho Chi Minh and the Communist Vietminh resistance movement simply absorbed all other movements. Anyone who resisted was liquidated. I was in that war, too. I was one of those human ants who carried the parts of the artillery to the mountain peaks around Dien Bien Phu where the French were crushed in 1954. Then came the Geneva Accords and also a new disaster. My country was divided—North and South."

"You went back to war?"

"Not immediately. There was a short window of peace. We waited for the referendum that was part of the Accords. When it was denied, because the Diem dynasty ruling the South knew they would lose it, we went back to war. The choice was the disgusting Diems and their corruption in the South or Ho and General Giap in the North. I had fought under Giap; I hero-worshiped him. I chose the Communists."

"You were still single?"

"No, I had married my first wife. We had three children."

"They are still there?"

"No, all dead."

"Disease?"

"B-52s."

"Go on."

"Then the first Americans came. Under Kennedy. Supposedly as advisers. But to us, the Diem regime had simply become another puppet government like the ones imposed under the Japanese and the French. So again, half my country was occupied by foreigners. I went back to the jungle to fight."

"When?"

"Nineteen sixty-three."

"Ten more years?"

"Ten more years. By the time it was over, I was forty-two and I had spent half my life living like an animal, subject to hunger, disease, fear, and the constant threat of death."

"But after 1972 you should have been triumphant," remarked Dexter. The Vietnamese shook his head.

"You do not understand what happened after Ho died in 1968. The party and the government fell into different hands. Many of us were still fighting for a country we hoped and expected would have some tolerance in it. The ones who took over from Ho had no such intention. Patriot after patriot was arrested and executed. Those in charge were Le Doan and Le Duc Tho. They had none of the inner strength of Ho, which could tolerate a humane approach. They had to destroy to dominate. The power of the secret police was massively increased. You remember the Tet Offensive?"

"Yes."

"You Americans seem to think it was a victory for us.

Not true. It was devised in Hanoi, wrongly attributed to General Giap, who was in fact impotent under Le Doan. It was imposed on the Vietcong as a direct order. It destroyed us. That was the intent. Forty thousand of our best cadres died in suicide missions. Among them were all the natural leaders of the South. With them gone, Hanoi ruled supreme. After Tet, the North Vietnamese army took control, just in time for the victory. I was one of the last survivors of the southern Nationalists. I wanted a free and reunited country, yes, but also with cultural freedom, a private sector, farm-owning farmers. That turned out to be a mistake."

"What happened?"

"Well, after the final conquest of the South in 1975, the real pogroms started. The Chinese. Two million were stripped of everything they possessed, either forced into slave labor or expelled, the Boat People. I objected and said so. Then the camps started for dissident Vietnamese. Two hundred thousand are now in camps, mainly southerners. At the end of 1975, the Cong Ang, the secret police, came for me. I had written one too many letters of objection, saying that for me, everything I had fought for was being betrayed. They didn't like that."

"What did you get?"

"Three years, the standard sentence for 'reeducation.' After that, three years of daily surveillance. I was sent to a camp in Hatay Province, about forty miles from Hanoi. They always send you far away from your home; it deters escape."

"But you made it?"

"My wife made it. She really is a nurse, as well as being a forger. And I really was a schoolmaster in the few years of peace. We met in the camp. She was in the clinic. I had developed abscesses on both legs. We talked. We fell in love. She smuggled me out of there; she had some gold trinkets, hidden, not confiscated. These bought us a ticket on a freighter. So now you know."

"And you think I might believe you?" asked Dexter.

"You speak our language. Were you there?"

"Yes, I was."

"Did you fight?"

"I did."

"Then I say as one soldier to another: You should know defeat when you see it. You are looking at complete and utter defeat. So, shall we go?"

"Where had you in mind?"

"Back to the Immigration people of course. You will have to report us."

Cal Dexter finished his coffee and rose. Maj. Nguyen Van Tran tried to rise also, but Dexter pressed him back into his seat. "Two things, Major. The war is over. It happened far away and long ago. Try to enjoy the rest of your life."

The Vietnamese was like one in a state of shock. He nodded dumbly. Dexter turned and walked away.

As he went down the steps to the street, something was troubling him. Something about the Vietcong officer, his face, the expression of frozen astonishment.

At the end of the street, passersby turned to look at the young lawyer who threw back his head and laughed at the madness of fate. Absently he rubbed his left hand where the one-time enemy's hot nut oil in the tunnel had scalded him.

It was November 22, 1978.

10
THE GEEK

By 1985, Cal Dexter had left Honeyman Fleischer, but not for a job that would lead to that fine house in Westchester. He joined the Legal Aid Society. It was not glamorous and it was not lucrative; but it gave him something he could not have achieved in corporate or tax law, and he knew it. It was called job satisfaction.

Angela had taken it well, better than he had hoped. In fact, she did not really mind. The Marozzi family were as close as grapes on the vine, and they were Bronx people through and through. Amanda Jane was in a school she liked, surrounded by her friends. A bigger and better job and a move upmarket was not required.

The new job meant working an impossible number of hours in a day and representing those who had slipped through a hole in the mesh of the American Dream. It meant defending in court those who could not begin to afford legal representation on their own account.

For Cal Dexter, poor and inarticulate did not necessarily mean guilty. He never failed to get a buzz when some dazed and grateful client who, whatever else his inadequacies, had not done what he was charged with, walked free. It was a hot summer night in 1988 when he met Washington Lee.

The borough of Manhattan alone handles over 110,000 criminal cases a year, and that excludes civil suits. The court system appears permanently on the verge of overload and a circuit blowout, but somehow it seems to survive. In those years part of the reason was the twenty-four-hour-a-day conveyor-belt system of court hearings that ran endlessly through the great granite block at 100 Center Street.

Like a good vaudeville show, the Criminal Courts Building could boast "We never close." It would probably be an exaggeration to say that "all life is here," but certainly the lower parts of Manhattan life showed up.

That night in July 1988, Dexter was working the night shift as an on-call attorney who could be allocated a client on the say-so of an overbusy judge. It was 2:00 A.M. and he was trying to slip away when a voice summoned him back to Court AR2A. He sighed; one did not argue with Judge Hasselblad.

He approached the bench to join an assistant district attorney already standing there clutching a file.

"You're tired, Mr. Dexter."

"I guess we all are, Your Honor."

"No dispute, but there is one more case I'd like you to take on. Not tomorrow, now. Take the file. This young man seems to be in serious trouble."

"Your wish is my command, Judge."

Hasselblad's face widened in a grin. "I just love deference," he rejoined.

Dexter took the file from the ADA, and they left the court together. The file cover read: *People of the State of New York v. Washington Lee.*

"Where is he?" asked Dexter.

"Right here in a holding cell," said the ADA.

As he had thought from the mug shot staring at him from the file, his client was a skinny kid with the air of bewildered hopelessness worn by the uneducated who are sucked in, chewed up, and spat out by any judicial system in the world. He seemed more bewildered than smart.

The accused was eighteen years old, a denizen of that charm-free district known as Bedford-Stuyvesant, a part of Brooklyn that is virtually a Black ghetto. That alone aroused Dexter's interest. Why was he being charged in Manhattan? He presumed the kid had crossed the river and stolen a car or mugged someone with a wallet worth stealing.

But no, the charge was bank fraud. So, passing a forged check, attempting to use a stolen credit card, even the old trick of simultaneous withdrawals at opposite ends of the counter from a dummy account? No.

The charge was odd, unspecific. The district attorney had laid a bare-bones charge alleging fraud in excess of ten thousand dollars. The victim was the East River Savings Bank headquartered in midtown Manhattan, which explained why the charge was not being pursued in Brooklyn. The fraud had been detected by the bank security staff, and the bank wished to pursue with maximum vigor according to corporate policy.

Dexter smiled encouragingly, introduced himself, sat down, and offered cigarettes. He did not smoke, but 99 percent of his clients dragged happily on the white sticks. Washington Lee shook his head.

"They're bad for your health, man."

Dexter was tempted to say that seven years in the state pen was not going to do great things for it either, but forbore. Mr. Lee, he noted, was not just homely, he was downright ugly. So how had he charmed a bank into handing over so much money? The way he looked, shuffled, slumped, he would hardly have been allowed across the Italian-marble lobby of the prestigious East River Savings Bank.

Calvin Dexter needed more time than was available to give the case file his full and proper attention. The immediate concern was to get through the formality of the arraignment and see if there was even a remote possibility of bail. He doubted it.

An hour later Dexter and the ADA were back in court. Washington Lee, looking completely bewildered, was duly arraigned.

"Are we ready to proceed?" asked Judge Hasselblad.

"May it please the court, I have to ask for a continuance," said Dexter.

"Approach," ordered the judge. When the two lawyers stood beneath the bench, he asked, "You have a problem, Mr. Dexter?"

"This is a more complex case than at first appears, Your Honor. This is not hubcaps. The charge refers to over ten thousand dollars, embezzled from a blue-chip bank. I need more study time."

The judge glanced at the ADA, who shrugged, meaning no objection.

"A week from today," said the judge.

"I'd like to ask for bail," said Dexter.

"Opposed, Your Honor," said the ADA.

"I'm setting the bail at the sum named in the charge, ten thousand dollars," said Judge Hasselblad.

It was out of the question, and they all knew it. Washington Lee did not have ten dollars, and no bail bondsman was likely to give him the time of day. It was back to a cell. As they left the court, Dexter asked the ADA for a favor.

"Be a sport, keep him in the Tombs, not the Island."

"Not a problem. Try and grab some sleep, huh?"

There are two short-spell remand prisons used by the Manhattan court system. The Tombs may sound like something underground, but it is in fact a high-rise remand center right next to the court buildings and far more convenient for defense lawyers visiting their clients than Rikers Island, way up the East River. Despite the ADA's advice for a bit of sleep, the file probably precluded that. If he was to confer with Washington Lee the next morning, he had some reading to do.

To the trained eye the wad of papers told the story of the detection and arrest of Washington Lee. The fraud had been detected internally and traced to Lee. The bank's head of security, one Dan Mitkowski, was a former detective with the NYPD, and he had prevailed on some of his former colleagues to go over to Brooklyn and arrest Washington Lee.

He had first been brought to, and lodged in, a precinct house in midtown. When a sufficient number of miscreants were gracing the cells of the precinct house, they were brought down to the Criminal Courts Building and relodged there on the timeless and unvarying diet of baloney and cheese sandwiches.

Then the wheels had ground their remorseless course. The rap sheet showed a short litany of minor street crime: hubcaps, vending machines, shoplifting. With that formality complete, Washington Lee was ready for arraignment. That was when Judge Hasselblad demanded that the youth be represented.

On the face of it, this was a youth born to nothing and with nothing, who would graduate from truancy to pilfering and thence a life of crime and frequent periods as a guest of the citizens of New York State somewhere "up the river." So how on earth had he sweet-talked the East River Savings Bank, which did not even have a branch in Bedford-Stuyvesant, out of ten thousand dollars? No answer. Not in the file. Just a bare-bones charge, and an angry and vengeful Manhattan-based bank. Grand larceny in the third degree. Seven years' hard time.

Dexter grabbed three hours' sleep, saw Amanda Jane off to school, kissed Angela good-bye, and came back to Center Street. It was in an interview room in the Tombs that he was able to drag his story out of the Black kid.

At school he excelled at nothing. His grades were a disaster. The future offered nothing but the road to dereliction, crime, and jail. And then one of the schoolteachers, maybe smarter than the others or just kinder, had allowed the graceless boy access to his Hewlett-Packard computer. (Here Dexter was reading between the lines of the halting narrative.)

It was like offering a young Yehudi Menuhin a chance to hold a violin. He stared at the keys, he stared at the screen, and he began to make music. The teacher, clearly a computer buff when personal machines were the exception rather than the norm, was intrigued. That was five years earlier.

Washington Lee began to study. He also began to save. When he opened and gutted vending machines, he did not smoke the proceeds or drink them or shoot them into his arm or wear them as clothes. He saved them until he could buy a cheap computer in a bankruptcy sale.

"So how did you swindle the East River Savings Bank?"

"I broke into their mainframe," said the kid.

For a moment Cal Dexter thought a jimmy might have been involved, so he asked his client to explain. For the first time the boy became animated. He was talking about the only thing he knew.

"Man, have you any idea how weak some of the defensive systems created to protect databases really are?"

Dexter conceded it was not a query that had ever detained him. Like most nonexperts, he knew that computer-system designers created "firewalls" to prevent unauthorized access to hypersensitive databases. How they did it, let alone how to outwit them, had never occurred to him. He teased the story out of Washington Lee.

The East River Savings Bank had stored every detail of every account holder in a huge database. As clients' financial situations are regarded by most clients as very private, access to those details involved bank officers punching in an elaborate system of coded signals. Unless these were absolutely correct, the computer screen would simply flash the message "Access Denied." A third erroneous attempt to break in would start alarm signals, which would flash at the head office.

Washington Lee had broken the codes without triggering the alarms, to the point where the main computer buried below the bank's headquarters in Manhattan would obey his instructions. In short, he had performed coitus noninterruptus on a very expensive piece of technology.

His instructions were simple. He ordered the computer to identify every savings and deposit account held by clients of the bank and the monthly interest paid into those accounts. Then he ordered it to deduct twenty-five cents from each interest payment and transfer it into his own account.

As he did not have one, he opened one at the local Chase Manhattan. Had he known enough to transfer the money to the Bahamas, he would probably have gotten away with it.

It is quite a calculation to ascertain interest due on one's deposit account because it will depend on the ambient interest rate over the earning period, and that will fluctuate; and to get it to the nearest twenty-five cents takes time. Most people do not have that time. They trust the bank to do the math and get it right.

Not Mr. Tolstoy. He may have been eighty, but his mind was still sharp as a pin. His problem was boredom, whiling away his hours in his tiny apartment on West 108th Street. Having spent his life as an actuary for a major insurance company, he was convinced that even nickels and dimes count, if multiplied enough times. He spent his time trying to catch the bank in error. One day, he did.

He became convinced his interest due for the month of April was twenty-five cents short. He checked the figures for March. Same thing. He went back two more months. Then he complained.

The local manager would have given him the missing dollar, but rules are rules. He filed the complaint. Head office thought it was a single glitch on a single account but ran random checks on half a dozen other accounts. Same thing. Then the tech staff was called in.

They established that the master computer had done this
to every checking account in the bank and had been doing
so for twenty months. They asked it why.

"Because you told me to," said the computer.

"No, we didn't," said the techies.

"Well, someone did," said the computer.

That was when they called in Dan Mitkowski. It did not
take very long. The transfers of all these quarters were to
an account at the Chase Manhattan over in Brooklyn. Client's name: Washington Lee.

"Tell me, how much did all this net you?" asked Dexter.

"Just shy of a million dollars."

The lawyer bit the end off his pencil. No wonder the
charge was so vague. "In excess of ten thousand dollars"
indeed. The very size of the theft gave him an idea.

Mr. Lou Ackerman enjoyed his breakfast. For him it was
the best meal of the day—never hurried like lunch, never
overrich like banquet dinners. He enjoyed the shock of the
icy juice, the crunch of the cereal flakes, the fluffiness of
well-scrambled eggs, the aroma of the freshly perked Blue
Mountain coffee. On his balcony above Central Park West,
in the cool of a summer morning before the real heat came
upon the day, it was a joy. And it was a shame for Mr.
Calvin Dexter to spoil it.

When his Filipino manservant brought the pasteboard
card to his terrace, he glanced at the words "attorney-at-
law," frowned, and wondered who his visitor might be. The
name rang a bell. He was about to tell his manservant to
ask the visitor to come to the bank later in the morning,
when a voice behind the Filipino said, "I know it's an impertinence, Mr. Ackerman, and for that I apologize. But if
you will give me ten minutes, I suggest you will be glad
we did not meet in the glare of attention at your office."

Ackerman shrugged and gestured to a chair across the
table.

"Tell Mrs. Ackerman I'm in conference at the breakfast

table," he instructed the Filipino. Then to Dexter, "Keep it short, Mr. Dexter."

"I will. You are pressing for the prosecution of my client, Mr. Washington Lee, for having allegedly skimmed almost a million dollars from your clients' accounts. I think it would be wise to drop the charges."

The CEO of the East River Savings Bank could have kicked himself. You show a little kindness and what do you get? A ball breaker ruining your breakfast.

"Forget it, Mr. Dexter. Conversation over. No way. The boy goes down. There must be deterrence to this sort of thing. Company policy. Good day."

"Pity. You see, the way he did it was fascinating. He broke into your computer mainframe. He waltzed through all your firewalls, your security guards. No one is supposed to be able to do that."

"Your time is up, Mr. Dexter."

"A few seconds more. There will be other breakfasts. You have about a million clients, checking accounts and deposit accounts. They think their funds are safe with you. Later this week a skinny Black kid from the ghetto is going to stand up in court and say that if he did it, any half-assed amateur could empty any of your clients' accounts after a few hours of electronic probing. How do you think your clients are going to like that?"

Ackerman put down his coffee and stared across the park. "It's not true, and why should they believe it?"

"Because the press will be there and the TV and radio media will be outside. I think up to 25 percent of your clients could decide to change banks."

"We'll announce we are installing a whole new safeguard system. The best on the market."

"But that's what you were supposed to have had before. And a kid from Bed-Stuy with no school grades broke it. You were lucky. You got the whole million dollars back. Supposing it happened again, for tens of millions in one awful weekend, and it went to the Caymans. The bank would have to reinstate. Would your board appreciate the humiliation?"

Lou Ackerman thought of his board. Some of the institutional shareholders were people like Shearson Lehman and Morgan Stanley, the sort of people who hated to be humiliated, the sort who might have a man's job.

"It's that bad, uh?"

"I'm afraid so."

"All right. I'll call the DA's office and say we have no further interest in proceeding, since we have all our money back. Mind you, the DA can still proceed if he wants to."

"Then you'll be very persuasive, Mr. Ackerman. All you have to say is: 'Scam, what scam?' After that, mum is the word, wouldn't you say?"

He rose and turned to leave. Ackerman was a good loser.

"We could always do with a good lawyer, Mr. Dexter."

"I've got a better idea. Take Washington Lee on the payroll. I'd have thought fifty thousand dollars a year is about right."

Ackerman was on his feet, Blue Mountain staining the table linen brown.

"What the hell should I want that lowlife on the payroll for?"

"Because when it comes to computers, he's the best. He's proved it. He sliced through a security system that cost you a mint to install, and he did it with a fifty-dollar sardine can. He could install for you a totally impenetrable system. You could make a sales point out of it: The safest database outside of Switzerland. He's much safer inside the tent pissing out."

Washington Lee was released twenty-four hours later. He was not quite sure why. Neither was the ADA. But the bank had had a bout of corporate amnesia, and the District Attorney's Office had its usual backlog. Why insist?

The bank sent a town car to the Tombs to pick up their new staffer. He had never been in one before. He sat in the back and looked at the head of his lawyer poking in the window.

"Man, I don't know what you did or how you did it. One day maybe I can pay you back."

"OK, Washington, maybe one day you will."

11

THE KILLER

When Yugoslavia was ruled by Marshal Tito it was virtually a crime-free society. Molesting a tourist was unthinkable, women safely walked the streets, and racketeering was nonexistent.

This was odd, considering that the six republics that made up Yugoslavia, cobbled together by the Western Allies in 1918, had traditionally produced some of the most vicious and violent gangsters in Europe.

The reason was that, post 1948, the Yugoslav government established a compact with the Yugoslav underworld. The deal was simple: You can do whatever you like, and we will turn a blind eye under one condition—you do it abroad. Belgrade simply exported its entire crime world.

The speciality targets for the Yugoslav crime bosses were Italy, Austria, Germany, and Sweden. The reason was

simple. By the mid-1960s, the Turks and the Yugoslavs had
become the first wave of "guest workers" in richer countries
to the north, meaning that they were encouraged to come
and do the mucky jobs that the overindulged indigenes no
longer wanted to do.

Every large ethnic movement brings its own crime world
with it. The Italian Mafia arrived in New York with the
Italian immigrants; Turkish criminals soon joined the Turkish "guest worker" communities across Europe. The Yugoslavs were the same, but here the agreement was more
structured.

Belgrade got it both ways. Its thousands of Yugoslavs
working abroad sent their hard currency home each week.
As a Communist state Yugoslavia was always an economic
mess, but the regular inflow of hard currency hid the fact.

So long as Tito repudiated Moscow, the United States
and NATO remained pretty relaxed about what else he did.
Indeed, he ranked as one of the leaders of the nonaligned
countries right through the Cold War. The beautiful Dalmatian coast along the Adriatic where the sun shone became a tourist Mecca, bringing in even more foreign
exchange.

Internally, Tito ran a brutal regime where dissidents or
opponents were concerned, but he kept it quiet and discreet.
The compact with the gangsters was run and supervised not
so much by the civil police but by the secret police, known
as State Security or DB.

It was the DB that laid down the terms. The gangsters
preying on the Yugoslav communities abroad could return
home for R and R with impunity, and they did. They built
themselves villas on the coast and mansions in the capital.
They made their donations to the pension funds of the
chiefs of the DB, and occasionally they were required to
carry out a "wet job" with no invoice and no trace back.
The mastermind of this cozy arrangement was the long-time
Intelligence boss, the fat and fearsome Slovenian Stane
Dolanc.

Inside Yugoslavia there was a little prostitution, but well

under local police control, and some lucrative smuggling, which again helped official pension funds. But violence, other than the state kind, was forbidden. Young delinquents reached the level of running rival district street gangs, stealing cars (not belonging to tourists) and brawling. If they wanted to get more serious than that, they had to leave.

Those hard of hearing on this issue could find themselves in a remote prison camp with the cell key dropped down a deep well. Marshal Tito was no fool, but he was mortal. He died in 1980, and things began to fall apart.

In the blue-collar Belgrade district of Zemun, a garage mechanic had a son in 1956 and named him Zoran. From an early age it became plain that the boy's nature was vicious and deeply violent. By the age of ten, Zoran Zilic's teachers shuddered at the mention of him. But he had one thing that would later set him apart from other Belgrade gangsters like Zeljko Raznatovic, alias Arkan. He was smart.

Skipping school from fourteen onward, Zilic became the leader of a teenage gang involved in the usual pleasures of stealing cars, brawling, drinking, and ogling the local girls. After one particular "rumble" between two gangs, three members of the opposing team had been so badly beaten with bicycle chains that they hovered between life and death for several days. The local police chief decided that enough was enough.

Zilic was hauled in, taken to the basement by two stalwarts with lengths of rubber hose, and beaten till he could not stand. There was no ill will involved; the police felt they needed him to concentrate on what they were saying.

The police chief then gave the youth a word of advice, or several. It was 1972, the boy was sixteen, and a week later he left the country. But he already had an introduction to take up. In Germany, he joined the gang of Ljuba Zemunac, whose surname was adopted, taken from the suburb of his birth. He also came from Zemun.

Zemunac was an impressively vicious mobster who would later be shot to death in the lobby of a German courthouse, but Zoran Zilic stayed with him for ten years, earning the older man's admiration as the most sadistic enforcer he had ever employed. In protection racketeering, the ability to inspire terror is vital. Zilic could do that and enjoy every moment of it.

In 1982, Zilic left and formed his own gang at the age of twenty-six. This might have caused a turf war with his old employer, but Zemunac shuffled off the mortal coil soon afterward. Zilic remained at the head of his gang in Germany and Austria for the next five years. He had long ago mastered German and English. But back home, things were changing.

There was no one to replace Marshal Tito, whose war record as a partisan against the Germans and sheer force of personality had kept together this unnatural six-province federation for so long.

The decade of the eighties was marked by a series of coalition governments that rose and fell, but the spirit of secession and separate independence was raging through Slovenia and Croatia in the north, and Macedonia in the south.

In 1987, Zilic cast his lot in with a shabby little ex-Communist Party hack whom others had overlooked or underestimated. He sported two qualities Zilic liked: an absolute ruthlessness in the pursuit of power, and a level of cunning and deviousness that would disarm rivals until it was too late. Zilic had spotted the coming man. From 1987, he offered to "take care" of the opponents of Slobodan Milosevic. There was no refusal and no charge.

By 1989, Milosevic had realized that communism was dead in the water; the horse to mount was that of extreme Serb nationalism. In fact, he brought not one but four horsemen to his country, those of the Apocalypse. Zilic served him almost to the end.

Yugoslavia was breaking up. Milosevic posed as the man to save the union, but he made no mention that he intended to do this through genocide, known as "ethnic cleansing." Inside Serbia, the province around Belgrade, his

popularity stemmed from the belief that he would save
Serbs everywhere from non-Serb persecution.

To do this, they first had to be persecuted. If the Croa-
tians or Bosnians were slow on the uptake, this had to be
arranged. A small local massacre would normally provoke
the resident majority to turn on the Serbs among them.
Then Milosevic could send in the army to save the Serbs.
It was the gangsters, turned paramilitary "patriots," who
acted as his agents provocateurs.

Where up until 1989 the Yugoslav state had kept its
gangster underworld at arm's length and abroad, Milosevic
took them into full partnership at home.

Like so many second-raters elevated to state power,
Milosevic became fascinated by money. The sheer size of
the sums involved acted on him like a snake charmer's pipe
to a cobra. It was not, for him, the luxury that money could
buy. He remained personally frugal to the end. It was
money as another form of power that hypnotized him. By
the time he fell, it was estimated by the successor Yugos-
lavian government that Milosevic and his cronies had embezzled and diverted to their own foreign accounts about
twenty billion dollars.

Others were not so frugal. These included his ghastly
wife and equally appalling son and daughter. The Milosevic
household made *The Munsters* look like *Little House on the
Prairie*.

Among those "full partners" was Zoran Zilic, who became the dictator's personal enforcer, a killer for hire. Reward under Milosevic was never in cash. It came in the
award of franchises for especially lucrative rackets, coupled
with the assurance of absolute immunity. The tyrant's cronies could rob, torture, rape, kill, and there was absolutely
nothing the regular police could do about it. He established
a criminal-cum-embezzler regime, posed as a patriot, and
the Serbs and Western European politicians fell for it for
years.

In all this brutality and bloodshed, he still did not save
the Yugoslav Federation or even his dream of a greater

Serbia. Slovenia left, then Macedonia and Croatia. By the
Dayton Agreement of November 1995, Bosnia was gone;
and by July 1999, he had not only effectively lost Kosovo,
but he had also provoked the partial destruction of Serbia
itself by NATO bombs.

Like Arkan, Zilic also formed a small squad of paramilitaries. There were others, like the sinister, shadowy, and brutal Frankie's Boys, the group of Frankie Stamatovic—
amazingly not even a Serb, but a renegade Croat from Istria.
Unlike the florid and ostentatious Arkan, gunned down in the
lobby of the Belgrade Holiday Inn, Zilic kept himself and his
group so low-profile as to be invisible. But on three occasions during the Bosnia war he took his group north and
raped, tortured, and murdered his way across that miserable
province until American intervention put a stop to it.

The third occasion was in April 1995. Where Arkan
called his group his Tigers and had a couple of hundred of
them, Zilic was content with Zoran's Wolves and he kept
the numbers small. On the third sortie, he had no more than
a dozen. They were all thugs who had operated before, save
one. He lacked a radio operator and one of his colleagues,
whose younger brother was in law school, said his brother
had a friend who had been an army R/T operator.

Contacted via the fellow student, the newcomer agreed
to forego his Easter vacation and join the Wolves.

Zilic asked what he was like. Had he seen combat? No,
he had done his military service in the Signal Corps, which
was why he was ready for some "action."

"If he has never been shot at, then he surely has never
killed anyone," said Zilic. "So this expedition should be
quite a learning experience."

The group set off for the north in the first week of May,
delayed by technical problems in their Russian-made vehicles. They went through Pale, the tiny former ski resort
now established as the capital of the self-styled Republika
Serbska, the third of Bosnia now so "cleansed" that it was
uniquely Serb. They skirted Sarajevo, once the proud host

of the winter Olympics, now a wreck, and went on into Bosnia proper, making their base at the stronghold of Banja Luka.

From there Zilic ranged outward, avoiding the dangerous Mujehadin, looking for softer targets among any Bosnian Muslim communities that might lack armed protection.

On May 14th, they found a small hamlet in the Vlasic range, took it by surprise, and wiped out the inhabitants, spent the night in the woods, and were back at Banja Luka by the evening of the 15th.

The new recruit left them the next day, screaming that he wanted to get back to his studies after all. Zilic let him go, after warning him that if he ever opened his mouth, he, Zilic, would personally cut off his dick with a broken wine glass and stuff both down his throat in that order. He did not like the boy anyway; he was stupid and squeamish.

The Dayton Agreement put an end to sport in Bosnia, but Kosovo was coming into season; and in 1998, Zilic was operating there also, claiming to be suppressing the Kosovo Liberation Army, in fact concentrating on rural communities and some seriously interesting looting.

But he never neglected his real reason for allying with Slobodan Milosevic. His service to the despot had paid rich dividends. His "business" dealings were a gangster's charter, the right to do what every mafioso has to dodge the law to achieve and yet do it with presidential immunity.

Chief among the franchises that paid dividends of several hundred percent were cigarettes and perfumes, fine brandies and whiskies, and all forms of luxury goods. These franchises he shared with Arkan, the only other gangster of comparable importance, and a few others. Even with sweeteners for all the necessary police and political "protection," he was a millionaire by the mid-nineties.

Then he moved into prostitution, narcotics, and arms dealing. With his fluent German and English he was better placed to deal with the international crime world than the others, who were monolinguistic.

Narcotics and arms were especially lucrative. His dollar

fortune entered eight figures. He also entered the files of
the American Drug Enforcement Administration (DEA),
the CIA, the Defense Intelligence Agency (DIA), and the
FBI.

Those around Milosevic, fat on embezzled money,
power, corruption, ostentation, luxury, and the endless syc-
ophancy to which they were subjected, became lazy and
complacent. They presumed the party would go on forever.
Zilic did not.

He avoided the obvious banks used by most of his cronies to store or export their fortunes. Almost every penny
he made, he stashed abroad but via banks no one in the
Serbian state knew anything about. And he watched for the
first cracks in the plaster. Sooner or later, he reasoned
acutely, even the awesomely weak politicians and diplo-
mats of the United Nations and the European Union would
see through Milosevic and call "time out." It happened over
Kosovo.

A largely agricultural province, Kosovo ranked with
Montenegro as all that was left of Serbia's fiefdoms within
the Yugoslav Federation. It contained about 180,000 Kosovars, who are Muslims and hardly distinguishable from
the neighboring Albanians, and 200,000 Serbs.

Milosevic had been deliberately persecuting the Kosovars for a decade until the once moribund Kosovo Liberation Army was back in being. The strategy was to be the
same as usual. Persecute beyond toleration, wait for the
local outrage, denounce the "terrorist," enter in force to
save the Serbs, and "restore order." Then NATO said it
would not stand by any more. Milosevic did not believe
them. Mistake. This time they meant it.

In the spring of 1999, the ethnic cleansing began, mainly
accomplished by the occupying Third Army, assisted by
the Security Police and the paramilitaries: Arkan's Tigers,
Frankie's Boys, and Zoran's Wolves. As foreseen, hundreds of thousands of Kosovars fled in terror over the borders into Albania and Macedonia. They were supposed to.

The West was supposed to take them all in as refugees. But they did not. They started to bomb Serbia.

Belgrade stuck it out for seventy-eight days. Up front, the local reaction was anti-NATO. Behind their hands, the Serbs began to mutter that it was the mad Milosevic who had brought this ruin upon them. It is always educational to note how the war fever fades when the roof falls in. Zilic heard this muttering.

On June 3, 1999, Milosevic agreed to terms. That was the way it was put. To Zilic it was unconditional surrender. He decided the moment had come to depart.

The fighting ended. The Third Army, having hardly taken a casualty from NATO's high-altitude bombing inside Kosovo, withdrew with all their equipment intact. The NATO allies occupied the province. The remaining Serbs began to flee into Serbia, bringing their rage with them. The direction of that rage began to move from NATO to Milosevic as the Serbs contemplated their shattered country.

Zilic began to slip more and more of his fortune beyond reach and to prepare for his own departure. Through the autumn of 1999 the protests against Milosevic grew and grew.

In a personal interview in November 1999, Zilic begged the dictator to observe the writing on the wall, conduct his own coup d'état while he had a loyal army to do it, and do away with any further pretense at democracy or opposition parties. But Milosevic was by then in his own private world, where his popularity was undiminished.

Zilic left his presence wondering yet again at the phenomenon that when men who have once held supreme power start to lose it, they go to pieces in every sense. Courage, will power, perception, decisiveness, even the ability to recognize reality—all are washed away as the tide sweeps away a sandcastle. By December, Milosevic was no longer exercising power; he was clinging to it. Zilic completed his preparations.

His fortune was no less than 500 million dollars; he had

a place to go where he would be safe. Arkan was dead, executed for falling out with Milosevic. The principal ethnic cleansers of Bosnia, Karadzic and General Mladic of the Srebrenitsa massacre, were being hunted like animals through Republika Serbska where they had taken refuge. Others had already been snatched for the new war crimes tribunal in The Hague. Milosevic was a broken reed.

As a matter of record, Milosevic declared on July 27, 2000, the coming presidential elections for September 24th. Despite copious rigging and a refusal to accept the outcome, he still lost. Crowds stormed the Parliament and installed his successor. Among the first acts of the new regime was to start investigating the Milosevic period: the murders and the 20 billion missing dollars.

The former tyrant holed himself up in his villa in the plush suburb of Dedinje. On April 1, 2001, President Kostunica was good and ready. The arrest team moved in at last.

But Zoran Zilic was long gone. In January 2000, he just disappeared. He said no good-byes and took no luggage. He went as one departing for a new life in a different world, where the old gewgaws would have no use. So he left them all behind.

He took nothing and no one with him, save his ultraloyal personal bodyguard, a hulking giant called Kulac. Within a week he had settled in his new hideout, which he had spent over a year preparing to receive him.

No one in the intelligence community paid attention to his departure, save one. A quiet, secretive man in America noted the gangster's new abode with considerable interest.

12
THE MONK

It was the dream, always the dream. He could not be rid of it, and it would not let him go. Night after night he would wake screaming, wet with sweat, and his mother would rush in to hold him and try to bring him comfort.

He was a puzzle and a worry to both his parents, for he could not or would not describe his nightmare; but his mother was convinced that he had never had such dreams until his return from Bosnia.

The dream was always the same. It was of the face in the slime, a pale disk ringed with lumps of excrement, some bovine, some human, screaming for mercy, begging for life. He couldn't understand English, as Zilic could, but words like "No, no, please, don't" are pretty international.

But the men with the poles laughed and pushed again.

And the face came back, until Zilic rammed his pole into the open mouth and pushed downward till the boy was dead under there somewhere. Then he would wake, shouting and crying, until his mother wrapped him in her arms, telling him it was all right, he was home in his own room at Senjak. But he could not explain what he had done, what he had been a part of, when he thought he was doing his patriotic duty to Serbia.

His father was less comforting, claiming he was a hardworking man who needed his sleep. By the autumn of 1995, Milan Rajak had his first session with a trained psychotherapist.

He attended twice a week at the gray-rendered, five-story psychiatric hospital on Palmoticeva Street, the best in Belgrade. But the experts at the Laza Lazarevic could not help either because he dared not confess.

Relief, he was told, comes with purging; but catharsis requires confession. Milosevic was still in power, but far more frightening were the feral eyes of Zoran Zilic that morning in Banja Luka when he said he wanted to quit and go home to Belgrade. Much more terrifying were the whispered words of mutilation and death if he ever opened his mouth.

His father was a dedicated atheist, raised under the Communist regime of Tito and a lifelong loyal servant of the Party. But his mother had kept her faith in the Serbian Orthodox Church, part of the Eastern communion with the Greek and Russian churches. Mocked by her husband and son, she had gone to her morning service down the years. By the end of 1995, Milan started to accompany her.

He began to find some comfort amid the ritual and the litany, the chants and the incense. The horror seemed to ebb in the church, just three blocks from where they lived and where his mother always went.

In 1996, he flunked his law exams to the outrage and despair of his father, who raged up and down the house for two days. If the news from the academy was not to his taste, what his son had to say took his breath away.

"I do not want to be a lawyer, Father. I want to enter the church."

It took time, but Rajak Senior calmed down and tried to come to terms with his changed son. At least the priesthood was a profession of sorts. Not given to wealth, but respectable. A man could still hold his head up and say, "My son is in the church, you know."

The priesthood itself, he discovered, would take years of study to achieve, most of that time in a seminary, but the son had other ideas. He wanted to live in seclusion and without delay. He wanted to become a monk, repudiating everything material in favor of the simple life.

Ten miles southeast of Belgrade he found what he wanted: the small monastery of Saint Stephen in the hamlet of Slanci. It contained no more than a dozen brothers under the authority of the abbot or *iguman*. The monks worked in the fields and barns of their own farm, grew their own food, accepted donations from a few tourists and pilgrims, meditated, and prayed. There was a waiting list to join and no chance of jumping it.

Fate intervened in the meeting with the *iguman*, Abbot Vasilije. He and Rajak Senior stared at each other in amazement. Despite the full black beard, flecked with gray, Rajak recognized the same Goran Tomic who had been at school with him forty years before. The abbot agreed to meet his son and discuss with him a possible career in the church.

The abbot's shrewd intelligence divined that his former schoolmate's son was a young man torn by some inner turmoil that could not find peace in the outer world. He had seen it before. He could not create a vacancy for an instant monk, he pointed out, but men from the city occasionally joined the monks for the purpose of a religious "retreat."

In the summer of 1996, with the Bosnian war over, Milan Rajak went to Slanci on an extended retreat to grow tomatoes and cucumbers, to meditate, and to pray. The dream ebbed away.

After a month Abbot Vasilije gently suggested that he confess, and he did. In whispered tones, by the light of a candle by the altar, under the gaze of the man from Naz-areth, he told the abbot what he had done.

The abbot crossed himself fervently and prayed—for the soul of the boy in the cesspit and for the penitent beside him. He urged Milan to go to the authorities and report those responsible.

But the grip of Milosevic was absolute, and the terror inspired by Zoran Zilic no less so. That the "authorities" would have lifted a finger against Zilic was inconceivable. And the killer's promised vengeance would, when carried out, raise not a ripple on the water. So the silence went on.

The pain began in the winter of 2000. He noticed that it intensified with each bodily motion. After two months he consulted his father, who presumed it was some passing "bug." Nevertheless, he arranged for tests at the Belgrade General Hospital, the Klinicki Centar.

Belgrade has always boasted medical standards among the highest in Europe, and the Belgrade General Hospital was up there among the best. There were three series of tests, and Milan was seen by specialists in proctology, urol-ogy, and oncology. It was the professor heading the third department who finally asked Milan Rajak to visit his suite of rooms at the clinic.

"I believe you are a trainee monk?" he asked.

"Yes."

"Then you believe in God?"

"Yes."

"I sometimes wish I could also. Alas, I cannot. But you must now test your faith. The news is not good."

"Tell me, please."

"It is what we call colorectal cancer."

"Operable?"

"I regret. No."

"Reversible? Chemotherapy."

"Too late. I am sorry, deeply sorry."

The young man stared out of the window. He had been sentenced to death. "How long, Professor?"

"That is always asked, and it's always impossible to an-

swer. With precautions, care, a special diet, some radio-
therapy . . . a year. Possibly less, possibly more. Not much
more."

It was March 2001. Milan Rajak went back to Slanci
and told the abbot. The older man wept for the one who
was now like the son he had never had.

On April 1st, the Belgrade police arrested Slobodan
Milosevic. Zoran Zilic had disappeared. Milan's father had
used his contacts high in the police force to confirm that
Yugoslavia's most successful and powerful gangster had
simply disappeared more than a year earlier and was now
living somewhere abroad, location unknown. His influence
had disappeared with him.

On April 2, 2001, Milan Rajak looked among his papers
for an old business card. He took a sheet of paper and,
writing in English, addressed a letter to London. The bur-
den of the letter was in the first sentence.

"I have changed my mind. I am prepared to testify."

Within twenty-four hours of receiving the letter three
days later, and after a quick call to Stephen Edmond in
Windsor, Ontario, the Tracker came back to Belgrade.

The statement was taken in English, in the presence of
a certified interpreter and notary public. It was signed and
witnessed.

> *Back then in 1995, young Serbian men were
> accustomed to believe what they were told, and
> I was no exception. It may be plain today what
> terrible things were done in Croatia and Bos-
> nia, and later in Kosovo, but we were told the
> victims were isolated communities of Serbs in
> these former provinces, and I believed this. The
> idea that our own armed forces were carrying
> out the mass murder of old people, women, and
> children was inconceivable. Only Croats and
> Bosnians did this sort of thing, we were told.
> Serbian forces were only concerned to protect
> and rescue Serbian minority communities.*

When in April 1995, a fellow law student told me that his brother and others were going to Bosnia to protect the Serbs up there and needed a radio operator, I suspected nothing.

I had done my military service as a radio operator, but miles from any fighting. I agreed to give up my spring vacation to help my fellow Serbs in Bosnia.

When I joined the other twelve, I realized they were rough types, but I put this down to their being hardened combat soldiers and blamed myself for being too spoiled and soft.

The column of four off-roads contained twelve men, including the leader, who joined us at the last minute. Only then did I learn he was Zoran Zilic, of whom I had vaguely heard but who had a fearsome and shadowy reputation. We drove for two days, north through Republika Serbska and into central Bosnia. We arrived at Banja Luka and that became our base, notably the Bosna Hotel where we took rooms and ate and drank.

We made three patrols north, east, and west of Banja Luka but found no enemy or threatened Serbian villages. On May 14th, we drove south into the Vlasic range of mountains. We knew that beyond the range lay Travnik and Vitez, both enemy territory for us Serbs.

In the late afternoon we were driving along a track in the woods when we came across two little girls in front of us. Zilic got out and talked to them. He was smiling. I thought he was being nice to them. One told him her name was Laila. I did not understand. It was a Muslim name. She had signed her own death warrant and that of her village.

Zilic took the girls aboard the leading vehicle, and they pointed out where they lived. It was a hamlet in a valley in the woods, nothing much, about twenty adults and a dozen children, seven cottages, some barns, and railed paddocks. When I saw the crescent above the tiny mosque, I realized they were Muslims, but they clearly posed no threat.

The others poured out of the off-roads and rounded up everyone in the hamlet. I suspected nothing when they began to search the cottages. I had heard of Muslim fanatics, Mujehadin from the Middle East, Iran, and Saudi Arabia, who also marauded through Bosnia and would kill any Serb on sight. Perhaps there were some hiding there, I thought.

When the search was over, Zilic walked back to the lead vehicle and took a position behind the machine gun mounted on a swivel behind the front seats. He shouted to his men to scatter and opened fire on the peasants huddled in the railed cattle pen.

It happened almost before I could believe it had happened. The peasants began to jump and dance as the heavy bullets hit them. The other soldiers opened up with their submachine guns. Some of the peasants tried to save their children, throwing their bodies over them. A few of the smaller children got away in this manner, darting between the adults and reaching the trees before the bullets took them. Later I learned there were six who had escaped.

I felt violently sick. There was a stench of blood and entrails in the air—you never get the stench in films from Hollywood. I had never seen people die before, but these were not even soldiers or partisans. One old shotgun, perhaps for killing rabbits and crows, had been found.

When it was over, most of the shooters were disappointed. There had been no alcohol found *nor anything of value. So they torched the houses and the barns, and we left them burning.*

We spent the night in the forest. The men had brought their own slivovitz and most got drunk on it. I tried to drink, but brought it all back up. In my sleeping bag, I realized I had made a terrible mistake. These were not patriots around me, but gangsters who killed because they enjoyed it.

The next morning, we began to drive down a series of mountain tracks, mainly along the face of the range, back toward the pass that would lead us over the mountains to Banja Luka. That was when we found the farmhouse. It was alone in another small valley amid the woods. I saw Zilic in the first off-road rise from his seat and hold up his hand in a "stop" signal. He gestured that we should cut our engines. The drivers did that, and there was silence. Then we heard voices.

Very quietly we got down from the vehicles, took guns, and crept to the edge of the clearing. About a hundred yards away were two grown males leading six children out of a barn. The men were not armed and not in uniform. Behind them was a fire-gutted farmhouse and to one side a new, black Toyota Landcruiser with the words "Loaves-n-Fishes" on the door panel. Both turned and stared when they saw us. The oldest of the children, a little girl of about ten, began to cry. I recognized her by her headscarf. It was Laila.

Zilic advanced toward the group with his gun raised, but neither made any attempt to fight. The rest of us fanned out and formed a horseshoe round the captives when we got close to them. The taller of the men spoke, and I realized one was American. So did Zilic. None of the others spoke a word of English. The American said, "Who are you guys?"

Zilic did not answer. He strolled over to examine the brand-new Landcruiser. At that moment the child Laila tried to make a run for it. One of the men grabbed but missed. Zilic turned from the off-road, drew his pistol, aimed, fired, and blew the back of her head away. He was very proud of his marksmanship with a pistol.

The American was ten feet from Zilic. He took two strides, swung a fist with all his power, and caught Zilic on the side of the mouth. If he had had any chance of survival, that finished it. Zilic was caught by surprise, as he might have been, because no one in all of Yugoslavia would have dared do that.

There were two seconds of complete disbelief as Zilic went down, blood pouring from his split lip. Then six of his men were on the American with boots, fists, gun butts. They beat him to a bloody pulp. I think they would have finished him off, but Zilic intervened. He was back up, dabbing the blood off his mouth. He told them to stop the beating.

The American was alive, shirt ripped open, torso red from kicking, face already swelling and cut. The open shirt revealed a broad money belt at his waist. Zilic gestured with one hand, and one of his men ripped it off. It was stuffed with one-hundred-dollar bills. Zilic examined the man who had dared hit him.

"Dear me," he said, "so much blood. You need a cold bath, my friend, something to freshen you up." He turned to his men. They were bewildered at his apparent concern for the American. But Zilic had seen something else in the clearing. The cesspit was brimming full, *partly from animal slurry but also from human waste. It had once served both purposes. If the passing years had solidified the mixture, the recent rains had reliquefied it. On Zilic's orders the American was thrown into it.*

The shock of the cold must have brought him to his senses. His feet found the bottom of the pit, and he began to struggle. There was a cattle pen nearby with post and rail fencing. It was old and broken, but some of the long poles were still whole. The men grabbed several and began to poke the American under the surface of the slime.

He began to scream for mercy each time his face appeared above the slime. He was begging for his life. About the sixth time, maybe it was seven, Zilic grabbed a pole and rammed the end into the American's gaping mouth, smashing most of the teeth. Then he pushed downward and kept pushing until the young man was dead.

I walked away to the trees and vomited up the sausage and black bread I had eaten for breakfast. I wanted to kill them all, but they were too many and I was too afraid. While I was being sick, I heard several volleys. They had killed the other five children and the Bosnian aid worker who had brought the American to that spot. All the bodies were thrown into the slime pit. Slowly they slithered below the surface and were gone. One of the men found that the words "Loaves-n-Fishes" on each front door of the Landcruiser were simply decals with adhesive backing. They peeled off quite easily.

When we drove away there was no sign, except the startlingly bright splashes of red, the children's blood on the grass, and the twinkling

*of a few brass cartridges. That evening Zoran
Zilic divided up the dollars. He gave a hundred
dollars to each man. I refused to take them, but
he insisted that I take a minimum of one note
to remain "one of the boys."*

*I tried to get rid of it in the bar that evening,
but he saw me and really lost his temper. The
next day I told him I was going home, back to
Belgrade. He threatened that if I ever spoke one
word of what I had seen, he would find me,
mutilate, and then kill me.*

*As I have long known, I am not a brave man,
and it was my fear of him that kept me silent
all these years, even when the Englishman
came asking questions in the summer of 1995.
But now I have made my peace and am prepared to testify in any court in Holland or
America, so long as God Almighty gives me the
strength to stay alive.*

*I swear by Him that all I have said is the
truth and nothing but the truth.*

*Given under my hand, Senjak District, Bel-
grade, this 7th day of April 2001.*

Milan Rajak.

That night the Tracker sent a long message to Stephen
Edmond in Windsor, Ontario, and the instructions that
came back were unequivocal: "Go wherever you must, do
whatever it takes, find my grandson or whatever is left of
him and bring him home."

13
THE PIT

Peace had come to Bosnia with the Dayton Agreement of November 1995, but over five years later, the scars of war were not even disguised, let alone healed.

It had never been a rich province. No Dalmatian coast to attract the tourists; no mineral reserves, just low-tech agriculture in the farmlands between the mountains and the forests.

The economic damage would take years more to recover from, but the social damage was far worse. Few could imagine that in less than a generation or two, Serb, Croat, and Bosnian Muslims would accept to live side by side with each other again, or even a few miles apart, save in armed, watchful compounds.

The international bodies spouted the usual blather about

reunification and restoring mutual trust, thus justifying the doomed attempts to put Humpty Dumpty back together again rather than facing the necessity of partition.

The task of governing the shattered entity went to the United Nations high representative, a sort of proconsul with near absolute powers, backed by the soldiers of UNPRO-FOR. Of all the unglamorous tasks that fell to the people who had no time for posturing on the political stage but who actually made things happen, the least charming went to the ICMP—the International Commission on Missing Persons.

This was run with impressive and quiet efficiency by Gordon Bacon, a former British policeman. To the ICMP fell the task of listening to the tens of thousands of relatives of the "disappeared ones" and taking their statements on the one hand, and tracing and exhuming the hundreds of minimassacres that had taken place since 1992. The third job was to try and match statements with relics and restore the skull and bundle of bones to the right relatives for final burial according to the religious creed or none.

The matching process would have been completely impossible without DNA, but the new technology meant that a swab of blood from the relative and a sliver of bone from the cadaver could provide proof of identity beyond doubt. By 2000, the fastest and most efficient DNA laboratory in Europe was not in some wealthy Western capital but in Sarajevo, set up and run on tiny funds by Gordon Bacon. It was to see him that the Tracker drove into the Bosnian city two days after Milan Rajak had signed his name.

He did not need to bring the Serb with him. Rajak had revealed that before he died, the Bosnian aid worker, Fadil Sulejman, had told his murderers that the farm had once been his family home. Gordon Bacon read the Rajak statement with interest but no sense of novelty.

He had read hundreds before, but always from the few survivors, never from one of the perpetrators, and never involving an American. He realized the mystery of what he knew as the Colenso file might be solved at last. He con-

tacted the ICMP commissioner for the Travnik zone and
asked for the fullest cooperation with Mr. Gracey when he
arrived. The Tracker spent the night in his fellow countryman's spare bedroom and drove north again in the morning.

It is just over two hours into Travnik, and he was there
by midday. He had talked with Stephen Edmond, and a
swab of the grandfather's blood was on its way from Ontario.

On April 11th, the exhumation team left Travnik for the
hills, aided by a local guide. Questions at the mosque had
quickly discovered two men who had known Fadil Sulejman, and one of them said he knew the farm in the upland
valley. He was in the leading off-road.

The digger team brought with them protective clothing,
breathing aids, shovels, soft brushes, sieves, and evidence
bags, all the needs of their grisly trade.

The valley was much as it must have been six years
earlier, but a bit more overgrown. No one had come to
reclaim it; the Sulejman family appeared to have ceased to
exist.

They found the sewage pit without difficulty. The spring
rains had been less than in 1995, and the contents of the
pit had hardened to malodorous clay. The diggers pulled
on garments like a fly fisherman's waders and jackets but
seemed immune to the smell.

Rajak had testified that on the day of the murder, the pit
was full to the brim, but if Ricky Colenso's feet had
touched bottom, it must be about six feet deep. Without
rain, the surface had receded two feet downward.

After three feet of slime had been shoveled out, the
ICMP commissioner ordered his men to throw down their
shovels and resume with hand trowels. An hour later the
first bones were visible, and after a further hour of work
with scraper and camel-hair brush, the massacre site was
exposed.

No air had penetrated to the bottom of the pit, so there
had been no maggots at work, since they depend on air.

The decomposition was uniquely due to enzymes and ba-
cilli.

Every fragment of soft tissue was gone, and when wiped
with a damp cloth, the first skull to emerge gleamed clean
and white. There were fragments of leather, from the boots
and belts of the two men; an ornate belt buckle, surely
American, plus metal studs from jeans and buttons from a
denim jacket.

One of the men on his knees down below called out and
passed up a watch. Seventy months had not affected the
inscription on the back: "Ricky, from Mom. Graduation.
1994."

The children had all been thrown in dead, and they had
sunk on top of, or close to, each other. Time and decomposition had made a jumble of the bones of the six corpses,
but the size of the skeletons proved who they had been.

Sulejman had also gone in dead; his skeleton lay on its
back, spread-eagled, the way the body had sunk. His friend
stood and looked down into the pit and prayed to Allah.
He confirmed his former classmate had been around five
feet, eight inches tall.

The eighth body was the big one, over six feet. It was
to one side, as if the dying boy had tried to crawl through
the blackness to the sidewall. The bones lay on their side,
hunched in a fetal position. The watch came from that pile
and the belt buckle. When the skull was passed up, the front
teeth were smashed, as Rajak had testified.

It was sundown when the last tiny bone was retrieved
and bagged. The two grown men were in separate bags; the
children shared their own, the reassembly of six small skeletons could be done in the mortuary down in the town.

The Tracker drove to Vitez for the night. The British
army was long gone, but he took a billet with the guest-
house he had stayed in before and which he knew. In the
morning he returned to the ICMP office in Travnik.

From Sarajevo, Gordon Bacon authorized the local commissioner to release the remains of Ricky Colenso to Captain Gracey for transportation to the capital.

The swab from Ontario had arrived. In a remarkably fast two days, the DNA tests were complete. The head of the ICMP in Sarajevo attested that the skeleton was indeed that of Richard "Ricky" Colenso. He needed formal authority from the next of kin to release the remains into the care of Philip Gracey of Andover, Hampshire, UK. That took two days to arrive.

In the interval, on instructions from Ontario, the Tracker bought a casket from Sarajevo's premier funeral parlor. The morticians arranged the skeleton with other materials to give heft and balance to the casket as if it contained a real cadaver. Then it was sealed forever.

It was on April 16th that the Canadian magnate's Grumman IV arrived with a letter of authority to take over. The Tracker consigned the casket and the fat file of paperwork to the captain and went home to the green fields of England.

Stephen Edmond was at Dulles to receive his own executive jet when it touched down on the evening of the 16th after a refueling stop at Shannon. An ornate hearse took the casket to a funeral parlor for two days while final arrangements for interment were completed.

On the 18th, the ceremony took place at the very exclusive Oak Hill Cemetery on R Street in Georgetown. It was small and private, in the Roman Catholic rite. The boy's mother, Mrs. Annie Colenso, née Edmond, stood with her husband's arm around her, weeping quietly. Professor Colenso dabbed at his eyes and occasionally glanced over at his father-in-law as if he did not know what to do and sought some guidance.

Across the grave the eighty-one-year-old Canadian stood in his dark suit like a pillar of his own pentlandite ore and looked unblinkingly down at the coffin of his grandson. He had not shown the report from the Tracker to his daughter or son-in-law and certainly not the testimony of Milan Rajak.

They knew only that a belated eyewitness had come forward who recalled seeing the black Landcruiser in a valley, and as a result, the two bodies had been found. But he had to concede that they had been murdered and buried. There was no other way of explaining the six-year gap.

The service ended, the mourners moved away to let the sextons work. Mrs. Colenso ran to her father and hugged him, pressing her face against the fabric of his shirt. He looked down and gently stroked the top of her head, as he had when she was a small girl and something frightened her.

"Daddy, whoever did this to my baby, I want him caught. Not killed quickly and cleanly. I want him to wake up in jail every morning for the rest of his life and know that he is there and will never come out again, and I want him to think back and know that it is all because he cold-bloodedly murdered my child."

The old man had already made up his mind. "I may have to move heaven," he rumbled, "and I may have to move hell. And if I must, I will."

He let her go, nodded to the professor, and strode away to his limousine. As the driver eased up the slope to the R Street gateway, Stephen Edmond took his phone from the console and dialed a number. Somewhere on Capitol Hill a secretary answered.

"Put me through to Sen. Peter Lucas," he said.

The face of the senior senator for New Hampshire lit up when he got the message. Friendships born in the heat of war may last an hour or a lifetime. With Stephen Edmond and Peter Lucas, it had been fifty-five years since they had sat on an English lawn on a spring morning and wept for the young men of both their countries who would never come home. But the friendship had endured, as though they were brothers. Each knew that, if asked, he would go to the wire for his friend. The Canadian was about to ask.

One of the aspects of the genius of Franklin Delano Roosevelt was that, although a convinced Democrat, he was quite prepared to use talent wherever he found it. It was just after Pearl Harbor that he summoned a conservative Republican, who happened to be at a football game, and asked him to form the Office of Strategic Services.

The man he summoned was Gen. William "Wild Bill" Donovan, the son of Irish immigrants, who had commanded the Fighting Sixty-ninth Regiment on the western front in World War I. After that, as a trained lawyer, he had become deputy attorney general under Herbert Hoover, then spent years as a Wall Street legal eagle. It was not his law skills that Roosevelt wanted; it was his sheer combativeness, the quality he needed to create the United States' first foreign intelligence and special forces unit.

Without much hesitation, the old warrior gathered around himself a corps of brilliant and well-connected young men as his gofers. They included Arthur Schlesinger, David Bruce, and Henry Hyde, who would all go on to high office.

At that time Peter Lucas, raised to New England wealth and privilege, was a sophomore at Princeton, and he decided on the day of Pearl Harbor that he, too, wanted to go to war. His father forbade any such thing.

In February 1942, the young man disobeyed and dropped out of college, all taste for study gone. He raced around trying to find something he really wanted to do; toyed with the idea of fighter pilot and took private flying lessons until he learned that he was constantly airsick.

In June 1942, the OSS was established. Peter Lucas offered himself at once and was accepted. He saw himself with blackened face, dropping by night far behind German lines. He attended a lot of cocktail parties instead. General Donovan wanted a first-class aide-de-camp, efficient and polished.

He saw at short range the preparations for the landings in Sicily and Salerno in which OSS agents were wholly involved and begged for action. Be patient, he was told. It was like taking a boy to a sweet shop but leaving him inside a glass box. He could see, but he couldn't touch.

Finally he went to the general with a flat ultimatum. "Either I fight under you, or I quit and join the Airborne."

No one gave "Wild Bill" Donovan ultimatums, but he stared at the young man and maybe saw something of himself a quarter of a century earlier. "Do both," he said, "in reverse order."

With Donovan's backing, all doors opened. Peter Lucas shrugged off the hated civilian suit and went to Fort Benning to become a "ninety-day wonder," a fast-track commission to emerge as a second lieutenant in the Airborne.

He missed the D-day Normandy landings, being still in parachute school. When he graduated, he returned to General Donovan. "You promised," he said.

Peter Lucas got his black-faced parachute drop one cold autumn night into the mountains behind the German lines in northern Italy. There he came across the Italian partisans who were dedicated Communists, and the British special forces who seemed too laid back to be dedicated to anything.

Within a couple of weeks he learned the "laid back" bit was an act. The Jedburgh group he had joined contained some of the war's most skilled and vicious killers.

He survived the bitter winter of 1944 in the mountains and almost made it to the end of the war intact. It was March 1945 when he and five others ran into a stay-behind squad of no-surrender SS men they did not know were still in the region. There was a firefight, and Lucas took two slugs from a Schmeisser submachine gun in the left arm and shoulder.

They were miles from anywhere, out of morphine, and it took a week of marching in agony to find a British forward unit. There was a patch-up operation on the spot, a morphine-dazed flight in a Liberator, and a much better reconstruction in a London hospital.

When he was fit enough to leave, he was sent to a convalescent home on the coast of Sussex. He shared a room with a Canadian fighter pilot nursing two broken legs. They played chess to while away the days.

Returning home, the world was his oyster. He joined his father's firm on Wall Street, took it over eventually, became a giant in the financial community, and ran for public office. In April 2001, he was in his fourth and last term as a Republican senator for New Hampshire, and he had just seen a Republican president elected.

When he heard who was on the line, he told his secretary to hold all calls.

"Steve. Good to hear you again. Where are you?"

"Right here in Washington. Peter, I need to see you. It's serious."

Catching his mood, the senator dropped the bonhomie. "Sure, pal. Wanna tell me?"

"Over lunch. Can you make it?"

"I'll clear the calendar. The Hay-Adams. Ask for my usual corner table. It's quiet. One o'clock."

They met when the senator strode into the lobby. The Canadian was waiting there.

"I just came from an interment up in Georgetown. I just buried my only grandson."

The senator stared and his face creased with shared pain. "Jesus, old friend, I am so sorry."

"Let's talk at the table. There's something I need you to read."

When they were seated, the Canadian answered his friend's question. "He was murdered. In cold blood. No, not here, and not now. Six years ago. In Bosnia."

He explained briefly about the boy's age, his desire back in 1995 to help alleviate the pain of the Bosnians, his odyssey through the capitals to the town of Travnik, his agreement to try to help his interpreter trace his family homestead. Then he passed over the Rajak confession.

Dry martinis came. The senator ordered smoked salmon platter, brown bread, chilled Meursault. Edmond nodded, meaning, the same.

Senator Lucas was accustomed to reading fast, but halfway through the report he gave a low whistle and slowed down.

While the senator toyed with the salmon and read the last pages, Steve Edmond glanced around. His friend had chosen well, a personal table just beyond the grand piano, secluded in a corner by a window through which the White House was visible. The Lafayette at the Hay-Adams was unique, more like a house set at the heart of an eighteenth-century country estate than a restaurant in the middle of a bustling capital city.

Senator Lucas raised his head. "I don't know what to say, Steve. This is perhaps the most awful document I have ever read. What do you want me to do?"

A waiter removed the plates and brought small black coffees and for each man a snifter of old Armagnac. They were silent while the young man was at the table.

Steve Edmond looked down at their four hands on the white cloth. Old men's hands, cord veined, sausage fingered, liver spotted. Hands that had thrown a Hurricane fighter straight down into a formation of Dornier bombers; that had emptied an M-1 carbine into a taverna full of SS men outside Bolzano; hands that had fought fights, caressed women, held firstborns, signed checks, created fortunes, altered politics, changed the world. Once.

Peter Lucas caught his friend's glance and understood his mood. "Yes, we are old now. But not dead yet. What do you want me to do?"

"Maybe we could do one last good thing. My grandson was an American citizen. The United States has the right to require this monster's extradition from wherever he is. Back here. To stand trial for Murder One. That means the Justice and State Departments, acting together on any government that harbors this swine. Will you take it to them?"

"My friend, if this government of Washington, D.C., cannot give you justice, then no one can."

He raised his glass. "One last good thing."

But he was wrong.

14
THE FATHER

It was only a family spat, and it should have ended with a kiss and make up. But it took place between a passionate Italian-blooded daughter and a doggedly tenacious father.

By the summer of 1991, Amanda Jane Dexter was sixteen and knockout attractive. The Naples-descended Marozzi genes had given her a figure to cause a bishop to kick a hole in a stained-glass window. The blond Anglo-Saxon lineage of Dexter had endowed her with a face like the young Bardot. The local boys were over her like a rash, and her father had to accept that. But he did not like Emilio.

He had nothing against Hispanics, but there was something sly and shallow about Emilio, even predatory and cruel behind matinee-idol looks. But Amanda Jane fell for him like a ton of bricks.

It came to a head during the long summer vacation. Emilio proposed to take her away for a holiday by the sea. He spun a good tale. There would be other young people, adults to supervise, beach sports, fresh air, and the bracing tang of the Atlantic. It sounded good; it sounded normal; it sounded innocent. But when Cal Dexter tried to make eye contact with the young man, Emilio avoided his gaze. Dexter's gut instinct told him there was something wrong. He said, "No."

A week later she ran away. There was a note to say they should not worry, everything would be fine, but she was a grown woman now and refused to be treated like a child. She never came back.

School holidays ended. She still did not appear. Too late, her mother, who had approved her request, listened to her husband. They had no address for the beach party, no knowledge of Emilio's background, parentage, or real home address. The Bronx address he had used turned out to be a lodging house. His car had Virginia number plates, but a check with Richmond told Dexter it had been sold for cash in July. Even the surname, Gonzalez, was as common as Smith.

Through his contacts, Cal Dexter consulted with a senior sergeant in the Missing Persons Bureau of the NYPD. The officer was sympathetic but resigned. "Sixteen is like grown-up nowadays, Counselor; they sleep together, vacation together, set up house together . . ." The department could only send out an all-points if there was evidence of threat, duress, forcible removal from the parental home, drug abuse, whatever.

Dexter had to concede there had been a single phone message. It had come at a time Amanda Jane would know that her father would be at work and her mother out. The message was on the answering machine.

She was fine, she said, very happy, and they should not worry. She was living her own life and enjoying it. She would be in touch when she was good and ready.

Cal Dexter traced the call. It had come from a mobile

phone, the sort that operates off a purchased SIM card and cannot be traced to the owner. He played the tape to the sergeant, and the man shrugged. Like all Missing Persons Bureaus in every force across the States, he had a case overload. This was not an emergency.

Christmas came, but it was bleak—the first in the Dexter household in sixteen years without their baby.

It was a morning jogger who found the body. His name was Hugh Lamport; he ran a small IT consultancy company; he was an honest citizen trying to keep in shape. For him that meant a three-mile run every morning between 6:30 and as near to 7:00 as he could make it, and that even included cold, bleak mornings like February 18, 1992. He was running along the grass verge of Indian River Road, Virginia Beach, which was where he lived. The grass was easier on the ankles than tarmac or concrete. But when he came to a bridge over a narrow culvert, he had a choice: cross via the concrete bridge or jump the culvert. He jumped.

He noticed something below him as he jumped, something pale in the predawn gloom. After landing, he turned and peered back into the ditch. She lay in the strange disjointed pose of death, half in and half out of the water.

Lamport glanced frantically round and saw, four hundred yards away through some trees, a dim light, another early riser brewing the morning cup. No longer jogging but sprinting, he arrived at the door and hammered hard. The coffee brewer peered through the window, listened to the shouted explanation, and let him in.

The 911 call was taken by the night-duty dispatcher in the basement switchboard at Virginia City's police headquarters on Princess Anne Road. She asked as a matter of urgency for the nearest patrol car, and the response came from the First Precinct's sole cruiser, which was a mile from the culvert. It made that mile in a minute, to find a man in sweats and another in a bathrobe marking the spot.

It took the two patrol officers no more than two minutes to call in for homicide detectives and a full forensic team. The householder fetched coffee, which was gratefully received, and all four waited.

That whole sector of eastern Virginia is occupied by six cities with contiguous boundaries, a community that extends for miles on both banks of the James River and Hampton Roads. It is a landscape studded with naval and air bases, for here the roads run out into Chesapeake Bay and thence the Atlantic.

Of the six cities—Norfolk, Portsmouth, Hampton (with Newport News), James City, and Chesapeake—the biggest by far is Virginia Beach. It covers 310 square miles and contains 430,000 citizens out of a total of 1.5 million. Of its four precincts, the Second, Third, and Fourth cover the built-up areas, while the First Precinct is large and mainly rural. Its 195 square miles run right down to the North Carolina border and are bisected by Indian River Road.

Forensics and Homicide arrived at the culvert around the same time, thirty minutes later. The medical examiner was five minutes after that. Dawn came, or what passed for dawn, and a drizzle set in.

Lamport was driven home to shower off and make a full statement. The coffee brewer made a statement, which is to say he could only aver that he had heard and seen nothing during the night.

The ME quickly established death, that the victim was a young Caucasian female, that death had almost certainly occurred somewhere else and the body been dumped, presumably from a car. After the police photographer took shots of the body in situ, he ordered the attendant ambulance to take the cadaver to the state morgue in Norfolk, a facility that served all six cities.

The local homicide detectives took time out to muse that if the perpetrator or perpetrators, who seemed to have a moral code on the level of a snake's navel and an IQ to match, had driven three miles farther on, they would have entered the swamp country at the head of Back Bay. Here, a weighted body could disappear forever and no one be the wiser. But they had seemingly run out of patience and dumped their grisly cargo where it would be found quickly and start a manhunt.

At Norfolk, two things happened with respect to the corpse: An autopsy was done to establish cause, time of death, and if possible, location, and an attempt was made to secure identification. The body itself yielded nothing to the second search: some skimpy but no longer provocative underwear, a badly torn and slinky dress. No medallions, bracelets, tattoos, or purse.

Before the forensic pathologist began his task, the face, which bore lesions and contusions compatible with a savage beating, was again photographed. The photo would be passed around the vice squads of all six cities, for the girl's clothing seemed to indicate a possibility that she had been involved with what is euphemistically called "night life."

The other two details the ID hunters needed and got were fingerprints and blood type. Then the pathologist started. It was the fingerprints the police pinned their hopes on.

The six cities came up negative on the prints. Details went to Richmond, where prints covering the whole of Virginia are stored. Days went by. The answer came back. Sorry. The next step up was the FBI, covering the entire United States. It uses IAFIS—the Integrated Automated Fingerprint Identification System.

The pathologist's report made even hardened homicide detectives queasy. The girl appeared not much more than eighteen, if that. She had once been pretty, but someone, plus her lifestyle, had put an end to that. Vaginal and anal dilation was so exaggerated that she had clearly been penetrated, and repeatedly, by instruments far larger than a normal male organ. The terminal beating had not been the only one; there had been others before. And heroin abuse, probably dating back no more than six months.

To both Homicide and Vice detectives in Norfolk, the report said "prostitution." It was no news to any of them

that recruitment into vice was often accompanied by nar-
cotic dependency, the pimp being the only source of the
drug. Any girl trying to escape the clutches of such a gang
would certainly be punished; such "lesson learning" could
involve forced participation in exhibitions featuring brutal
perversions and bestiality. There were creatures prepared to
pay for this, and thus creatures prepared to supply it.

The post-autopsy body went into the cold room, while
the search for the girl's identity continued. She was still
Jane Doe. Then a Vice detective in Portsmouth thought he
recognized the circulated photograph, despite the damage
and discoloration. He thought that she might have been a
hooker going under the name of Lorraine.

Inquiries revealed that "Lorraine" had not been seen for
several weeks. Prior to that she had worked for a notori-
ously vicious Hispanic gang, who recruited by using good-
looking gang members to pick up girls in the cities to the
north and entice them south with promises of marriage, a
lovely vacation, whatever it took.

The Portsmouth Vice Squad worked on the gang but
with no result. The pimps claimed they had never known
Lorraine's real name, that she had been a professional when
she arrived, and that she had left voluntarily to return to
the West Coast. The photograph was simply not clear
enough to prove otherwise.

But Washington did identify the girl. They came up with
a firm ID based on the prints. Amanda Jane Dexter had
tried to fool the security of a local supermarket and shoplift
an item. The security camera won. The juvenile court judge
accepted her story, backed by five classmates, and let her
go with a caution. But her fingerprints were taken. They
were with the NYPD and had been passed on to IAFIS.

"I think," muttered Sergeant Austin of the Portsmouth
Vice Squad when he heard the news, "I might be able to
get those bastards at last."

It was another filthy winter morning when the phone
rang in the apartment in the Bronx, but perhaps a good
enough morning to ask a father to drive three hundred miles

to identify his only child. Cal Dexter sat on the edge of the
bed and wished he had died in the tunnels of Cu Chi rather
than take this kind of pain. He finally told Angela and held
her while she sobbed. He rang his mother-in-law, and she
came over at once.

He could not wait for a flight out of La Guardia for
Norfolk International; he could not have sat and waited if
there had been a flight delay due to fog, rain, hail, or con-
gestion. He took his car and drove. Out of New York,
across the bridge to Newark, on through the country he
knew so well as he had been hauled from one construction
site to another; out of New Jersey, through a chunk of
Pennsylvania and another of Delaware, then south and ever
more south past Baltimore and Washington, D.C., to the
end of Virginia.

At the morgue in Norfolk he stared down at the once
lovely and much loved face and nodded dumbly to the
homicide detective with him. They went upstairs. Over coffee he ascertained the basic outlines. She had been beaten
by a person or persons unknown. She had died of severe
internal hemorrhaging. The "perps" had seemingly put the
body in the trunk of a car, driven into the most rural part
of the First Precinct, Virginia City, and dumped it. "Inquiries are proceeding, sir." He knew it was a fraction of
the truth.

He made a long statement, told them all about "Emilio,"
but it rang no bells with the detectives. He asked for his
daughter's body. The police had no further objections, but
approval had to come from the Coroner's Office. It took
time. Formalities. Procedures. He took his car back to New
York, returned, and waited. Eventually he escorted his
daughter's body, riding in the hearse, back home to the
Bronx.

The casket was sealed. He did not want his wife or any
of the Marozzis to see what was inside. The funeral was
local. Amanda Jane was interred just three days short of
her seventeenth birthday. A week later Dexter returned to
Virginia.

Sergeant Austin was in his office in the Portsmouth police headquarters at 711 Crawford Street, when the front desk phoned to say there was a Mr. Dexter who wished to see him. The name did not ring a bell. He did not connect it with his recognition of a battered face in a photograph as the departed hooker, Lorraine. He asked what Mr. Dexter wanted and was told the visitor might have a contribution to make in an ongoing inquiry. On that basis, the visitor was shown up.

Portsmouth is the oldest of the six cities; it was founded by the British well before the Revolution. Today it slumps on the southwest side of the Elizabeth River, mainly low-built redbrick buildings, staring across the water at the high-rise modern glitz of Norfolk on the other side. But it is the place many of the servicemen go if they are looking for "a good time" after dark. Sergeant Austin's Vice Squad was not there for decoration.

The visitor did not look like much compared to the muscular bulk of the former linebacker turned detective. He just stood in front of the desk and said, "You remember the teenager, turned to heroin and prostitution, gang raped and beaten to death four weeks back? I'm her father."

Alarm bells began to tinkle. The sergeant had risen and extended a hand. He withdrew it. Angry, vengeful citizens had his fullest sympathy and could expect nothing more. To any working cop, they are tiresome and can be dangerous.

"I'm sorry about that, sir. I can assure you that every effort . . ."

"At ease, Sergeant. I just want to know one thing. Then I'll leave you in peace."

"Mr. Dexter, I understand what you must be feeling, but I am not in a position . . ."

The visitor had put his right hand in his jacket pocket and was pulling something out. Had front desk security screwed up? Was the man armed? The sergeant's own piece was an uncomfortable ten feet away in a desk drawer.

"What are you doing, sir?"

"I'm putting some bits of metal on your desk, Sergeant Austin."

He went on until he was finished. Sergeant Austin had been in the military, for they were of a similar age, but had never left the States. He found himself staring down at two Silver Stars, three Bronze Stars, the Army Commendation Medal, and four Purple Hearts. He had never seen anything like it.

"Far away and long ago, I paid for the right to know who killed my child. I bought that right with my blood. You owe me that name, Sergeant Austin."

The Vice detective walked to the window and looked across at Norfolk. It was irregular, completely irregular, worth his job on the force.

"Madero. Benyamin 'Benny' Madero. Headed up a Latino gang. Very violent, very vicious. I know he did it, but I just don't have enough for an arrest warrant."

"Thank you," said the man behind him. He collected his bits of metal.

"But in case you're thinking of paying him a private visit, you're too late. I'm too late. We're all too late. He's gone. He's back in his native Panama."

A hand pushed open the door of the small emporium of Oriental art off Madison at Twenty-eighth Street, Manhattan. Above the portal a bell jangled with the movement of the door.

The visitor looked around at the shelves stacked with jade and celadon, stone and porcelain, ivory and ceramic; at elephants and demigods, panels, wall hangings, parchments, and innumerable Buddhas. At the rear of the shop a figure emerged.

"I need to be someone else," said Calvin Dexter.

It had been fourteen years since he had given the gift of a new life to the former Vietcong jungle fighter and his wife. Major Nguyen did not hesitate for a second; he inclined his head. "Of course," he said, "please come with me."

15
THE SETTLEMENT

The fast fishing boat *Chiquita* slipped away from the quay in the resort port of Golfito just before dawn and headed down the channel for the open sea.

At her helm was owner and skipper Pedro Arias, and if he had reservations about his American charter party he kept them to himself. The man had turned up the previous day on a trail bike with local Costa Rican plates. In fact, it had been bought, secondhand but in excellent condition, farther up the Pan American Highway at Palmar Norte where the tourist had arrived via a local flight from San Jose.

The man had strolled up and down the pier, checking out the various moored game-fishing boats before making his choice and his approach. With the trail bike chained to a nearby lamppost and his haversack over his shoulder, the man looked like a mature backpacker.

But there was nothing "backpacker" about the block of dollars he laid on the cabin table. This was the sort of money that caught a lot of fish. However, the man did not want to go fishing, which was why the rods were all racked along the cabin ceiling as the *Chiquita* cleared the headland at Punta Voladera and emerged into the Golfo Dulce. Arias set her head due south to clear Punta Banco an hour away.

What the gringo actually accounted for were the two plastic drums of extra fuel strapped onto the stern of the fishing deck. He wanted to be run out of Costa Rican waters, around the headland at Punta Burica, and into Panama. His explanation that his family was vacationing in Panama City and that the visitor wished to "see some of the Panamanian countryside" by riding the length of the country struck Pedro Arias as being as substantial as the sea mist now dissolving in the rising sun.

Still, if a gringo wanted to enter Panama on a trail bike off a lonely beach without passing through certain formalities, Señor Arias was a man of wide tolerances, especially where neighboring Panama was concerned. At the breakfast hour the *Chiquita*, a thirty-one-foot Bertram Moppie, cruising happily at twelve knots over calm water, cleared Punta Banco and emerged into the swell of the real Pacific. Arias pulled her forty degrees to port to follow the coast two more hours to Burica Island and the unmarked border.

It was 10:00 A.M. when they saw the first finger of Burica Island lighthouse jutting above the horizon and half past the hour as they turned the corner and veered back to the northeast.

Pedro Arias swept his arm toward the land to their left, the eastern coast of the Burica Peninsula. "Now all is Panama," he said.

The American nodded his thanks and studied the map. He jabbed with a forefinger. "*Por aqui*," he said.

The area he indicated was a stretch of coast where no towns or resorts were indicated, just a place that would

have some abandoned empty beaches and some tracks back
into the jungle. The skipper nodded and changed course to
cut a straighter and shorter line across the Bay of Charco
Azul. Twenty-five miles, a tad over two hours.

They were there by 1:00. The few fishing boats they had
seen on the broad expanse of the bay had taken no notice
of them.

The American wanted to cruise along the coast a hundred yards offshore. Five minutes later, east of Chiriqui
Viejo, they saw a sandy beach with a brace of straw huts,
the sort local fishermen use when they wish to stay over-
night. That would mean a track leading inland. Not feasible
for a vehicle, even an off-road, but manageable with a trail
bike.

It took some grunting and pushing to get the bike down
into the shallows; then the haversack was on the beach, and
they parted company. Half at Golfito and half on delivery.
The gringo paid up.

He is a strange one, thought Arias, but his dollars were
as good as everyone else's when it came to feeding four
hungry kids. Arias backed the *Chiquita* off the sand and
headed out to sea. A mile offshore he emptied the two
drums into his fuel tanks and gunned her south for the
headland and home.

On the beach Cal Dexter took a screwdriver, unfastened
the Costa Rican plates, and hurled them far into the sea.
From his haversack he took the plates a Panamanian mo-
torcycle would carry and screwed them on. His paperwork
was perfect. Thanks to Mrs. Nguyen he had an American
passport, but not in the name of Dexter, which already bore
an entry stamp apparently applied a few days earlier at Panama City airport, plus a driver's license to match.

His halting Spanish, picked up around the courts and
remand centers of New York, where 20 percent of his clients were Hispanic, was not good enough to pretend to be
Panamanian. But a visiting American is allowed to ride up-
country to look for a fishing resort.

It was just over two years since, in December 1989, the

United States had turned parts of Panama into an ashtray to topple and capture the dictator Noriega, and Dexter suspected most Panamanian cops had retained the basic message.

The narrow trail led back from the beach through dense rain forest to become, ten miles inland, a track. This turned into a dirt road with occasional farms, and there he knew he would find the Pan American Highway, that feat of engineering that runs from Alaska to the tip of Patagonia.

At David City he filled the tank again and set off down the Pan American for the 310-mile run to the capital. Darkness came. He ate at a wayside stop with truck drivers, tanked up again, and rolled on. He crossed the toll bridge to Panama City, paid in pesos, and cruised into the suburb of Balboa as the sun rose. Then he found a park bench, chained the bike, and slept for three hours.

The afternoon was for the extended survey. The huge-scale city map he had purchased in New York gave him the layout of the city and the tough slum of Chorillo where Noriega and Madero had grown up a few blocks from each other.

But successful lowlifes prefer the high life, if they can get it, and Madero's reported watering holes were two he part owned in upscale Paitilla, across the bay from the slums of Old Town.

It was two in the morning when the repatriated thug decided he was tired of the Papagayo Bar and Disco and wished to leave. The anonymous black door with discreet brass plaque, grille, and eyehole opened and two men came out first—heavily built bodyguards, his personal gorillas.

One entered the Lincoln limousine by the curb and started the engine. The other scanned the street. Sitting hunched on the curb, feet in the gutter, the tramp turned and grinned a smile of rotting or missing teeth. Greasy gray locks fell to his shoulders; a fetid raincoat clothed his body. Slowly he eased his right hand into a brown paper bag clutched to his chest. The gorilla slipped his hand beneath his left armpit and tensed. The hobo slowly pulled a bottle of cheap rum from his bag, took a swig, and with the generosity of the very drunk, held it out to the gorilla.

The man hawked, spat on the pavement, withdrew his own hand empty from beneath his jacket, relaxed, and turned away. Apart from the wino, the pavement was empty and safe. He tapped on the black door. Emilio, who had recruited Dexter's daughter, was the first out, followed by his boss. Dexter waited till the door closed and self-locked before he rose. The hand that came out of the paper bag a second time held a shortened-barrel .44 magnum Smith & Wesson.

The gorilla who had spat never knew what hit him. The fired slug broke into four flying parts; all four penetrated at the ten-foot range and performed considerable mischief inside his torso.

Drop-dead handsome Emilio did exactly that, mouth open to scream, when the second discharge took him in the face and neck, one shoulder, and one lung simultaneously.

The second gorilla was halfway out of the car when he met his Maker in an unforeseen rendezvous with four spinning, tumbling metal fragments entering the side of his body exposed to the shooter.

Benyamin Madero was back at the black door, screaming for admission when the fourth and fifth shots were fired. Some bold spirit inside had the door two inches open when a splinter went through his marcelled hair and the door shut in a hurry.

Madero fell, still hammering for admittance, sliding down the high-gloss panel work, leaving long red smears from his soaked Guayabara tropical shirt.

The tramp walked over to him, showing no panic or particular hurry, stooped, turned him on his back, and looked into his face. He was still alive but fading.

"Amanda Jane, *mi hija*," said the gunman and used the sixth shot to shred the entrails.

Madero's last ninety seconds of life were no fun at all.

A housewife in an upper window across the street later told the police she saw the tramp jog away around a corner and heard the *put-put* of a scooter engine moving away. That was all.

Before sunrise the trail bike was propped against a wall two boroughs away, unchained, ignition key in place. It would survive no more than an hour before entering the food chain.

The wig, the prosthetic teeth, and the raincoat were bundled into a trashcan in a public park. The haversack, relieved of its remaining clothes, was folded and tossed into a builder's Dumpster.

At 7:00 an American business executive in loafers, chinos, Polo shirt, and lightweight sports jacket, clutching a soft Abercrombie and Fitch travel bag, hailed a cab outside the Miramar Hotel and asked for the airport.

Three hours later the same American lifted off in Club Class on the regular Continental Airlines flight for Newark, New Jersey.

And the gun, the Smith & Wesson adapted to fire slugs that split in four lethal fragments for close-quarter work; that was down a storm drain somewhere in the city now dropping beneath the wingtip.

It might not have been allowed in the tunnels of Cu Chi, but twenty years later it worked like a dream on the streets of Panama.

Dexter knew there was something wrong when he entered his latchkey in his own door in the Bronx. It opened to reveal the face of his mother-in-law, Mrs. Marozzi, her cheeks streaked with tears.

Along with the grief, it was the guilt. Angela Dexter had approved of Emilio as a suitor for her daughter; she had agreed to the "vacation" by the sea that the young Panamanian had proposed. When her husband said he had to leave for a week to take care of unfinished business, she assumed he meant some legal work.

He should have stayed. He should have told her. He should have understood what was in her mind. Leaving her parents' house where she had stayed since her daughter's funeral, Angela Dexter had returned to the apartment with an oversupply of barbiturates and ended her own life.

The ex–hard hat, soldier, student, lawyer, and father went into a deep depression. Finally he came to two conclusions. The first was that he had no further life in the Office of the Public Defender, scurrying from court to remand center and back again. He handed in his papers, sold the apartment, bid a tearful farewell to the Marozzi family, who had been good to him, and went back to New Jersey.

He found the small town of Pennington, content in its leafy landscape, but with no local lawyer. He bought a small, one-man office and hung up his shingle. He bought a frame house on Chesapeake Drive and a pickup truck in lieu of the city sedan. He began to train in the brutal discipline of the triathlon to take away the pain.

His second decision was that Madero had died too easily. His just deserts should have been to stand in a U.S. court and hear a judge sentence him to life without parole; to wake up each day and never see the sky; to know that he would pay until the end of his days for what he had done.

Calvin Dexter knew that the U.S. Army and two tours in the stinking hell under the jungle floor of Cu Chi had given him dangerous talents. Silence, patience, near-invisibility, the skill of a hunter, the relentlessness of a born tracker.

He heard via the media of a man who had lost his child to a murderer who had vanished abroad. He made covert contact, obtained the details, went out beyond the borders of his native land and brought the killer back. Then he vanished, becoming the genial and harmless lawyer of Pennington, New Jersey. Three times in seven years he hung the CLOSED FOR VACATION notice on his Pennington office and went out into the world to find a killer and claw him back into the range of "due process." Three times he alerted the United States Marshals Service and slipped back into obscurity.

But each time it landed on his mat, he checked the small want ads section of *Vintage Airplane* the only way the tiny few who knew of his existence could make contact.

He did it again that sunny morning of May 13, 2001. The ad read: "AVENGER. Wanted. Serious offer. No price ceiling. Please call."

16

THE FILE

Sen. Peter Lucas was an old hand on Capitol Hill. He knew that if he were going to secure any official action as a result of the file on Ricky Colenso and the confession of Milan Rajak, he would have to take it high, right to the top.

Operating with section or department heads would not work. The entire mind-set of civil servants at that level was to pass the buck to another department. It was always someone else's job. Only a flat instruction from the top floor would achieve a result.

As a Republican senator and friend over many years of George Bush Sr., Peter Lucas could get to the secretary of state, Colin Powell, and the new attorney general, John Ashcroft. That would cover State and Justice, the two departments likely to be able to do anything.

Even then, it was not that simple. Cabinet secretaries did not want to be brought problems and questions; they preferred problems and solutions. Extradition was not his specialty. He needed to find out what the United States could do and ought to do in such a situation. That needed research, and he had a team of young interns for precisely that purpose. He set them to work. His best ferret, a bright girl from Wisconsin, came back a week later. "This animal Zilic is arrestable and transferable to the United States under the Comprehensive Crime Control Act of 1984," she said.

The passage she had discovered came from the Congressional Hearing on Intelligence and Security of 1997. Specifically the speaker had been Robert M. Bryant, assistant director of the FBI, addressing the House Committee on Crime.

"I've highlighted the relevant passages, Senator," she said. He thanked her and looked at the text she laid before him.

"The FBI's extraterritorial responsibilities date back to the mid-1980s when Congress first passed laws authorizing the FBI to exercise federal jurisdiction overseas when a U.S. national is murdered," Mr. Bryant had said four years earlier.

Behind the bland language was a staggering act that the rest of the world had largely ignored and most U.S. citizens as well. Prior to the Comprehensive Crime Control Act of 1984, the global presumption was that if a murder was committed, whether in France or in Mongolia, only the French or Mongolian governments had jurisdiction to pursue, arrest, and try the killer. That applied whether the victim was French, Mongolian, or a visiting American.

The United States had simply arrogated to itself the right to decide that if you kill an American citizen anywhere in the world, you might as well have killed him on Broadway. Meaning U.S. jurisdiction covers the whole planet. No international conference conceded this; the United States simply said so. Then Mr. Bryant went further.

". . . and the Omnibus Diplomatic Security and Antiterrorism Act of 1986 established a new extraterritorial statute pertaining to terrorist acts conducted abroad against U.S. citizens."

Not a problem, thought the senator. *Zilic was not a Yugoslav army serviceman nor a policeman. He was freelance, and the title of terrorist will stick. He can be extradited to the United States under both statutes.*

He read on: "Upon the approval of the host country, the FBI has the legal authority to deploy FBI personnel to conduct extraterritorial investigations in the host country where the criminal act was committed, enabling the United States to prosecute terrorists for crimes committed abroad against U.S. citizens."

The senator's brow furrowed. This did not make sense. It was incomplete. The key phrase was, "Upon the approval of the host country . . ." But cooperation between police forces was nothing new. Of course the FBI could accept an invitation from a foreign police force to fly over and help them out. It had been going on for years. And why were two separate acts needed, in 1984 and 1986?

The answer, which he did not have, was that the second act went a mile farther than the first, and the phrase "Upon the approval of the host country . . ." was just Mr. Bryant being comforting to the committee. What he was hinting at but not daring to say was the word "rendition."

In the 1986 act, the United States awarded itself the right to ask politely for the murderer of an American to be extradited back to the States. If the answer was "No," or seemingly endless delay amounting to a snub, that was the end of "Mr. Nice Guy." The United States had entitled itself to send in a covert team of agents, snatch the "perp," and bring him back for trial.

As FBI terrorist-hunter John O'Neill put it when the act was passed, "From now on, host country approval has got jack shit to do with it." A joint CIA/FBI snatch of an alleged murderer of an American is called a rendition. There had been ten such very covert operations since the act was

passed under Ronald Reagan, and it all began because of
an Italian cruise liner.

In October 1985, the *Achille Lauro*, out of Genoa, was
cruising along the north coast of Egypt, with further stops
on the Israeli coast in prospect, and carrying a mixed cargo
of tourists, including some Americans. She had been secretly boarded by four Palestinians from the Palestine Liberation Front, a terrorist group attached to Yasser Arafat's
PLO, then in exile in Tunisia.

The terrorists' aim was not to capture the ship but to
disembark at Ashdod, a stopping point in Israel, and take
Israeli hostages there. But on October 7th, between Alexandria and Port Said, they were in one of their cabins,
checking their weapons, when a steward walked in, saw the
guns, and started yelling. The four Palestinians panicked
and hijacked the liner. There followed four days of tense
negotiations. In from Tunis flew Abu Abbas, claiming to
be Arafat's negotiator. Tel Aviv would have none of it,
pointing out that Abu Abbas was the boss of the PLF, not
a benign mediator. Eventually a deal was struck; the terrorists would get passage off the ship and an Egyptian airliner back to Tunis. The Italian captain confirmed at
gunpoint that no one had been hurt. He was forced to lie.
Once the ship was free, it became clear that on day three
the Palestinians had murdered a seventy-nine-year-old,
wheelchair-bound New Yorker, Leon Klinghoffer. They
had shot him in the face and thrown him and his chair into
the sea.

For Ronald Reagan that was it; all deals were off. But
the killers were airborne, on their way home, in an airliner
of a sovereign state, friendly to America and in international airspace; that is, untouchable. Or maybe not. The flat-
top USS *Saratoga* happened to be steaming south down the
Adriatic carrying F-14 Tomcats. As darkness fell, the Egyptian airliner was found off Crete, heading west for Tunis.
Out of the gloom four Tomcats suddenly flanked the airliner. The terrified Egyptian pilot asked for an emergency
landing at Athens. Permission was denied. The Tomcats

signaled the pilot that he should accompany them or face the consequences. The same EC2 Hawkeye, also off the *Saratoga*, that had found the Egyptian plane, passed the messages between the fighters and the airliner.

The diversion ended when the airliner, with the killers and Abu Abbas, their leader, on board, landed under escort at the U.S. base at Sigonella, Sicily. Then it became complicated.

Sigonella was a shared base: U.S. Navy and Italian air force. Technically it is Italian sovereign territory; the United States only pays rent. The government in Rome, in a pretty high state of excitement, claimed the right to try the terrorists. The *Achille Lauro* was theirs; the air base theirs. It took a personal call from President Reagan to the U.S. Special Forces detachment at Sigonella to order them to back off and let the Italians have the Palestinians.

In due course, back in Genoa, home city of the liner, the small fry were sentenced. But their leader, Abu Abbas, flew out free as air on October 12th and went on to hide for years on the outskirts of Baghdad.* The Italian defense minister resigned in disgust. The premier at the time was Bettino Craxi. He later died in exile, also in Tunis, wanted for massive embezzlement while in office.

Reagan's response to this perfidy was the Omnibus Act, nicknamed the "Never Again" Act. It was not finally the bright kid from Wisconsin but the veteran FBI terrorist hunter, Oliver "Buck" Revell, in retirement, who took a good dinner off the old senator and told him about "renditions."

Even then it was not thought that for Zilic a "rendition" would ever be needed. Post-Milosevic Yugoslavia was keen to return to the community of civilized nations. She needed large loans from the International Monetary Fund and elsewhere to rebuild her infrastructure after seventy-eight days of NATO bombing. Her new president, Kostunica, would surely regard it as a bagatelle to have Zilic arrested and

*Abbas was captured by American special forces on April 14, 2003.

extradited to the United States. That certainly was the request Senator Lucas intended to proffer to Colin Powell and
John Ashcroft. If worse came to worst, he would ask for a
covert rendition to be authorized.

He had his writer team prepare from the full 1995 report
of the Tracker a one-page synopsis to explain everything
from Ricky Colenso's departure to Bosnia to try and help
pitiful refugees to his presence in a lonely valley on May
15, 1995.

What happened in the valley that morning, as described
by Milan Rajak, was compressed into two pages, the most
distressing passages heavily highlighted. Fronted by a personal letter from Lucas, the file was edged and bound for
easy reading.

That was something else Capitol Hill had taught him.
The higher the office, the shorter the brief should be. In
late April, he got his face-to-face with both Cabinet secretaries.

Each listened with grave visage and pledged to read the
brief and pass it to the appropriate department within their
departments. And they did.

The United States has thirteen major intelligence-
gathering agencies. Among them they probably garner 90
percent of all the intelligence, licit and illicit, on the entire
planet in any twenty-four-hour period.

The sheer volume makes absorption, analysis, filtration,
collation, storage, and retrieval a problem of industrial pro-
portions. Another problem is that they do not talk to each
other.

American intelligence chiefs have been heard to mutter
in a late-night bar that they would give their pensions for
something like the British Joint Intelligence Committee
(JIC).

The JIC meets weekly in London under the chairman-
ship of a veteran and trusted bureaucrat to bring together
the smaller country's four agencies: the Secret Intelligence
Service MI6 (foreign), the Security Service MI5 (home),
the Government Communications Headquarters (SIGINT

satellites, the listeners), and Scotland Yard's Special
Branch.

Sharing intelligence and progress can prevent duplica-
tion and waste, but its main aim is to see if fragments of
information learned in different places by different people
could form the jigsaw puzzle that makes up the picture
everyone is looking for.

Senator Lucas's report went to six of the agencies, and
each obediently scoured their archives to see what, if anything, they had learned and filed about a Yugoslav gangster
called Zoran Zilic.

The Bureau of Alcohol, Tobacco and Firearms, known
as ATF, had nothing. He had never operated in the United
States and ATF rarely, if ever, goes abroad.

The other five were the Defense Intelligence Agency
(DIA), which has an interest in any arms dealer; the National Security Agency (NSA), the biggest of them all,
working out of their "Black Chamber" at Fort Meade,
Maryland, listening to trillions of words a day, spoken,
E-mailed or faxed, with technology almost beyond science
fiction; the Drug Enforcement Administration (DEA),
which has an interest in anyone who has ever trafficked
narcotics anywhere in the world; the FBI (of course); and
the CIA. Both the latter spearhead the permanent search for
knowledge about terrorists, killers, warlords, hostile regimes, whatever. It took a week or more, and April slipped
into May. But because the order came right from the top,
the searches were thorough.

The people at Defense, Drugs, and Fort Meade all came
up with fat files. In various capacities they had known about
Zoran Zilic for years. Most of their entries concerned his
activities since he became a major player on the Belgrade
scene as enforcer to Milosevic, racketeer in drugs and arms,
profiteer, and general lowlife.

That he had murdered an American boy during the Bosnian war they had not known, and they took it seriously.
They would have helped if they could, but their files all
had one thing in common; they ran out fifteen months be-

fore the senator's inquiry. Zilic had vanished, vaporized, disappeared. Sorry.

At the CIA, enveloped in summer foliage just off the Beltway, the director passed the query on to the deputy director of operations. He consulted downward to five subdivisions: Balkans, Terrorism, Special Ops, and Arms Dealing were four. He even asked, more as a formality than anything else, the small and obsessively secret office formed less than a year earlier after the massacre of the seventeen sailors on the USS *Cole* in Aden Harbor, known as Peregrine.

But the answer was the same. Sure we have files; but nothing after fifteen months ago. We agree with all our colleagues. He is no longer in Yugoslavia, but where he is, we do not know. He has not come to our attention for two years, so there has been no reason to expend time and treasure.

The other major hope would have been the FBI. Surely, somewhere in the huge Hoover Building at Pennsylvania and Ninth, there would be a recent file describing exactly where this cold-blooded killer could now be found, detained, and brought to justice?

Dir. Robert Mueller, recently appointed successor to Louis Freeh, passed the file and request downward with his "Action Without Delay" tag, and it found the desk of Assistant Director Colin Fleming.

Fleming was a lifelong Bureau man who could never remember the time, even as a boy, when he did not want to be a G-Man. He came from Scottish Presbyterian stock, and his faith was as unflinching as his concept of law, order, and justice.

On the work of the Bureau, he was a fundamentalist. Compromise, accommodation, concession—in the manner of crime these were mere excuses for appeasement. This he despised. What he may have lacked in subtlety, he made up for in tenacity and dedication.

He came from the granite hills of New Hampshire where the boast is that the rocks and the men vie for toughness.

He was a staunch Republican, and Peter Lucas was his senator. Indeed, he had campaigned locally for Lucas and had made his acquaintance.

After reading the skimpy report, he rang the senator's office to ask if he might read the full report by the Tracker and the complete confession of Milan Rajak. A copy was messengered over to him that same afternoon. He read the files with growing anger. He, too, had a son to be proud of, a navy flier, and the thought of what had happened to Ricky Colenso filled him with righteous wrath. The Bureau had to be the instrument of bringing Zilic to justice either via extradition or a rendition. As the man heading the desk covering all terrorism from overseas sources, he would personally authorize the rendition team to go and get the killer.

But the Bureau could not because the Bureau was in the same position as the rest. Even though his gangsterdom, drugs, and arms dealing had brought him to the attention of the Bureau as a man to watch, he had never been caught in an act of anti-American terrorism or support thereof; so when he had vanished, the Bureau had not pursued it. Its file had run out fifteen months before. It was with the deepest personal regret that Fleming had to join the others in the intelligence community in admitting they did not know where Zoran Zilic was.

Without a location, there could be no application to a foreign government for extradition. Even if Zilic were now sheltering in a "failed" state where the writ of normal governmental authority did not run, a snatch operation could only be mounted if the Bureau knew where he was. In his personal letter to the senator, Assistant Director Fleming apologized that it did not. Fleming's tenacity came with his Highland genes. Two days later he sought out and lunched with Fraser Gibbs. The FBI has two retired senior officers of almost iconic status, who can pack the student lecture halls at the Bureau's Quantico training facility when they go.

One is the towering ex-footballer, former marine pilot, "Buck" Revell; the other is Fraser Gibbs, who spent his career penetrating organized crime as an undercover agent, about as dangerous work as you can get, crushing the Cosa Nostra down the eastern seaboard. When restored to Washington after a bullet in the leg left him with a limp, he was given the desk covering freelancers, mercenaries, and guns for hire. He considered Fleming's query with a furrowed brow.

"I did hear something once," he conceded. "A manhunter. Sort of a bounty hunter. Had a code name."

"A killer himself? You know government rules absolutely forbid that sort of thing."

"No, that's the point," said the old veteran. "The rumor was, he doesn't kill. Kidnaps, snatches, brings them back. Now, what the hell was his name?"

"It could be important," said Fleming.

"He was terribly secretive. My predecessor tried to identify him. Sent in an undercover man as a pretend client. But he smelled a trick somehow, made an excuse, left the meeting, and disappeared."

"Why didn't he just fess up and come clean?" asked Fleming. "If he wasn't in the killing business . . ."

"I guess he figured that as he operated abroad, and as the Bureau doesn't like freelancers operating on its own turf, we'd have sought top-level instruction and been ordered to close him down. And he'd probably have been right. So he stayed in the shadows, and I never hunted him down."

"The agent would have filed a report."

"Oh, yes. Procedure. Probably under the man's code name. Never got any other name. Ah, that's it. Avenger. Punch up 'Avenger.' See what comes up."

The file the computer disgorged was indeed slim. An ad had to be run in a technical magazine for vintage airplane buffs, seemingly the only way the man would communicate. A story had been spun, a rendezvous agreed upon.

The bounty hunter had insisted on sitting in deep shadow behind a bright lamp, which shone forward away from him.

The agent reported he was of medium height, slim build, probably no more than 160 pounds. He never saw the face, and within three minutes the man suspected something. He reached out, killed the light, leaving the agent with no night vision, and when the agent had quit blinking the man was gone.

All the agent could report was that as the bounty hunter's hand lay on the table between them, his left sleeve had ridden up to reveal a tattoo on the forearm. It appeared to be a rat grinning over its shoulder while showing the viewer its bottom.

None of this would have been of the slightest interest to Senator Lucas or his friend in Canada. But the least Colin Fleming thought he could do was pass on the code name and the method of contact. It was a one-in-a-hundred chance, but it was all he had.

Three days later in his office in Ontario, Stephen Edmond opened the letter sent by his friend in Washington. He had already heard the news from the six agencies and had virtually given up hope.

He read the supplementary letter and frowned. He had been thinking of the mighty United States using its power to require a foreign government to bring forth its murderer, snap handcuffs on his wrists, and send him back to the United States.

It had never occurred to him that he was too late; that Zilic had simply vanished; that all the billion-dollar agencies of Washington simply did not know where he was and therefore could do nothing.

He thought it over for ten minutes, shrugged, and pressed the intercom.

"Jean, I want to run an ad in the wanted section of an American magazine. You'll have to check it out. I've never heard of it. It's called *Vintage Airplane*. Yeah, the text. Make it: 'AVENGER. Wanted. Serious offer. No price ceiling. Please call.' Then put my cell-phone number and private line. OK, Jean?"

Twenty-six men in intelligence agencies in and around Washington had seen the request. All had responded that they did not know where Zoran Zilic was.

One of them had lied.

PART TWO

PART TWO

17

THE PHOTO

Since the attempt by the FBI to unmask him six years earlier, Dexter had decided there was no need for face-to-face meetings. Instead, he built up several defensive lines to mask his location and his identity.

One of these was a small, one-bedroom apartment in New York, but not the Bronx where he might be recognized. He rented it furnished, paid by the quarter, regular as clockwork, and always in cash. It attracted no official attention, and neither did he when he was in residence.

He also used mobile phones only of the type using SIM pay-as-you-talk cards. These he bought in bulk out of state, used once or twice, and consigned to the East River. Even the NSA, with the technology to listen to a phone call and trace the exact source, cannot identify the purchaser of these use-and-jettison SIM mobiles nor direct police to the location of the call if the user is on the move, keeps the call short, and gets rid of the technology afterward.

Another ploy is the old-fashioned public phone booth. Numbers called from a booth can, of course, be traced; but there are so many millions of them that unless a specific booth or bank of them is suspected, it is very hard to pick up the conversation, identify the caller as a wanted man, trace the location, and get a police car there in time.

Finally he used the much-maligned U.S. mails, with his letters being sent to a "drop" in the form of an innocent Korean-run fruit and vegetable shop two blocks from his apartment in New York City. This would be no protection if the mail or the shop was targeted and put under surveillance, but there was no reason why it should be.

He contacted the placer of the ad on the cell phone listed. He did so from a single-use mobile phone, and he drove far into the New Jersey countryside to do it.

Stephen Edmond identified himself without demur, and in five sentences described what had happened to his grandson. Avenger thanked him and hung up.

He then logged onto LexisNexis. There was enough to confirm who Stephen Edmond was, and there had been two articles concerning the disappearance years ago of his grandson while a student-aid worker in Bosnia, both from the *Toronto Star*. This caller seemed to be genuine.

Dexter called the Canadian back and dictated terms: considerable operating expenses, a fee on account, and a bonus on delivery of Zilic to U.S. jurisdiction, not payable in the event of failure.

"That's a lot of money for a man I have not met and apparently will not meet. You could take it and vaporize," said the Canadian.

"And you, sir, could go back to the U.S. government, where I presume you have already been."

There was a pause. "All right, where should it be sent?"

Dexter gave him a Caymanian account number and a New York mailing address. "The money order to the first, every line of research material already done to the second," he said, and hung up.

The Caribbean bank would shift the credit through a dozen different accounts within its computer system but would also open a line of credit to a bank in New York. This would be in favor of a Dutch citizen who would identify himself with a perfect Dutch passport.

Three days later, a file arrived in a stout envelope at a Korean fruit shop in Brooklyn. It was collected by the addressee, Mr. Armitage. It contained a photocopy of the entire report from the Tracker, that of 1995 and of that same spring of 2001, including the confession of Milan Rajak. None of the files on Zoran Zilic in the archives of the various United States intelligence agencies had ever been shown to the Canadian, so his knowledge of Zilic was sketchy. Worst of all, there was no picture.

Dexter went back to his media archives. Unlike the publicity-hungry Zeljko "Arkan" Raznatovic, Zilic had an abhorrence of being photographed. He clearly went out of his way to avoid publicity of any kind. In this he resembled some of the Palestinian terrorists like Sabri al-Banna, known as Abu Nidal.

Dexter came up with one major *Newsweek* feature going back to the Bosnian war. It was about all the Serbian so-called warlords, but within it Zilic had only a few passing mentions, probably for lack of material.

There was one photograph of a man at a cocktail party of some sort, clearly cropped and blown up, which made it slightly hazy. The other was of a teenager; it came from the Belgrade police files, and clearly went back to the days of the street gangs of Zemun. Either man could walk straight past him in the street, and he would not recognize the Serbian.

The Englishman, the Tracker, mentioned a private investigation agency in Belgrade. It was now postwar, post-Milosevic. The Yugoslav capital, where Zilic had been born and raised, and from which he had vanished, seemed the place to start. Dexter flew New York to Vienna and on to

Belgrade, and checked into the Hyatt. From his tenth-floor window, the battered Balkan city stretched out beneath him. Half a mile away he could see the hotel in whose lobby Raznatovic had been shot to death despite his covey of bodyguards.

A taxi brought him to the agency called Chandler, still run by Dragan Stojic, the Philip Marlowe wannabe. Dexter's cover was a publishing commission from the *New Yorker* asking for a ten-thousand-word biography of Raznatovic. Stojic nodded and grunted.

"Everyone knew him. Married a pop singer, glamorous girl. So what do you want from me?"

"The fact is, I have just about all I need for this piece," said Dexter, whose American passport revealed him as Alfred Barnes. "But there is a sort of afterthought I should give mention to. A one-time contemporary of Arkan in the Belgrade underworld. Name of Zoran Zilic."

Stojic let out a long puff of air.

"Now that was a nasty piece of work," he said. "He never liked being written about, photographed, or even talked about. People who upset him in that area were . . . visited. There's not much on file about him."

"I accept that. So what is Belgrade's premier clippings agency for written material?"

"Not a problem, there's really only one. It's called VIP. It's got an office in Vracar, and the editor-in-chief is Slavko Markovic."

Dexter rose.

"That's it?" asked the Balkan Marlowe. "Hardly worth an invoice."

The American took a hundred-dollar bill and laid it on the desk. "All information has a price, Mr. Stojic. Even a name and address."

Another cab took him to the VIP clippings agency. Mr. Markovic was at lunch so Dexter found a café and toyed with a light lunch and a glass of local red wine until he came back.

Markovic was as pessimistic as the private eye. But he

punched up his in-house database to see what he had.

"One piece," he said, "and it happens to be in English."

It was the *Newsweek* piece from the Bosnian war.

"That's it?" queried Dexter. "This man was powerful, important, prominent. Surely there must be some trace of him?"

"That's the point," said Markovic, "he was all those things. And violent. Under Milosevic there was no argument. He seems to have cleaned out every record of himself before he quit. Police and court records, state TV, media, the lot. Family, school contemporaries, former colleagues, no one wants to talk about him. Warned off. Mr. No-face, that's him."

"Do you recall when the last attempt was made to write anything about him?"

Markovic thought for a while.

"Now you mention it, I heard a rumor that someone tried. But it came to nothing. After Milosevic fell, and with Zilic vanished, someone tried to do a piece. I think it was canceled."

"Who was it?"

"My talking canary said it was a magazine here in Belgrade called *Ogledalo*. That means '*The Mirror*.' "

The Mirror still existed, and its editor was still Vuk Kobac. Even though it was print day, he agreed to give the American a few minutes of his time. He lost his enthusiasm when he heard the inquiry.

"That bloody man," he said. "I wish I had never heard of him."

"What happened?"

"It was a young freelancer. Nice kid. Keen, eager. Wanted a staff job. I hadn't got one vacant, but he pleaded for a chance. So I gave him a commission. Name of Petrovic, Srechko Petrovic. Only twenty-two, poor kid."

"What happened to him?"

"He got run over, that's what happened to him. Parked his car opposite the apartment block where he lived with his mother, went to cross the road. A Mercedes came round the corner and ran him over."

"Careless driver."

"Very careless. Managed to run him over twice. Then drove off."

"Discouraging."

"And permanent. Even in exile, he can still order and pay for a 'hit' to be done in Belgrade."

"Any address for the mother?"

"Hold on. We sent a wreath. Must have sent it to the flat."

He found it and bade his visitor good-bye.

"One last question," said Dexter. "When was this?"

"Six months ago. Just after New Year. A word of advice, Mr. Barnes. Stick to writing about Arkan. He's safely dead. Leave Zilic alone. He'll kill you. Must rush, it's print day."

The address said Block 23, Novi Beograd. He recognized Novi Beograd, or New Belgrade, from the city map he had bought in the hotel bookshop. It was the rather bleak district in which the hotel itself stood, on a peninsula flanked by the rivers Sava and Dunav, the Danube itself, which was emphatically not blue. It stood across both rivers from downtown Belgrade.

In the Communist years, the taste had been for huge, high-rise apartment blocks for the workers. They had gone up on vacant lots in Novi Beograd, great poured concrete beehives, each cavity a tiny flat with its door opening to a long, open-sided passage, lashed by the elements.

Some had survived better than others. It depended on the level of prosperity of the inhabitants, and thus the level of maintenance. Block 23 was a roach-infested horror. Mrs. Petrovic lived on the ninth floor, and the elevator was out of order. Dexter could take them at a run, but he wondered how senior citizens coped, the more so as they all seemed to be chain smokers.

There was not much point in going up to see her alone. There was no chance she would speak English, and he did not know Serbo-Croat. It was one of the pretty and bright girls behind the reception desk at the Hyatt who accepted his offer to help him out. She was saving to get married, and two hundred dollars for an hour's extra work at the end of her shift was quite acceptable.

They arrived at seven and just in time. Mrs. Petrovic was an office cleaner and left each evening at eight to work through the night in the offices across the river.

She was one of those who have quite simply been defeated by life, and the lined and exhausted face told its own story. She was probably in her mid-forties going on seventy, her husband killed in an industrial accident with almost no compensation, her son murdered beneath her own window. As always with the very poor approached by the apparently rich, her first reaction was suspicion.

He had brought a large bunch of flowers. It had been a long, long time since she had had flowers. Anna, the girl from the hotel, arranged them in three displays around the tiny, shabby room.

"I want to write about what happened to Srechko. I know it cannot bring him back, but I can perhaps expose the man who did this to him. Will you help me?"

She shrugged. "I know nothing," she said. "I never asked about his work."

"The night that he died . . . was he carrying anything with him?"

"I don't know. The body was searched. They took everything."

"They searched the body? Right there on the street?"

"Yes."

"Did he have papers? Did he have notes that he left behind? Here in the flat?"

"Yes, he had bundles of papers. With his typewriter and his pencils. But I never read them."

"Could I see them?"

"They are gone."

"Gone?"

"They took them. Took them all. Even the ribbon from the typewriter."

"The police?"

"No, the men."

"Which men?"

"They came back. Two nights later. They made me sit in the corner there. They searched everywhere. They took everything he had had."

"There is nothing left at all of what he was working on for Mr. Kobac?"

"Only the photo. I had forgotten about that."

"Please tell me about the photo."

It came out in small details, all via Anna, from language to language. Three days before he died, Srechko, the cub reporter, had attended a New Year's party, and red wine had been spilled on his denim jacket. His mother had put it in the laundry bag for washing later.

When he was dead, there was no point. She, too, forgot about the laundry bag, and the gangsters never thought to ask. When she was making a pile of her dead son's clothes, the wine-stained denim jacket fell out. She felt the pockets quickly to see if her son had forgotten any money, but felt something semistiff. It was a photograph.

"Do you still have it? May I see it?" asked Dexter.

She nodded and crept away like a mouse to a sewing box in the corner. She came back with the photo.

It was of a man, caught unawares, who had seen the photographer at the last minute. He was trying to raise his outspread hand to cover his face, but the shutter had clicked just in time. He was full face, upright, in a short-sleeved shirt and slacks.

The picture was in black and white, not of professional clarity, but with enlargement and enhancement was as good as he was ever likely to get. He recalled the teenage picture and the cocktail party photo he had found in New York and carried in the lining of his attaché case. They were all a bit grainy, but it was the same man—Zilic.

"I would like to buy this picture, Mrs. Petrovic," he said. She shrugged and said something in Serbo-Croat.

"She says you may have it. It is of no interest to her. She does not know who he is," said Anna.

"One last question. Just before he died, did Srechko go away for a while?"

"Yes, in December. He was away a week. He would not say where he had been, but he had a sunburn on his nose."

She escorted them to her door and the landing exposed to the winds, which led to the nonfunctioning lift and the stairwell. Anna went first. When she was out of earshot, Dexter turned to the Serbian mother who had also lost her child, and spoke gently in English.

"You can't understand a word I say, lady, but if I ever get this swine into a slammer in the States, it's partly for you. And it's on the house."

Of course she did not understand, but she responded to the smile and said, "Hvala." In a day in Belgrade he had learned that it means "Thank you."

He had instructed the taxi to wait. He dropped Anna, clutching her two hundred dollars, at her home in the suburbs, and on the way back to the center he studied the picture again.

Zilic was standing on what looked like an open expanse of concrete or tarmac. Behind him were big, low buildings like warehouses. Over one of the buildings a flag floated, extended by the breeze, but part of it was off the picture.

There was something else sticking into vision out of frame, but he could not work it out. He tapped the taxi driver on the shoulder.

"Do you have a magnifying glass?" He did not understand, but elaborate pantomime cleared up the mystery. He nodded. He kept one in the glove compartment for studying his A–Z city road map if need be.

The long, flat object jutting into the picture from the left came clear. It was the wingtip of a plane, but no more than six feet off the ground. So not an airliner, but a smaller craft.

Then he recognized the buildings in the background. Not warehouses, hangars. Not the huge structures required for sheltering airliners, but the sort needed for private planes, executive jets, whose tail fins rarely top more than thirty feet. The man was on a private airfield or the executive section of an airport.

They helped him at the hotel. Yes, there were several cybercafés in Belgrade, all open late. He dined in the snack bar and took a taxi to the nearest. When he was logged on to his favorite search engine, he asked for all the flags of the world.

The flag fluttering above the hangars in the dead reporter's photo was only in monochrome, but clearly it had three horizontal stripes of which the bottom one was so dark it looked black. If not, then a very dark blue. He opted for black.

As he ran through the world's flags, he noted that a good half of them had some kind of logo, crest, or device superimposed on the stripes. The one he sought had none. That cut the choice down to the other half.

Those who had horizontal stripes and no logo were no more than two dozen, and those with a black or near-black bottom stripe were five.

Gabon, the Netherlands, and Sierra Leone all had three horizontal stripes of which the lowest was deep blue, which could show up black in a monochrome photograph. Only two had a bottom stripe of three that was definitely black: Sudan and one other. But the Sudan had a green diamond up against the flagpole as well as three stripes. The remaining one had a vertical stripe nearest the flagpole. Peering at his photo, Dexter could just make out the fourth stripe, not clear, but it was there.

One vertical red stripe by the flagpole; green, white, and black horizontals running out to the flapping edge. Zilic was standing at an airport somewhere in the United Arab Emirates.

Even in December a pale-skinned Slav could get a badly burned nose in the UAE.

18

THE GULF

There are seven emirates in the UAE, but only the three biggest and richest, Dubai, Abu Dhabi, and Sharjah spring readily to mind. The other four are much smaller and almost anonymous.

They all occupy the peninsula at the southeastern tip of the Saudi landmass, that tongue of desert that separates the Persian Gulf to the north and the Gulf of Oman to the south.

Only one, Al Fujayrah, faces west onto the Gulf of Oman and thence the Arabian Sea; the other six are strung in a line along the northern coast, staring at Iran across the water. Apart from the seven capitals, there is the desert oasis town of Al Ain that also has an airport.

While still in Belgrade, Dexter found a portrait photographic studio with the technology to rephotograph the pic-

ture of Zoran Zilic, increase its clarity, and then blow it up
from playing card to softcover book size.

While the photographer worked on one task, Dexter returned to the cybercafé, inquired after the United Arab
Emirates, and downloaded everything he could get. The
following day he took the JAT regular service via Beirut
to Dubai.

The wealthy emirates derive their riches mainly from oil,
although they have all tried to broaden the base of their
economies to include tourism and duty-free trade. Most of
the oil deposits are offshore.

Rigs have to be resupplied constantly, and although the
vehicles used for heavy cargoes are seaborne lighters, personal transfers are faster and easier by helicopter.

The oil companies operating the rigs have their own
helicopters, but there is still ample room for charter firms,
and the Internet revealed three such, right in Dubai. The
American Alfred Barnes had become a lawyer when he
visited the first. He picked the smallest, on the grounds it
was probably the least concerned with formalities and the
most interested in wads of dollar bills. He was right on
both counts.

The office was a Portakabin out at Port Rashid, and the
proprietor and chief pilot turned out to be a former British
Army Air Corps flier trying to make a living. They do not
come much more informal than that.

"Alfred Barnes, attorney-at-law," said Dexter, extending
his hand. "I have a problem, a tight schedule, and a large
budget."

The British ex-captain raised a polite eyebrow. Dexter
pushed the photo across the cigarette-scorched desk.

"My client is, or rather was, a very wealthy man."

"He lost it?" asked the pilot.

"In a way. He died. My law firm is the chief executor.
And this man is the chief beneficiary. Only he doesn't know
it, and we cannot find him."

"I'm a charter pilot, not Missing Persons. Anyway, I've
never seen him."

"No reason why you should. It's the background to the picture. Look carefully. An airport or airfield, right? The last I heard he was working in civil aviation here in the UAE. If I could identify that airport, I could probably find him. What do you think?"

The charter pilot studied the background.

"Airports here have three sections; military, airlines, and private flyers. That wing belongs to an executive jet. There are scores, maybe hundreds of them, in the Gulf. Most have company livery, and most are owned by wealthy Arabs. What do you want to do?"

What Dexter wanted to buy was the charter captain's access to the flying side to all these airports. It came at a price and took two days. The cover was that he had to pick up a client. After sixty minutes inside the executive jet compound, when the fictional client failed to show up, the captain told the tower he was breaking off the charter and leaving the circuit.

The airports at Abu Dhabi, Dubai, and Sharjah were huge, and even the private aviation sector of each was far bigger than the background in the photograph.

The emirates of Ajman and Umm al Qaywayn had no airport at all, being cheek by jowl with Sharjah airport. That left the desert town of Al Ain, Al Fujayrah out on the far side of the peninsula facing the Gulf of Oman, and, right up in the north, the least known of them all, Ra's al Khaymah.

They found it on the morning of the second day. The Bell Jetranger swerved in across the desert to land at what the British called Al K, and there were the hangars with the flag fluttering behind them.

Dexter had taken the charter for two full days and brought his suitcase with him. He settled up with a fistful of hundred-dollar bills, stepped down, and watched the Bell lift away. Looking around, he realized he was standing almost where Srechko Petrovic must have been when he snapped the photo that sealed his fate. An official stepped from an administration building and beckoned him to clear the area.

The arrival and departure building for both airline and private jet passengers was neat, clean, and small, with the accent on small. Named after the Emiral family, Al Qassimi International Airport had clearly never disturbed those airlines, whose names are famous worldwide.

On the tarmac in front of the terminal building were Russian-built Antonovs and Tupolevs. There was an old Yakovlev single-prop biplane. One airliner bore the livery and logo of Tajikistan Airlines. Dexter went up one floor to the roof café and ordered a coffee.

The same floor contained the administration offices, including the supremely optimistic Public Relations Department. The sole inhabitant was a nervous young lady robed from head to toe in a black chador, with only her hands and pale oval face visible. She spoke halting English.

Alfred Barnes had now become a development officer for tourism projects with a major U.S. company and wished to inquire about the facilities Ra's al Khaymah could offer to the executives seeking an exotic conference center; especially, he needed to know if they could be offered airport facilities for the executive jets in which they would arrive.

The lady was polite but adamant. All inquiries regarding tourism should be addressed to the Department of Tourism in the Commercial Center, right next to Old Town.

A taxi brought him there. It was a small cube of a building on a development site, about five hundred yards from the Hilton and right on the edge of the brand-new, deepwater harbor. It did not appear to be under siege from those seeking to develop tourism.

Mr. Hussein al Khoury would have regarded himself, if asked, as a good man. That did not make him a contented man. To justify the first, he would have said that he only had one wife but treated her well. He tried to raise his four children as a good father should. He attended mosque every Friday and gave alms to charity according to his ability and according to Scripture.

He should have progressed far in life, *Insh'Allah*. But it seemed Allah did not smile upon him. He remained stuck in the middle ranks of the Tourism Ministry; specifically, he remained stuck in a small brick cube on a development site next to the deep-water harbor, where no one ever called. Then one day the smiling American walked in.

He was delighted. An inquiry at last, and the chance to practice the English over which he had spent so many hundreds of hours. After several minutes of courteous pleasantries—how charming of the American to realize that Arabs do not like to delve straight into business—they agreed that as the air-conditioning had broken down and the outside temperature was nudging 100 degrees, they might use the American's taxi to adjourn to the coffee lounge of the Hilton.

Settled in the pleasant cool of the Hilton bar, Mr. al Khoury was intrigued that the American seemed in no hurry to proceed to his business. Eventually the Arab asked, "Now, how can I help you?"

"You know, my friend," said the American with seriousness, "my whole life's philosophy is that we are put upon this earth by our mighty and merciful Creator to help one another. And I believe that it is I who am here to help you."

Almost absentmindedly the American began to fumble in his jacket pockets for something. Out came his passport, several folded letters of introduction, and a block of one-hundred-dollar bills that took Mr. al Khoury's breath away.

"Let us see if we cannot help each other."

The civil servant stared at the dollars. "If there is anything I can do . . . ," he murmured.

"I should be very honest with you, Mr. al Khoury. My real job in life is as a debt collector. Not a very glamorous job, but necessary. When we buy things, we should pay for them. Not so?"

"Assuredly."

"There is a man who flies into your airport now and again in his own executive jet. This man."

Mr. al Khoury stared at the photo for a few seconds, then shook his head. His gaze returned to the block of dollars. Four thousand? Five? To put Faisal through university . . .

"Alas, this man did not pay for his plane. In a sense, therefore, he stole it. He paid the deposit, then flew away and was never seen again. Probably changed the registration number. Now, these are expensive things. Twenty million dollars each. So the true owners would be grateful, in a very practical way, to anyone who could help them find their aircraft."

"But if he is here now, arrest him. Impound the aircraft. We have laws . . ."

"Alas, he has gone again. But every time he lands here, there is a record. Stored in the files at Al Qassimi Airport. Now, a man of your authority could see those archives."

The civil servant dabbed his lips with a clean handkerchief.

"When was it here, this plane?"

"Last December."

Before leaving Block 23, Dexter had learned from Mrs. Petrovic that her son had been away from December 13th to the 20th. Calculating that Srechko had snapped his photograph, been seen, knew he had been seen, and had left immediately for home, he would have been in Ras al Khaymah about the 18th. How he had known to come here, Dexter had no idea. He must have been a good, or very lucky, reporter. Kobac should have taken him on.

"There are many executive jets that come here," said Mr. al Khoury.

"All I need are the registration numbers, and the types, of every privately or corporately owned executive jet, specifically owned by Europeans, hopefully this one, parked here between the 15th and 19th of December. Now I would think, in those four days . . . what? . . . Ten?"

He prayed the Arab would not ask how he did not know the make of the jet if he represented the vendors. He began to peel off one-hundred-dollar bills.

"As a token of my good faith, and my complete trust in you, my friend. And the other four thousand later."

The Arab still looked dubious, torn between desire for such a magnificent sum and fearful of discovery and dismissal. The American pressed his case.

"If you were doing anything to harm your country, I would not dream of asking. But this man is a thief. Taking away from him what he has stolen can surely only be a good thing. Does not the Koran praise justice against the wrongdoer?"

Mr. al Khoury's hand covered the thousand dollars.

"I'll check in here now," said Dexter. "Just ask for Mr. Barnes when you are ready."

The call came two days later. Mr. al Khoury was taking his new role as secret agent rather seriously. He phoned from a booth from a public place.

"It is your friend," said a breathless voice in the mid-morning.

"Hello, my friend, do you wish to see me?" asked Dexter.

"Yes. I have the package."

"Here or at the office?"

"Neither. Too public. The Al Hamra Fort. Lunch."

His dialogue could not have been more suspicious had anyone been eavesdropping, but Dexter doubted the Ra's al Khaymah Secret Service was on the case.

He checked out and ordered a taxi. The Al Hamra Fort Hotel was out of town, ten miles down the coast but in the right direction, heading back toward Dubai, a luxurious conversion from an old turreted Arab fortress into a five-star beachside resort.

He was there at midday, much too early for a Gulf lunch, but found a low-slung club chair in the vaulted lobby, ordered a beer, and watched the entrance arch. Mr. al Khoury appeared, hot and dripping even from the one-hundred-yard walk from his car in the parking lot, just after 1:00 P.M. Of the five restaurants, they selected the Lebanese with its cold buffet.

"Any problems?" asked Dexter, as they took their plates and moved down the groaning trestle tables.

"No," said the civil servant. "I explained my department was contacting all known visitors to send them a brochure explaining the new and extra leisure facilities now available in Ra's al Khaymah."

"That is brilliant," Dexter said, beaming. "No one thought it odd?"

"On the contrary, the officials in Air Traffic took out all the flight plans for December and insisted on giving me the whole month."

"You mentioned the importance of the European owners?"

"Yes, but there are only about four or five who are not well-known oil companies. Let us sit."

They took a corner table and ordered two beers. Like many modern Arabs, Mr. al Khoury had no problem with alcoholic drinks.

He clearly enjoyed his Lebanese food. He had piled his plate with mezzah, hummus, moutabel, lightly grilled halloumi cheese, sambousek, kibbeh, and stuffed vine leaves. He handed over a sheaf of paper and began to eat.

Dexter ran through the listings of filed flight plans for December, along with the time of landing and duration of stay before departure, until he came to December 15th. With a red felt-tip pen he bracketed those appearing then and covering the period to December 19th. There were nine.

Two Grumman 3s and a 4 belonged to internationally known U.S. oil companies. A French Dassault Mystere and a Falcon were down to Elf Aquitaine. That left four.

A smaller Lear jet was known to belong to a Saudi prince, and a larger Cessna Citation to a multimillionaire businessman from Bahrain. The last two were an Israeli-built Westwind that arrived from Bombay and a Hawker 1000 that came in from Cairo and departed back there. Someone had noted something in Arab script beside the Westwind.

"What does that mean?" asked Dexter.

"Ah, yes, that one is regular. It is owned by an Indian film producer. From Bombay. He stages through on his way to London or Cannes or Berlin. All the film festivals. In the tower, they know him by sight."

"You have the picture?"

Al Khoury handed back the borrowed photograph.

"That one, they think he comes from the Hawker."

The Hawker 1000 had a registration number listed as P4-ZEM and was down as owned by the Zeta Corporation of Bermuda.

Dexter thanked his informant and paid over the promised balance of four thousand dollars. It was a lot for a sheaf of paper, but Dexter thought it might be the lead he needed.

On his drive back to Dubai airport, he mused on something he had once been told. That when a man changes his entire identity, he cannot always resist the temptation to keep back one tiny detail for old time's sake.

ZEM just happened to be the first three letters of Zemun, the district in Belgrade where Zoran Zilic was born and raised. And Zeta just happened to be Greek for the letter Z.

But Zilic would have hidden himself and his covering corporations, not to mention his plane, if indeed the Hawker was his, behind layers of protection. The records would be out there somewhere, but they would be stored in databases of the type not available to the innocent seeker of knowledge.

Dexter could manage a computer as well as the next man, but there was no way he could hack into a protected database. But he remembered someone who could.

19

THE CONFRONTATION

When it came to matters of right and wrong, of sin and righteousness, FBI assistant director Colin Fleming was a fundamentalist. The concept of "No Surrender" was in his bones and his genes, brought across the Atlantic a hundred years ago from the cobbled streets of Portadown. Two hundred years before that, his ancestors had brought their Presbyterian code across to Ulster from the western coast of Scotland.

When it came to evil, to tolerate was to accommodate, to accommodate was to appease, and to appease was to concede defeat. That he could never do.

When Fleming read the synthesis of the Tracker's report and the Serbian confession, and when he reached the details of the death of Ricky Colenso, he determined that the man responsible should, if at all possible, face due process in a court of law in the greatest country in the world, his own.

Of all those in the various agencies who read the circulated report and the joint request from Secretary Powell and Attorney General Ashcroft, he had taken it almost personally that his own department had no current knowledge of Zoran Zilic and could not help.

In a final bid to do something, he had circulated a full-face picture of the Serbian gangster to the thirty-eight "legats" posted abroad.

It was a far better picture than had been contained in any press archive, though not as recent as the one that a charlady in Block 23 had given to Avenger. The reason for its quality was that it had been taken in Belgrade by a long-lens camera on the orders of the CIA station chief five years earlier, when the elusive Zilic was a mover and shaker in the court of Milosevic.

The photographer had caught Zilic emerging from his car; in the act of straightening up, head raised, gaze toward the lens he could not see a quarter of a mile away. Inside the Belgrade Embassy, the FBI legat had obtained a copy from his CIA colleague, so both agencies possessed the same photo.

Broadly speaking, the CIA operates outside the United States and the FBI inside. But for all of that, in the ongoing fight against espionage, terrorism, and crime, the Bureau has no choice but to collaborate intensively and extensively with foreign countries, especially allies, and to that end maintains its legal attachés abroad.

It may look as if the legal attaché is some kind of diplomatic appointment, answering to the Department of State. Not so. The "legat" is the FBI representative inside the U.S. Embassy. Every one of them had received the photo of Zilic from Assistant Director Fleming, with an instruction to display it in hope of a lucky break. It came in the unlikely form of Inspector Bin Zayeed.

Insp. Moussa Bin Zayeed would also, if asked, have replied that he, too, was a good man. He served his emir, Sheikh Maktoum of Dubai, with complete loyalty, took no bribes, honored his god, and paid his taxes. If he moon-lighted by passing useful information to his friend at the American Embassy, this was simple cooperation with his country's ally and not to be confused with anything else.

Thus it was that he found himself, with the outside temperature in July over one hundred degrees, sheltering in the welcome cool of the air-conditioned embassy lobby and waiting for his friend to descend and take him out for lunch. His eyes looked over at the bulletin board.

He rose and strolled over to it. There were the usual notices of coming events, functions, arrivals, departures, and invitations to various club memberships. Among the clutter was a photograph and the printed question: HAVE YOU SEEN THIS MAN?

"Well, have you?" asked a cheery voice behind him, and a hand clapped him on the shoulder. It was Bill Brunton, his contact, lunch host, and the legal attaché. They exchanged friendly greetings.

"Oh yes," said the Special Branch officer, "two weeks ago."

Brunton's bonhomie dropped away. The fish restaurant out at Jumeirah could wait awhile.

"Let's step right back to my office," he suggested.

"Do you remember where and when?" asked the legat, back in his office.

"Of course. About two weeks ago. I was visiting a relative in Ra's al Khaymah. I was on the Faisal Road; you know it? The seafront road out of town between the Old Town and the Gulf."

Brunton nodded.

"Well, a truck was trying to maneuver backward into a narrow work site. I had to stop. To my left was a café terrace. There were three men at the table. One of them was this one." He gestured to the photograph now faceup on the legat's desk.

"No question about it?"

"None. That was the man."

"He was with two others?"

"Yes."

"You recognized them?"

"One by name. The other only by sight. The one by name was Bout."

Bill Brunton sucked in his breath. Vladimir Bout needed no introduction to virtually anyone in a Western or East bloc intelligence service. He was widely notorious, a former KGB major who had become one of the world's leading black market arms dealers, a merchant of death of the first rank. That he was not even born a Russian, but a half-Tajik from Dushanbe, attests to his skill in the arts of the underworld. The Russians are nothing if not the most racist people on earth, and back in the old USSR referred to denizens of the non-Russian republics collectively as *chorny,* meaning "blacks"; and it was not a compliment. Only White Russians and Ukrainians could escape the term and rise through the ranks on an equal par with an ethnic Russian. For a half-breed Tajik to graduate out of Moscow's prestigious Military Institute of Foreign Languages, a KGB-front training academy, and make it to the rank of major, was unusual.

He was assigned to the Navigation and Air Transport Regiment of the Soviet Air Force, another covert "front" for shipping arms consignments to anti-Western guerrillas and Third World regimes opposed to the West. Here he could use his mastery of Portuguese in the Angolan civil war. He also built up formidable contacts in the air force.

When the USSR collapsed in 1991, chaos reigned for several years and military inventories were simply abandoned as unit commanders sold off their equipment for almost any price they could get. Bout simply bought the sixteen Ilyushin IL-76s of his own unit for a song and went into the air charter and freight business.

By 1992, he was back in his native south; the Afghan civil war had started just across the border from his native Tajikistan, and one of the prime contestants was his fellow Tajik, General Dostum. The only "freight" the barbarous Dostum wanted was arms; Bout provided them.

By 1993, he showed up in Ostend, Belgium, a jumping-off point to move into Africa via the Belgian ex-colony, the permanently war-torn Congo. His source of supply was limitless, the vast weapons pool of the old USSR, still operating on fictional inventories. Among his new clients were the Interahamwe, the genocidal butchers of Rwanda and Burundi.

This finally upset even the Belgians, and he was hounded out of Ostend, appearing in 1995 in South Africa to sell to both the UNITA guerrillas in Angola and their enemies in the MPLA government. But with Nelson Mandela occupying the South African presidency, things went bad for him there, too, and he had to leave in a hurry.

In 1998, Bout showed up in the UAE and settled in Sharjah. The British and Americans put his dossier in front of the emir, and three weeks before Bill Brunton sat in his office with Inspector Bin Zayeed, Bout had been kicked out yet again.

But his recourse was simply to move ten miles up the coast and settle in Ajman, taking a suite of rooms in the Chamber of Commerce and Industry Building. With only forty thousand people, Ajman had no oil and little industry and could not be as particular as Sharjah.

For Bill Brunton the sighting was important. He did not know why his superior, Colin Fleming, was interested in the missing Serb, but this report was certainly going to earn him a few brownie points in the Hoover Building.

"And the third man?" he asked. "You say you know him by sight? Any idea where?"

"Of course. Here. He is one of your colleagues."

If Bill Brunton thought his surprises for the day were over, he was wrong. He felt his stomach perform some gentle aerobatics. Carefully, he withdrew a file from the bottom drawer of his desk. It was a compendium of the embassy staff. Insp. Bin Zayeed was unhesitating in pointing to the face of the cultural attaché.

"This one," he said. "He was the third man at the table. You know him?" Brunton knew him alright. Even though

cultural exchanges were few and far between, the cultural
attaché was a very busy man. This was because behind the
façade of visiting orchestras, he was the station chief for
the CIA.

The news from Dubai left Colin Fleming incandescent with
rage. It was not that the secret agency out at Langley was
conferring with a man like Vladimir Bout. That might be
necessary in the course of information gathering. What had
angered him was that someone high in the CIA had clearly
lied to the secretary of state and to his own superior, the
attorney general. A lot of rules had been broken here, and
he was pretty sure he knew who had broken them. He
called Langley and asked for a meeting as a matter of some
urgency.

The two men had met before. They had clashed in front
of the national security adviser, Condoleezza Rice, and
there was little love lost between them. Occasionally, op-
posites attract, but not in this case.

Paul Devereaux III was the scion of a long line of those
families who come as near to being aristocracy as the Commonwealth of Massachusetts has had for a long time. He
was born a Boston Brahmin to his boot heels. He was
showing his intellectual brilliance way before school age
and sailed through Boston College High School, the main
feeder unit to one of the foremost Jesuit academies in
America. His grades when he came out were summa cum
laude.

At Boston College, the tutors had him marked out as a
high flyer, destined one day to join the Society of Jesus
itself, if not to hold high office somewhere in academia.

He read for a B.A. in Humanities, with strong compo-
nents being philosophy and theology. He read them all,
devoured them; from Ignatius Loyola, of course, to Teil-
hard de Chardin. He wrangled late into the night with his
senior tutor in theology over the concept of the doctrine of
the lesser evil and the higher goal: that the end may justify

the means and yet not damn the soul, providing the para-
meters of the impermissible are never breached.

In 1966, he was nineteen. It was the pinnacle of the Cold
War when world communism still seemed capable of rolling up the Third World and leaving the West a beleaguered
island. That was when Pope Paul VI appealed to the Jesuits
and entreated them to spearhead the task of combating atheism.

For Paul Devereaux the two were synonymous: Atheism
was not always communism, but communism was atheism.
He would serve his country not in the church or in academia but in that other place quietly mentioned to him at the
country club by a pipe-smoking man introduced by a colleague of his father.

A week after graduating from Boston College, Paul Devereaux was sworn into the ranks of the Central Intelligence
Agency. For him it was the poet's bright, confident morning. The great scandals were yet to come. With his patrician
background and contacts, he rose in the hierarchy, blunting
the shafts of jealousy with a combination of easy charm
and sheer cleverness. He also proved that he had a buck-
etful of the most prized currency of them all in the Agency
in those years: He was loyal. For that a man can be forgiven
an awful lot, maybe sometimes a bit too much. He spent
time in the three major divisions: Operations (Ops), Intelligence (Analysis), and Counterintelligence (Internal Security). His career hit the buffers with the arrival of John
Deutsch as director.

The two men simply did not like each other. It happens.
Deutsch, with no background in intelligence gathering, was
the latest in a long and, with hindsight, pretty disastrous
line of political appointees. He believed Devereaux, with
seven fluent languages, was quietly looking down on him;
and he could have been right.

Devereaux regarded the new DCI (Director of Central
Intelligence) as a politically correct nincompoop appointed
by the Arkansan president whom, although a fellow Democrat, he despised, and that was before Paula Jones and

Monica Lewinsky. It was not a marriage made in heaven, and it almost became a divorce when Devereaux came to the defense of a division chief in South America accused of employing unsavory contacts.

The entire agency had swallowed Executive Order 12333 with good grace, except for a few dinosaurs who went back to World War II. This was the EO brought in by Pres. Ronald Reagan that forbade any more "terminations."

Devereaux had considerable reservations but was too junior to be sought out for his counsel. It seemed to him that in the thoroughly imperfect world occupied by covert intelligence gathering there would arise occasions where an enemy, in the form of a betrayer, might have to be "terminated" as a preemption. Put another way, one life may have to be terminated to preserve a likely ten.

As to the final judgment in such a case, Devereaux believed that if the director himself was not a man of wholly sufficient moral integrity to be entrusted with such a decision, he should not be director at all.

But under Clinton, in the by-now veteran agent's view, political correctness went quite lunatic with the instruction that disreputable sources were not to be used as informants. He felt it was like being asked to confine one's sources to monks and choirboys.

So when a man in South America was threatened with the wreckage of his career for using ex-terrorists to inform on functioning terrorists, Devereaux wrote a paper so sarcastic that it circulated throughout the grinning staffers of Ops Division like illegal samizdat in the old Soviet Union.

Deutsch wanted to require the departure of Devereaux at that point, but his deputy director, George Tenet, advised caution and eventually it was Deutsch who went, to be replaced by Tenet himself.

Something happened in Africa that summer of 1998 that caused the new director to need the mordant but effective intellectual, despite his views on their joint commander in chief. Two U.S. embassies were blown up. It was no secret to the lowliest cleaner that since the end of the Cold War in 1991, the new cold war had been against the steadily growing rise of terrorism, and the "happening" unit within Ops Division was the Counterterrorism Center.

Paul Devereaux was not working in the CT Center. Because one of his languages was Arabic, and his career included three stints in Arabic countries, he was Number Two in the Middle East at the time.

The destruction of the embassies brought him out of there and into the leadership of a small task force dedicated to one task and answering only to the director himself. The job in hand was called Project Peregrine, after that falcon who hovers high and silent above his prey until he is certain of a lethal hit and then descends with awesome speed and accuracy.

In the new office Devereaux had no-limits access to any information from any other source that he might want and a small but expert team. For his Number Two he chose Kevin McBride, not an intellectual patch on himself, but experienced, willing, and loyal. It was McBride who took the call and held his hand across the mouthpiece.

"Assistant Director Fleming at the Bureau," he said. "Doesn't sound happy. Shall I leave?"

Devereaux signaled for him to stay.

"Colin . . . Paul Devereaux. What can I do for you?"

His brow furrowed as he listened. "Why surely, I think a meeting would be a good idea."

It was a safe house, always convenient for a row. Daily "swept" for bugs every word recorded with the full knowledge of the conference participants, refreshments on immediate call.

Fleming thrust the report from Bill Brunton under Devereaux's nose and let him read it. The Arabist's face remained impassive.

"So?" he queried.

"Please don't tell me the Dubai inspector got it wrong," said Fleming. "Zilic was the biggest arms trafficker in Yugoslavia. He quit, disappeared. Now he is seen conferring

with the biggest arms trafficker in the Gulf and Africa. Totally logical."

"I wouldn't dream of trying to fault the logic," said Devereaux.

"And in conference with your man covering the Persian
Gulf."

"The Agency's man covering the Gulf," said Devereaux
mildly. "Why me?"

"Because you virtually ran the Mid East, although you
were supposed to be second string. Because back then all
company staff in the Gulf would have reported to you. Because even though you are now in some kind of special
project, that situation has not changed. Because I very much
doubt that two weeks ago was Zilic's first visit to that neck
of the woods. My guess is that you knew exactly where
Zilic was when the request came through or at least that he
would be in the Gulf and available for a snatch on a certain
day. And you said nothing."

"So? Even in our business, suspicions are a long way
from proof."

"This is more serious than you seem to think, my friend.
By any count, you and your agents are consorting with
known criminals and of the filthiest hue. Against the rules,
flat against all the rules."

"So. Some foolish rules have been breached. Ours is not
a business for the squeamish. Even the Bureau must have
a comprehension of the smaller evil to obtain the greater
good."

"Don't patronize me," snapped Colin Fleming.

"I'll try not," drawled the Bostonian. "All right, you're
upset. What are you going to do about it?"

There was no need to be polite any more. The gloves
were off and lying on the floor. "I don't think I can let this
ride," said Fleming. "This man Zilic is obscene. You must
have read what he did to that boy from Georgetown. But
you're consorting. By proxy, but consorting for all that.
You know what Zilic can do; what he's already done. All
on file and I know you must have read it. There's testimony

that as a gangster he hung a nonpaying shopkeeper from his heels six inches above a two-bar electric fire until his brains boiled. He's a raving sadist. What the hell are you using him for?"

"If indeed I am, then it's classified. Even from an assistant director of the Bureau."

"Give the swine up. Tell us where we can find him."

"Even if I knew, which I do not admit, no."

Colin trembled with rage and disgust. "How can you be so bloody complacent?" he shouted. "Back in 1945 the CIC in occupied Germany cut deals with Nazis who were supposed to help in the fight against communism. We should never have done that. We should not have touched those swine with a barge pole. It was wrong then; it's wrong now."

Devereaux sighed. This was becoming tiresome and had long been pointless. "Spare me the history lesson," he said. "I repeat, what are you going to do about it?"

"I'm taking what I know to your director," said Fleming.

Paul Devereaux rose. It was time to go. "Let me tell you something. Last December I'd have been toast. Today, I'm asbestos. Times change."

After a tiresome imbroglio in the vote-counting booths of Florida, the president sworn in in January 2001 was one George W. Bush, whose most enthusiastic cheerleader was none other than CIA director George Tenet.

"This is not the end of it," Fleming called at the departing back. "He'll be found and brought back if I have anything to do with it."

Devereaux thought over the remark in his car on the way back to Langley. He had not survived the snakepit of the company for thirty years without developing formidable antennae. He had just made an enemy, maybe a bad one.

"He'll be found." By whom? How? And what could the Hoover Building moralist have to do with it? He sighed. An extra care in a stress-filled planet. He would have to watch Colin Fleming like a hawk . . . at any rate like a peregrine falcon. The joke made him smile, but not for long.

20

THE JET

When he saw the house, Cal Dexter had to appreciate the occasional irony of life. Instead of the GI-turned-lawyer getting the fine house in Westchester County, it was the skinny kid from Bedford-Stuyvesant. In thirteen years, Washington Lee had evidently done well.

When he opened the door that Sunday morning in late July, Dexter noted he had had the buck teeth fixed, the beaky nose sculpted back a bit, and his wild Afro was down to a neat trim. This was a thirty-two-year-old businessman with a wife and two small children, a nice house, and a modest but prosperous computer consultancy.

All that Dexter once had he had lost; all that Washington Lee never hoped for, he had earned. After tracing him, Dexter had called to announce his coming.

"Come on in, Counselor," said the ex-hacker.

They took soda in canvas chairs on the back lawn. Dexter offered Lee a brochure. Its cover showed a twinjet executive airplane banking over a blue sea.

"That's public domain, of course. I need to find one of that model. A specific example. I need to know who bought it, when, who owns it now, and most of all where that person resides."

"And you think they don't want you to know?"

"If the proprietor is living openly and under his own name, I have it wrong. Bum steer. If I am right, he will be holed up out of sight under a false name, protected by armed guards and layers of computerized identity protection."

"And it's the layers you want pulled away."

"Yep."

"Things have got a lot tougher in thirteen years," said Lee. "Dammit, I'm one of the ones that made them tougher, from the technical standpoint. The legislators have done the same from the legal standpoint. What you are asking for is a break-in. Or three. Totally illegal."

"I know."

Washington Lee looked around him. Two little girls squealed as they splashed in a plastic pool at the far end of the lawn. His wife, Cora, was in the kitchen making lunch.

"Thirteen years ago I was staring at a long stretch in the pen," he said. "I'd have come out and gone back to sitting on tenement steps in the ghetto. Instead I got a break. Four years with a bank, nine years as my own boss inventing the best security systems in the United States, even if I do say so myself. Now it's payback time. You got it, Counselor. What do you want?"

First they looked at the plane. The name of Hawker went back in British aviation to World War I. It was a Hawker Hurricane that Stephen Edmond had flown in 1940. The last frontline fighter was the ultraversatile Harrier. By the seventies, smaller companies simply could not afford the research and development costs of devising new warplanes in isolation. Only the American giants could do that, and even they amalgamated. Hawker moved increasingly into civil aircraft.

By the nineties, just about all the UK airplane companies were under one roof, BAE or British Aerospace. When the board decided to downsize, the Hawker Division was bought by the Raytheon Company of Wichita, Kansas. They kept on a small sales office in London and the servicing facility at Chester.

What Raytheon got for their dollars was the successful and popular HS 125 short-range twinjet executive runabout; the Hawker 800, and the top-of-the-range, three-thousand-mile Hawker 1000 model.

But Dexter's own research in the public domain showed that the 1000 model had gone out of production in 1996, so if Zoran Zilic owned one, it would be secondhand. More, only fifty-two had ever been made, and thirty of them were with an American-based charter fleet.

He was looking for one of the remaining twenty-two that had changed hands in the last two years, three at most. There were a handful of secondhand dealers who moved in the rarefied atmosphere of airplanes that expensive, but it was ten-to-one that during the owner changeover it had undergone a full servicing, and that probably meant going back to Raytheon's Hawker Division. Which made it likely they handled the sale.

"Anything else?" asked Lee.

"The registration. P4-ZEM. It's not with one of the main international civil aviation registers. The number refers to the tiny island of Aruba."

"Never heard of it," said Lee.

"Former Dutch Antilles, along with Curaçao and Bonaire. They all do secret bank accounts, company registrations, that sort of thing. It's a pain in the ass for international fraud regulations, but it's a cheap income for an otherwise no-resource island. Aruba has a tiny oil refinery. Otherwise, its income is tourism based on some great coral; plus secret bank accounts, gaudy stamps, and dodgy number plates. I would guess my target changed the old registration number to the new one."

"So Raytheon would have no record of P4-ZEM?"

"Almost certainly not. That apart, they do not divulge client details. No way."

"We'll see," muttered Washington Lee.

In thirteen years the computer genius had learned a lot, in part because he had invented a lot. Most of America's real computer geeks are out in Silicon Valley; and for the eggheads of the valley to hold an East Coaster in some awe, he had to be good.

The first thing Lee had told himself a thousand times was: Never get caught again. As he contemplated the first illegal task he had attempted in thirteen years, he determined there was no way anyone was ever going to trace a trail of cyberclues back to a home in Westchester.

"How big is your budget?" he asked.

"Adequate. Why?"

"I want to rent a Winnebago motor home. I need full domestic circuit power, but I need to transmit, close down, and vanish. Two, I need the best personal computer I can get; and when this is over I have to deep-six it into a major river."

"Not a problem. Which way are you going to attack?"

"All points. The tailplane register of the Aruba government. They have to cough up what that Hawker was called when Raytheon last saw it. Second, the Zeta Corporation in the Bermuda company's register. Head office, destination of all communications, money transfers. The lot. Third, those flight plans it filed. They must have come to that emirate, what did you call it . . . ?"

"Ra's al Khaymah."

"Right, Ra's al Whatever. They must have reached there from somewhere."

"Cairo. They came in from Cairo."

"So its flight plan is logged in the Cairo Air Traffic Control archives. Computerized. I'll have to visit. The good news is I doubt if they will have too many firewalls to protect them."

"You need to go to Cairo?" asked Dexter.

Washington Lee looked at him as if he were mad. "*Go* to Cairo? Why would I go to Cairo?"

"You said, 'visit.' "

"I mean in cyberspace. I can visit the Cairo database from a picnic site in Vermont. Look, why don't you go home and wait, Counselor? This is not your world."

Washington Lee rented his motor home and bought his PC, plus the software he needed for what he had in mind. It was all for cash, despite the raised eyebrows, except for the motor home, which needed a driver's license, but renting a motor home does not necessarily mean a hacker is at work. He also bought a gas-powered generator, to give him standard domestic "juice" whenever he needed to plug in and log on.

The first and easiest was to crack the Aruba tailfin registration bank, which operated out of an office in Miami. Rather than use a weekend, where an unauthorized visit would show up on Monday morning, he broke into the archive on a busy working day when the database was answering many questions and his would get lost in the clutter.

Hawker 1000 P4-ZEM had once been VP-BGG, and that meant it had been registered somewhere in the British registration zone.

He was using a system designed to hide its own identity and location called PGP, standing for "Pretty Good Privacy," which is a system so secure that it is actually illegal. He had set up two lines, public and private. He had to send on the public line because that line can only encrypt; receiving answers would be on his private line, because that one can only decrypt. The advantage from his point of view was that the encryption system, worked out by some patriot who did pure theoretical math as a hobby, was so impenetrable that it would be unlikely anyone could find out who he was or where he was located. If he kept time-on-line short and location mobile, he should get away with it.

His second line of defense was much more basic; he would communicate by E-mail only through Web cafés in the towns he passed through. Cairo Air Traffic Control revealed that Hawker 1000 P4-ZEM, when it passed through with a refueling stop in the Land of the Pharaohs, came in from the Azores—every time.

The very fact that the line across the world ran from west to east via the mid-Atlantic Portuguese islands to Cairo thence to Ra's al Khaymah indicated that P4-ZEM was starting its journey somewhere in the Caribbean basin or South America. It was not proof, but it made sense. From a rest stop in North Carolina, Washington Lee persuaded the Portuguese/Azores air traffic database to admit that P4-ZEM arrived from the west but was based at a private field owned by the Zeta Corporation. That made the line of pursuit via the filed flight plans into an impasse. The British colony of Bermuda also operated a system of banking secrecy and corporate confidentiality for the benefit of clients who were prepared to pay top dollar for top security, and it prided itself on being very top notch indeed.

The database in Hamilton could not eventually resist the Trojan horse decoy system fed into it by Washington Lee and conceded that the Zeta Corporation was indeed registered and incorporated in the islands. But it could only yield three local nominees as directors, all of unimpeachable respectability. There was no mention of any Zoran Zilic, no Serbian-sounding name.

Back in New York, Cal Dexter, armed with the suggestion from Washington Lee that the Hawker was based somewhere around the Caribbean, had contacted a charter pilot he had once defended when a passenger had become violently airsick and tried to sue on the grounds that the pilot should have picked better weather.

"Try the FIRs," said the pilot, "flight information registers. They know who is based in their areas."

The FIR for the southern Caribbean is in Caracas, Venezuela, and they confirmed that Hawker 1000 P4-ZEM was

based right there. For a moment Dexter thought he might
have been wasting his time on all the other lines of inquiry.
It seemed so simple. Ask the local FIR and they tell you.

"Mind you," said his charter pilot friend, "it doesn't
have to live there. It's just registered as being there."

"I don't follow."

"Easy," said the pilot. "A yacht can have Wilmington,
Delaware, all over its stern because it is registered there.
But it can spend its whole life chartering in the Bahamas.
The hangar this Hawker lives in could be miles from Ca-
racas."

Washington Lee proposed the last resort and briefed
Dexter. Two days of hard driving brought Lee to the city
of Wichita, Kansas. He called Dexter when he was ready.

The vice president of sales took the New York call in
his office on the fifth floor of the headquarters building.

"I am ringing on behalf of the Zeta Corporation of Bermuda," said the voice. "You recall you sold us a Hawker
1000 tailfin number VP-BGG, you know, the British-owned
one, some months back? I'm the new pilot."

"I surely do, sir. And who am I speaking with?"

"Only Mr. Zilic is not happy with the internal cabin
configuration and would like it made over. Can you offer
that facility?"

"Why certainly. We do cabin interiors right here at the
works, Mr . . . er . . ."

"And it could have the necessary engine overhauls at the
same time."

The executive sat bolt upright. He recalled the sale very
well. Everything had been serviced to give a clear run of
major items for a couple of years. Unless the new owner
had been almost constantly airborne, the engines would not
be due for overhaul for up to a year.

"May I inquire exactly who I am talking to? I do not
think those engines are anywhere near to needing another
overhaul," he said.

The voice at the other end lost its self-confidence and

began to stutter. "Really? Aw, jeez. Sorry about that. Must have the wrong airplane."

The caller hung up. By now the vice president of sales was consumed with suspicion. To his recall he had never mentioned the sale of the registration of the British-sourced Hawker offered for sale by the firm of Avtech of Biggin Hill, Kent. He resolved to ask security to trace that call and try to establish who had made it.

He would be too late, of course, because the SIM-based mobile was heading into the East River. But in the meantime, he recalled the delivery pilot from the Zeta Corporation who had come up to Wichita to fly the Hawker to its new owner.

A very pleasant Yugoslav, a former colonel in that country's air force, with papers in perfect order, including the full FAA (Federal Aviation Administration) records of the U.S. flight school where he had converted to the Hawker. He checked his sales records, Capt. Svetomir Stepanovic, and an E-mail address. He composed a brief E-mail to alert the captain of the Hawker to the weird and troubling phone call and sent it. Across the landscaped grounds that surrounded the headquarters building, parked behind a clump of trees, Washington Lee scanned his electromagnetic emanation monitor, thanked his stars the sale executive was not using the Tempest system to shield his computer from such monitors, and watched the EEM (Electronic Engineers Master) intercept the message. The text was immaterial to him. It was the destination he wanted.

Three days later in New York, the motor home returned to the charter company, hard drive and software somewhere in the Missouri River.

Washington Lee pored over a map and pointed with a pencil tip. "It's here," he said. "Republic of San Martin. About fifty miles east of San Martin City. And the airplane captain is a Yugoslav. I think you have your man, Counselor. And now, if you'll forgive me, I have a home, a wife, two kids, and a business to attend to. Good luck."

The Avenger got the biggest definition maps he could find
and blew them up even larger. Right at the bottom of the
lizard-shaped isthmus of land that links North and South
America, the broad mass of the South begins with Colom-
bia to the west and Venezuela dead center.

East of Venezuela lie the four Guianas. First is the former British Guiana, now called just Guyana. Next comes
former Dutch Guiana, now Suriname. Farthest east is
French Guiana, home of Devil's Island and the story of
Papillon, now home to Kourou, the European space-launch
complex. Sandwiched between Suriname and the French
territory, Dexter found the triangle of jungle that was once
Spanish Guiana, named, postindependence, San Martin.

Further research revealed it was regarded as the last of
the true banana republics, ruled by a brutal military dictator,
ostracized, poor, squalid, and malarial, the sort of place
where money could buy a bucket of protection.

A week into August, the Piper Cheyenne II flew along
the coast at a sedate 1,250 feet, high enough not to arouse
too much suspicion as little more than an executive proceeding from Suriname to French Guiana, but just low
enough to allow good photography.

Chartered out of the airport at Georgetown, Guyana, the
Piper's twelve-hundred-mile range would take it just over
the French border and back home again. The client, whose
passport revealed him as U.S. citizen Alfred Barnes, now
purported to be a developer of vacation resorts looking for
possible locations. The Guyanese pilot privately thought he
would pay not to vacation in San Martin, but who was he
to turn down a perfectly good charter, paid for in dollars?

As requested, he kept the Piper just offshore, so that his
passenger, sitting in the right-hand copilot seat could keep
his zoom lens ready for use out of the window if occasion
arose.

After Suriname, and its border the Commini River,
dropped away, there were no suitable sandy beaches for

miles. The coast was a tangle of mangrove, creeping
through brown, snake-infested water from the jungle to the
sea. They passed over the capital, San Martin City, asleep
in the blazing soggy heat.

The only beach was east of the city, at La Bahia, but
that was the reserved resort of the rich and powerful of San
Martin, basically the dictator and his friends. At the end of
the republic, ten miles short of the banks of the Maroni
River and the start of French Guiana, was El Punto. A
triangular peninsula, like a shark's tooth jutting from the
land into the sea, protected from the landward side by a
sierra or cordillera of mountains from coast to coast, bisected by a single track over a single mountain pass. But
it was inhabited.

The pilot had never been this far east, so the peninsula
was, to him, simply a coastal triangle on his nav maps. He
could see there was a kind of defended estate down there.
His passenger began to take photographs. Dexter was using
a 35-mm Nikon F5 with a motor drive that would give him
five frames a second and get through his roll in seven seconds to change film, but he absolutely could not afford to
start circling.

He was set for a very fast shutter speed, due to the aircraft vibration, which at any slower than five hundred per
second would cause blurring. With 400 ASA film and his
aperture set at F8, it was the best he could do.

On the first pass he got the mansion on the tip of the
peninsula, with its protective wall and huge gate, plus the
fields being tended by estate workers; rows of barns and
farm buildings; and the chain-link fencing that separated
the fields from the cluster of cuboid white cabanas that
seemed to be the workers' village.

Several people looked up, and he saw two in uniform
start to run. Then they were over the estate and heading for
French territory. On the pass back, he had the pilot fly
inland so that from the right-hand seat he could see the
estate from the landward angle. He was looking down from
the peaks of the sierra at the estate running away to the

mansion and the sea, but there was a guard in the mountain pass below the Piper who took its number. He used up his second roll on the private airstrip running along the base of the hills, shooting the residences, workshops, and the main hangar. There was a tractor pulling a twin-engined executive jet into the hangar and out of sight. The tailfin was almost gone. Dexter got one brief look at the fin before it was enveloped in the shadows. The number was P4-ZEM.

21
THE JESUIT

Paul Devereaux, for all that he was confident the FBI would not be allowed to dismantle his Project Peregrine, was perturbed by the acrimonious meeting with Colin Fleming. He underestimated neither the other man's intelligence, influence, or passion. What worried him was the threat of delay.

After two years at the helm of a project so secret that it was known only to CIA director George Tenet and White House antiterrorist expert Richard Clarke, he was close, enticingly close, to springing the trap he had moved heaven and earth to create.

The target was simply called UBL. This was because the whole intelligence community in Washington spelled the man's first name, Usama, using the letter *U* rather than the *O* favored by the media.

By the summer of 2001, that entire community was obsessed by and convinced of a forthcoming act of war by UBL against the United States. Ninety percent thought the onslaught would come against a major U.S. interest outside America; only 10 percent could envisage a successful attack inside the territorial United States.

The obsession ran through all the agencies, but mostly through the antiterrorist departments of the CIA and the FBI. Here the intention was to discover what UBL had in mind and then prevent it.

Regardless of presidential edict 12333 forbidding "wet jobs," Paul Devereaux was not trying to prevent UBL; he was trying to kill him. Early on in his career, the scholar from Boston College had realized that advancement inside the company would depend on some form of specialization. In his younger days, in the blaze of Vietnam and the Cold War, most debutantes had chosen the Soviet Division. The enemy was clearly the USSR; the language to be learned was Russian. The corridors became crowded. Devereaux chose the Arab world and the wider study of Islam. He was regarded as crazy.

He turned his formidable intellect to mastering Arabic until he could virtually pass for an Arab, and studied Islam to the level of a Koranic scholar. His vindication came on Christmas Day 1979; the USSR invaded a place called Afghanistan and most of the agents inside CIA headquarters at Langley were reaching for their maps.

Devereaux revealed that apart from Arabic, he spoke reasonable Urdu, the language of Pakistan, and had a knowledge of Pashto, spoken by the tribesmen throughout Pakistan's Northwest Frontier and into Afghanistan.

His career really took off. He was one of the first to argue that the USSR had bitten off far more than it knew; that Afghan tribes would not concede any foreign occupation; that Soviet atheism offended their fanatical Islam; that with U.S. material help, a fierce mountain-based resistance could be fomented that would eventually bleed white Gen. Boris Gromov's Fortieth Army.

Before it was over, quite a bit had changed. The Mujehadin had indeed sent more than twenty-five thousand Russian recruits back home in caskets; the occupation army,
despite the infliction of hideous atrocities on the Afghans,
had seen their grip pried loose and their morale gutted.

It was a combination of Afghanistan and the arrival of
Mikhail Gorbachev that between them put the USSR on the
final skid toward dissolution and ended the Cold War. Paul
Devereaux had switched from Analysis to Ops, and with
Milt Bearden had helped distribute one billion dollars a
year of U.S. guerrilla hardware to the "mountain fighters."

While living rough, running, fighting through the Afghan mountains, he had observed the arrival of hundreds
of young, idealistic, anti-Soviet volunteers from the Middle
East, speaking neither Pashto nor Dari, yet prepared to fight
and die far from home if need be.

Devereaux knew what he was doing there; he was fighting a superpower that threatened his own. But what were
the young Saudis, Egyptians, and Yemenis doing there?
Washington ignored them, and Devereaux's reports.

But they fascinated him. Listening for hours to their con-
versations in Arabic, pretending he had no more than a
dozen words of a language he spoke fluently, the CIA man
came to appreciate that they were fighting, not communism,
but atheism.

More, they also entertained an equally passionate hatred
and contempt for Christianity, the West, and most specifically the United States. Among them was a febrile, tem-
peramental, spoiled, offspring of a hugely rich Saudi
family, who distributed millions running training camps in
the safety of Pakistan; funding refugee hostels; buying and
distributing food, blankets, and medicines to the other Mujehadin. His name was Usama.

He wanted to be taken as a great warrior, like Ahmad
Shah Massoud, but in fact he was only in one scrap, in late
spring 1987, and that was it. Milt Bearden called him a
spoiled brat, but Devereaux watched him carefully. Behind
the younger man's endless references to Allah, there was a

seething hatred that would one day find a target other than the Russians.

Paul Devereaux returned home to Langley and a cascade of laurels. He had chosen not to marry, preferring scholarship and his job to the distractions of wife and children. His deceased father had left him wealthy; his elegant town house in Old Town Alexandria boasted a much-admired collection of Islamic art and Persian carpets.

He tried to warn against the foolishness of abandoning Afghanistan to its civil war after the defeat of Gromov, but the euphoria as the Berlin Wall came down led to a conviction that with the USSR collapsing into chaos, the Soviet satellites breaking westward for freedom and world communism dead in the water, the last and final threats to the world's only remaining superpower were evaporating as mist before the rising sun.

Devereaux was hardly home and settled in when, in August 1990, Saddam Hussein invaded Kuwait. At Aspen, President Bush and Margaret Thatcher, victors of the Cold War, agreed they could not tolerate such impudence. Within forty-eight hours, the first F-15 Eagles were airborne for Thumrait in Oman, and Paul Devereaux was heading for the U.S. Embassy in Riyadh, Saudi Arabia.

The pace was furious and the schedule grueling, or he might have noticed something. A young Saudi, also back from Afghanistan, claiming to be the leader of a group of guerrilla fighters and an organization called simply "The Base," offered his services to King Fahd in the defense of Saudi Arabia from the belligerent neighbor to the north.

The Saudi monarch probably also did not notice the military mosquito or his offer; instead, he permitted the arrival in his country of half a million foreign soldiers and airmen from a coalition of fifty nations to roll the Iraqi army out of Kuwait and protect the Saudi oil fields. Ninety percent of those soldiers and airmen were infidels, meaning Christians, and their combat boots marched upon the same soil as contained the Holy Places of Mecca and Medina. Almost 400,000 were Americans.

For the zealot, this was an insult to Allah and His prophet Muhammad that simply could not be tolerated. He declared his own private war, first against the ruling house that could do such a thing. More important, the seething rage that Devereaux had noticed in the mountains of the Hindu Kush had finally found its target. UBL declared war on America and began to plan.

If Paul Devereaux had been transferred to Counterterrorism the moment the Gulf War was over and won, the course of history might have been changed. But CT was a too-low priority in 1992; and both the CIA and the FBI entered the worst decade of their twin existences. In the CIA's case, that meant the shattering news that Aldrich Ames had been betraying his country for over eight years. Later it would be learned that the FBI's Robert Hanssen was still doing it. At what ought to have been the hour of victory after four decades of struggle against the USSR, both agencies suffered crises of leadership, morale, and incompetence.

The lingering scandals of Irangate and the illicit aid to the Nicaraguan Contras caused the new masters a crisis of nerves. Good men left in droves; bureaucrats and bean counters were elevated to chiefs of departments. Men with decades of frontline experience were disregarded.

At eclectic dinner parties, Paul Devereaux smiled politely as congressmen and senators preened themselves to announce that at least the Arab world loved the United States. They meant the ten princes they had just visited. The Jesuit had moved for years like a shadow through the Muslim streets. Inside him a small voice whispered, "No, they hate our guts."

On February 26, 1993, four Arab terrorists drove a rented van into the second level of the basement garage below the World Trade Center. It contained between twelve and fifteen hundred pounds of a homemade, fertilizer-based explosive called urea nitrate. Fortunately for New York, it is far from the most powerful explosive known.

For all that, it made a big bang. What no one knew for

certain, and no more than a dozen even suspected, was that the blast constituted the salvo at Fort Sumter in a new war.

Devereaux was by then the deputy chief for the entire Middle East Division, based at Langley but traveling constantly. It was partly what he saw in his travels and partly what came to him in the torrent of reports from the CIA stations throughout the world of Islam that caused his attention to wander away from the chancelleries and palaces of the Arab world, which were his proper concern, into another direction.

Almost as a sideline, he began to ask for supplementary reports from his stations; not about what the local prime minister was doing, but about the mood in the street, in the souks, in the medinas, in the mosques, and in the teaching schools, the *madrassahs* that churn out the next generation of locally educated Muslim youths. The more he watched and listened, the more the alarm bells rang.

"They hate our guts," his voice told him, "they just need a talented coordinator." Researching on his own time, he picked up the trail once again of the Saudi fanatic, UBL. He learned that the man had been expelled from Saudi Arabia for his impertinence in denouncing the monarch for permitting infidels onto the sacred sand.

He learned that UBL was based in the Sudan, another pure Islamist state where fundamentalist fanaticism was in power. Khartoum offered to hand the Saudi zealot over to the United States, but no one was interested. Then he was gone, back to the hills of Afghanistan where the civil war had ended in favor of the most fanatical faction, the ultra-religious Taliban.

Devereaux noted that the Saudi arrived with huge largesse, endowing the Taliban with millions of dollars in personal gifts, and rapidly became a major figure in the land. He arrived with almost fifty personal bodyguards and found several hundred of his foreign (non-Afghan) Mujehadin still in place. Word spread in the bazaars of the Pakistani border towns of Quetta and Peshawar that the returnee had begun two frantic programs: building elaborate cave complexes in a dozen places and constructing training camps. The camps were not for the Afghan military; they were for volunteer terrorists. The word came back to Paul Devereaux. Islamist hatred of his country had found its coordinator.

The misery of the Somali slaughter of the U.S. Army Rangers came and went, caused by rotten intelligence. But there was more. Not only was the opposition of the warlord, Aideed, underestimated, but there were others fighting there; not Somalis but more skilled Saudis. In 1996, a huge bomb destroyed the Al Kobar towers in Dhahran, Saudi Arabia, killing nineteen U.S. servicemen and injuring many others.

Paul Devereaux went to see Dir. George Tenet. "Let me go over to Counterterrorism," he begged.

"CT is full, and it's doing a good job," said the DCI.

"Six dead in Manhattan, nineteen in Dhahran. It's Al Qaeda. It's UBL and his team who are behind it, even if they don't actually plant the bombs."

"We know that, Paul. We're working on it. So is the Bureau. This is not being allowed to lie fallow."

"George, the Bureau knows diddly about Al Qaeda. They don't have the Arabic, they don't know the psychology. They're good on gangsters; but east of Suez might as well be the dark side of the moon. I could bring a new mind to this business."

"Paul, I want you in the Middle East. I need you there more. The king of Jordan is dying. We don't know who his successor will be. His son Abdullah or his brother Hassan? The dictator in Syria is failing; who takes over? Saddam is making life more and more intolerable for the weapons inspectors. What if he throws them out? The whole Israel-Palestine thing is going south in a big way. I need you in the Middle East."

It was in 1998 that Devereaux secured his transfer. On August 7th, two huge bombs were detonated outside two U.S. embassies in Africa; at Nairobi and Dar es Salaam.

Two hundred and thirteen people died in Nairobi, with 4,722 injured. Of the dead, 12 were Americans. The explosion in Tanzania was not as bad: 11 were killed, 72 injured. No Americans died, but 2 were crippled. The organizing force behind both bombs was quickly identified as the Al Qaeda network. Paul Devereaux handed his Middle East duties over to a rising young Arabist he had taken under his wing, and he moved to Counterterrorism.

He carried the rank of assistant director, but he did not displace the existing incumbent. It was not an elegant arrangement. He hovered on the fringe of Analysis as a kind of consultant but quickly became convinced the rule of only employing sources of upright character as informants was complete madness.

It was the sort of madness that had led to the fiasco of the response to Africa. Cruise missiles destroyed a pharmaceutical factory on the outskirts of Khartoum, capital of Sudan, because it was thought the long-departed UBL was manufacturing chemical weapons there. It turned out to be a genuine aspirin factory.

Seventy more Tomahawk cruise missiles were poured into Afghanistan to kill UBL. They turned a lot of big rocks into little rocks at several million dollars a pop, but UBL was at the other end of the country. It was out of this failure and the advocacy of Devereaux himself that Peregrine was created.

It was generally agreed around Langley that he must have called in a few markers to get his terms accepted. Project Peregrine was so secret that only Director Tenet knew what Devereaux intended. Outside the building, the Jesuit had to confide in one other, White House antiterrorist chief, Richard Clarke, who had started under George Bush Sr., and continued under Clinton.

Clarke was loathed at Langley for his blunt and abrasive criticisms, but Devereaux wanted and needed Clarke for several reasons. The White House man would agree to the sheer ruthlessness of what Devereaux had in mind; he could keep his mouth shut when he wanted; more, he could secure Devereaux the tools he needed when he needed them.

But first, Devereaux was given permission to throw in

the trash can all talk of not being allowed to kill the target or use to that end "assets" who might be utterly loathsome, if that is what it took. From that moment Paul Devereaux was performing his own very private high-wire act, and no one was talking safety nets.

He secured his own office and picked his own team. He headhunted the best he could get, and the DCI overruled the howls of protest. Having never been an empire builder, he wanted a small, tight unit, and every one a specialist. He secured a suite of three offices on the sixth floor of the main building, facing over the birch and osier toward the Potomac, just out of sight, save in winter when the trees were bare.

He needed a good, reliable, right-hand man; solid, trustworthy, loyal; one who would do as asked and not second-guess. He chose Kevin McBride. Except that both men were career "lifers," who had joined the company in their mid-twenties and served thirty years, they were as chalk and cheese. The Jesuit was lean and spare, working out daily in his private gym at home; McBride had thickened with the passing years, fond of his six-pack of beer on a weekend, most of the hair gone from the top and crown of his head. His annual "vetting" records showed he had a rock-stable marriage to Molly, two youngsters who had just left home, and a modest house in a residential development out beyond the Beltway. He had no private fortune and lived frugally off his salary.

Much of his career had been in foreign embassies, but never rising to chief of station. He was no threat, but a first-class Number Two. If you wanted something done, it would be done. You could rely on him. There would be no pseudointellectual philosophizing. McBride's values were traditional, down-home, American.

On October 12, 2000, twelve months into Project Peregrine, Al Qaeda struck again. This time the perpetrators were two Yemenis, and they committed suicide to achieve their goal. It was the first time the concept of suicide bomber had been evoked against U.S. armed forces since

1983 in Beirut. At the Twin Towers, Mogadishu, Dhahran, Nairobi, and Dar es Salaam, UBL had not demanded the supreme sacrifice. At Aden, he did. He was upping the stakes.

The USS *Cole*, a Burke-class destroyer, was moored in the harbor at the old British coaling station and one-time garrison at the tip of the Saudi peninsula. Yemen was the birthplace of UBL's father. The U.S. presence must have rankled.

Two terrorists in a fast inflatable packed with TNT roared through the flotilla of supply boats, rammed between the hull and the quay, and blew themselves up. Due to the compression between the hull and the concrete, a huge hole was torn. Inside the vessel, seventeen sailors died and thirty-nine were injured.

Devereaux had studied terror, its creation and infliction. He knew that whether imposed by the state or a nongovernmental source, it always divides into five levels.

At the top are the plotters, the planners, the authorizers, the inspirers. Next come the enablers, the facilitators, without whom no plan can work. They are in charge of recruiting, training, funding, supply. Third come the doers, those deprived of normal moral thought, who push the Zyklon B pellets into the gas chambers, plant the bombs, pull the triggers. At slot four are the active collaborators, those who guide the killers, denounce the neighbors, reveal the hiding places, betray the one-time school friends. At the bottom are the broad masses; bovine, stupid, saluting the tyrant, garlanding the murderers.

In the terror against the West in general, and the United States. in particular, Al Qaeda fulfilled the first two functions. Neither UBL nor his ideological Number Two, the Egyptian Ayman Al Zawahiri, not his Ops chief, Mohamed Atef, nor his international emissary, Abu Zubaydah, would ever need to plant a bomb or drive a truck.

The mosque schools, the *madrassahs*, would provide a stream of teenage fanatics, already impregnated with a deep hatred of the whole world that was not fundamentalist, plus a garbled version of a few distorted extracts of the Koran. To them could be added a few more mature converts, tricked into thinking that mass murder guaranteed Koranic paradise.

Al Qaeda would then simply devise, recruit, train, equip, direct, fund, and watch.

On his way back in the limousine from his blazing row with Colin Fleming, Devereaux once again examined the morality of what he was doing. Yes, the disgusting Serb had killed one American. Somewhere out there was a man who had killed fifty, and more to come.

He recalled that Fr. John Heaney had taxed him with a moral problem! "A man is coming at you, with intent to kill you. He has a knife. His total reach is four feet. You have the right of self-defense. You have no shield, but you have a spear. Its reach is nine feet. Do you lunge or wait?"

He would put pupil against pupil, each tasked to argue the opposite viewpoint. Devereaux never hesitated. The greater good against the lesser evil. Had the man with the spear sought the fight? No. Then he was entitled to lunge, not counterstrike; that came after surviving the initial strike. But preemptive strike. In the case of UBL, he had no qualms. To protect his country, Devereaux would kill, no matter how appalling the allies he had to call in aid. Fleming was wrong. He needed Zilic.

For Paul Devereaux there was an abiding enigma about his own country and its place in the world's affections, and he believed he had resolved it. About 1945, when he was born, and for the next decade through the Korean War and the start of the Cold War, the United States was not simply the richest and most militarily powerful country in the world, it was also the most loved, admired, and respected.

After fifty years, the first two qualities remained. The United States was stronger and richer than ever, the only remaining superpower, apparently mistress of all she surveyed.

And through great swathes of the world, black Africa, Islam, left-wing Europe, she was loathed with a passion.

What had gone wrong? It was a quandary that defied Capitol Hill and the media.

Devereaux knew his country was far from perfect; it made mistakes, often far too many. But it was in its heart as well meaning as any, and better than most. As a world traveler, he had seen a lot of that "most" at close range. Much of it was deeply ugly.

Most Americans could not comprehend the metamorphosis between 1951 and 2001, so they pretended it had not happened, accepting the Third World's polite mask for its inner feeling.

Had not Uncle Sam tried to preach democracy against tyranny? Had he not given away at least a trillion dollars in aid? Had he not picked up the hundred-billion-dollar-a-year defense tab for Western Europe for five decades? What justified the hate-you-hate-you demonstrations, the sacked embassies, the burnt flags, the vicious placards?

It was an old British spymaster who explained it to him in a London club in the late sixties as Vietnam became nastier and nastier and the riots erupted.

"My dear boy, if you were weak, you would not be hated. If you were poor, you would not be hated. You are not hated despite the trillion dollars; you are hated *because* of the trillion dollars."

The old bureaucrat gestured toward Grosvenor Square, where left-wing politicians and bearded students were massing to stone the embassy. "The hatred of your country is not because it attacks theirs; it is because it keeps theirs safe. Never seek popularity. You can have supremacy or be loved but never both. What is felt toward you is ten percent genuine disagreement and ninety percent envy. Never forget two things! No man can ever forgive his protector. There is no loathing that any man harbors more intense than that toward his benefactor."

The old spy was long dead, but Devereaux had seen the truth of his cynicism in half a hundred capitals. Like it or not, his country was the most powerful in the world. Once the Romans had that dubious honor. They had responded to the hatred with ruthless force of arms.

A hundred years ago, the British Empire had been the rooster. They had responded to the hatred with languid contempt. Now the Americans had it, and they wracked their consciences to ask where they had gone wrong. The Jesuit scholar and the secret agent had long made up his mind. In defense of his country, he would do what he believed had to be done and one day go to his Maker and ask forgiveness. Until then the America haters could take a long walk off a short jetty.

When he arrived at his office, Kevin McBride was waiting for him and his face was gloomy. "Our friend has been in touch," he said. "In a rage and a panic. He thinks he is being stalked."

Devereaux thought, not of the complainant, but of Fleming at the FBI. "Damn the man," he said. "Damn and blast him to hell. I never thought he'd do it and certainly not this fast."

22
THE PENINSULA

There was a secure computer link between a guarded enclave on the shore of the Republic of San Martin and a machine in McBride's office. Like Washington Lee, it used the Pretty Good Privacy (PGP) system of unbreakable cybercodes to keep communications from prying eyes; the difference was that this one had authority.

Devereaux studied the full text of the message from the south. It had clearly been written by the estate's head of security, the South African Van Rensberg. The English was overformal, as of one using their second language.

The meaning was clear enough. It described the Piper Cheyenne of the previous morning; its double pass, heading eastward toward French Guiana and then back again twenty minutes later. It reported the flash of sunlight off a camera lens in the right-hand window and even the registration number when it passed too low over the mountain pass in the escarpment. "Kevin, trace that aircraft. I need to know who owns it, who operates it, who flew it yesterday, and who was the passenger. And hurry."

In his anonymous apartment in Brooklyn, Cal Dexter had developed his seventy-two frames and blown them up to prints as large as he could before losing too much definition. From the same original negatives he had also made slides that he could project onto the wall screen for closer study. From the prints he had created, a single wall map running the length of the living room and from ceiling to floor. He sat for hours studying the wall, checking occasionally on a small detail with the appropriate slide. Each slide gave better and clearer detail, but only the wall gave the entire target. Whoever had been in charge of the project had spent millions and made of that once-empty peninsula a fearsome and ingenious fortress.

Nature had helped. The tongue of land was quite different from the hinterland of steamy jungle that made up much of the small republic. It jutted out from the main shore like a triangular dagger blade, but it was guarded on its landward side by the chain of hills that some primeval force had thrown up millions of years ago. The chain ran from the sea to the sea, and at each end dropped to the blue water in vertical cliffs. No one would ever walk round the ends to stroll from the jungle onto the peninsula.

On the landward side, the hills climbed gently from the littoral plain to about a thousand feet, with slopes covered in dense vegetation. Over the crests, on the seaward side, the slope was a vertiginous escarpment, denuded of any foliage, whether by nature or the hand of man. From the estate, anyone with binoculars looking up at the escarpment would easily see anything trying to descend onto the forbidden side.

There was one single col, or mountain pass, in the chain. A narrow track ran up to it from the hinterland then twisted and turned down the escarpment until it reached the estate below. In the mountain pass was a barrier and guardhouse, which Dexter had seen too late as it flashed below his window.

Dexter began to make a list of the equipment he would need. Getting in would not be a problem. It was getting out, bringing the target with him, and against a good-sized force of armed guards, *that* would be close to impossible.

"It belongs to a one-plane, one-man charter firm based at Georgetown, Guyana," said Kevin McBride that evening. "Lawrence Aero Enterprises, owned and run by George Lawrence, Guyanese citizen. It looks perfectly legitimate, the sort foreigners can charter to fly into the interior . . . or along the coast in this case."

"Is there a number for this Mr. Lawrence?" asked Devereaux.

"Sure. Here."

"Did you try to contact him?"

"No. The line would have to be open. And why would he discuss a client with a complete stranger on the phone? He might just tip the client off."

"You're right. You'll have to go. Use scheduled flights. Have Cassandra get you on the first flight. Trace Mr. Lawrence. Pay him if you have to. Find out who our inquisitive friend with the camera was and why he was there. Do we have a station in Georgetown?"

"No, next door. Caracas."

"Use Caracas for secure communications. I'll clear it with the station chief."

Studying his wall-sized photo montage, Cal Dexter's eye moved from the escarpment into the peninsula known simply as El Punto. Running along the base of the escarpment wall was a runway, taking up two-thirds of the fifteen hundred yards available. On the estate side of the runway was a chain-link fence that enclosed the entire airfield, hangar, workshops, fuel store, generator house, and all.

Using a pair of compasses and estimating the hangar length at one hundred feet, Dexter was able to start calculating and marking distances between points. These put the cultivated farmland at around three thousand acres. It was clear that centuries of wind-borne dust and bird droppings had created a rich soil, for he could see grazing herds and a variety of lush crops. Whoever had created El Punto had gone for complete self-sufficiency behind the ramparts of escarpment and ocean. The irrigation problem was solved by a glittering stream that erupted from the base of the hills and flowed through the estate before tumbling in a cataract into the sea. It could only originate in the high inland plateau and flow through the protective wall in an underground flue. Dexter noted the words: "Swim in?" Later he would cross them out. Without a rehearsal, it would be crazy to attempt a passage through an unknown underground tunnel. He recalled the terror inspired by crawling through the water traps of the tunnels of Cu Chi, and they were only a few yards long. This one could be miles, and he did not even know where it began.

At the base of the runway, beyond the wire, he could see a settlement of perhaps five hundred small white blocks, clearly dwelling units of some kind. There were dirt streets, some larger buildings for mess halls, and a small church. It was a village of sorts; but it was odd that, even with the men away in the fields and barns, there were no women or children on the streets. No gardens, no livestock. More like a penal colony. Perhaps those who served the man he sought had little choice in the matter.

He turned his attention to the main body of the agricultural estate. This contained all the cultivated fields, the flocks, barns, granaries, and a second settlement of low, white buildings. But a uniformed man standing outside indicated these were barracks for the security staff, guards, and overseers. By the look and the number and the size of the quarters, and the likely occupancy rate, he put the guards alone at around one hundred. There were five more substantial villas, with gardens, apparently for the senior officers and flight personnel.

The photographs and the slides were serving their purpose, but he needed two things more. One was a concept of three dimensions; the other was a knowledge of routines and procedures. The first would need a scale model of the whole peninsula; the second would require days of silent observation.

Kevin McBride flew the next morning from Dulles direct to Georgetown, Guyana, landing at 2:00 P.M. Formalities at the airport were simple, and with only a suitcase for a one-night stay, he was soon in a taxi.

Lawrence Aero Enterprises was not hard to find. Its small office was in a back alley off Waterloo Street. The American knocked several times, but there was no reply. The moist heat was beginning to drench his shirt. He peered through the dusty window and rapped again.

"Ain't no one there, man," said a helpful voice behind him. The speaker was old and gnarled; he sat a few doors away in a patch of deep shade and fanned himself with a disc of palm leaves.

"I'm looking for George Lawrence," said the American.

"You Briddish?"

"American."

The old-timer considered this as if the availability of charter pilot Lawrence was entirely down to nationality.

"Friend of yours?"

"No. I was thinking of chartering his plane for a flight, if I can find him."

"Ain't been there since yesterday," said the old man. "Not since they took him away."

"Who took him away, my friend?"

The old man shrugged, as if the abduction of neighbors was usual enough.

"The police?"

"No. Not them. They were white. Came in a rental car."

"Tourists . . . clients?" asked McBride.

"Maybe," admitted the sage. Then he had an idea. "You could try the airport. He keeps his plane there."

Fifteen minutes later, a sweat-drenched Kevin McBride was heading back to the airport. At the desk for private aviation he asked for George Lawrence. Instead he met Floyd Evans. Inspector Evans of the Georgetown Police Department.

He was taken back downtown yet again, this time in a patrol car, and was shown into an office where the air-conditioning was like a long-delayed cold bath and delicious. Inspector Evans toyed with his passport.

"What exactly are you doing in Guyana, Mr. McBride?" he asked.

"I was hoping to pay a short visit with a view to bringing my wife on vacation later," said the agent.

"In August? The salamanders shelter in August down here. Do you know Mr. Lawrence?"

"Well, no. I have a pal in Washington. He gave me the name. Said I might like to fly into the interior. Said Mr. Lawrence was about the best charter pilot. I just went to his office to see if he was available for charter. That's all. What did I do wrong?"

The inspector closed the passport and handed it back. "You arrived from Washington today. That seems clear enough. Your tickets and entry stamp confirm it. The Meridien Hotel confirms your one-night reservation."

"Look, Inspector, I still don't understand why I was brought here. Do you know where I can find George Lawrence?"

"Oh yes. Yes, he's in the mortuary down at our general hospital. Apparently he was taken from his office yesterday by three men in a rented 4 × 4. They checked it back in last night and flew out. Do these three names mean anything to you, Mr. McBride?" He passed a slip of paper over the desk. McBride glanced at the three names, all of which he knew to be false because he had issued them.

"No, sorry, they mean nothing to me. Why is Mr. Lawrence in the morgue?"

"Because he was found at dawn today by a vegetable seller coming to market, dead in a ditch by the roadside just out of town. You, of course, were still in the air."

"That's awful. I never met him, but I'm sorry."

"Yes, it is. We have lost our charter pilot. Mr. Lawrence lost his life and, as it happens, eight of his fingernails. His office has been gutted, and all records of past clients removed. What do you think his captors wanted of him, Mr. McBride?"

"I have no idea."

"Of course, I forgot. You are just a traveling salesman, are you not? Then I suggest you travel back home to the States, Mr. McBride. You are free to go."

"These people are animals," protested McBride to Devereaux down the secure line from Caracas Station to Langley.

"Come on home, Kevin," said his superior. "I'll ask our friend in the south what, if anything, he discovered."

Paul Devereaux had long cultivated a contact inside the FBI on the grounds that no man in his line of business could ever have too many sources of information and the Bureau was not likely to share with him the very gems that would constitute true brotherly love.

He had asked his "asset" to check in the archive database for files withdrawn by Assistant Director (Investigative Division) Colin Fleming since the request from on high had circulated regarding a murdered boy in Bosnia. Among the withdrawals was one marked simply AVENGER. Kevin McBride, weary and travel stained, arrived home the following morning.

Paul Devereaux was in his office as early as usual and crisply laundered. He handed a file to his subordinate. "That's him," he said, "our interloper. I spoke with our friend in the south. Of course, it was three of his thugs who

brutalized the charter pilot. And you were right. They are
animals. But right now they are vital animals. Pity, but
unavoidable."

He tapped the file. "Code name Avenger. Age around
fifty. Height, build . . . it's all in the file. There is a brief
description. Now masquerading as U.S. citizen Alfred
Barnes. That was the man who chartered the deeply unfor-
tunate Mr. Lawrence to fly him over our friend's hacienda.
And there is no Alfred Barnes matching that description on
State Department files as a U.S. passport holder. Find him,
Kevin, and stop him. In his tracks."

"I hope you don't mean terminate."

"No, that is forbidden. I mean, identify. If he uses one
false name, he may have others. Find the one he will try
to use to enter San Martin. Then inform the appalling but
efficient Colonel Moreno in San Martin. I am sure he can
be relied on to do what has to be done."

Kevin McBride retired to his own office to read the file.
He already knew the chief of the secret police of the Republic of San Martin. Any opponent of the dictator falling
into his hands would die, probably slowly. He read the
Avenger file with his habitual great care.

Over two hundred miles away, in New York City, the passport of Alfred Barnes was consigned to the flames. Dexter
had not a clue or shred of proof that he had been seen, but
as he and charter pilot Lawrence had flown over the mountain pass in the sierra, he had been jolted to see a face
staring up at him, close enough to take the Cessna's number. So, just in case, Alfred Barnes ceased to exist.

That done, he began to build his model of the fortress
hacienda. Across the city, in downtown Manhattan, Mrs.
Nguyen Van Tran was myopically poring over three new
passports.

It was August 3, 2001.

23

THE VOICE

If it is not available in New York, it probably doesn't exist. Cal Dexter used a lumber shop to create a trestle table with a top of inch-thick ply that almost filled his living room.

Art shops furnished enough paints to create the sea and the land in ten different hues. Green baize from fabric shops made fields and meadows. Wooden building blocks were used for scores of houses and barns; Model Makers Emporium provided balsa wood, fast-drying glue, and paste-on designs of brickwork, doors, and windows.

The runaway Serb's mansion at the tip of the peninsula was made of LEGOs from a children's store, and the rest of the landscape was down to a magical warehouse providing for model railway enthusiasts.

Railway modelers want entire landscapes, with hills and

valleys, cuttings and tunnels, farms and grazing animals. Within three days Dexter had fashioned the entire hacienda to scale. All he could not see was what was out of sight to his airborne camera: booby traps, pitfalls, the work force, security locks, gate chains, the full strength of the private army, their equipment, and all interiors.

It was a long list and most of the queries on it could only be solved by days of patient observation. Still, he had decided his way in, his battle plan, and his way out. He went on a buying spree.

Boots, jungle clothing, K rations, cutters, the world's most powerful binoculars, a new cell phone . . . He filled a haversack that finally weighed close to eighty pounds. And then there was more; for some he had to go out of state to places in the United States with more lax laws, for others he had to dive into the underworld, and others were quite legal but raised eyebrows. By August 10th, he was ready and so were his first ID papers.

"Spare a moment, Paul?"

Kevin McBride's yeoman face came around the edge of the door and Devereaux beckoned him in. His deputy brought with him a large-scale map of the northern coast of South America, from Venezuela east to French Guiana. He spread it out and tapped the triangle between the Commini and Maroni Rivers, the Republic of San Martin.

"I figure he'll go in by the overland route," said McBride.

"Take the air route. San Martin City has the only airport, and it is small. Served only twice daily and then only by local airlines coming from Cayenne to the east or Paramaribo to the west." His finger stabbed at the capitals of French Guiana and Suriname.

"It's such a god-awful place politically that hardly any businessmen go and no tourists. Our man is white, American, and we have his approximate height and build, both from the file and from what that charter pilot described

before he died. Colonel Moreno's goons would have him
within minutes of debarkation. More to the point, he'd have
to have a valid visa and that means visiting San Martin's
only two consulates: Paramaribo and Caracas. I don't think
he'll try the airport."

"No dispute. But Moreno should still put it under night
and day surveillance. He might try a private plane," said
Devereaux.

"I'll brief him on that. Next, the sea. There is just one
port; San Martin City again. No tourist craft ever puts in
there, just freighters and not many of them. The crews are
Indians, Filipinos, or Creoles; he'd stand out like a sore
thumb if he tried to come in openly as a crewman or passenger."

"He could come in off the sea in a fast inflatable."

"Possible, but that would have to have been hired or
bought in either French Guiana or Suriname. Or he could
be dropped offshore from a freighter whose captain he has
bribed for the job. He could motor in from twenty miles
off the coast, dump the inflatable, puncture it, sink it. Then
what?"

"What indeed?" murmured Devereaux.

"I figure he will need equipment, a heavy load of it.
Where does he make landfall? There are no beaches along
San Martin's coast, except here at La Bahia. But that's full
of the villas of the rich with bodyguards, night watchmen,
and dogs.

"Apart from that, the coast is tangled mangrove, infested
with snakes and crocodiles. How is he to march through
all that? If he gets to the main east-west road, what then?
I don't think it's on, even for a Green Beret."

"Could he land off the sea right on our friend's peninsula?"

"No, Paul, he couldn't. It's girded on all seaward sides
by cliffs and pounding surf. Even if he got up the cliffs
with grappling irons, the roaming dogs would hear the
noise and have him."

"So he comes in by land. From which end?"

McBride used his forefinger again. "I reckon from the west, from Suriname, on the passenger ferry across the Commini, straight into the San Martin border post, on four wheels, with false papers."

"He'd still need a San Martin visa, Kevin."

"And where better to get it than right there in Suriname, one of the only two consulates they run? I reckon that's the logical place for him to acquire his car and his visa."

"So what's your plan?"

"The Suriname Embassy here in Washington and the consulate in Miami. He'll need a visa to get in there as well. I want to put them both on full alert to go back a week, and from now on pass me details of every single applicant for a tourist visa. Then I check every one with the passport section at State."

"You're putting all your eggs in one basket, Kevin."

"Not really. Colonel Moreno and his Ojos Negros can cover the eastern border, the airport, the docks, and the coast. I'd like to back my hunch our interloper will logically try to get all his kit into San Martin by car out of Suriname. It's far and away the busiest crossing point."

Devereaux smiled at McBride's attempt at Spanish. The San Martin Secret Police were known as "Black Eyes" because they and their wraparound black sunglasses struck terror into the peons of San Martin. He thought of all the U.S. aid heading in that direction. There was no doubt the Suriname Embassy would cooperate to the full.

"OK, I like it. Go for it. But hurry."

McBride was puzzled. "We have a deadline, boss?"

"Tighter than you know, my friend."

The port of Wilmington, Delaware, is one of the largest and busiest on the East Coast of the United States. High at the top of the long Delaware Bay that leads from the river to the Atlantic, it has miles of sheltered water, which, apart from taking the big ocean liners, also plays host to thousands of small coastal freighters.

The Carib Coast Ship and Freight Company was an
agency handling cargoes for scores of such smaller ships
and the visit of Mr. Ronald Proctor caused no surprise. He
was friendly, charming, convincing, and his rented U-Haul
pickup was right outside with the crate in the rear.

The freight clerk who handled his inquiry had no reason
to doubt his veracity, all the more so when, in response to
the query, "Do you have documentation, sir?" he produced
precisely that.

His passport was not only in perfect order, it was a diplomatic passport at that. Supporting letters and movement
orders from the State Department proved that Ronald Proctor, a professional U.S. diplomat, was being transferred to
his country's embassy in Paramaribo, Suriname.

"We have a cost-free allowance, of course, but what with
my wife's passion for collecting things on our travels, I
fear we're one crate over the limit. I'm sure you know what
wives are like? Boy, can they collect stuff."

"Tell me about it," agreed the clerk. Few things bond
male strangers like commiserating about their wives. "We
have a freighter heading down to Miami, Caracas, and
Parbo in two days."

He gave the capital of Suriname its shorter and more
common name. The consignment was agreed and paid for.
The crate would be seaborne within two days and in a
bonded warehouse by Parbo docks by the twentieth. Being
diplomatic cargo, it would be customs exempt when Mr.
Proctor called to collect it.

The Suriname Embassy in Washington is at 4301 Con-
necticut Avenue, and it was there that Kevin McBride
flashed his identity as a senior officer of the Central Intelligence Agency and sat down with an impressed consular
official in charge of the visa section. It was probably not
the busiest diplomatic office in Washington, and one man
handled all visa applications.

"We believe he deals in drugs and consorts with terrorists," said the CIA man. "So far he remains very shady. His name is not important because he will certainly apply, if at all, under a false identity. But we do believe he may try to slip into Suriname as a way of cutting across to Guyana and thence to rejoin his cronies in Venezuela."

"You have a photo of him?" asked the official.

"Alas, not yet," said McBride. "That is where we hope you might be able to help us if he comes here. We have a description of him."

He slipped a sheet of paper across the desk with a short, two-line description of a man of about fifty; five feet, eight inches; compact; muscular build; blue eyes; sandy hair.

McBride left with photocopies of the nineteen applications for visas to Suriname that had been lodged and granted in the previous week. Within three days all had been checked out as legitimate U.S. citizens whose details and passport photos lodged with the State Department fully matched those presented to the Suriname Consulate.

If the elusive Avenger of the file Devereaux had ordered him to memorize was going to show up, he had not done so yet.

In truth, McBride was in the wrong consulate. Suriname is not large and certainly not rich. It maintains consulates in Washington and Miami, plus Munich (but not in the German capital of Berlin) and two in the former colonial power, the Netherlands. One is in The Hague, but the bigger office is at 11 De Cuserstraat, Amsterdam.

It was in this office that Ms. Amelie Dykstra, a locally recruited Dutch lady paid for by the Dutch Ministry of Foreign Affairs, was being so helpful to the visa applicant before her.

"You are British, Mr. Nash?"

The passport she had in her hand showed that Mr. Henry Nash was indeed British, and his profession was that of businessman.

"What is the purpose of your visit to Suriname?" asked Ms. Dykstra.

"My company develops new tourist outlets, notably resort hotels in coastal situations," said the Englishman. "I am hoping to see if there are any openings in your country, well, Suriname, that is, before moving on to Venezuela."

"You should see the Ministry of Tourism," said the Dutch girl, who had never been to Suriname.

From what Cal Dexter had researched about that malarial coast, such a ministry was likely to be an exercise in optimism over reality.

"Precisely my intention, as soon as I get there, dear lady."

He pleaded a last flight waiting at Schiphol Airport, paid his thirty-five guilders, got his visa, and left. In truth, his plane was not for London but for New York.

McBride headed south again, to Miami and Suriname. A car from San Martin met the CIA officer at Parbo airport and he was driven east to the Commini River crossing point. The Ojos Negros who escorted him simply drove to the head of the queue, commandeered the ferry, and paid no toll to cross to the San Martin side.

During the crossing, McBride stepped out of the car to watch the sluggish brown liquid passing down to the aquamarine sea, but the haze of mosquitoes and the drenching heat drove him back to the interior of the Mercedes and its welcome cool air. The secret policemen sent by Colonel Moreno permitted themselves wintry smiles at such stupidity. But behind the black glasses, their eyes were blank.

It was forty miles over bumpy, potholed, road from the river border to San Martin City. The road ran through jungle on both sides. Somewhere to the left of the road, the jungle would give way to the swamps, the swamps to the mangrove tangle, and eventually to the inaccessible sea. To the right the dense rain forest ran away inland, rising gently, to the confluence of the Commini and the Maroni, and thence into Brazil. *A man,* thought McBride, *could be lost in there within half a mile.* Occasionally he saw a track running off the road and into the bush, no doubt to some small farm or plantation not far from the road. Down the highway they passed a few vehicles, mostly pickups or battered Land Rovers clearly used by better-off farmers and occasionally a cyclist with a basket of produce above the rear wheel, his livelihood on its way to market.

There were a dozen small villages along the journey, and the man from Washington was struck at the different ethnic type of the San Martin peasant from those one republic back. There was a reason. All the other colonial powers, conquering and trying to settle virtually empty landscapes, planted their estates and then looked for a labor force. The local Indios took one peek at what was in store and vaporized into the jungle.

Most of the colonialists imported African slaves from the properties they already owned or traded with along the West African coast. The descendants of these, usually mixing the genes with the Indios and whites, had created the modern populations. But the Spanish Empire was almost totally New World, not African. They did not have an easy source of black slaves, but they did have millions of landless Mexican peons; and the distance from Yucatan to Spanish Guiana was much shorter.

The wayside peasants McBride was seeing through the windows of the Mercedes were walnut-hued from the sun, but they were not black nor Creole. The whole labor force of San Martin was still genetically Hispanic.

When Shakespeare's Caesar expressed the wish to have fat men around him, he presumed they would be jolly and amiable. He was not thinking of Col. Hernan Moreno.

The man who was credited with keeping the gaudy and massively decorated President Muñoz in the palace on the hill behind the capital of this last banana republic was fat like a brooding toad, but he was not jolly. The torments practiced on those he suspected of sedition, or to be in possession of details of such people, were hinted at only in the lowest whispers and the darkest corners.

There was a place, up-country it was rumored, for such
things, and no one ever came back. Dumping cadavers at
sea, like the secret police of Galtieri in Argentina, was not
necessary; it was not even required to break a sweat with
a shovel and pick. A naked body pegged out in the jungle
would attract fire ants, and fire ants can do to soft tissue in
a night what normal nature needs months or years to
achieve.

He knew the man from Langley was coming and chose
to offer him lunch at the yacht club. It was the best restaurant in town, certainly the most exclusive, and it was located at the base of the harbor wall facing out over a
glittering blue sea. More to the point, the sea winds at last
triumphed over the stench of the back streets.

Unlike his employer, the secret police chief avoided ostentation, uniforms, medals, and glitz; his pinguid frame
was encased in a black shirt and black suit. If there had
been a hint of nobility in his features, thought the CIA man,
he might have resembled Orson Welles toward the end. But
the face was more Hermann Goering.

Nevertheless, his grip on the small and impoverished
country was absolute, and he listened without interruption.
He knew exactly the relationship between the refugee from
Yugoslavia who had sought sanctuary in San Martin and
now lived in an enviable mansion at the end of a piece of
property Moreno himself hoped one day to acquire, as did
the president. He knew of the huge wealth of the refugee
and the annual fee he paid to President Muñoz for sanctuary
and protection, even though that protection was really provided by himself.

What he did not know was why a very senior hierarchy
in Washington had chosen to bring together the refugee and
the tyrant. It mattered not. The Serb had spent over five
million dollars building his mansion and another ten on his
estate. Despite the inevitable imports to achieve such a feat,
half that money had been spent inside San Martin, with tidy
percentages going to Colonel Moreno on every contract.

More directly, Moreno took a fee for providing the slave

labor force and keeping the numbers topped off with fresh arrests and detainees. So long as no peon ever escaped or came back alive, it was a lucrative and safe arrangement. The CIA man did not need to beg for his cooperation.

"If he sets one foot inside San Martin," he wheezed, "I will have him. You will not see him again, but every piece of information he divulges will be passed on to you. On that you have my word."

On his way back to the river crossing and the waiting plane at Parbo, McBride thought of the mission the unseen bounty hunter had set himself; he thought of the defenses, and the price of failure—death at the hands of Colonel Moreno and his Black-Eyed experts in pain. He shuddered, and it was not from the air-conditioning.

Thanks to the wonders of modern technology, Calvin Dexter did not need to return to Pennington to collect any messages left on the answering machine attached to his office telephone. He could make the collections from a public phone booth in Brooklyn. He did so on August 15th. The cluster of messages was mainly from voices he knew before the speakers identified themselves. Neighbors, legal clients, local businessmen, mainly wishing him a happy fishing vacation and asking when he would be back at his desk.

It was the second to last message that almost caused him to drop the phone, to stare, unseeing, at the traffic rushing past the glass of the booth. When he had replaced the handset, he walked for an hour trying to work out how it had happened, who had leaked his name and business, and, most important of all, whether the anonymous voice was that of a friend or a betrayer.

The voice did not identify the speaker. It was flat, monotone, as if coming through several layers of paper tissue. It said simply: "Avenger, be careful. They know you are coming."

24
THE PLAN

When Prof. Medvers Watson left the Surinamese consul, the official was feeling slightly breathless, so much so, he very nearly excluded the academic from the list of visa applicants he was sending to Kevin McBride at a private address in the city.

"Callicore maronensis," beamed the professor when asked for the reason he wished to visit Suriname. The consul looked blank. Seeing his perplexity, Professor Watson delved into his attaché case and produced Andrew Neild's masterwork: *The Butterflies of Venezuela.*

"It's been seen, you know. Unbelievable."

He whipped open the reference work at a page of colored photographs of butterflies that, to the consul, looked pretty similar, barring slight variations of marking to the back wings.

"One of the Limenitidinae, you know. Subfamily, of course. Like the Charaxinae. Both derived from the Nymphalidae."

The bewildered consul found himself being educated in the descending order of family, subfamily, genus, species, and subspecies.

"But what do you want to do about them?" asked the consul. Prof. Medvers Watson closed his almanac with a snap. "Photograph them, my dear sir. Find them and photograph them. Apparently there has been a sighting. Until now the *Agrias narcissus* was about as rare as it gets in the jungles of your hinterlands, but the Callicore maronensis? Now that would make history. That is why I must go without delay. The autumn monsoon, you know. Not far off."

The consul stared at the U.S. passport. Stamps for Venezuela were frequent. Others for Brazil, Guyana. He unfolded the letter on the headed paper of the Smithsonian Institution. Professor Watson was warmly endorsed by the head of the Department of Entomology, Division Lepidoptera. He nodded slowly. Science, environment, ecology, these were the things not to be gainsaid or denied in the modern world. He stamped the visa and handed back the passport.

Professor Watson did not ask for the letter, so it stayed on the desk.

"Well, good hunting," the consul said weakly.

Two days later Kevin McBride walked into the office of Paul Devereaux with a broad smile on his face. "I think we have him," he said. He laid down a completed application form of the type issued by the Suriname Consulate and filled out by the applicant for a visa. A passport-sized photo stared up from the page.

Devereaux read through the details. "So?"

McBride laid a letter beside the form. Devereaux read that as well. "And?"

"And he's a phoney. There is no U.S. passport holder in the name of Medvers Watson. State Department is adamant on that. He should have picked a more common name.

This one sticks out like a sore thumb. The scholars at the Smithsonian have never heard of him. No one in the butterfly world has ever heard of Medvers Watson."

Devereaux stared at the picture of the man who had tried to ruin his covert operation and thus had become, albeit unwittingly, his enemy. The eyes looked owlish behind the glasses, and the straggly goatee weakened instead of strengthened the face.

"Well done, Kevin. Brilliant strategy. But then, it worked; and of course all that works becomes brilliant. Every detail immediately to Colonel Moreno in San Martin, if you please. He may move quickly."

"And the Suriname government in Parbo."

"No, not them. No need to disturb their slumbers."

"Paul, they could arrest him the moment he flies into Parbo airport. Our embassy boys could confirm the passport is a forgery. The Surinamese can charge him with passport fraud and put him on the next plane back with two of our marines as escort. We arrest him on touchdown, and he's in the slammer, out of harm's way."

"Kevin, listen to me. I know it's rough, and I know the reputation of Moreno. But if our man has a big stack of dollars, he could elude arrest in Suriname. Back here he could bail within a day, then skip."

"But, Paul, Moreno is an animal. You wouldn't send your worst enemy into his grip. . . ."

"And you don't know how important the Serb is to all of us. Nor his paranoia. Nor how tight his schedule may be. He has to know the danger to himself is over, totally eliminated, or he will bow out of what I need him for."

"And you still can't tell me?"

"Sorry, Kevin. No, not yet."

His deputy shrugged, unhappy but obedient. "OK, on your conscience, not mine."

And that was the problem, thought Paul Devereaux when he was once again alone in his office staring out at the thick green foliage between him and the Potomac.

Could he square his conscience with what he was doing? He had to. The lesser evil, the greater good.

The unknown man with the false passport would not die easily, "upon the midnight with no pain." But he had chosen to swim in hideously dangerous waters, and it had been his decision to do so.

That day, August 18th, America sweltered in the summer heat, and half the country sought relief in the seas, rivers, lakes, and mountains. Down on the north coast of South America there was 100 percent humidity sweeping in from the steaming jungles behind the coast, adding ten more degrees to the hundred caused by the sun.

In Parbo docks, ten miles up the teak-brown Suriname River from the sea, the heat was like a tangible blanket lying over the warehouses and quays. The pye-dogs tried to find the deepest shade to pant away the hours until sundown. Humans sat under slow-moving fans, which merely moved the discomfort around a bit.

The foolish tossed down sugary drinks, sodas and colas, which merely made the thirst and dehydration worse. The experienced stayed with piping hot, sweet tea, which may sound crazy but was discovered by the British empire builders two centuries earlier to be the best rehydrator of them all.

The fifteen-hundred-ton freighter, *Tobago Star*, crept up the river, docked at her assigned pier, and waited for dark. In the cooler dusk, she discharged her cargo, which included a bonded crate in the name of U.S. diplomat Ronald Proctor. This went into a chain-link fenced section of the warehouse to await collection.

Paul Devereaux had spent years studying terrorism in general and the types that emanated from the Arab and Muslim world, not necessarily the same type in particular. He had long come to the conclusion that the conventional whine in the West, that terrorism stemmed from the poverty and destitution of those whom Fanon had called "the wretched of the earth" was convenient and politically correct psycho-babble.

From the anarchists of tsarist Russia to the IRA of 1916, from the Irgun and the Stern Gang to the EOKA in Cyprus, from the Baader-Meinhof group in Germany, the CCC in Belgium, the Action Directe in France, the Red Brigades in Italy, the Red Army Faction again in Germany, the Rengo Sekigun in Japan, through to the Shining Path in Peru to the modern IRA in Ulster or the ETA in Spain, terrorism came from the minds of the comfortably raised, well-educated, middle-class theorists with a truly staggering personal vanity and a developed taste for self-indulgence.

In the Devereaux theory, those who could order another to plant a bomb in a food hall and gloat over the resultant images all had one thing in common. They possessed a fearsome capacity for hatred. This was the genetic "given." The hatred came first; the target could come later and usually did.

The motive also came second to the capacity to hate. It might be the Bolshevik Revolution, national liberation, or a thousand variants thereof, from amalgamation to secession; it might be anticapitalist fervor; it might be religious exaltation.

But the hatred came first, then the cause, then the target, then the methods, and finally the self-justification. And Lenin's "useful dupes" always swallowed it.

Devereaux was utterly convinced that the leadership of Al Qaeda ran precisely true to form. Its cofounders were a construction millionaire from Saudi Arabia and a qualified doctor from Cairo. It mattered not whether their hatred of Americans and Jews was secular based or religiously fueled. There was nothing, absolutely nothing that America or Israel could do, short of complete self-annihilation, that would even begin to appease or satisfy them.

None of them, for him, cared a damn for the Palestinians save as vehicles and justifications. They hated his country, not for what it did, but for what it was.

He recalled the old British spy chief in the window table

at White's as the left-wing demonstrators went by. Apart
from the usual snowy-haired British socialists who could
never quite get over the death of Lenin, there were the
British boys and girls who would one day get a mortgage
and vote Conservative, and there were the torrents of students from the Third World.

"They'll never forgive you, dear boy," the old man had
said. "Never expect it, and you'll never be disappointed.
Your country is a constant reproach. It is rich to their poor,
strong to their weak, vigorous to their idle, enterprising to
their reactionaries, ingenious to their bewildered, can-do to
their sit-and-wait, thrusting to their timid.

"It only needs one demagogue to arise and shout, 'Everything the Americans have they stole from you,' and
they'll believe it. Like Shakespeare's Caliban, their zealots
stare in the mirror and roar in rage at what they see. That
rage becomes hatred; the hatred needs a target. The working
class of the Third World does not hate you; it is the pseudo-
intellectuals. If they ever forgive you, they must indict
themselves. So far their hatred lacks the weaponry. One day
they will acquire that weaponry. Then you will have to fight
or die. Not in tens but in tens of thousands."

Thirty years down the line, Devereaux was sure the old
Brit had got it right. After Somalia, Kenya, Tanzania,
Yemen, his country was in a new war and did not know it.

The Jesuit had asked for the front line and got it. Now
he had to do something with his command. His response
was Project Peregrine. He did not intend to seek to negotiate with UBL, nor even respond after the next strike. He
intended to try to destroy his country's enemy before that
strike. In Father Heaney's analogy, he intended to use his
spear to lunge, before the knife tip came in range. This
problem was: where? Not more or less, not "somewhere in
Afghanistan," but where to ten yards by ten yards, and
when to thirty minutes.

He knew a strike was coming. They all did. Dick Clarke
at the White House, Tom Pickard at the Bureau headquarters in the Hoover Building, George Tenet one floor above

his head at Langley. All the whispers out on the street said
"a big one" was in preparation. It was the where, when,
what, how, they did not know, and thanks to the crazy rules
forbidding them to ask nasty people, they were not likely
to find out. That, plus the refusal to collate what they did
have.

Paul Devereaux was so disenchanted with the whole lot
of them that he had prepared his Peregrine plan and would
tell no one what it was. In his reading of tens of thousands
of pages about terror in general and Al Qaeda in particular,
one theme had come endlessly through the fog. The Islamist terrorists would not be satisfied with a few dead Americans from Mogadishu to Dar es Salaam. UBL would want
hundreds of thousands. The prediction of the long-gone
Britisher was coming true.

For those kind of figures, the Al Qaeda leadership would
need a technology they did not yet have but endlessly
sought to acquire. Devereaux knew that in the cave complexes of Afghanistan, which were not simply holes in
rocks but subterranean labyrinths including laboratories, ex-
periments had been started with germs and gases. But they
were still miles from the methods of mass dissemination.

For Al Qaeda, as for all the terror groups in the world,
there was one prize beyond rubies: fissionable material.
Any one of at least a dozen killer groups would give their
eye teeth, take crazy risks, to acquire the basic element of
a nuclear device.

It would never have to be an ultramodern "clean" war-
head; indeed, the more basic, the "dirtier" in radiation
terms, the better. Even at the level of their in-house scientists, the terrorists knew that enough fissionable element,
jacketed within enough plastic explosive, would create
enough lethal radiation over enough square miles to make
a city the size of New York uninhabitable for a generation.
And that would be apart from the three million people ir-
radiated into an early cancerous grave.

It had been a decade, and the underground war had been
costly and intense. So far the West, assisted by Moscow

more recently, had won it and survived. Huge sums had
been spent buying up any fragment of uranium 235 or plu-
tonium that came near to private sale. Entire countries, former Soviet republics, had handed over every gram left
behind by Moscow, and the local dictators, under the pro-
visions of the Nunn-Lugar Act, had become very wealthy.
But there was too much, far too much, quite simply missing.

Just after he founded his own tiny section in Counterterrorism at Langley, Paul Devereaux noticed two things.
One was that a hundred pounds of pure, weapons-grade
uranium 235 was lodged at the secret Vinca Institute in the
heart of Belgrade. As soon as Milosevic fell, the United
States began to negotiate its purchase. Just a third of it,
thirty-three pounds or fifteen kilograms, would be enough
for one bomb.

The other thing was that a vicious Serbian gangster and
intimate at the court of Milosevic wanted out before the
roof fell in. He needed "cover," new papers, protection, and
a place to disappear to. Devereaux knew that place could
never be the United States. But a banana republic . . . Devereaux cut him a deal, and he cut him a price. The price
was collaboration.

Before he quit Belgrade, a thumbnail-sized sample of
uranium 235 was stolen from the Vinca Institute, and the
records were changed to show that a full fifteen kilograms
were really missing.

Six months earlier, introduced by the arms dealer, Vladimir Bout, the runaway Serb had handed over his sample
and documentary proof that he possessed the remaining fifteen kilos.

The sample had gone to Al Qaeda's chemist and physicist, Abu Khabab, another highly educated and fanatical
Egyptian. It had necessitated his leaving Afghanistan and
quietly traveling to Iraq to secure the equipment he needed
to test the sample properly.

In Iraq, another nuclear program was underway. It also
sought weapons-grade uranium 235, but was making it the

slow, old-fashioned way, with calutrons like the ones used in 1945 at Oak Ridge, Tennessee. The sample caused great excitement.

Just four weeks before the circulation of that damnable report compiled by a Canadian magnate concerning his long-dead grandson, word had come through that Al Qaeda would deal. Devereaux had to force himself to stay very calm.

For his killing machine, he had wanted to use an un-manned, high-altitude drone called the Predator, but it had crashed just outside Afghanistan. Its wreckage was now back in the United States, but the hitherto unarmed UAV was being "weaponized" by the fitting of a Hellfire missile so that it could in future, not only see a target from the stratosphere, but blow it to bits as well. But the conversion would take too long. Paul Devereaux revamped his plan, but he had to delay it while different weaponry was put in place. Only when they were ready could the Serb accept the invitation to journey to Peshawar, Pakistan, there to meet with Kawaheri, Atef, Zubaydah, and the physicist Abu Khabab. He would carry with him fifteen kilos of uranium, but not weapons grade. Yellowcake would do, normal re-actor fuel, isotope 235, 3 percent refined, not the needed 88 percent.

At the crucial meeting, Zoran Zilic was going to pay for all the favors he had been accorded. If he did not, he would be destroyed by a single phone call to Pakistan's lethal and pro–Al Qaeda secret service, the ISI. He would suddenly double the price and threaten to leave if his new price was not met. Devereaux was gambling there was only one man who could make that decision, and he would have to be consulted.

Far away in Afghanistan, UBL would have to take that phone call. High above, rolling in space, a listener satellite linked to the National Security Agency would hear the call and pinpoint its destination to a place ten feet by ten feet.

Would the man at the Afghan end wait around? Could he contain his curiosity to learn whether he had just become

the owner of enough uranium to fulfill his most deadly
dreams?

Off the Baluchi coast, the nuclear sub USS *Columbia*
would open her hatches to emit a single Tomahawk cruise
missile. Even as it flew, it would be programmed by the
Global Positioning System (GPS) plus Terrain Contour
Matching (TERCOM) and Digital Scene Matching Area
Correlation (DSMAC).

Three navigational systems would guide it to that
hundred-square-foot target and blow the entire area con-
taining the mobile phone to pieces, including the man
waiting for his callback from Peshawar. For Devereaux, the
problem was time. The moment when Zoran would have
to leave for Peshawar, pausing at Ra's al Khaymah to pick
up the Russian, was moving ever closer. He could not afford to let Zoran panic and withdraw on the grounds that
he was a hunted man and thus their deal was null and void.
Avenger had to be stopped and probably destroyed. Lesser
evil, greater good.

It was August 20th. A man descended from the Dutch KLM
airliner straight in from Curaçao to Paramaribo airport. It
was not Prof. Medvers Watson, for whom a reception committee waited further down the coast.

It was not even the U.S. diplomat, Ronald Proctor, for
whom a crate waited at the docks.

It was the British resort-developer, Henry Nash. With
his Amsterdam-delivered visa, he passed effortlessly
through Customs and Immigration and took a taxi into
town. It would have been tempting to book in at the To-
rarica, far and away the best hotel in town. But he might
have met real Britishers there, so he went to the Krasnopolsky on the Dominiestraat. His room was on the top floor,
with a balcony facing east. The sun was behind him when
he went out for a look over the city. The extra height gave
a hint of breeze to make the dusk bearable. Far to the east,
seventy miles away and over the river, the jungles of San
Martin were waiting.

PART THREE

25
THE JUNGLE

It was the American diplomat, Ronald Proctor, who leased the car. It was not even from an established agency but from a private seller advertising in the local paper.

The Cherokee was secondhand but in good repair and with a bit of work and a thorough service, which its U.S. Army–trained new owner intended to give it, it would do what it had to.

The deal he made the vendor was simple and sweet. He would pay ten thousand dollars in cash. He would only need the vehicle for a month, until his own 4×4 came through from the States. If he returned it absolutely intact in thirty days, the vendor would take it back and reimburse five thousand dollars.

The seller was looking at an effort-free five thousand

dollars in a month. Given that the man facing him was a charming American diplomat, and the Cherokee might come back in thirty days, it seemed foolish to go through all the trouble of changing the documents. Why alert the tax man? Proctor also rented the lock-up garage and storage shed behind the flower and produce market. Finally, he went to the docks and signed for his single crate, which went into the garage to be carefully unpacked and repacked in two canvas knapsacks. Then Ronald Proctor simply ceased to exist.

In Washington, Paul Devereaux was gnawed by anxiety and curiosity as the days dragged by. Where was this man? Had he used his visa and entered Suriname? Was he on his way?

The easy way to indulge the temptation would be to ask the Suriname authorities directly, via the U.S. Embassy on Redmondstraat, but that would trigger Surinamese curiosity. They would want to know why. They would pick him up themselves and start asking questions. The man called Avenger could arrange to be set free and start again. The Serb, already becoming paranoid at the thought of going to Peshawar, could panic and call the deal off. So Devereaux paced and prowled and waited.

Down in Paramaribo the tiny consulate of San Martin had been tipped off by Colonel Moreno that an American pretending to be a collector of butterflies might apply for a visa. It was to be granted immediately, and he was to be informed at once.

But no one called Medvers Watson appeared. The man they sought was sitting at a terrace café in the middle of Parbo with his last purchases in a sack beside him. It was August 24th.

What he had bought had come from the town's only camping and hunting shop, the Tackle Box on Zwarten Hovenbrug Street. As the London businessman, Henry Nash, he had brought almost nothing that would be useful across the border. But with the contents of the diplomat's crate and what he had acquired that morning, he could think of nothing he might be missing. So he tilted back his Parbo beer and enjoyed the last he was going to have for some time.

Those who waited were rewarded on the morning of the 25th. The line at the river crossing was, as ever, slow, and the mosquitoes, as ever, dense. Those crossing were almost entirely locals, with pedal bikes, motorcycles, and rusty pickups, all loaded with produce.

There was only one smart car in the line on the Suriname side, a black Cherokee, with a white man at the wheel. He wore a creased seersucker jacket in cream, off-white Panama hat, and heavy-rimmed glasses. Like the others he sat and swatted, then moved a few yards forward as the chain ferry took on a fresh cargo and cranked back across the Commini.

After an hour he was at last on the flat iron deck of the ferry, handbrakes on, able to step down and watch the river. On the San Martin side, he joined the line of six cars awaiting clearance.

The San Martin checkpoint was tighter, and there seemed to be a tension among the dozen guards who milled around. The road was blocked by a stripped pole laid over two recently added oil drums weighted with concrete. In the shed to one side, an immigration officer studied all papers, his head visible through the window. The Surinamese, here to visit relatives or buy produce to sell back in Parbo, must have wondered why, but patience has never been rationed in the Third World nor information a glut. They sat and waited again. It was almost dusk when the Cherokee rolled to the barrier. A soldier flicked his fingers for the needed passport, took it from the American, and handed it through the window.

The off-road driver seemed nervous. He sweated in rivers. He made no eye contact but stared ahead. From time to time he glanced sideways through the booth window. It was during one of these glances that he saw the immigration officer start violently and grab his phone. That was when the traveler with the wispy goatee panicked.

The engine suddenly roared; the clutch was let in. The heavy black 4×4 threw itself forward, knocked a soldier flying with the rearview mirror, tossed the stripped pole in the air, and burst through, swerving crazily around the trucks ahead and charging off into the dusk.

Behind the Cherokee there was chaos. Part of the flying pole had whacked the army officer in the face. The immigration official came out of his booth shouting and waving an American passport in the name of Prof. Medvers Watson.

Two of Colonel Moreno's secret police goons, who had been standing behind the immigration officer in the shed, came running out with handguns drawn. One went back and began to gabble down the phone lines to the capital, forty miles east.

Galvanized by the army officer who was clutching his broken nose, the dozen soldiers piled into the olive-drab truck and set off in pursuit. The secret policemen ran to their own blue Land Rover and did the same. But the Cherokee was around two corners and gone.

In Langley, Kevin McBride saw the flickering bulb flash on the desk phone that linked him to the office of Colonel Moreno in San Martin City. He took the call, listened carefully, noted what was said, asked a few questions, and noted again. Then he went to see Paul Devereaux.

"They've got him," he said.

"In custody?"

"Almost. He tried to come in as I thought, over the river from Suriname. He must have spotted the sudden interest in his passport, or the guards made too much of a fuss. Whatever, he smashed down the barrier and roared off. Colonel Moreno says there is nowhere for him to go. Jungle both sides; patrols on the roads. He says they'll have him by morning."

"Poor man," said Devereaux, "he really should have stayed at home."

Colonel Moreno was overly optimistic. It took two days. In fact, the news was brought by a bush farmer who lived two miles up a track running off the right-hand side of the highway into the jungle.

He said he recalled the noise of a heavy engine growling past his homestead the previous evening, and his wife had caught sight of a big and almost new off-road going up the track.

He naturally assumed it must be a government vehicle, since no farmer or trapper would dream of being able to afford such a vehicle. Only when it did not come back by the following night did he trudge down to the main road. There he found a patrol and told them.

The soldiers found the Cherokee. It had made one further mile beyond the farmer's shack when, trying to push onward into the rain forest, it had nosed into a gully and stuck at forty-five degrees. Deep furrows showed where the fleeing driver had tried to force his way out of the gully, but his panic had merely made matters worse. It took a crane truck from the city to get the 4×4 out of the hole, turned around, and heading for the road. Colonel Moreno himself came. He surveyed the churned earth, the shattered saplings and torn vines.

"Trackers," he said. "Get the dogs. The Cherokee and everything in it to my office. Now."

But darkness came down. The trackers were simple folk, not able to face the darkness when the spirits of the forest were abroad. They began next morning at dawn and found the quarry by noon.

One of Moreno's men was with them and had a cell

phone. Moreno took the call in his office. Thirty minutes later, Kevin McBride walked into Devereaux's office.

"They found him. He's dead."

Devereaux glanced at his desk calendar. It revealed the date was August 27th.

"I think you should be there," he said.

McBride groaned.

"It's a hell of a journey, Paul. All over the bloody Caribbean."

"I'll sanction a company plane. You should be there by breakfast tomorrow. It's not just me who has to be satisfied this damn business is over for good. Zilic has to believe it, too. Go down there, Kevin. Convince us both."

The man Langley knew only by his code name of Avenger had spotted the track off the main road when he flew over the region in the Piper. It was one of a dozen that left the highway between the river and the capital forty miles to the east. Each track serviced one or two small plantations or farms, then petered out into nothing.

He had not thought to photograph them at the time, saving all his film for the hacienda at El Punto. But he remembered them. And on the flight back with the doomed charter pilot Lawrence, he had seen them again. The one he chose to use was the third from the river. He had a start of half a mile over his pursuers when he slowed in order not to leave visible skid marks, and then eased the Cherokee up the track. Around a bend, engine off, he heard the pursuers thunder past.

The drive to the farmstead was easy, first-gear, four-wheel work. After the farm, it was all slog. He got the vehicle an extra mile through dense jungle, descended in the darkness, walked ahead, found a gully, and crashed it. He left what he intended the trackers to find and took the rest. It was heavy. The heat, even in the night, was oppressive. The notion that jungles at night are quiet places is a fallacy. They rustle, they croak, they roar, but they do not have spirits.

Using his compass and flashlight, he marched west, then south, for about a mile, slashing with one of his machetes to create a kind of path. After a mile he left the other part of what he intended the pursuers to find and, lightened at last to a small haversack, water bottle, flashlight, and second machete, pressed on toward the river bank.

He reached the Commini at dawn, well upstream of the crossing point and ferry. The inflatable airmattress would not have been his crossing of choice, but it sufficed. Prone on the navy-blue canvas, he paddled with both hands, withdrawing them from the water when a deadly cottonmouth, or it might have been a water moccasin, glided past. The beady, lidless eye gazed at him from a few inches away, but the snake pressed on downstream.

An hour's paddling and drifting brought him to the Suriname bank. The trusty airmattress was stabbed into oblivion and abandoned. It was midmorning when the stained, streaked, wet figure, mottled with mosquito bites and hung with leeches, stumbled onto the road back to Parbo. After five miles a friendly market trader allowed him to ride the cargo of watermelons the last fifty miles to the capital.

Even the kind souls at the Krasnopolsky would have raised an eyebrow at their English businessman turning up in such a state, so he changed in the lock-up store, used a garage washroom and a gas lighter to burn off the leeches, and returned to his hotel for a lunch of steak and fries, plus several bottles of Parbo. Then he slept.

Thirty thousand feet up, the company Lear jet drifted down the eastern seaboard of the United States with Kevin McBride as its only passenger. "This," he mused, "is the kind of transportation I really could force myself to get used to."

They refueled at the spook-haven air base of Eglin, northern Florida, and again at Barbados. There was a car waiting at San Martin City airfield to bring the CIA man to Colonel Moreno's secret police headquarters in an oil palm forest on the outskirts of town.

The fat colonel greeted his visitor in his office with a bottle of whiskey.

"I guess a tad early for me, Colonel," said McBride.

"Nonsense, my friend, never too early for a toast. Come . . . I propose. Death to our enemies."

They drank. McBride, at that hour and in that heat, would have preferred a decent coffee.

"What have you got for me, Colonel?"

"A little exposition. Better I show you."

There was a conference room next to the office, and it had clearly been arranged for the colonel's grisly "exposition." The central long table was covered with a white cloth, which contained one exhibit. Around the walls were four other tables with collections of mixed items. It was one of the smaller tables that Colonel Moreno approached first.

"I told you our friend, Mr. Watson, first panicked, drove down the main road, swerved up a track at the side, and attempted to find escape by driving straight through the jungle? Yes? Impossible. He crashed his off-road into a gully and could not get out. Today it stands in the yard beneath these windows. Here is part of what he abandoned in it."

Table one contained mainly heavy-duty clothing, spare boots, water pannikins, mosquito netting, repellent, and water-purification tablets. Table two had a tent, pegs, lantern, and a canvas basin on a tripod, along with miscellaneous toiletries.

"Nothing I wouldn't have on any normal camping trip," remarked McBride.

"Quite right, my friend. He obviously thought he would be hiding in the jungle for some time, probably making an ambush for his target on the road out of El Punto. But that target hardly ever leaves by road at all, and when he does it is in an armored limousine. This assassin was not very good. Still, when he abandoned his gear, he also abandoned this. Too heavy, perhaps."

At table three the colonel whisked a sheet off the contents. It was a Remington 30-06, with a huge Rhino scope sight and a box of shells. Purchasable in American gun stores as a hunting rifle, it would also take a human head away with no problem at all.

"Now," explained the fat man, enjoying his mastery of his list of discoveries, "at this point your man leaves the car and 80 percent of his equipment. He sets off on foot, probably aiming for the river. But he is not a jungle fighter. How do I know? No compass. Within three hundred meters he was lost, heading south into deeper jungle, not west to the river. When we found him, all this was scattered about."

The last table contained a water can (empty), bush hat, machete, flashlight. There were tough-soled combat boots, shreds of camouflage trousers and shirt, bits of a completely inappropriate seersucker jacket, a leather belt with brass buckle and sheath knife still looped onto the belt.

"That was all he was carrying when you found him?"

"That was all he was carrying when he died. In his panic, he left behind what he should have taken—his rifle. He might have defended himself at the end."

"So your men caught up with him and shot him?"

Colonel Moreno threw up both hands, palms forward, in a gesture of surprised innocence.

"Us? Shoot him? Unarmed? Of course not. We wanted him alive. No, no. He was dead by the midnight of the night he fled. Those who do not understand the jungle should not venture into it. Certainly not ill-equipped, at night, seized by panic. That is a deadly combination. Look." With self-adoring theatricality, he whipped the sheet off the center table. The skeleton had been brought from the jungle in a body bag, feet still in the boots, rags still around the bones. A hospital doctor had been summoned to rearrange the bones in the right order. The dead man, or what was left of him, had been picked clean to the last tiny fragment of skin, flesh, and marrow.

"The key to what happened is here," said Colonel Moreno, tapping with his forefinger. The right femur had been snapped cleanly through the middle.

"From this we can deduce what happened, my friend. He panicked, he ran. By flashlight only, blindly, without a compass. He made it about a mile from the stranded car, then he caught his foot in a root, a hidden tree stump, a tangled vine. Down he went. Snap. One broken leg.

"Now he cannot run, he cannot walk, he cannot even crawl. With no gun he cannot even summon help. He can only shout, but to what end? You know we have jaguars in these jungles?

"Well, we do. Not many, but if one hundred and fifty pounds of fresh meat insists on shouting its head off, chances are a jaguar will find it. That's what happened here. The main limbs were scattered over a small clearing. It's a larder out there. The racoon eats fresh meat. Also the puma and the coati. Up in the tree canopy, the daylight will bring the forest vultures. Ever seen what they can do to a corpse? No? Not pretty, but thorough. At the end of them all, the fire ants.

"Nature's most fantastic cleaners. Fifty yards from the remains, we found the ants' nest. They send out scouts, you know. They cannot see, but their sense of smell is amazing; and, of course, within twenty hours he would have smelt to high heaven. Enough?"

"Enough," said McBride. Early though it might be; he fancied a second whiskey. Back in the colonel's office, the secret policemen laid out some smaller items. One steel watch, engraved MW on the back. A signet ring, no inscription.

"No wallet," said the Colonel. "One of the predators must have snatched it if it was made of leather. But tucked down one of the boots, still intact, we found this."

It was a U.S. passport in the name of Medvers Watson. The profession was given as scientist. The same face McBride had seen before from the visa application form stared at him: eyeglasses, wispy goatee, slightly helpless expression. The CIA man reckoned, quite rightly, that no one would ever see Medvers Watson again.

"May I contact my superior in Washington?"

"Please," said Colonel Moreno, "be my guest. I will leave you your privacy."

McBride took his laptop from his attaché case and contacted Paul Devereaux, tapping in a sequence of numbers that would keep the exchange from prying ears. With his cell phone plugged into the laptop, he waited until Devereaux came on line.

He told his superior the gist of what Colonel Moreno reported, and what he had seen. There was silence for a while.

"I want you to come home," said Devereaux.

"Not a problem," said McBride.

"Moreno can keep all the toys, including the rifle, but I want that passport. Oh, and something else."

McBride listened.

"You want . . . what?"

"Just do it, Kevin. Godspeed."

McBride told the colonel what he had been ordered to do. The fat secret police chief shrugged. "Such a short visit. You should stay. Lobster for lunch on my boat out at sea? Cold Soave? No? Oh well . . . the passport of course. And the rest . . ."

He shrugged. "If you wish, take them all."

"I'm told just one will do."

26

THE TRICK

McBride arrived back in Washington on August 29th. That same day, down in Paramaribo, Henry Nash, with his passport issued by Her Majesty's Principal Secretary of State for Foreign and Commonwealth Affairs, to give him his full title, walked into the Consulate of the Republic of San Martin and asked for a visa.

There was no problem. The consul in the one-man office knew there had been a flap several days earlier when a refugee from justice had tried to enter his homeland, but the alarm had been stood down. The man was dead. He issued the entry visa.

That was the trouble with August. You could never get anything done in a hurry, not even in Washington, not even if your name was Paul Devereaux. The excuse was always the same: "I'm sorry, sir, he's on vacation. He'll be back next week." And thus it was as the month of August finally trickled away into September.

It was on the 3rd that Devereaux received the first of the two answers he sought.

"It's probably the best forgery we've ever seen," said the man from the State Department's passport division. "Basically, it was once genuine and was printed by us. But two vital pages were removed by an expert and two fresh pages from another passport inserted. It is the fresh pages that bear the photo and name of Medvers Watson. To our knowledge there is no such person. This passport number has never been issued."

"Could the holder of this passport fly into and out of the States?" asked Paul Devereaux. "Is it that good?"

"Out of, yes," said the expert. "Flying out would mean it would only be checked by airline staff. No computer database involved. Flying in . . . that would be a problem if the INS officer chose to run the number through the database. The computer would reply: No such number."

"Can I have the passport back?"

"Sorry, Mr. Devereaux. We like to try and help you guys, but this masterpiece is going into our Black Museum. We'll have entire classes studying this beauty."

And still there was no reply from the forensic pathology unit at Bethesda, the hospital where Devereaux had a few useful contacts.

It was on the 4th that Henry Nash, at the wheel of a modest little rented compact, with a suitcase of summer clothes and toiletries, British passport in hand, and San Martin visa stamped inside it, rolled onto the ferry at the Commini River border crossing.

His British accent might not have fooled Oxford or Cambridge, but among the Dutch-speaking Surinamese and, he assumed, the Spanish-speaking San Martinos, there would be no problem. There was not.

Avenger watched the brown river flowing beneath his

feet one last time and vowed he would be a happy man if he never saw the damned thing again. On the San Martin side, the stripped pole was gone, as were the secret police and soldiers. The border was back to its usual sleepy self. He descended, passed his passport through the side window of the booth, beamed an inane smile, and fanned himself while he waited.

Running in an undershirt in all weathers meant he habitually had a slight tan; two weeks in the tropics had deepened it to a mahogany brown. His fair hair had received the attention of a barber in Paramaribo and was now so dark brown as to be almost black, but that simply matched the description of Mr. Nash of London.

The glance through the trunk of his car and his valise of clothes was perfunctory, his passport went back into the top pocket of his shirt, and he rolled on down the road to the capital.

At the third track on the right, he checked that no one was watching and turned into the jungle again. Halfway to the farmstead he stopped and turned the car around. The giant baobab tree was not hard to locate, and the tough black twine was still deep inside the cut he had sliced in the trunk a week earlier.

As he paid out the twine, the camouflaged Bergen knapsack came down from the branches where it had hung unseen. It contained all he hoped he would need for several days crouched on the crest of the cordillera above the hacienda of the runaway Serb and for his descent into the fortress itself.

The customs officer at the border post had taken no notice of the ten-liter plastic can in the trunk. When the Englishman said, "*Agua,*" he merely nodded and closed the lid. With the water added to the Bergen, the load would take even a triathlete to his limit for mountain climbing, but two liters a day would be vital.

He drove quietly through the capital, past the oil-palm forest where Colonel Moreno sat at his desk, and on to the east. He went into the resort village of La Bahia just after lunch, at the hour of siesta, and no one stirred.

The plates on the car were by now those of a San Martin national. He recalled the adage: Where do you hide a tree? In the forest. Where do you hide a rock? In the quarry. He put the compact in the public car park, hefted the Bergen, and marched eastward out of town. Another backpacker.

Dusk descended. Ahead of him he saw the crest of the cordillera that separated the hacienda from the enveloping jungle. Where the road curved away inland to loop around the hills and go on to the Maroni and the border to French Guiana, he left the road and began to climb. He saw the narrow track snaking down from the mountain pass, and angled away from it toward a peak he had selected from the photographs taken from the plane. When it became simply too black to move, he set down his Bergen, took a supper of high-value hard rations, a cup of the precious water, leaned against the haversack, and slept.

In the camping stores of New York he had declined the U.S. Army–derived MREs or Meals Ready to Eat, recalling that in the Gulf War they were so deeply awful that the GIs dubbed them Meals Rejected by Ethiopians. He made up his own concentrates to include beef, raisins, nuts, and dextrose. He would be passing rabbit pellets, but he would keep his strength for when he needed it.

Before dawn he came awake, nibbled again, sipped again, and climbed on. At one point, down the mountain and through a gap in the trees, he saw the roof of the guardhouse in the mountain pass far below.

Before the sun rose, he made the crest. He came out of the forest two hundred yards from where he wanted, so he crabbed sideways until he found the spot in the photograph.

His eye for terrain had not let him down. There was a slight dip in the line of the crest, screened by the last fuzz of vegetation. With camouflaged shirt and bush hat, daubed face, and olive-colored binoculars, motionless under the leaves, he would be invisible from the estate below.

When he needed a break, he could slither backward off the crest and stand up again. He made the small camp that

would be home for up to four days, smeared his face, and
crawled into the hideout. The sun pinked the jungles over
French Cayenne, and the first beam slipped across the peninsula below. El Punto lay spread out like the scale model
that had once graced the sitting room of his apartment in
Brooklyn, a shark tooth jabbing into the glittering sea. From
below came a dull clang as someone smashed an iron bar
into a hanging length of railway track. It was time for the
forced laborers to rise.

It was not until the 4th that the friend Paul Devereaux had
contacted in the Department of Pathology at Bethesda
called back.

"What on earth are you up to, Paul?"

"Enlighten me. What am I up to?"

"Grave robbing by the look of it."

"Tell me all, Gary. What is it?"

"Well, it's a femur all right. A thighbone, right leg.
Clean break at the midsection. No compound fracture, no
splinters."

"Sustained in a fall?"

"Not unless the fall involved a sharp edge and a hammer."

"You're fulfilling my worst fear, Gary. Go on."

"Well, the bone is clearly from an anatomical skeleton,
purchasable in any medical store, used by students since
the Middle Ages. About fifty years old. The bone was broken recently with a sharp blow, probably across a bench.
Did I make your day?"

"No, you just ruined it. But I owe you anyway."

As with all his calls, Devereaux had recorded it. When
Kevin McBride listened to the playback his jaw dropped.

"Good God."

"For the sake of your immortal soul, I hope he is, Kevin.
You goofed. It's phoney. He never died. He choreographed
the whole damn episode, duped Moreno and Moreno convinced you. He's alive. Which means he's coming back, or

he's back already. Kevin, this is a major emergency. I want
the company plane to take off in one hour, and I want you
on it.

"I will brief Colonel Moreno myself while you fly.
When you get there Moreno will be checking every single
possibility that this goddamn Avenger came back or is on
his way. Now, go."

On the 5th, Kevin McBride faced Colonel Moreno again.
Any veneer of amiability he may have used before was
gone. His toadlike face was mottled with anger.

"This is one clever man, *mi amigo.* You did not tell me
this. Hokay, he fool me once. Not again. Look."

Since the moment Prof. Medvers Watson had burst
through the border controls, the Secret Police chief had
checked every possible entrant into San Martin.

Three game fishermen out of St. Laurent on the French
side had suffered an engine breakdown at sea and been
towed into San Martin Marina. They were in detention and
not happy.

Four more non-Hispanics had entered from the Suriname
direction. A party of French technicians from the Kourou
space-launch facility in French Guiana had come over the
Maroni River looking for cheap sex and were undergoing
an even cheaper stay in jail.

Of the four from Suriname, one was Spanish and two
Dutch. All their passports had been confiscated. Colonel
Moreno slapped them onto his desk.

"Which one is false?" he asked.

Eight French, two Dutch, one Spanish. One missing.

"Who was the other visitor from the Suriname side?"

"An Englishman. We can't find him."

"Details?"

The colonel studied a sheet with the records from the
San Martin Consulate in Parbo and the crossing point on
the Commini.

"Nash. Señor Henry Nash. Passport in order; visa in order. No luggage except a few summer clothes. Small compact car, rented. Unsuitable for jungle work. With this he gets nowhere off the main road or the capital city. Drove in on the 4th, two days ago."

"Hotel?"

"He told our consulate in Parbo he would be staying in the city, the Camino Real Hotel. He had a reservation, faxed from the Krasnopolsky in Parbo. He never checked in."

"Looks suspicious."

"The car is also missing. No foreign car can be found in San Martin. It has not been found, yet it cannot drive off the main highway. So I say to myself, a garage somewhere in the country. The country is being scoured."

McBride looked at the pile of foreign passports.

"Only their own embassies could verify these as forgeries or genuine. And the embassies are in Suriname. It means a visit for one of your men."

Colonel Moreno nodded glumly. He prided himself on absolute control of the small dictatorship. Something had gone wrong.

"Have you Americans told our Serbian guest?"

"No," said McBride. "Have you?"

"Not yet."

Both men had good reasons. For the dictator, President Muñoz, his asylum seeker was extremely lucrative. Moreno did not want to be the one who caused him to quit and take his fortune with him.

For McBride, it was a question of orders. He did not know it, but Devereaux feared Zoran Zilic might panic and refuse to fly to Peshawar to meet the chief of Al Qaeda. Sooner or later someone was either going to have to find the manhunter or tell him.

"Please keep me posted, Colonel," he said, as he turned to leave. "I'll stay at the Camino Real. It seems they have a spare room."

"There is one thing that puzzles me, Señor," said Moreno as McBride reached the door.

He turned. "Yes?"

"This man, Medvers Watson. He tried to enter the country without a visa."

"So?"

"He would have needed a visa to get in. He must have known that. He did not even bother."

"You're right," said McBride. "Odd."

"So I ask myself, as a policeman, why? And you know what I answer, Señor?"

"Tell me."

"I answer: Because he did not intend to enter legally; because he did not panic at all; because he intended to do exactly what he did—to fake his own death and find his way back to Suriname. Then quietly return."

"Makes sense," admitted McBride.

"Then I say to myself: So he knew we were waiting for him, but how did he know?"

McBride's stomach turned over at the full implication of Moreno's reasoning.

Meanwhile, invisible in a patch of scrub on the flank of a mountain, the hunter watched, noted, and waited. He waited for the hour that had not yet come.

27
THE VIGIL

Dexter was impressed as he studied the triumph of security and self-sufficiency that a combination of nature, ingenuity, and money had accomplished on the peninsula below the escarpment. Were it not dependent on slave labor, it would have been admirable.

The triangle jutting out to sea was larger than he had imagined in the scale model in his New York apartment.

The base, on which he now looked down from his mountain hideout, was about two miles from side to side. It ran, as his aerial photos had shown, from sea to sea and at each end the mountain range dropped to the water in vertical cliffs.

The sides of the isosceles triangle he estimated at about three miles, giving a total land area of almost six square

miles. The area was divided into four parts, each with a
different function.

Below him, at the base of the escarpment, was the private airstrip and the workers' village. Three hundred yards
out from the cliff a twelve-foot-high chain-link fence
topped with razor wire ran across the land from edge to
edge. Where it met the sea, he could observe through his
binoculars in the growing light, the fence jutted over the
cliff and ended in a tangle of rolls of razor wire. No way
of slipping around the end of the fence; no way of going
over the top.

Two-thirds of the strip created between the escarpment
and the wire was dedicated to the airfield. Below him,
flanking the runway, was a single large hangar, a marshal-
ing apron, and a range of smaller buildings that had to be
workshops and fuel stores. Toward the far end, near the sea
to catch the cooler breezes, were half a dozen small villas,
which he presumed to be the home of the aircrew and maintenance staff.

The only access and egress to and from the airfield was
a single steel gate set in the chain-link fence. There was no
guardhouse near the gate, but a pair of visible rods and
small steel wheels beneath the leading edge indicated it was
electrically powered and would open to the command of
the appropriate remote control. At half past six, nothing
moved on the airfield.

The other third of the strip was consigned to the village.
It was segregated from the airfield by another fence, running from the escarpment outward and also topped with
razor wire. The peasants were clearly not allowed on or
near the airfield.

The clanging of the iron bar on the railway track stopped
after a minute, and the village stumbled into life. Dexter
watched the first figures, clad in off-white trousers and
shirts, with rope-soled espadrilles on their feet, emerge
from the groups of tiny cabanas and head for the communal
washhouses. When they were all assembled, the watcher
estimated there were about twelve hundred of them.

Clearly there were some staff who ran the village and would not go to work in the field. He saw them working in open-fronted, lean-to kitchens, preparing a breakfast of bread and gruel. Long trestle tables and benches formed the dining hall under palm-thatch shelters, which would protect against occasional rain but more usually against the fierce sun.

At a second beating of the iron rail, the farm workers took bowls and a half loaf and sat down to eat. There were no gardens, no shops, no women, no children, no school. This was not a true village, but a labor camp. The only remaining buildings were what appeared to be a food store, a general clothing and bedding store, and the church with the priest's house attached. It was functional; a place to work, eat, sleep, pray for release, and nothing else.

If the airfield was a rectangle trapped between the escarpment, the wire, and the sea, so was the village. But there was one difference. A pitted and rutted track zigzagged down from the single mountain pass in the whole mountain range, the only access by road to the rest of the republic. It was clearly not suitable for heavy-duty trucks. Dexter wondered how resupply of weighty essentials like gasoline, engine diesel, and aviation fuel would take place. When the visibility lengthened, he found out.

At the extremity of his vision, hidden in the morning mist, was the third portion of the estate, the walled five-acre compound at the end of the foreland. He knew from his aerial pictures it contained the magnificent white mansion in which the former Serbian gangster lived; half a dozen villas in the grounds for guests and senior staff; tonsured lawns, flower beds, and shrubbery; and along the inner side of the fourteen-foot-high protecting wall, a series of lean-to cottages and stores for domestic staff: linen, food, and drink.

In his pictures and on his scale model, the huge wall also went from cliff edge to cliff edge, and at this point the land was fifty feet above the sea, which surged and thumped on the rocks below.

A lone but massive double gate penetrated the wall at
its center with a road of pounded rubble leading up to it.
There was a guardhouse inside that controlled the gate-
opening machinery, and a parapet ran along the inside of
the wall to enable armed guards to patrol its entire length.
Everything between the chain-link fence below the watcher
and the wall over two miles away was the food-producing
farm. As the light rose, Dexter could confirm what his photos had told him; the farm produced almost everything the
community within the fortress could need. There were grazing herds of beef and lamb. Sheds would certainly contain
pigs and poultry. There were fields of arable crops, grains,
legumes, tubers; orchards producing ten kinds of fruit; and
acre after acre of vegetables either in the open or under
long domes of polyethylene. He surmised the farm would
produce every conceivable kind of salad and fruit, along
with meat, butter, eggs, cheese, oil, bread, and rough red
wine. The fields and orchards were studded with barns and
granaries, machine stores, and facilities to slaughter the
beasts, mill the grain, bake the bread, and press the grapes.

To his right, near the cliff edge but inside the farm, was
a series of small barracks for the guard staff, with a dozen
better-quality chalets for their officers and two or three
company shops.

To his left, also at the cliff edge, also inside the farm,
were three large warehouses and a gleaming aluminum fuel
storage farm. Right at the very edge of the cliff were two
large cranes or derricks. That solved one problem: Heavy
cargoes came by sea and were hefted or pumped from the
ship below to the storage facilities forty feet above the
freighter's deck.

The peons finished their morning meal and again came
the harsh clang as the iron bar smashed against the hanging
length of rail. This time there were several reactions.

Uniformed guards spilled from their barracks farther up
the coast to the right. One put a silent whistle to his lips.
Dexter heard nothing, but out of the farmland a dozen lop-
ing Dobermans emerged in obedience to the call and en-

tered their fenced compound near the barracks. Clearly they had not eaten for twenty-four hours; they hurled themselves at the plates of raw offal set out and tore the meat to pieces.

That told Dexter what happened each sundown. When every staffer and slave was closed off in their respective compounds, the dogs would be released to hunt and prowl the three thousand acres of farmland. They must have been trained to leave the calves, sheep, and pigs alone, but any wandering burglar would simply not survive. They were far too many for a single man to begin to combat. Entry by night was not feasible.

The watcher had buried himself so deeply in the undergrowth that anyone below, raising his or her eyes to the crest of the range, would see no glint of sun off the lens, nor would he catch a glimpse of the motionless, camouflaged man.

At half past six, when the farming estate was ready to receive them, the iron clang summoned the laborers to work. They trooped toward the high gate that separated the village from the farm.

This gate was a far more complicated affair than the one from the airfield to the estate. It opened inward to the farmland in two halves. Beyond the gate, five tables had been set up and guards sat behind each. Others stood over them. The peons formed into five columns.

On a shouted command, they shuffled forward. Each man at the head of the line stooped at the table to offer a dog tag round his neck to the seated official. The number on the tag was checked and tapped into a database.

The workers must have lined up in the right column, according to their type of number, for after they were nodded through, they reported to a foreman beyond the tables. In groups of about a hundred, they were led away to their tasks, pausing at a number of tool sheds beside the main track to pick up what they needed.

Some were for the fields, some for the orchards, others were destined for animal husbandry, or the grain mill, the slaughterhouse, the vineyard, or the huge kitchen garden.

As Dexter watched, the enormous farm came to life. But the security never slackened. When the village was finally empty, the double gate closed, and the men dispersed to their stations. Dexter concentrated on that security and looked for his opening.

It was mid-morning that Colonel Moreno heard back from the two emissaries he had sent out with foreign passports in their hands.

In Cayenne, capital of French Guiana to the east, the authorities had wasted no time. They were not pleased that three innocent game fishermen had been detained for the crime of breaking down at sea, nor that five technicians had been picked up and detained without good cause. All eight French passports were pronounced 100 percent genuine and an urgent request was lodged that their owners be released and sent home.

To the west, in Paramaribo, the Dutch Embassy said exactly the same about their two nationals: The passports were genuine, the visas in order, what was the problem?

The Spanish Embassy was closed, but Colonel Moreno had been assured by the man from the CIA that the fugitive was about five feet, eight inches tall, while the Spaniard was over six feet. That just left the missing Mr. Henry Nash of London.

The Secret Police chief ordered his man in Cayenne to come home, and the man in Parbo to hunt through every car-rental agency to find out what kind of car the Londoner had rented and its registration number.

By mid-morning the heat on the hills was intense. A few inches from the unmoving watcher's face a lizard with red, erect ruff behind its head, walking on stones that would fry an egg, stared at the stranger, detected no threat, and scuttled on its way. There was activity out by the cliff-top derricks.

Four muscular young men wheeled a thirty-foot aluminum patrol boat to the rear of a Land Rover and hitched up. The Land Rover towed the vessel to a gas pump where it was fueled. It could almost have passed for a leisure craft except for the .30-caliber Browning machine gun mounted in the midsection. When the boat was ready for sea, it was towed beneath one of the derricks. Four webbing bands suspended from a rectangular frame ended in four tough steel cleats. These were fixed into strong points on the boat's hull.

With the crew on board, the patrol boat was lifted off the hard pad, swung out to sea, and lowered to the ocean. Dexter saw it go out of sight. Minutes later he saw it again out at sea. The men on board hauled up and emptied two fish traps and five lobster pots, rebaited them, threw them back, and resumed their patrol.

Dexter had noted that everything in front of him would collapse into ruin without two life-giving elixirs. One was gasoline that would power the generator plant situated behind the warehouses of the dock. This provided the electricity that would power every device and motor on the whole estate, from the gate to a power drill to a bedside light. The other elixir was water; fresh, clean, clear water in a limitless supply. It came from the mountain stream that he had first seen in the aerial photographs.

That stream was now below him and slightly to his left. It bubbled out of the mountainside, having made its way from somewhere deep in the rain forests of the interior.

It emerged twenty feet above the peninsula, tumbled down several rock falls, and then entered a concrete-sided channel that had clearly been created for it. From that point, man took over from nature.

To reach the farmland it had to flow under the runway below the hunter. Clearly strong, square culverts had been inserted below the runway when it was built. Emerging from below the runway on the other side, the now-marshaled water flowed under the chain-link fence as well. Dexter had little doubt there was an impenetrable grille there as well. Without a grille anyone could have slipped into the stream within the airfield, gone under the wire, and used the gully and the flowing water to elude the wandering dogs. Whoever designed the defenses would not have allowed that.

In the mid-morning two things happened right below his aerie. The Hawker 1000 was towed out of the hangar into the sun. Dexter feared it might be needed to fly the Serb somewhere, but it was only pulled from the hangar to make space. What followed was a small helicopter of the sort traffic police use to monitor flow. It could hover barely inches away from the rock face if required, and he would have to be invisible to avoid being spotted. But it remained below him with its rotors folded while the engine was serviced.

The other thing was that a four-wheeler came from the farm to the electric gate. Using a remote to open the gate, the man on the four-wheeler motored in, waved a cheery greeting to the mechanics on the apron, and went up the runway to where the stream passed under it.

He stopped the quad, took a wicker basket from the back, and looked down at the flowing water. Then he tossed several chicken carcasses into the water. He did this on the upstream side of the runway. Then he crossed the tarmac and looked down into the water again. The carcasses must have been carried by the flow to press up against the grille at the departure side.

Whatever was in that water between the escarpment and the grille, it ate meat. Dexter could only think of one freshwater denizen of those parts that ate meat, and that was the piranha. If they could eat hens, they could eat swimmers. It mattered not if the water touched the roof longer than he could hold his breath; it was already a three-hundred-yard-long piranha pool.

After the chain-link fence, the stream ran down through the estate, feeding a glittering tracery of irrigation channels. Other taps underground would duct some of the flow to the workers' village, the villas, the barracks, and the master mansion.

The rest, having served all parts of the estate, curved back toward the farm end of the runway, there to tumble over the edge and into the sea.

By early afternoon, the heat lay on the land like a great, heavy, suffocating blanket. Out on the estate the workers had toiled from seven until twelve. They were then allowed to find shade and eat what they had brought in small cotton tote bags. Until four they were allowed to take a siesta before the last three hours' labor, from four to seven.

Dexter lay and panted, envying the salamander basking on a rock a yard away, immune to the heat. It was tempting to throw pints of precious water down his throat to achieve relief, but he knew it must be rationed simply to prevent dehydration, rather than gulped down for pleasure.

At four, the clang of the iron rail told the workers to go back to the fields and barns. Dexter struggled to the edge of his escarpment and watched the tiny figures in rough cotton shirts and pants, nut-brown faces hidden under straw sombreros, take up their hoes and mattocks again to keep the model farm weed-free.

To his left a battered-looking pickup rolled to the space between the derricks and stopped, after reversing its rear toward the sea. A peon in bloodstained overalls hauled a long steel chute from the back, fixed it to the tailgate, and with a pitchfork began to hoist something onto the steel slide. Whatever it was slithered off and fell into the sea. Dexter adjusted his focus. The next forkful gave the game away. It was a black hide with the bullock's head still attached.

Back in New York, examining the photos, he had been struck that even with the cliffs there was nevertheless no attempt to make any access to the beautiful blue sea. No steps down, no diving platform, no moored raft, no beach, no jetty. Seeing the offal go in, he understood why. The water around the whole peninsula would be alive with hammerheads, tigers, and great whites. Anything swimming, other than a fish, would last only a few minutes.

About that time Colonel Moreno took a call on a cell phone from his man across the border in Suriname. The Englishman, Nash, had rented his car from a small private and local company, which is why it had taken so long to trace. But he had it at last. It was a Ford Fiesta. He dictated the number.

The secret policeman issued his order for the morning. Every car park, every garage, every driveway, every track was to be scoured for a Fiesta with this Surinamese registration number. Then he changed his orders. Any Ford with any registration number was to be traced, searching was to start at dawn.

Dusk and dark come in the tropics with bewildering speed. The sun had passed behind Dexter's back an hour earlier, bringing relief at last. He watched the estate workers come home, dragging weary feet. They handed in their tools; they were checked through the double gate one by one, in their five columns, two hundred per column.

They came back to the village to join the two hundred who had not gone to the fields. In the villas and the barracks, the first lights came on. At the far end of the triangle, a white glow revealed where the Serb's mansion was floodlit.

The mechanics on the airfield closed up and took their motorbikes to ride to the villas at the far end of the runway. When all was fenced and locked, the Dobermans were released, the world said farewell to September 6th, and the manhunter prepared to go down the escarpment.

28

THE VISITOR

In a day of peering over the edge of the escarpment, Dexter had realized two things about it that had not showed up on his photographs. One was that it was not steep all the way down. The slope was perfectly climbable until about a hundred feet from the level plain, at which point it dropped sheer. But he had brought more than that length of good climbing rope.

The other was that the nudity of all weeds and shrubs was done through an act of man, not of nature. Someone, preparing the defenses, had had teams of men come over the edge of the drop in rope cradles to rip every twig and shrub out of the crevices in the slope, so as to give no leaf cover at all. Where the saplings were slim enough to be entirely ripped out, they had been. But some had had a stem that was simply resistant to the pull of a man on a rope's end. These had been sawn off short, but not short enough. The stumps formed hundreds of hand-and-toe holds for a climber going down or up.

In daylight such a climber would have been instantly visible but not in darkness.

By 10:00 P.M. the moon was up, a sickle moon, just enough to give dim light to the climber, not enough to make him visible against the shale face. Delicacy would be needed not to cause a rockfall. Moving from stump to stump, Dexter began to ease his way down to the airfield below.

When the slope became too steep even for climbing, Dexter used the coiled rope around his shoulders to rappel the rest.

He spent three hours on the airfield. Years earlier another of his "clients" from the Tombs in New York had taught him the gentlemanly art of picking locks, and the set of picks he carried with him had been made by a master. The padlock on the doors of the hangar he left alone. The double doors would have rumbled if they were rolled back. There was a smaller door to one side, with a single Yale-type locking mechanism and it cost him no more than thirty seconds.

It takes a good mechanic to repair a helicopter and an even better one to sabotage it in such a manner that a good mechanic could not find the fault and mend it or even notice the tampering.

The mechanic the Serb employed to look after his helicopter was good, but Dexter was better. Up close he recognized the bird as an EC 120 Eurocopter, the single-engine version of the twin EC 135. It had a big Perspex bubble at the front end with excellent all-around, up-and-down observation for the pilot and the man beside him, plus room for three more behind them.

Dexter concentrated not on the main rotor mechanism but on the smaller tail rotor. If that malfunctioned, the "chopper" would simply not be fit to fly. By the time he had finished, it was certainly going to malfunction and be very hard to repair.

The door of the Hawker 1000 was open, so he had a chance to inspect the interior and ensure that the executive jet had had no serious internal reconfiguration.

When he locked up the main hangar, he broke into the mechanics' store, took what he wanted, but left no trace. Finally, he jogged gently to the far end of the runway, close to the backs of the residential villas, and spent his last hour there. In the morning one of the mechanics would notice with irritation that someone had borrowed his bicycle from where it leaned against the back fence.

When he had done all he came to do, Dexter found his hanging rope and climbed back to the stout stump where it was tied. Beyond that, he climbed, moving from root to root until he was back in his aerie. He was soaked to the point where he could have wrung the sweat from his clothes. He consoled himself with the thought that body odor was one thing no one was going to notice in that part of the world. To replace the moisture, he allowed himself a full pint of water, checked the level of the remaining liquid, and slept. The tiny alarm in his watch woke him at six in the morning, just before the iron bar began to clang against the hanging rail far below.

At 7:00, Paul Devereaux raised McBride in his room at the Camino Real Hotel.

"Any news?" asked the man from Washington.

"None," said McBride. "It seems pretty sure he came back masquerading as an Englishman, Henry Nash, resort developer. Then he vaporized. His car has been identified as a rented Ford from Suriname. Moreno is starting a countrywide trawl for it about now. Should have news sometime today."

There was a long pause from the Counterterrorism chief, still sitting in a robe in his breakfast room in Alexandria, Virginia, before leaving for Langley.

"Not good enough," said Devereaux. "I'm going to have to alert our friend. It will not be an easy call. I'll wait till 10:00. If there is any news of a capture, or imminent capture before then, call me at once."

"You got it," said McBride.

There was no such news. At 10:00, Devereaux made his call. It took ten minutes for the Serb to be summoned from the swimming pool to the radio shack, a small room in his basement that, despite its traditional name, was no shack and contained some highly modern and eavesdrop-free communications equipment.

At 10:30, Dexter noticed a flurry of activity on the estate below him. Off-roads streamed from the mansion on the foreland, leaving trails of dust behind them. Below him the EC 120 was wheeled out of the hangar and its main rotors spread and locked into flying mode.

"Someone," he mused, "appears to have hit the alarm."

The helicopter crew arrived from their homes at the end of the runway on two motor scooters. Within minutes they were at the controls, and the big rotors began slowly to turn. The engine kicked into life, and the rotor rate rapidly increased to warm-up speed.

The tail rotor, vital to stop the whole machine from spinning around its own main axis, was also whirring around. Then something in its core bearings seemed to snag. There was a grinding of suffering metal, and the spinning hub destroyed itself. A mechanic waved frantically to the two men inside the Perspex bubble and drew his hand across his throat.

The pilot and observer had been told by the instrument panel that they had a major bearing failure in the tail. They closed down. The main rotors ground to a halt, and the crew climbed back out. A group formed around the tail, staring upward at the damaged prop.

Uniformed guards poured into the village of the absent peons and began to search the cabanas, stores, even the church. Others, on four-wheelers, went off across the estate to spread the word to the gang masters to keep an eye open for any signs of an intruder. There were none. Such signs as there had been eight hours earlier had been too well disguised.

Dexter put the uniformed guards at around one hundred. There was a community of about a dozen on the airfield and the twelve hundred workers. Given more security personnel, plus domestic staff out of sight in the grounds of the mansion, and twenty more technicians at the generating station and various repair shops, Dexter now had an idea how many he was up against. And he still had not seen the mansion itself and its no doubt complex defenses.

Just before midday, Paul Devereaux called his man in the storm center.

"Kevin, you have to go over and visit with our friend. I have spoken to him. He is in a high state of temper. I cannot stress enough how vital it is that this wretch plays his part in Project Peregrine. He must not duck out now. One day I'll be able to tell you how vital he is. For the moment, stand by him until the intruder is caught and neutralized. Apparently our friend's helicopter is malfunctioning. Ask the colonel for a Jeep to get you over the sierra. Call me when you get there."

At midday, Dexter watched a small coaster approach the cliffs. Holding stationary in the water just clear of the rocks, the freighter discharged crates from its deck and holds, which the derricks hoisted to the concrete apron, where flatback pickups awaited them. Clearly they were for those luxuries the hacienda could not produce.

The last item was a thousand-gallon fuel tank, an aluminum canister the size of a fuel tanker. An empty one was lowered to the boat's deck, and it steamed away across the blue ocean.

Just after one o'clock, below him and to his right, an off-road—having been checked through the guardhouse in the defile—grunted and coughed down the track to the village. It was in San Martin police markings, with a passenger beside the driver.

Traversing the village, the blue Land Rover came to the chain-link gates and stopped. The police driver descended to offer his ID to the guards manning it. They made a phone call, presumably to the mansion for clearance.

In the pause, the man in the passenger seat also descended and gazed around with curiosity. He turned to look back at the sierra he had just descended. High above, a pair of binoculars adjusted and settled on his face.

Like the unseen man above him on the crest, Kevin McBride was impressed. He had been with Paul Devereaux on Project Peregrine for two years, from the first contact to recruitment of the Serbian. He had seen the files, knew, he thought, everything there was to know about him, yet they had never met. Devereaux had always reserved that dubious pleasure for himself.

The blue-liveried police off-road drove toward the high defending wall of the foreland compound, which towered over them as they approached the gate. A small door in the gate opened, and a burly man in slacks and a sea island cotton shirt stepped out. The shirt flapped over the waistband, and for a reason. It obscured the Glock 9mm. McBride recognized him from the file: Kulac, the only one the Serb gangster had brought from Belgrade with him, his perpetual bodyguard.

The man approached the passenger door and beckoned. After two years away from home, he still spoke nothing but Serbo-Croat.

"*Muchas gracias. Adios,*" said McBride to his police driver. The man nodded, keen to get back to the capital.

Inside the giant timber gates, made of beams the size of rail sleepers and machine operated, was a table. McBride was expertly frisked for concealed weapons, then his suitcase was searched on the table. A white-starched butler descended from an upper terrace and waited until the precautions were complete.

Kulac grunted that he was satisfied. With the butler in the lead, carrying the suitcase, the three went up the steps. McBride got his first real glimpse of the mansion.

It was three stories tall, set in manicured lawns. Two peons in white tunics could be seen at a distance, intent on their gardening. The house was not unlike some of the more luxurious residences seen along the French, Italian, and Croatian Rivieras, each upper room balconied but steel shuttered against the heat.

The flagged patio on which they stood may have been several feet above the base of the gate they had entered, but it was still below the top of the protective wall. One could see over the wall to the cordillera through which McBride had come, but no sniper in the near ground was going to be able to fire over the wall to hit someone on the terrace.

Set into the patio was a gleaming blue swimming pool, and beside the pool a large table of white Carrara marble on stone supports was set for lunch. Silver and crystal glittered.

To one side, a cluster of easy chairs surrounded a table on which an ice bucket played host to a bottle of Dom Perignon. The butler gestured that McBride should sit. The bodyguard remained upright and alert. From the deep shade of the villa a man emerged in white slacks and cream silk safari shirt.

McBride hardly recognized the man who had once been Zoran Zilic, gang enforcer from Zemun District, Belgrade; mobster of a dozen underworld rackets in Germany and Sweden; killer in the Bosnian war; runner of prostitutes, drugs, and arms out of Belgrade; embezzler of the Yugoslav treasury; and eventually fugitive from justice.

The new face bore little resemblance to the one in the CIA file. That spring the Swiss surgeons had done a good job. The Baltic pallor was replaced by a tropical tan, and only the fine white lines of scars refused to darken. But McBride had once been told that ears, like fingerprints, were totally distinctive to each human being and, short of surgery, never change. Zilic's ears were the same, and his fingerprints, and when they shook hands McBride noticed the hazel, wild animal eyes.

Zilic sat at the marble table and nodded to the only other vacant setting. McBride sat. There was a rapid exchange in Serbo-Croat between Zilic and the bodyguard. The muscular thug ambled away to eat somewhere else. A very young and pretty Martino girl in a blue maid's uniform filled two flutes of champagne. Zilic proposed no toast; he studied the amber liquid, then downed it without pause.

"This man," he said in good if not flawless English, "who is he?"

"We do not exactly know. He is a private contractor. Very secretive. Known only by his own chosen code name."

"And what is that?"

"Avenger."

The Serb considered the word, then shrugged. Two more girls began to serve the meal. There were quail egg tartlets and asparagus in melted butter.

"All made on the estate?" asked McBride.

Zilic nodded.

"Bread, salads, eggs, milk, olive oil, grapes . . . I saw them all as we drove through."

Another nod.

"Why does he come after me?" asked the Serb.

McBride thought. If he gave the real reason, the Serb might decide there was no point in further cooperation with the U.S. or any part of its establishment on the grounds that they would never forgive him anyway. His charge from Devereaux was to keep the loathsome creature inside the Peregrine team.

"We do not know," he said. "He was contracted by somebody else, perhaps an old enemy from Yugoslavia."

Zilic thought it through, then shook his head.

"Why did you leave it so late, Mr. McBride?"

"We knew nothing of this man until you complained of the plane flying over your estate and taking pictures. You took the registration number. Fine. Then you sent men to Guyana to intervene. Mr. Devereaux thought we could find the interloper, identify him, and stop him. He slipped through the net."

The lobsters were cold in mayonnaise, also from local ingredients. To round off there were Muscat grapes and peaches, with strong black coffee.

The butler offered Cohiba Cuban cigars and waited until both were drawing well before leaving. The Serb seemed lost in thought.

The three pretty waitresses were lined up against the wall of the house.

Zilic turned in his chair, pointed at one, and snapped his fingers. The girl went pale but turned and entered the house, presumably to prepare herself for her master's arrival. "I take a siesta at this hour. It is a local custom and quite a good one. Before I leave, let me tell you something. I designed this fortress with Major Van Rensberg, whom you will meet. I regard it as probably the safest place on earth.

"I do not believe your mercenary will even be able to get in here. If he does, he will never leave alive. The security systems here have been tested. This man may have gotten past you; he will not get past my systems and near to me. While I enjoy my rest, Van Rensberg will show you around. Then you can tell Mr. Devereaux his crisis is over. Until later."

He rose and left the table. McBride stayed on. Below the terrace the door in the main gate opened and a man walked up the steps to the flagstones. McBride knew him from the files, but pretended not to.

Adriaan Van Rensberg was another man with a history. During the period when the National Party and its apartheid policies ruled South Africa, he had been an eager recruit to the Bureau of State Security, the dreaded BOSS, and had

risen through the ranks due to his dedication to the extreme
forms of that body's excesses.

After the arrival of Nelson Mandela, he had joined the
extreme-right AWB Party led by Eugene Terre Blanche,
and when that collapsed he thought it would be wiser to
flee the country. After several years hiring out his services
as steward and security expert to a number of European
fascist factions, he had caught the eye of Zoran Zilic and
landed the plum job of devising, designing, building, and
commanding the fortress hacienda of El Punto. Unlike Colonel Moreno, the South African's size was not due to fat
but muscled bulk. Only the belly folding over the broad
leather belt betrayed a taste for beer and plenty of it.

McBride noted that he had designed himself a uniform
for the part, combat boots, jungle camouflage, leopard skin–
ringed bush hat, and flattering insignia.

"Mr. McBride? The American gentleman?"

"That's me."

"Major Van Rensberg, head of security. I am instructed
to give you a tour of the estate. Shall we say tomorrow
morning? Eight-thirty?"

In the car park at the resort of La Bahia, one of the policemen found the Ford. The plates were local but forged
and made up in a garage elsewhere. The manual in the
glove compartment was in Dutch. As in Suriname. Much
later someone recalled seeing a backpacker with a large,
camouflaged Bergen haversack trekking away from the resort on foot. He was heading east. Colonel Moreno called
back his entire police force and the army to their barracks.
In the morning, he said, they would climb and sweep the
cordillera from the landward side, from the road to the
crest.

29

THE TOUR

It was the second sunset and fall of darkness that Dexter had witnessed from his invisible prone position on the peak of the sierra, and it would be his last.

Still motionless, he watched the last lights snuff in the windows of the peninsula below him, then he prepared to move. They rose early down there and slept little. For him as well there would be, again, precious little sleep.

He feasted off the last of his field rations, packing down two days' supply of vitamins and minerals, fiber, and sugar. He was able to finish off the last of his water, giving his body a reservoir for the next twenty-four hours. The big Bergen, the scrim netting, and rain cape could be abandoned. What he needed he had either brought with him or stolen the previous night. They all fit into a smaller backpack. Only the coiled rope across his shoulders would remain bulky and would have to be hidden where it would not be found.

It was past midnight when he made what was left of his encampment as invisible as possible and left it.

Using a branch to brush out the tracks left by his own feet, he worked his way slowly to his right until he was over the laborers' village rather than the airfield. It took him half a mile and cost an hour. But he timed it right. The sickle moon rose. The sweat began to soak his clothes again.

He made his way slowly and carefully down the scarp, from handhold to handhold, stump to stump, root to root, until he needed the rope. This time he had to double it and hang the loop over a smooth root where it would not snag when he pulled from below.

He rappeled the rest of the way, avoiding athletic leaps that might dislodge pebbles, but simply walking backward, pace by pace, until he arrived in the cleft between the cliffs and the rear of the church. He hoped the priest was a good sleeper; he was only a few yards from his house.

He tugged gently on one strand of the double rope. The other slipped over the stump high up the face and at last cascaded down around him. He coiled it around his shoulder and left the shadows of the church.

Latrine facilities were communal and single sex. There were no women in the labor camp. He had watched the men at their ablutions from above. The base of the latrine was a long trench covered by boards to mask the inevitable stench, or at least the worst of it. In the boards were circular holes covered by circular lids. There was no concession to modesty. Taking a deep breath, Dexter lifted one of the lids and dropped his coiled rope into the black interior. With luck, it would simply disappear forever, even if it were searched for, which was extremely unlikely.

The shacks in which the men lived and slept were small squares, little more than a police cell, but each worker had one to himself. They were in rows of fifty, facing another fifty and thus forming a street. Each group of one hundred ran outward from a main highway, and that was the residential section.

The main road led to the square, flanked by the washing units, the kitchens, and the thatch-topped dining hall tables. Avoiding the moonlight of the main square, sticking to the shadows of the buildings, Dexter returned to the church. The lock on the main door detained him for no more than a few minutes.

There was not much to it, as churches go, but for those running the labor camp it was a wise precaution to provide a safety valve in this deeply Catholic country. Dexter wondered idly how the resident priest could square his job with his creed.

He found what he wanted at the far back, behind the altar and to one side, in the vestry. Leaving the main door unlocked, he went back to the rows of huts where the workers snored away their few hours of repose.

From above, he had memorized the location of the cabin he wanted. He had seen the man emerge for his breakfast. Fifth cabin down, left-hand side, third street off the main road after the plaza. There was no lock, just a simple wooden latch. Dexter stepped inside and froze motionless to accustom his eyes to the almost complete darkness after the pale moonlight outside.

The hunched figure on the bunk snored on. Three minutes later, with complete night vision, Dexter could see the low hump under the coarse blanket. He crouched to remove something from his knapsack, then went toward the bed. The sweet odor of chloroform came up to him from the soaked pad in his hand.

The peon grunted once, tried to roll from side to side for a few seconds, then lapsed into deeper sleep. Dexter kept the pad in place to ensure hours of insensibility. When he was ready, he hefted the sleeping man over his shoulder in a fireman's lift and flitted silently back the way he had come to the church.

In the doorway of the coral stone building he stopped again and waited to hear if he had disturbed anyone, but the village slept on. When he found the vestry again, he used stout masking tape to bind the peon's feet and ankles and to cover his mouth, while leaving the nose free to breathe. As he relocked the main door, he glanced with satisfaction at the notice beside it on the blackboard. The notice was a lucky "plus."

Back in the empty shack he risked a penlight to examine the laborer's worldly possessions. They were not many. There was a portrait of the Virgin on one wall and stuck into the frame a faded photo of a smiling young woman. Fiancée, sister, daughter? Through powerful binoculars the man had looked about Dexter's age, but he might have been younger. Those caught up in Colonel Moreno's penal system and sent to El Punto would age fast. Certainly he was of the same height and build, which was why Dexter had picked him.

No other wall decorations, just pegs on which hung two sets of work clothes, both identical—coarse cotton trousers and a shirt of the same material. On the floor were a pair of rope-soled espadrilles, stained and worn but tough and reliable. Other than that, a sombrero of plaited straw completed the work clothes. There was a canvas bag with a drawstring for carrying lunch to the plantation. Dexter snapped off his flashlight and checked his watch. Five past four.

He stripped down to boxer shorts, selected the items he wanted to take with him, wrapped them in his sweaty T-shirt, and bundled them into the lunch bag. The rest he would have to lose. This surplus was rolled into the knapsack and disposed of during a second visit to the latrines. Then he waited for the clang of the iron bar on the hanging length of railway track. It came as ever at 6:30, still dark but with a hint of pink in the east. The duty guard, standing outside the village just beyond the chain-link double gates of the farmland, was the source. All around Dexter the village began to come to life.

He avoided the run to the latrines and wash troughs and hoped no one would notice. After twenty minutes, peering through a slit in the boards of the door, he saw that his alley was empty again. Chin down, sombrero tilted forward, he scurried to the latrines, one figure in sandals, pants, and shirts among a thousand.

He crouched over an open hole while the others took their breakfast. Only when the third clang summoned the workers to the access gate did he join the line.

The five checkers sat at their tables, examined the dog tags, checked the work manifests, punched the number into the records of those admitted that morning, and to which labor gang he was assigned, and waved the laborer through to join his foreman and be led away to collect tools and start the allocated tasks.

Dexter reached the table attending to his line, offered his dog tag between forefinger and thumb, like the others, leaned forward and coughed. The checker pulled his face away sharply to one side, noted the tag number, and waved him away. The last thing the man wanted was a face full of chili odor. The new recruit shuffled off to draw his hoe; the assigned task was weeding the avocado groves.

At 7:30, Kevin McBride breakfasted alone on the terrace. The grapefruit, eggs, toast, and plum jam would have done credit to any five-star hotel.

At 8:15, the Serb joined him. "I think it would be wise for you to pack," he said. "When you have seen what Major Van Rensberg will show you, I hope you will agree that this mercenary has a one percent chance of getting here, even less of getting near me, and none of getting out again. There is no point in your staying. You may tell Mr. Devereaux that I will complete my part of our arrangement, as agreed, at the end of the month."

At 8:30, McBride threw his suitcase into the rear of the South African's open Jeep and climbed beside the major.

"So, what do you want to see?" asked the head of security.

"I am told it is virtually impossible for an unwanted

visitor to get in here at all. Can you tell me why?"

"Look, Mr. McBride, when I designed all this I created two things: One, it is an almost completely self-sufficient farming paradise. Everything is here. Second, it is a fortress, a sanctuary, a refuge, safe from almost all outside invasion or threat.

"Now, of course, if you are talking about a full military operation, paratroopers, armor, of course it could be invaded. But one mercenary acting alone? Never."

"How about arrival by sea?"

"Let me show you."

Van Rensberg let in the clutch and they set off, leaving a plume of rising dust behind them. The South African pulled over and stopped near a cliff edge.

"You can see from here," he said, as they climbed out. "The whole estate is surrounded by sea, at no point less than twenty feet below the cliff top, in most areas fifty feet. Sea-scanning radar, disguised as TV dishes, warn us of anything approaching by sea."

"Interception?"

"Two fast patrol boats, one at sea at all times. There is a one-mile limit of forbidden water around the whole peninsula. Only the occasional delivery freighter is allowed in."

"Underwater entry? Amphibious special forces?"

Van Rensberg snorted derisively. "A special force of one? Let me show you what would happen."

He took his walkie-talkie, called the radio basement, and was patched through to the slaughterhouse. The rendezvous was across the estate, near the derricks. McBride watched a bucket of offal go down the slide and drop into the sea thirty feet below.

For several seconds there was no reaction. Then the first scimitar fin sliced the surface. Within sixty seconds there was a feeding frenzy. Van Rensberg laughed.

"We eat well here. Plenty of steak. My employer does not eat steak, but the guards do. Many of them, like me, are from the old country, and we like our *braai*—or barbecue as you Americans call it."

"So?"

"When a beast is slaughtered, lamb, goat, pig, steer, about once a week, the fresh offal is thrown into the ocean. And the blood. That sea is alive with sharks. Blacktip, whitefin, tiger, giant hammerhead, they're all there. Last month one of my men fell overboard. The boat swerved back to pick him up. They were there in thirty seconds. Too late."

"He didn't come out of the water?"

"Most of him did. But not his legs. He died two days later."

"Burial?"

"Out there."

"So the sharks got him after all."

"No one makes mistakes around here."

"What about crossing the sierra, the way I came in yesterday?"

In answer Van Rensberg handed McBride a pair of field glasses. "Have a look. You cannot climb around the edges of it. It's sheer to the water. Come down the escarpment in daylight, and you'll be seen in seconds."

"But at night?"

"So you reach the bottom. Your man is outside the razor wire, over two miles from the mansion and outside the wall. He is not a peon, not a guard; he is quickly spotted and . . . taken care of."

"What about that stream I saw? Could one come in down the stream?"

"Good thinking, Mr. McBride. Let me show you."

Van Rensberg drove to the airfield, entered with his own remote for the chain-link gate, and motored to where the stream from the hills ran under the runway. They dismounted. There was a long patch of water open to the sky between the runway and the fence. The clear water ran gently over grasses and weeds on the bottom."

"See anything?"

"Nope," said McBride.

"They're in the cool, in the shade, under the runway."

It was clearly the South African's party piece. He kept

a small supply of beef jerky in the Jeep. When he tossed a
piece in, the water seethed. McBride saw the piranha sweep
out of the shadow and the wad of beef was shredded by a
myriad of needle-sharp teeth.

"Enough? I'll show you how we husband the water supply here and never lose security. Come."

Back in the farmland, Van Rensberg followed the stream
for most of its meandering course through the estate. At a
dozen points, spurs had been taken off the main current to
irrigate various crops or top up different storage ponds, but
they were always blind alleys.

The main stream curved hither and yon but eventually
came back to the cliff edge near the runway but beyond the
wire. There it increased in speed and rushed over the cliff
into the sea.

"Right near the edge I have a plate of spikes buried,"
said Van Rensberg. "Anyone trying to swim through here
will be taken by the current and swept along, out of control,
between smooth walls of concrete, toward the sea. Passing
over the spikes, the helpless swimmer will enter the sea
bleeding badly. Then what? Sharks, of course."

"But at night?"

"Ah, you have not seen the dogs? A pack of twelve.
Dobermans and deadly. They are trained not to touch anyone in the uniform of the estate guards and another dozen
of the senior personnel no matter how dressed. It is a question of personal odor.

"They are released at sundown. After that every peon
and every stranger has to remain outside the wire or survive
for a few minutes until the roaming dogs find him. After
that there is no chance for him. So this mercenary of yours.
What is he going to do?"

"I haven't the faintest idea. If he's got any sense, I guess
he's gone by now."

Van Rensberg laughed again.

"Very sensible of him. You know, back in the old country, up in the Caprivi Strip, we had a camp for *mundts* who
were causing a lot of trouble in the townships. I was in

charge of it. And you know what, Mr. CIA-man? I never lost a single kaffir. Not one. By which I mean, no escapers. Never."

"Impressive, I'm sure."

"And you know what I used? Landmines? No. Search-lights? No. Two concentric rings of chain-link fencing, buried six feet deep, razor-topped, and between the rings wild animals. Crocs in the ponds, lions in the grassland. One covered tunnel in and out. I love Mother Nature."

He checked his watch. "Eleven o'clock. I'll drive you up the track to our guardhouse in the gap in the hills. The San Martin police will send a Land Rover to meet you there and take you back to the hotel."

They were driving back across the estate from the coast to the gate giving access to the village and the climbing track when the major's radio crackled. He listened to the message from the duty operator in the cellar beneath the mansion. It pleased him. He switched off and pointed to the crest of the sierra.

"Colonel Moreno's men scoured the jungle this morning from the road to the crest. They've found the American's camp. Abandoned. You could be right. I think he's seen enough and chickened out."

In the distance McBride could see the great double gate and beyond it the white of the buildings of the worker village.

"Tell me about the laborers, Major."

"What about them?"

"How many? How do you get them?"

"About twelve hundred. They are all offenders within San Martin's penal system. Now don't get holier-than-thou, Mr. McBride. You Americans have prison farms. So this is a prison farm. Considering all things, they live pretty well here."

"And if they have served their sentences, when do they go back home?"

"They don't," said Van Rensberg.

A one-way ticket, thought the American, *courtesy of Col-*

*onel Moreno and Major Van Rensberg. A life sentence. For
what offenses? Jay-walking? Littering? Moreno would have
to keep the numbers up—on demand.*

"What about guards and mansion staff?"

"That's different. We are employed. Everyone needed
inside the mansion wall lives there. Everybody stays inside
when our employer is in residence. Only uniformed guards
and a few senior staff like me can pass through the wall.
Never a peon. Pool cleaners, gardeners, waiters, maids—
all live inside the wall. The peons who work the estate,
they live in their township. They are all single men."

"No women, no children?"

"None. They are not here to breed. But there is a church.
The priest preaches one text only—absolute obedience." He
forbore to mention that for lack of obedience he retained
the use of his rhino-hide sjambok whip as in the old days.

"Could a stranger come into the estate posing as part of
the workforce, Major?"

"No. Every evening the workforce for the next day is
selected by the estate manager who goes to the village.
Those selected walk to the main gate and report at sunrise,
after breakfast. They are checked through one by one. So
many desired, so many admitted. Not a single one more."

"How many come through?"

"About a thousand a day. Two hundred with some technical skill for the repair shops, mill, bakery, slaughterhouse,
tractor shed; eight hundred for hacking and weeding. About
two hundred remain behind each day. The genuinely sick,
garbage crews, cooks."

"I think I believe you," said McBride. "This loner
doesn't have a chance, does he?"

"Told you so, Mr. CIA-man. He's chickened out."

He had hardly finished when the radio crackled again.
His brow furrowed as he listened to the report. "What kind
of flap? Well, tell him to calm down. I'll be there in five
minutes."

He replaced the set. "Father Vicente, at the church. In
some kind of a panic. I'll have to drive by on our way to

the mountains. A delay of a few minutes no doubt."

On their left they passed a row of peons, aching backs bent over mattocks and hoes in the raging heat. Some heads lifted briefly to watch the passing vehicle bearing the man who had the power of life and death over them. Gaunt, stubbled faces, coffee-brown eyes under straw brims, but one pair of eyes was blue.

30

THE BLUFF

He was hopping up and down at the top of the church steps by the open door, a short, tubby man with porcine eyes and a none-too-clean white soutane. Father Vicente, pastoral shepherd of the wretched, forced laborers.

Van Rensberg's Spanish was extremely basic and habitually only expressed abrupt commands; that of the priest attempting English was not much better.

"Come queek, Coronel," he said and darted back inside. The two men dismounted, ran up the steps, and followed him.

The soiled cassock swept down the aisle, past the altar, and on to the vestry. It was a tiny room, its main feature a wall cupboard of basic carpentry, assembled and screwed to the wall to contain his vestments. With a theatrical gesture he threw the door open and cried, "Mira."

They looked. The peon was still exactly as Father Vicente had found him. No attempt had been made to release him. His wrists were firmly bound with tape in front of him; his ankles the same; a broad band of tape covered his mouth, from behind which came protesting mumbles. Seeing Van Rensberg, his eyes indicated that he was terrified.

The South African leaned forward and tore away the gag without ceremony. "What the hell is he doing here?"

There was a babble of terrified explanation from the man, and an expressive shrug from the priest.

"He says he not know. He says he go to sleep last night; he wake up in here. He has headache; he remember nothing more."

The man was naked but for a pair of skimpy shorts. There was nothing for the South African to grab but the man's upper arms, so he seized these and brought the peon to his feet.

"Tell him he'd better start remembering!" he shouted at the priest, who translated.

"Major," said McBride quietly, "first things first. What about a name?"

Father Vicente caught the sense. "He is called Ramon."

"Ramon what?"

The priest shrugged. He had over a thousand parishioners; was he supposed to remember them all?

"Which cabin does he come from?" asked the American.

There was another rapid exchange of local Spanish. McBride could decipher written Spanish slowly, but the local San Martin patois was nothing like Castilian.

"It is three hundred meters from here," said the priest.

"Shall we go and look?" said McBride. He produced a penknife and cut the tape from Ramon's wrists and ankles. The intimidated worker led the major and the American across the plaza, down the main street, and thence to his alley. He pointed to his door and stood back.

Van Rensberg went in, followed by McBride. There was nothing to find, save one small item which the American discovered under the bed. It was a pad of compressed cotton wool. He sniffed it and handed it to the major, who did the same.

"Chloroform," said McBride. "He was knocked out in his sleep. Probably never felt a thing. Woke up bound hand and foot, locked in a cupboard. He's not lying, just bewildered and terrified."

"So what the hell was that for?"

"Didn't you mention dog tags on each man, checked when they went through the gate to work?"

"Yes. Why?"

"Ramon isn't wearing one. And it's not here on the floor. Somewhere in there I think you have a ringer."

It sank in. Van Rensberg strode back to the Land Rover in the square and unhooked the walkie-talkie on the dash. "This is an emergency," he told the radio operator who answered. "Sound the 'escaped prisoner' siren. Seal the gate of the mansion to every one except me. Then use the PA to tell every guard on the estate, on or off duty, to report to me at the main gate."

Seconds later the long, wailing sound of the siren rolled over the peninsula. It was heard in field and barn, shed and orchard, kitchen, garden, and pigsty.

Every one out there raised his head from what he was doing to stare toward the main gate. When their undivided attention had been secured, the voice of the radio operator in the basement beneath the mansion was heard.

"All guards to main gate. Repeat, all guards to main gate. On the double."

There were over sixty on day shift and the rest on layover in their barracks. From the fields, riding four-wheelers from the farthest reaches, jogging on foot from the barracks a quarter mile from the main gate, they converged in response to the emergency.

Van Rensberg took his off-road back through the gate and waited for them, standing on the hood, bullhorn in hand.

"We don't have an escape," he told them when they

stood in front of him. "We have the reverse. We have an
intruder. Now he's masquerading as a laborer. Same
clothes, same sandals, same sombrero. He's even got a stolen dog tag. Day shift: Round up and bring in every single
laborer. No exceptions. Off-duty shift: Search every barn,
cowshed, stable, workshop. Then seal and mount guard.
Use your radios to stay in touch with squad commanders.
Junior leaders, stay in touch with me. Now get to it. Anyone in prisoner uniform seen running away, shoot on sight.
Now go."

The hundred men began to fan out over the estate. They
had the midsection to cover: from the chain-link fence sep-
arating the village and airfield from the farmland up to the
mansion wall. A big territory; too big even for a hundred
men. And it would take hours.

Van Rensberg had forgotten that McBride was leaving.
He ignored the American, busy with his own planning.
McBride sat and puzzled. There was a notice by the church,
right next to the door. It said: OBSEQUIAS POR NUESTRO
HERMANO PEDRO HERNANDEZ. ONCE DE LA MAÑANA.

Even with his labored Spanish, the CIA man could work
out that that meant: "Funeral service for our brother Pedro
Hernandez. Eleven in the morning." Did Avenger not see
it? Could he not work out the sense? It would be reasonable
that the priest would not normally visit his vestry until Sunday. But today was different. At exactly ten to eleven he
would open his vestry cupboard and see the prisoner.

Why not dump him somewhere else? Why not tape him
to his own cot where no one would find him till sundown
or not even then?

He found the major speaking to the airfield mechanics.

"What's wrong with it? Screw the tail rotor. I need it
back up in the air. Well, hurry it up."

He flicked off his machine, listened to McBride, glared
and snapped, "Your fellow countryman simply made a mistake, that is all, an expensive mistake. It's going to cost
him his life."

An hour passed. Even without field glasses McBride could see the first columns of white cotton-clad workers being force-marched back to the double gates to their village. Beside the lines of men, the uniformed guards were shouting them on. Midday. The heat was a hammer on the back of the head.

The milling crowd of men in front of the gates grew ever bigger. The chitchat on the radio never stopped, as sector after sector was cleared of workers, buildings searched, declared clear, sealed, and manned from inside.

At 1:30 the number checking began. Van Rensberg insisted on the five checkers resuming their places behind the tables and passing the workers through, one after another, two hundred per column.

The men normally worked in the cool of the dawn or the evening. They were baking alive in the heat. Two or three peons fainted and were helped through by friends. Every tag was checked until its number matched one passed through that same morning. When the last white-bloused figure stumbled toward the village, rest, shade, and water, the senior checker nodded.

"One missing," he called.

Van Rensberg walked to his desk to peer over his shoulder.

"Number five-three-one-oh-eight."

"Name?"

"Ramon Gutierrez."

"Release the dogs."

Van Rensberg strolled across to McBride. "Every single technician must by now be inside, locked in, and guarded. The dogs will never touch my men, you know. They recognize the uniform. That leaves one man out there. A stranger, white cotton pants and floppy shirt, wrong smell. It's like a lunch bell to the Dobermans. Up a tree? In a pond? They'll still find him. Then they will surround him and bay until the handlers come. I give this mercenary half an hour to get up a tree and surrender, or die."

The man he sought was in the middle of the estate, running
lightly between rows of maize higher than his own head.
He judged the direction of his run by the sun and crests of
the sierra.

It had taken two hours of steady jogging earlier in the
morning to bring him from his allotted work patch to the
base of the mansion's protective wall. Not that the distance
was a problem for a man accustomed to half a marathon,
but he had to dodge the other work parties and the guards.
He was still dodging.

He came to a track across the maize field, dropped to
his belly, and peered out. Down the track, two guards on
four-wheelers roared away in the direction of the main gate.
He waited till they were around a corner, then sprinted
across the track and was lost in a peach orchard. His study
of the layout of the estate from above had given him a route
that would take him from where he had started near the
mansion wall to where he wanted to be, without ever
crossing a knee-high crop.

The equipment he had brought in that morning, either
in his supposed lunch bag or inside the tight briefs he wore
beneath the boxer shorts, was almost expended. The tough
dive watch was back on his wrist, his belt round his waist,
and his knife was up against the small of his back, out of
the way but easy to reach. The bandage, sticky plaster, and
the rest were in the flat pouch forming part of his belt.

He checked the peaks of the hills again, altered course
by a few degrees, and stopped, tilting his head until he
heard the gurgle of the flowing water ahead. He came to
the stream's edge, backtracked fifteen yards, then stripped,
retaining only belt, knife, and briefs.

Across the crops, in the dull, numbing heat, he heard
the first hounds baying toward him. What little sea breeze
there was would take his odor to the muzzles of the hounds
in a few more minutes.

He worked carefully but fast, until he was satisfied, then

tiptoed away toward the stream, slipped into the cool water, and began to let the current take him, slanting across the estate toward the airfield and the cliff.

Despite his assertion that the killer dogs would never touch him, Van Rensberg had wound all the windows up as he drove slowly down one of the main avenues from the gate into the heartland.

Behind him came the deputy dog handler at the wheel of a truck with a completely enclosed rear made of steel-wire mesh. The senior handler was beside him in the Land Rover, head stuck out on the passenger side. It was he who heard the sudden change in pitch of his hounds' baying, from deep-throated bark to excited yelping.

"They have found something," he shouted.

Van Rensberg grinned. "Where, man, where?"

"Over there."

McBride crouched in the rear, glad of the walls and windows on the Land Rover Defender. He did not like savage dogs, and for him twelve was a dozen too many.

The dogs had found something all right, but their yelping was more from pain than excitement. The South African came upon the entire pack after swerving round the corner of a peach orchard. They were milling around the center of the track. A bundle of bloody clothes was the object of their attention.

"Get them into the truck," shouted Van Rensberg. The senior handler got down, closed the door, and whistled his pack to order. Without protest, still yelping, they bounded into the rear of the dog truck and were locked in. Only then did Van Rensberg and McBride descend.

"So, this is where they caught him," said Van Rensberg.

The handler, still puzzled by the behavior of his pack, scooped up the bloodstained cotton blouse and held it to his nose. Then he jerked his face away.

"Bloody man!" he screamed. "Chili powder, fine-ground green chili powder. It's stiff with the stuff. No wonder the poor bastards are screaming. That's not excitement; they're in pain."

"When will their muzzles work again?"

"Well, not today, boss, maybe not tomorrow."

They found the cotton pants, also impregnated with chili powder, and the straw hat, even the canvas espadrilles. But no body, no bones, nothing but the stains on the shirt.

"What did he do here?" Van Rensberg asked the handler.

"He cut himself, that's what the swine did. He cut himself with a knife, then bled over the shirt. He knew that would drive the dogs crazy. Man blood always does when they're on a kill patrol. So they would smell the blood, and inhale the chili."

Van Rensberg counted up the items of clothing.

"He also stripped down," he said. "We're looking for someone stark naked."

"Maybe not," said McBride.

The South African had outfitted his force along military lines. They all wore the same uniform. Into canvas, mid-calf combat boots, they tucked khaki drill trousers. Each had a broad leather belt with a buckle. Above the waist each man had a shirt in the pale African-bush camouflage known as "leopard." Sleeves were cut at the midforearm, then rolled up to the bicep and ironed flat.

One or two inverted chevrons indicated corporal or sergeant, while the four junior officers had cloth "pips" on the epaulets of their shirts.

What McBride had discovered, snagged on a thorn near the path where evidently a struggle must have taken place, was an epaulet, ripped off a shirt. It had no pips.

"I don't think our man is naked at all," said McBride. "I think he's wearing a camouflage shirt, minus one epaulet, khaki drill pants, and combat boots. Not to mention a bush hat like yours, Major."

Van Rensberg was the color of raw terra-cotta. But the evidence told its own story. Two scars along the grit showed where a pair of heels had apparently been dragged

through the long grass. At the end of the trail was the
stream.

"Throw a body in there," muttered the major, "it'll be
over the cliff edge by now."

And we all know how you love your sharks, thought
McBride, but said nothing.

The full enormity of his predicament sank into Van
Rensberg's mind. Somewhere, on a six-thousand-acre estate, with access to weapons and a four-wheeler, face
shaded by a broad-brimmed bush hat, was a professional
mercenary contracted, so he presumed, to blow his employer's head off.

He said something in Afrikaans, and it was not nice.
Then he got on the radio. "I want twenty extra and fresh
guards to the mansion. Other than them, let no one in but
me. I want them fully armed, scattered immediately
throughout the grounds around the house. And I want it
now." They drove back, cross-country, to the walled mansion on the foreland. It was 3:45.

31

THE STING

After the searing heat of the sun on bare skin, the water of the stream was like balm. But it was dangerous water, for its speed was slowly increasing as it rushed between concrete banks to the sea.

At the point where he entered the water, it would still have been possible for Dexter to climb out the other side. But he was too far from the point he needed to be, and he heard the dogs far away. Also, he had seen the tree from his mountaintop and even earlier in the aerial photographs.

His last piece of unused equipment was a small, folding grappling hook and a twenty-foot twine lanyard. As he swept between the banks, along a twisting course, he unfolded the three prongs, locked them rigid and slipped the loop of the lanyard around his right wrist.

He came around a corner in the torrent and saw the tree

ahead. It grew on the bank, at the airfield side of the water, and two heavy branches leaned over the stream. As he approached, he reared out of the water, swung his arm, and hurled the grappling hook high above him.

He heard the crash as the metal slammed into the tangle of branches, swept under the tree, felt the pain in his right arm socket as the hooks caught and the rush downriver stopped abruptly.

Hauling himself back on the twine, he crabbed his way to the bank and pulled his torso out. The water pressure eased, confined to his legs. With his free hand digging into the earth and grass, he dragged the rest of his body onto terra firma.

The grappling hook was lost in the branches. He simply reached as high as he could, sliced the lanyard with his knife and let it flutter above the water. He knew he was a hundred yards from the airfield wire that he had cut forty hours earlier. There was nothing for it but to crawl. He put the nearest hounds at still a mile away and across the stream. They would find the bridges but not just yet.

When he was lying in the darkness by the airfield's chain-link fence two nights earlier, he had cut a vertical and horizontal slice, to create two sides of a triangle, but left one thread intact to maintain the tension. The bolt cutters he had pushed under the wire into the long grass, and that was where he found them.

The two cuts had been retied with thin, green plastic-coated gardener's wire. It took not a minute to unlace the cuts; he heard a dull twang as the tension wire was sliced, and he crawled through. Still on his belly, he turned and laced it up again. From only ten yards the cuts became invisible.

On the farmland side, the peons cut hay for forage on spare tracts of grassland, but on each side of the runway it grew a foot long. Dexter found the bicycle and the other things he had stolen, dressed himself so as not to burn in the sun, and lay motionless to wait. A mile away, through the wire, he heard the hounds find the bloodied clothes.

· · ·

By the time Major Van Rensberg, at the wheel of his Land
Rover, reached the mansion gate, the fresh guards he had
ordered were already there. A truck was stopped outside
and the men jumped down, heavily armed and clutching
M-16 assault carbines. The young officer lined them up in
columns as the oaken gates swung apart. The column of
men jogged through and quickly dispersed across the parkland. Van Rensberg followed, and the gates closed.

The steps McBride had mounted to the pool terrace
when he arrived were ahead of them, but the South African
pulled to the right, around the terrace to the side. McBride
saw doorways at the lower level and the electrically operated gates of three underground garages.

The butler was waiting. He ushered them inside, and
they followed him down a passage, past doors leading to
the garages, up a flight of stairs, and into the main living
area.

The Serb was in the library. Although the late afternoon
was balmy, he had chosen discretion over valor. He sat at
a conference table with a cup of black coffee and gestured
for his two guests to sit down. His bodyguard, Kulac,
loomed in the background, back against a wall of unread
first editions, watchful.

"Report," said Zilic, without ceremony.

Van Rensberg had to make his humiliating confession
that someone, acting alone, had slipped into his fortress;
gained access to the farmland by posing as a laborer; and
escaped death by the dogs by killing a guard, dressing in
his uniform, and tossing the body into the fast-flowing
stream.

"So where is he now?"

"Between the wall around this park and the chain link
protecting the village and airfield, sir."

"And what do you intend to do?"

"Every single man under my command, every man who

wears that uniform, will be called up by radio and checked for identity."

"*Quis custodiet ipsos custodes?*" asked McBride. The other two looked at him blankly. "Sorry. Who guards the guardians themselves? In other words, who checks the checkers? How do you know the voice on the radio isn't lying?"

There was silence.

"Right," said Van Rensberg. "They will have to be recalled to the barracks and checked on sight by their squad commanders. May I go to the radio shack and issue the orders?"

Zilic nodded dismissively.

It took an hour. Outside the windows the sun set across the chain of crests. The tropical plunge to darkness began. Van Rensberg came back.

"Every one accounted for at the barracks. All eighty attested to by their junior officers. So he's still out there somewhere."

"Or inside the wall," suggested McBride. "Your fifth squad is the one patrolling this mansion."

Zilic turned to his security chief. "You ordered twenty of them in here without identity checks?" he asked icily.

"Certainly not, sir. They are the elite squad. They are commanded by Janni Duplessis. One strange face and he would have been seen immediately."

"Have him report here," ordered the Serb.

The young South African appeared at the library door several minutes later, snapping smartly to attention.

"Lieutenant Duplessis, in response to my order you chose twenty men, including yourself, and brought them here by truck two hours ago?"

"Yes, sir."

"You know every one of them by sight?"

"Yes, sir."

"Forgive me, but when you jog through the gate, what was your formation of march?" asked McBride.

"I was at the head. Sergeant Gray behind me. Then the

men, three abreast, six per column. Eighteen men."

"Nineteen," said McBride. "You forgot the tailender."

In the silence the mantelpiece clock seemed intrusively loud.

"What tailender?" whispered Van Rensberg.

"Hey, don't get me wrong, guys. I could have been mistaken. I thought I saw a nineteenth man come around the corner of the truck and jog through at the rear. Same uniform. I thought nothing of it."

At that moment the clock struck 6:00, and the first bomb went off. They were no bigger than golf balls and completely harmless, more like bird scarers than weapons of war. They had eight-hour-delay timers, and Dexter had hurled all ten of them over the wall around 10:00 A.M. He knew exactly where the thickest shrubbery dotted the parkland around the house from the aerial photographs, and in his teenage years he had been quite a good pitcher. The crackers did, nevertheless, make a sound on detonation remarkably similar to the *whack-whump* of a high-powered rifle shot.

In the library someone shouted, "Cover," and all five men hit the floor.

Kulac rolled, came up, and stood over his master with his gun out. Then the first guard outside, believing he had spotted the gunman, fired back. Two more bomblets detonated, and the exchange of rifle fire intensified. A window shattered. Kulac fired back toward the darkness outside.

The Serb had had enough. He ran at a crouch through the door at the back of the library, along the corridor, and down the steps to the basement. McBride followed suit, with Kulac bringing up the rear, facing backward.

The radio room was off the lower corridor. The duty operator, when his employer burst in, was white-faced in the neon light, trying to cope with a welter of shouts and yells on the waveband of the guards' breast-pocket radios.

"Speaker, identify. Where are you? What is going on?" he shouted.

No one listened as the firefight in the darkness intensified. Zilic reached forward to his console and threw a switch. Silence descended.

"Alert the airfield. All pilots, all ground staff. I want my helicopter, and I want it now."

"It's not serviceable, sir.

"Then the Hawker. I want it airworthy."

"Now, sir?"

"Now. Not tomorrow, not in an hour, now!"

The crackle of fire in the far distance brought the man in the long grass to his knees. It was the deepest dusk before complete darkness, the hour when the eyes play tricks and shadows become threats. He lifted the bicycle to its wheels, put the toolbox in the front basket, pedaled across the runway to the escarpment side, and began to cycle the mile and a half to the hangars at the far end. The mechanic's coveralls with the "Z" logo of the Zeta Corporation on the back were unnoticeable in the dusk, and with a panic about to be launched, no one would remark on them for the next thirty minutes either.

The Serb turned to McBride. "This is where we part company, Mr. McBride. I fear you will have to return to Washington by your own means. The problem here will be sorted, and I shall be getting a new head of security. You can tell Mr. Devereaux I shall not renege on our deal. For the moment I intend to kill the intervening days enjoying the hospitality of friends of mine in the emirates."

The garage was at the end of the basement corridor, and the Mercedes was armored. Kulac drove, his employer seated in the rear. McBride stood helplessly in the garage as the door rolled up and back. The limousine slid under it, across the gravel, and out of the still-opening gates in the wall. By the time the Mercedes had rolled up to it, the hangar was ablaze with light. The small tractor was hitched to the nosewheel assembly of the Hawker 1000 to tow it out onto the apron.

The last mechanic fastened down the last hatch on the engines, clattered down the gantry, and pulled the structure away from the airframe. In the illuminated cockpit, Captain Stepanovic, with his young French copilot beside him, was checking instruments, gauges, and systems on the strength of the auxiliary power unit.

Zilic and Kulac watched from the shelter of the car. When the Hawker was out on the apron, the door opened, the steps hissed down, and the copilot could be seen in the opening.

Kulac left the car alone, jogged the few yards of concrete, and ran up the steps into the sumptuous cabin. He glanced to his left toward the closed door of the flight deck. Two strides took him to the lavatory at the rear. He flung the door open. Empty. Returning to the top of the steps, he beckoned to his employer. The Serb left the car and ran to the steps. When he was inside, the door closed, locking them in to comfort and safety.

Outside, two men donned earmuffs. Captain Stepanovic started his engines. The two Pratt & Whitney 300s began to turn, then whine, then howl.

The second man stood way out front where the pilot could see him, a neon-lit bar in each hand. He guided the Hawker clear of the hangars and out to the edge of the apron.

Captain Stepanovic lined her up, tested the brakes one last time, released them, and powered both throttles.

The Hawker began to roll, faster and faster. To one side, miles away, the floodlights around the mansion flickered out, adding to the chaos. The nose lifted toward the sea and the north. To the left, the escarpment raced by. The twinjet eased off the tarmac, the faint rumbling stopped, the cliff-edge villas went under the nose, and she was out over the moonlit sea.

Captain Stepanovic brought up his undercarriage,

handed over to the Frenchman, and began to work out the flight plan and track for a first fuel stop in the Azores. He had flown to the UAE several times, but never at thirty minutes' notice. The Hawker tilted to starboard, moving from her northwest takeoff heading toward northeast, and passed through ten thousand feet.

Like most executive jets, the Hawker 1000 had a small but luxurious lavatory, right at the back, occupying the whole hull from side to side. And like some, the rear wall was a movable partition giving access to an even smaller cubbyhole for light luggage. Kulac had checked the lavatory but not the luggage bay.

Five minutes into the flight, the crouching man in the mechanic's coveralls eased the partition aside and stepped into the washroom. He removed the Sig Sauer 9mm automatic from the toolbox, checked the mechanism yet again, eased off the safety catch, and walked into the main cabin. The two men in the rawhide club chairs facing each other stared at him in silence.

"You'll never dare use it," said the Serb. "It will penetrate the hull and blow us all away."

"The slugs have been doctored," said Dexter evenly. "One-quarter charge. Enough to punch a hole in you, stay inside, and kill you, but never go through the hull. Tell your boy I want his piece out, finger and thumb, on the carpet."

There was a short exchange in Serbo-Croat. His face, dark with rage, the bodyguard eased out his Glock from the left armpit holster and dropped it.

"Kick it toward me," said Dexter. Zilic complied.

"And the ankle gun."

Kulac wore a smaller backup gun taped round his left ankle under the sock. This was also kicked out of range. Avenger produced a pair of handcuffs and tossed them to the carpet.

"Your pal's left ankle. Do it yourself. In vision all the time or you lose a kneecap. And, yes, I am that good."

"A million dollars," said the Serb.

"Get on with it," said the American.

"Cash, any bank you like."

"I'm losing patience."

The handcuff went on.

"Tighter."

Kulac winced as the metal bit.

"Around the seat stanchion. And to the right wrist."

"Ten million. You're a fool to say no."

The answer was a second pair of cuffs. . . .

"Left wrist, through your friend's chain, then right wrist. Back up. Stay in my vision or you're the one saying adios to the kneecap."

The two men crouched, side by side, on the floor, tethered to each other and the assembly holding the seat to the floor, which Dexter hoped would be stronger even than the giant bodyguard.

Avoiding their grip, he stepped round them and walked to the cabin door. The captain assumed the opening door was his owner coming forward to ask for progress. The barrel of the gun nudged his temple.

"It is Captain Stepanovic, isn't it?" said a voice. Washington Lee, who had intercepted the E-mail from Wichita, had told him.

"I have nothing against you," said the hijacker. "You and your friend here are simply professionals. So am I. Let's keep it that way. Professionals do not do stupid things if they can be avoided. Agreed?"

The captain nodded. He tried to glance behind him into the cabin.

"Your owner and his bodyguard are disarmed and chained to the fuselage. There will be no help coming. Please do just as I say."

"What do you want?"

"Alter course." Dexter glanced at the electronic flight instrument system just above the throttles. "I suggest Three-One-Five degrees, compass true, should be about right. Skirt the eastern tip of Cuba, as we have no flight plan."

"Final destination?"

"Key West, Florida."

"The United States?"

"Land of my fathers," said the man with the gun.

32

THE RENDITION

Dexter had memorized the route from San Martin to Key West, but there was no need. The avionics on the Hawker are so clear that even a nonflier can follow the liquid crystal display showing intended course and line of track.

Forty minutes out from the coast he saw the blur of Grenada's light slip under the starboard wing. Then came the two-hour overwater haul to make landfall on the south coast of the Dominican Republic.

After two more, between the coast of Cuba and the Bahamas' biggest island, Andros, he leaned forward and touched the Frenchman's ear with the tip of the automatic.

"Disconnect the transponder now."

The copilot looked across at the Yugoslav, who shrugged and nodded. The copilot switched it off. With the transponder—designed to pulse out an endlessly repeated identification signal—disconnected, the Hawker was reduced simply to a speck on the radar screen of someone looking very closely indeed. To anyone not looking that closely, it had ceased to exist. But it had also announced it was a suspect intruder.

South of Florida, reaching far out over the sea, is the air defense identification zone, designed to protect the southeastern flank of the United States from the continuous assault of the drug smugglers. Anyone entering ADIZ without a flight plan was playing hide-and-seek with some very sophisticated metal.

"Drop to four hundred feet above the sea," said Dexter. "Dive and dive now. All navigation and cabin lights off."

"That is very low," said the pilot, as the nose dropped through thirty thousand feet. The aircraft went dark.

"Pretend it's the Adriatic. You've done it before."

It was true. As a fighter pilot in the Yugoslav Air Force, Colonel Stepanovic had led dummy attacks against the Croatian coast at well below four hundred feet to slip under the radar. Still, he was right.

The moonlit sea at night is mesmerizing. It can lure the low-flying pilot down and down until he flips the surface of the waves, rolls in, and dies. Altimeters under five hundred feet have to be dead accurate and constantly checked. Ninety miles southeast of Islamorada, the Hawker leveled at four hundred feet and raced over the Santaren Channel toward the Florida Keys. Coming in at sea level, those last ninety miles almost fooled the radar.

"Key West Airport, runway Two-Seven," said Dexter. He had studied the layout of his chosen landfall. Key West Airport faces east-west, with one runway along that axis. All the passenger and ops buildings are at the eastern end. To land heading west would put the entire length of the runway between the Hawker and the vehicles racing toward it. Runway Two-Seven means it pointed to compass heading 270, or due west.

At fifty miles from touchdown, they were spotted.

Twenty miles north of Key West is Cudjoe Key, home to a huge balloon tethered to a cable and riding twenty thousand feet in the sky. Where most coastal radars look outward and up, the Cudjoe eye-in-the-sky looks down. Its radars can see any plane trying to slip in under the net.

Even balloons need occasional maintenance, and the one at Cudjoe is brought down at random intervals, which are never announced. It had been down that evening by chance and was heading back up. At ten thousand feet it saw the Hawker coming out of the black sea, transponder off, no flight plan. Within seconds, two F-16s on duty alert at Elgin Air Force Base in Pensacola were barreling down the runway, going straight to afterburn once they cleared the deck.

Climbing and breaking the sound barrier, the Fighting Falcons formated and headed south for the last of the Keys. Thirty miles out, Captain Stepanovic was down to two hundred knots and lining up. The lights of Cudjoe and Sugarloaf Keys twinkled to starboard. The fighters' radars picked up the intruder, and the pilots altered course to come in from behind. Against the Hawker's two hundred knots, the Falcons were moving at over a thousand.

As it happened, George Tanner was duty controller at Key West that night and was within minutes of closing the airport down when the alarm was raised. The position of the intruder indicated it was actually trying to land, which was the smart thing to do. Darkened intruders with lights and transponder switched off are given, after fighter interception, one warning to do as they are told and land where they are told. There are no second warnings: The war against the drug smugglers is too serious for games. Still and all, a plane can have an onboard emergency and deserves a chance to land. The light stayed on. Twenty miles out, the crew of the Hawker could see the lights of the runway glowing ahead of them. Above and behind, the F-16s began to drop and brake. For them, two hundred knots was almost landing speed.

Ten miles from touchdown, the Falcons found the darkened Hawker by the red glow from the jet efflux on each side of its tail. First the aircrew in the cabin knew, the deadly fighters were riding on each wingtip.

"Unidentified twin jet, look ahead and land. I say look ahead and land," said a voice in the captain's ear.

The undercarriage came down, with one-third flap. The Hawker adopted its landing posture. Chica Key Naval Air Station swept past to the right. The Hawker's main wheels felt for the touchdown markings, found the concrete, and it was down on U.S. territory.

For the last hour Dexter had had the spare earphones over his head and the mike in front of his mouth. As the wheels hit the tarmac, he keyed the transmit button.

"Unidentified Hawker jet to Key West tower, do you read?"

The voice of George Tanner came clearly into his ears.

"Read you, five."

"Tower, this airplane contains a mass murderer and a killer of an American in the Balkans. He is manacled to his seat. Please inform your police chief to exercise close custody and await the federal marshals."

Before waiting for a reply, he disconnected and turned to Captain Stepanovic.

"Go right to the far end, stop there, and I'll leave you," said the hijacker. He rose and pocketed his gun. Behind the Hawker, the Crash/Fire/Rescue trucks left the airport buildings and came after them.

"Door open, please," said Dexter.

He left the flight deck and walked back through the cabin as the lights came on. The two prisoners blinked in the glare. Through the open door, Dexter could see the trucks racing toward them. Flashing red/blues indicated police cars. The wailing sirens were faint but getting closer.

"Where are we?" shouted Zoran Zilic.

"Key West," said Dexter.

"Why?"

"Remember in a meadow? In Bosnia? Spring of Ninety-five? An American kid pleading for his life? Well, pal, all this"—he waved his hand outside—"is a present from the boy's grandpa."

He walked down the steps and strode to the nose wheel assembly. Two bullets blew out the tires. The boundary fence was twenty yards away. The dark coveralls were soon lost in the blackness as he vaulted the chain link and walked away through the mangrove.

The airport lights behind him dimmed through the trees, but he began to make out the flashes of car and truck headlights on the highway beyond the swamp. He pulled out a cell phone and dialed by the glow of the tiny screen. Far away in Windsor, Ontario, a man answered.

"Mr. Edmond?"

"This is he?"

"The package from Belgrade that you asked for has landed at Key West Airport, Florida."

He said no more and barely heard the yell at the other end before disconnecting. Just to be sure, the cell phone spun away into the brackish swamp water beside the track to be lost forever.

Ten minutes later, a senator in Washington was roused from his dinner, and within an hour two officers from the Federal Air Marshal Bureau in Miami were speeding south.

Before the marshals were through Islamorada, a teamster driving north, just out of Key West, on US1, saw a lone figure by the roadside. Thinking the coveralls meant a stranded trucker, he stopped.

"I'm going up as far as Marathon," he called down. "Any use?"

"Marathon will do just fine," said the man. It was 11:40 P.M.

It took Kevin McBride the whole of the 9th to find his way home. Major Van Rensberg, still trying to find the missing impostor, consoling himself that at least his employer was

safe, dispatched the CIA man as far as the capital city.
Colonel Moreno fixed him a passage from the airport to
Paramaribo. A KLM flight ferried him to Curaçao. There
was a connector to Miami International and thence the last
flight to Washington. He landed very late and very tired.
On Monday morning, he was early when he walked into
Paul Devereaux's office, but his chief was already there.

He looked ashen. He seemed to have aged. He gestured
McBride to a seat and wearily pushed a sheet across the
desk.

All good reporters go out of their way to maintain an
excellent contact with the police forces of their area. They
would be crazy not to. The Key West correspondent of the
Miami Herald was no exception. The events of Saturday
night were leaked to him by friends on the Key West force
by Sunday noon, and his report was filed well in time for
the Monday edition. It was a synopsis of the story that
Devereaux found on his desk that Monday morning—the
tale of a Serbian warlord and suspected mass murderer detained in his own jet after an emergency landing at Key
West International had made the third lead on the front
page.

"Good Lord," whispered McBride as he read. "We
thought he had escaped."

"No. It seems he was hijacked," said Devereaux. "You
know what this means, Kevin? Project Peregrine is dead.
Two years of work down the Potomac. It cannot go forward
without him."

Line by line, Devereaux explained the conspiracy he had
devised to accomplish the greatest antiterrorist strike of the
century.

"When was he due to fly to Karachi and on to the Peshawar meeting?"

"The twentieth. I just needed that extra ten days."

He rose and walked to the window, gazing out at the
trees, his back to McBride.

"I have been here since dawn, when a phone call woke

AVENGER 337

me with the news, asking myself: How did he do it, this
goddamn Avenger?"

McBride was silent, mute in his sympathy.

"Not a stupid man, Kevin. I will not have it that I was
bested by a stupid man. Clever, more than I could have
thought. Always just one step ahead of me. . . . He must
have known he was up against me. Only one man could
have told him. And you know who that was, Kevin?"

"No idea, Paul."

"Some sanctimonious bastard in the FBI called Colin
Fleming. But even tipped off, how did he beat me? He must
have guessed we would engage the cooperation of the Suriname Embassy here. So he invented Prof. Medvers Watson, butterfly hunter extraordinaire. And fictional. And a
decoy. I should have spotted it, Kevin. The professor was
a phoney, and he was meant to be discovered. Two days
ago I got news from our people in Suriname. Know what
they told me?"

"No, Paul."

"That the real cover name, the Englishman Henry Nash,
got his visa in Amsterdam. We never thought of Amsterdam. Clever, clever bastard. So Medvers Watson went in
and died in the jungle. As intended. And it bought the man
six days while we proved it was a sting. By then he was
inside and watching the estate from the mountaintop. Then
you went in."

"But I missed him too, Paul."

"Only because that idiot South African refused to listen
to you. Of course the chloroformed peon had to be discovered in the mid-morning. Of course the alarm had to be
raised. To bring the dogs in. To permit the third sting, the
presumption that he had murdered a guard and taken his
place."

"But I was at fault as well, Paul. I honestly thought I
saw an extra guard trotting into the mansion grounds in the
dusk. Apparently there wasn't one. By dawn they were all
accounted for."

"By then it was too late. He had hijacked the aircraft."

Devereaux turned from the window and walked over to his deputy. He held out his hand. "Kevin, we all slipped up. He won; I lost. But I appreciate everything you did and tried to do. As for Colin Fleming, the moralizing bastard who tipped him off, I'll deal with him in my own time. For the moment, we have to start again. UBL is still out there. Still planning. Still plotting. I want the whole team in here tomorrow at eight. Autopsy and forward planning. Where we go from here."

McBride turned to go.

"You know," said Devereaux, as McBride reached the door, "if there's one thing that thirty years in this agency has taught me, it's this. There are some levels of loyalty that command us beyond even the call of duty."

EPILOGUE
THE LOYALTY

Kevin McBride walked down the hall and turned into the executive washroom. He felt drained. Days of traveling, worrying, not sleeping, had left him exhausted.

He stared at his tired face in the mirror above the hand basins and wondered at Devereaux's last Delphic remark. Would Project Peregrine have worked? Would the Saudi master terrorist have fallen for it? Would his acolytes have showed up in Peshawar in ten days? Would they have made the vital phone call for the listening NSA to intercept?

Too late now. Zilic would never travel again, save to a U.S. courtroom and thence to a maximum security jail. What was done was done.

He dunked his face a dozen times and stared at the man in the mirror. Fifty-six, going on fifty-seven. A thirty-year man, due to take his pension at the end of December.

In the spring, he and Molly would do what he had long promised. Their son and daughter were through college and making their own careers. He wanted his daughter and her husband to make him a grandchild whom he could spoil rotten.

While waiting, they would buy the big motor home he had promised Molly and go see the Rockies. He knew he had a rendezvous with some serious cutthroat trout up in Montana.

A much younger agent, a newly joined GS 12, came out of a cubicle and began to wash his hands two basins down. One of the team. They nodded and smiled. McBride took paper towels and dabbed his face dry.

"Kevin," said the youngster.

"Yep."

"Mind if I ask you a question?"

"Ask away."

"It's kind of personal."

"Then maybe I won't answer it."

"The tattoo on your left arm. The grinning rat with his pants down. What does it mean?"

McBride was still looking in the mirror, but he seemed to see two young GIs, rat-assed on beer and wine, laughing in the warm Saigon night, and a white Petromax lamp hissing, and a Chinese tattooist at work. Two young Americans who would part company but be bound by a bond that nothing could ever break. And he saw a slim file a few weeks earlier, which mentioned a tattoo of a grinning rat on the left forearm. And he heard the order to find the man and have him killed.

He slipped his watch back on his wrist and flipped his sleeve back down. He checked the day-date window. September 10, 2001.

"It's quite a story, son," said the Badger, "and it all happened long ago and far away."